NEPTUNE CROSSING

NEPTUNE CROSSING

VOLUME I

OF

THE CHAOS CHRONICLES

JEFFREY A. CARVER

TOR®

A Tom Doherty Associates Book
New York

NEPTUNE CROSSING

Copyright © 1994 by Jeffrey A. Carver

Edited by James Frenkel

A Tor Book
Published by Tom Doherty Associates, Inc.
175 Fifth Avenue
New York, N.Y. 10010

Tor ® is a registered trademark of Tom Doherty Associates, Inc.

Design by Lynn Newmark

Library of Congress Cataloging-in-Publication Data

Carver, Jeffrey A.
    Neptune Crossing / Jeffrey A. Carver.
        p.   cm.
    "A Tom Doherty Associates Book."
    ISBN 0-312-85640-7
    1. Life on other planets—Fiction.   I. Title.
PS3553.A7892N46   1994
813'.54—dc20   93-44423
                                                    CIP

First edition: April 1994

Printed in the United States of America

0 9 8 7 6 5 4 3 2 1

For Julia Dakota Carver . . .
there's a galaxy waiting for you out there.

ACKNOWLEDGMENTS

FOR SCIENTIFIC AND technical advice concerning Triton, I gratefully acknowledge the assistance of Dr. Robert H. Brown of NASA's Jet Propulsion Laboratory, as well as JPL's public information office. I am, of course, grateful for the Voyager 2 spacecraft itself, which sent back so many fine photos of my distant subject. I would also like to acknowledge the editors and contributors to *The Planetary Report, Science News,* and *Ad Astra,* who provided inspiration and information in ways too numerous to list. Finally, I must acknowledge James Gleick's book, *Chaos,* which is a wonderful introduction to the strange and fascinating science of chaos—and Charles Carver, who first showed it to me.

Many thanks to Amy Stout and Jim Frenkel, sharp editors and good friends, and my stalwart agent Richard Curtis, who helped steer this project to publication despite some difficult and unexpected complications. And special thanks to Tom Doherty, who gave me a vote of confidence when it was needed most.

And need I say it? The writing group, as always; and most of all, my family, for giving me reason and sanity for writing the book in the first place. Thanks.

Chaos . . .

. . . (L. *chaos* < Gk. vast chasm, abyss, void) n. 1. *Common usage.* Disorder; infinite formlessness. 2. *Human science.* Seemingly disordered or turbulent systems from which hidden order may emerge. Consequences arising from sensitive dependence on initial conditions may be unpredictable, even theoretically. 3. *Alien science.* Energetic potential for growth and development in the Universal Order, which may be amplified by selective intervention in highly complex and apparently disordered systems, esp. living systems.

PRELUDE

AWAKENING IN DEEP TIME

 THE CAVERN WAS cold, even in the slow energy flux of the translator's alien mechanisms. The quarx did not *feel* the near-absolute-zero cold, but was aware of it, as it awakened to the silence of a still world. Its first impression was not of place but of time, vast corridors of time through which it had floated in an almost coffinlike existence.

What did millions of years mean when one was asleep, when one's life process was held like a cup of electrons in the hands of an angel? What did the passage of time mean—except that once more, all the mortal lives it had known were gone?

The awakening was difficult and confusing. There was so much to remember . . . and so much more to learn. The quarx's translator had anticipated its confusion and was ready with information and explanations—not too much at once, but enough. They were in the planetary system of a yellow sun, though at such a remove that the sun was a mere fleck of light in the sky. But there were other planets, closer to the sun; and there was life there, venturing outward.

The quarx and its translator watched, and listened, with growing interest. There was much to know, but always with the mission to be considered. The mission. The quarx trusted that the translator knew what the mission *was*. The quarx, who had known the translator for millions of years, still did not entirely understand the mind of the thing . . . or the minds of its creators. It might have understood those things once; but much of what the quarx had once known, it had forgotten. How many worlds had it visited, how many suns, how many life-forms? It didn't know, couldn't remember.

But it knew enough to trust. It was the translator that swept the skies with its tendrils of awareness, the translator that computed the almost infinitely complex algorithms of chaos . . . the translator that recalled in its deepest memories just what it was they had been sent here to do.

○

Footsteps! Visitors! It had been only a short wait—no time at all, compared to the eons that had passed before. The translator had seen to it that remnants of the moon's past had convected upward to its icy surface, where traces might be noticed. Once the visitors were nearby, the quarx and its translator kept their hushed silence, but began searching . . . for the right individual, for one who would be willing to sacrifice everything for the sake of the mission.

The mission. The quarx already felt a sense of urgency. The computations were proceeding, but not yet complete. But it knew that lives were at stake—as ever—more lives than it could count. And it knew that its own life—as ever—was expendable.

And it knew that it could not act alone.

There were few enough candidates with the right combination of qualities—the right *potential*. But they needed just one. And soon. They had grown accustomed to the glacial slowness of geologic time, but things were about to change drastically; things were about to happen with lightning speed . . .

○

One individual came into sharper focus. The more the quarx and its translator watched this one, the more hopeful they became. Here was one who *knew* the presence of others in his mind, who felt at home with the tidal movement of dataflow and the slow seep of intermingled consciousnesses. This one had recently *lost* that presence, and suffered for the loss.

He was drawing near now—unwittingly near. There might be no better opportunity to try. He was in a period of disruptive suffering; but perhaps that would help—make it easier to draw him in, like an animal into a snare.

○

Sometimes the quarx wished that it didn't always have to happen this way.

1

TRITON SURVEY

JOHN BANDICUT COULDN'T have said exactly what made him drive his buggy past the invisible STOP HERE line, east of navpoint Wendy. It was almost as if the stately blue crescent of Neptune, overhead, were beckoning him onward, a deity calling him toward some mystical assignation among the rills and ravines of Triton. It was almost as if he had no choice.

That was lunacy, of course. Bandicut took the rover across into the unsurveyed sector because he was half out of his mind with silence-fugue. Though he was still perfectly capable of operating the equipment, he was hallucinating intermittently; and in some small corner of his mind he was aware that there was no way he should be out on the Triton surface risking his life, or for that matter the company's equipment. Now, Bandicut cared about company equipment the way he cared about cockroaches; but where his own life was concerned, he generally—in more lucid moments—had a pretty strong survival instinct.

But with each passing second, a little more of that lucidity was being swept away by the silence-fugue, by the terrible emptiness that was devouring the inside of his head. It was not that there wasn't plenty of information pouring through his senses: a clear view of the Triton landscape through his visor, occasional comm chatter in his helmet, the metallic stink of recycled air in his nostrils, the taste of bile in his throat, the bouncing of the buggy under his seat. But *inside,* deep in his thoughts, there lurked a dark, echoing, reverberating silence. This was the worst he had ever had the fugue; it felt as if some outside power were sucking his mind dry of even the *memory* of the flow and chatter and swarm of the neuro, stretching the inner silence as taut as a wire. He felt as if there were a black hole in his skull, and the only way to escape its awful hold was to flee physically across the Triton landscape.

He twitched the joystick and steered the rover down a shallow ravine, racing away from the sector that he was supposed to be detail-mapping. It was not a visibly hazardous direction; he was not looking for danger but for escape. He should have known, of course, that he was escaping nothing; but he wasn't thinking, he was just responding— to a desperate siren call in his mind, in the awful silence, a call to drive his buggy toward the planet Neptune, floating before him.

In time, he became aware of the exo-op calling him. The voice clanged in his headset like a hammer striking a metal pole. "UNIT ECHO, UNIT ECHO—DO YOU COPY? UNIT ECHO, BASE CAMP—WHAT IS YOUR PRESENT LOCATION? ECHO—*BANDICUT, ARE YOU THERE? FOR CHRISSAKE, ANSWER—*"

He reached for the comm control, as if to respond. Then he watched his hand turn the volume down to inaudibility. Now why had he done that? The thought and the question were carried away on the waves of emptiness and silence. He was riding on a tide, and there was no denying its mastery now. He nudged the joystick over and steered around a hump of ice and kept on rolling.

Neptune hung huge and majestic in the sky, her crescent a great blue scythe, her presence unsoftened by the tenuous nitrogen and methane atmosphere of Triton. Forget the old guy with the trident; this planet was a lady, seductive in her blue gown, beckoning him on. As he peered up at her through the scratches in his visor, he couldn't help reflecting how much more real she seemed in person than in the telepresence holos—more real, yet more remote. He had his light-augment turned off, so she appeared dim, ghostly, almost watery in the dark sky. The sun, not quite overhead, was little more than a bright star, viewed here from the edge of the solar system.

The Triton surface was a grayish-orangish brown, a frozen composite of nitrogen and methane ice and oxides barely illumined by the pale sunlight. This moon of Neptune was a buckled and broken place, ravaged by time, by impact, by gravity. It was impossible to gaze across Triton's face without wondering what stories were hidden in its history, what beings had once walked its surface, eons in the past. Beings *had,* of course; that was why humans were here with their mining encampment now. But as for who or what they had been, that remained a matter for speculation . . . and imagination.

John Bandicut's imagination was indeed racing now, as he nudged the joystick for another burst of power. With a disconnected part of his mind he recognized the approaching peak of the fugue; visions of aliens danced just beyond reach, their voices garbled and faint as they tried to communicate with him, tried to cross over that impregnable boundary of the missing neurolink. It was hopeless, of course; he was in silence, cut off from the datanet forever.

The buggy crested a rise and jerked over a ridged surface before nosing downward again into a low, narrow valley. He eased back on the power and coasted bumpily down the slope of the frozen terrain, almost relieved by the physical sensation. Off to his left, a soft dark plume rose into the thin air. It was a cryogeyser, dirty ice vapors erupting from beneath the surface, to be gently carried along by the thin Triton winds. Bandicut felt himself fixated on the eruption; it was an explosion of alien data, swept away by the winds before it could be drawn into the net. Madness: he knew it was all madness, but there was no stopping it. The alien datastorm hissed like static in the center of his mind, defying interpretation.

He felt a sickening lurch, followed by a floating sensation, then a thump back down in the seat of his pants. He blinked rapidly and pulled the power off. Too late. The lurch was a shifting of the ice beneath his buggy, and he knew he was already caught: he could feel one or more wheels mushing into a sinkhole. The underframe shuddered as it ground into the pebbly ice. He flicked the joystick into reverse, and the two right wheels chewed uselessly into snowy dust while the left two bit and slewed the buggy around. He was only digging the right side in even deeper.

Damn damn damn . . . His mind whirled in the void. He rocked the power forward and back, hoping that in the weak Triton gravity he would be able to dislodge the buggy. The effort was futile; a gravity of one-thirteenth gee meant poor traction, as well. More madness: how could there be a sinkhole in this frozen wasteland?

Cursing into the emptiness, he killed the power and unbuckled his harness. The alien hiss was gone. All he heard now was a choir of accusing voices, telling him how badly he had screwed up. The silence-fugue was fading; his thoughts were returning, shakily, to cold reality. He glanced at his suit's reserves, then disconnected from the buggy's life support. He raised the bubble canopy and stumbled out of the rover—to the left, to avoid the soft rut that had swallowed his right wheels. Peering around cautiously in his bulky suit and helmet, he only half wondered if alien shapes would loom over the horizon. He blinked hard, and with a silent curse, set about taking stock. He shuffled forward to inspect the vehicle from the front, to see how badly he had ground himself in.

His intention was to kneel carefully and peer beneath the buggy. He planted his modest weight on his left foot, on a solid patch of ice, and lifted his right foot to take a step past the bumper. With a sudden implosion, the ice collapsed beneath him. His body, the ice, everything twisted, and before he could even gasp in alarm, he felt himself falling through a glittering cloud of snow . . . falling into a hole that had not been there a moment ago . . . tumbling in slow motion, head over heels, falling.

He seemed to fall a long, long way into the thundering, silent darkness before he lost consciousness.

*

He awoke with his head pounding, wheeling with dizziness. The headache was almost welcome; whatever else had happened, the silence-fugue episode was over. The dizziness was another matter. He took several slow breaths, and finally realized that he was not just dizzy, but the world actually seemed to be spinning around him, in a strange, carousellike movement. He blinked and shifted his gaze around. He was underground, lying on his back in some sort of cavern. His visor's light-augmentation had kicked on automatically. An arched, translucent nitrogen-ice ceiling glowed faintly overhead. Around him, glinting back icily, were solid walls . . . solid, except for the great, ponderous, inexorable movement with which they were wheeling around him.

He took a deep breath and moved his head—or tried. He felt a sharp stab of pain in his neck, and his helmet did not budge. Terrified, he froze, moving only his eyes for a moment. He wiggled his fingers and toes, and felt them move painlessly inside his suit. Next he lifted his arms, then his legs. No problem there. But when he attempted to push himself up to a sitting position, he found that he was glued in place, stuck to the ice. The pain hit him in the neck, as before, but this time it seemed an ache rather than a stabbing pain. A bruise, probably, from the suit collar. Good.

Bruises he could handle; it was broken bones and spinal damage that scared him. He scissored his legs, trying to roll over. He might as well have tried rolling out from under an anvil.

He gazed up at the ceiling, trying to evaluate his predicament. He had never been in a cavern quite like this before. The ceiling was a flawed bluish ice with a tinge of reddish-orange methane coloration. It was at least fifteen or twenty meters above him. The walls, also ice, were steep and slick. They were still wheeling around him, and it made him dizzy to try to focus on them for longer than a moment or two. Nevertheless, he glimpsed, as it revolved past, an almost vertical trough in the wall, which was probably where he'd slid down. Directly over that trough was a dark shadow on the ceiling, perhaps the buggy atop the ice. He could not see the opening he'd fallen through. He hoped it was visible from the surface, because if it wasn't, search parties from the base would never find him. Not unless he could think of a way to climb out of here unaided.

The thought made him shiver. He didn't much care for the idea of lying here in a near-absolute-zero environment, waiting for his lifepack to expire. He pictured himself as a part of the moon's lifeless deposits, one day to be revealed by the vaporizing heat of the company's mining lasers. He shuddered, not just with fear but with fury at himself for the insanity that had led him to this. *The damn silence-fugue.* Prior to this, he'd had some episodes of loss of concentration and fleeting, moderate hallucination, when the neural silence became too great—but never anything he couldn't control by effort of will. It had never hit him like this before, never actually put his life in jeopardy.

He shut his eyes, trying to think. He wondered how long he could safely lie flat on this supercold surface. The suit was not intended for prolonged contact in that position. How long had he been unconscious? How much longer would the power unit hold out?

With the neuro, he would already have had the answers pouring directly into his thoughts. But in the silence, he could not ask the questions merely by thinking them. Blinking his eyes open, he squinted at the tiny red numbers glowing in the corner of his faceplate. Either his eyes were watering or the numbers themselves were swimming; he couldn't read a thing. He tried to speak his questions, but all that came out of his throat was a thin, desperate rasp.

He struggled not to panic. He drew several deep breaths.

He knew this much: he could have been unconscious for as little as a few seconds, or as long as a few hours. But given the absence of warning flashers in his visor, he figured that at worst he had another forty-five minutes, and at best several hours more—assuming that he hadn't broken anything mechanical in his fall. That was a risky assumption, of course, considering that he had plowed his way to a landing, ending up flat on his back.

Flat on his back . . .

Covering up his exhaust ports.

Christ—all this time he'd been lying here, his heat exhaust had been slowly melting into the ice, embedding him!

No time to panic! he thought. No time to panic. He tried to think calmly. There were no datanet voices to help him; he would have to find his own answers.

Think, damn you.

The silence in his head echoed like a tomb. But in his ears, he heard the sound of his suit ventilator. He wasn't entirely alone. He cleared his throat carefully and tried his voice again. "Hello!" he grunted. "Suit control."

Beep.

"Thank God," he whispered. "Suit control—what are my power reserves?"

Beep. "Forty-two percent," chirped the suit.

He cleared his throat again. Could have been better, could have been worse. He had a couple of hours left. A couple of hours to get free, call for help, be rescued. "Suit control—transmit." He heard the click of the comm switch and drew a tight breath. "Base Camp, Echo Unit. Base Camp, Echo Unit. Do you read?" He listened to the hiss of static; he swallowed with difficulty. "Base camp? Bandicut. Can you hear me? Anyone?"

He exhaled, and tried hard not to be upset. It would have been miraculous for any signal to have gotten out of this deep cavern, especially with his antenna buried in the ice under his back. Nevertheless, it frightened him not to get a response. He felt himself starting to hyperventilate, and he fought to control his breathing—slow and shallow. He took a sip of water from his feeder tube, then spoke again. "Mayday, Mayday, Mayday! This is Unit Echo. Bandicut. I've fallen through ice and am trapped underground. My location—" he struggled to remember "—two clicks east of position Wendy. Does *anyone* hear me?"

The only answer was a hiss of static.

He scissored his legs again, trying to roll; then he scissored the other way. He rocked just enough to give him some hope. Probably there was some melted ice directly beneath his heat exhaust. But even a few centimeters out from it, the nitrogen was almost certainly refrozen, binding him in place. If only there were some way of melting it again . . . but he was as helpless as a turtle on its back, kicking and thrashing. He had hands and tools, all of which were useless to him. His mind spun, ratcheting in the silent emptiness. What would the voices of the datanet have said to him?

What could this lone, struggling mind come up with?

Suddenly he blinked furiously. Perhaps there was a way.

"Suit control," he murmured. "Raise internal temperature to maximum." He waited, holding his breath. An instant later, he felt heat pouring in around his torso, then his extremities. He waited for the heat to taper off. It seemed to take forever; sweat ran into his eyes, and he felt like a fool cooking in a sauna. He began moving his arms and legs in fast chops, adding body heat. Finally he heard a *beep,* and the influx of heat stopped.

"Suit control," he grunted, "reduce internal temperature to minimum. *Fast.*" He felt a change in the suit's mechanical hum, and drew a sharp, painful breath as a blast of icy air flashed down his front. Within seconds, he was shuddering, his teeth chattering. He counted to three—then began scissoring his legs violently from side to side. Something creaked, and he felt a breath of hope. He wasn't free yet, but his suit was pumping all that excess heat out through the port beneath his back, and he could feel the ice melting.

He hoped he wasn't just melting himself in deeper.

He kept rolling, heedless of his bruises. Something kept catching, keeping him from going all the way over. The icy blast was tapering off; he had only seconds before it would all refreeze. He swung his left leg over *hard,* and dug his right elbow down sharply and levered himself up with the last of his strength. Something broke free, and he lurched, and suddenly was partway up, supported on his right elbow. Before he could fall backward again, he pitched himself forward to his hands and knees. He was free.

"S-suit c-control," he gasped. "Temperature . . . n-normal! Fast!" Heat poured back into the suit, sending new shudders down his spine.

For a moment he didn't even try to move. Then, as he caught his breath he struggled to his feet, supporting himself on an outcropping of ice. The low gravity helped, but he was fighting dizziness as much as weight. When he felt steadier, he told his suit to turn on his helmet lamp, and he played it over the cavern walls.

He nearly threw up at the sight of the walls spinning through the spotlight. He lowered the beam hastily and found that the movement stopped, closer to him. The spinning occurred only beyond a certain radius, about four meters from where he stood. Though he was sure that it must be only a visual illusion, he knew he had to keep from looking at it. He stared at the ground instead. In his headlight beam, the ice under his feet appeared solid and stable. Thank God. He turned around slowly to see what was behind him. He raised his gaze cautiously.

His headlight flashed crazily among some darkened ice formations—and his breath went out with a shuddering gasp, as he saw it. *It.* A machine of some sort.

¯A machine made by no one human.

Bandicut blinked hard and felt an almost overpowering urge to rub his eyes behind his visor. The artifact, a few meters from his outstretched hand, seemed to be *squirming* in his headlight beam. It seemed to consist of a great many spheres, some jet black and some iridescent, intersecting like clusters of soap bubbles. They were moving and sinking *through* one another, disappearing and re-emerging in different positions, at various rates of speed. Beneath their mirror sheens, the spheres appeared to be spinning. The assemblage was about as tall as he was, standing on the ice floor, balanced on a single spinning bubble. It was strangely hard to focus his eyes upon.

It looked almost . . . alive.

In the silence of his mind, one word reverberated in his thoughts. *Alien.* And he knew, despite the violence of the silence-fugue that had brought him to this place, that the fugue had passed, and that this object, and its alienness, were no hallucination of the fugue-state.

It hurt his eyes to stare at it. He glanced away, and that was when he realized that *it* was at the center of the visual disturbance that made the cavern seem to spin. He clutched again at the ice outcropping, fiercely trying to suppress a new wave of dizziness.

It was at that moment that he felt something new pass through the silence—a whisper of something in his mind. He felt it for just a moment, then it was gone. A tingle ran up his spine, and for an instant it reawakened the blinding headache that he'd felt at the end of his fugue episode. But the tingle ended in a quick shiver, and the headache was gone as suddenly as it had appeared.

But the inner awareness was not.

He didn't know whether this *object* was alive or not, but one thing he did know—he felt it in his bones, like a creeping chill that had nothing to do with temperature.

He was not alone in this cavern.

2

THE QUARX

He COULDN'T TELL if the feeling came directly from the object or not. Something made him feel that he was being watched from behind. He turned partway around, but saw nothing except the spinning ice walls and their rocky protrusions. He shuffled awkwardly back around to stare at the alien object, and shivered.

This time the feeling came purely from within. He felt as if something had blown open in his mind, like a shutter in a strong wind. The wind was sighing through his head now, rustling his inner order like so many fluttering leaves. It reminded him of the feeling of silence-fugue, but this was different. This was something from the outside touching him—and yet touching him within, intimately and profoundly. He had a feeling of a great door swinging silently open somewhere in his mind, and slamming shut again behind him as he passed over some invisible threshold.

He let out a startled breath. The curious inner feeling faded away, and was replaced by cold, outward reality. He was trapped in an underground cavern, with no idea how to get out. And he was standing in front of . . . the discovery of the century. An alien machine! It was what the Neptune/Triton explorers had looked for in vain, for years—an intact, and possibly functioning, artifact of the long-vanished alien race, the slag of whose technology laced the crust of this moon. This could be a discovery beyond price or measure, a discovery that could make him famous, possibly even rich. A discovery that could redeem him for his idiocy in falling into this cavern in the first place.

If, that is, he lived to tell anyone about it.

He was breathing fast again, thinking about it, wondering what knowledge was contained in that machine, what history, what capabilities. What power. And even, perhaps . . . what consciousness. Though he no longer felt the tangible sensation, an awareness that he was *not alone* continued to bubble inside him. He exhaled, flexing his hands in his gloves, trying to relax, trying to maintain an edge of alertness.

He was keenly aware that this machine, whatever its purpose or nature, could well be dangerous—despite the fact that it undoubtedly had been here for millennia. He had to assume that it was dangerous. He was in enough peril already, trapped here underground, without compounding his danger by triggering some ancient defense mechanism. Unless, of course, he already had triggered it.

He tried to think.

First: don't move any closer until you know what you're doing. Your antenna's free of the ice. Call for help again. Don't try to handle this alone.

Of course, he was still deep underground, and for that matter he might well have broken his antenna in his fall. But there was only one way to find out. "Suit," he said. "Comm—"

Before he could finish saying "on," he felt a sharp poke in the center of his forehead. It was followed immediately by a startling sensation, almost like being connected to a datanet . . . in a flickering, tenuous way, as if a single, remote voice had caught him in midaction, and out of the vast darkness had whispered, *Don't.*

What the hell? he thought. Was he hallucinating again? Or . . .

Had this thing just spoken to him?

He shivered with a sudden chill, and stared at the object with a mixture of fear and fascination. Had it just told him not to call for help?

"Is that it?" He spoke aloud, his voice reverberating in his helmet. "Are you telling me not to call?" There was no answer.

If he didn't call, he could be stuck here forever. Survive first, ask questions later.

"Suit," he muttered again, a little more determinedly. *"Comm on, trans—"*

NO.

The jab was sharper this time. He tried to keep speaking anyway, to overcome the resistance—and found that he couldn't. He could exhale and inhale, but was mute, as if stricken by a physical impediment. His breath hissed loudly in his helmet as he struggled to regain his voice.

"What do you want?" he thought—and heard his voice again, croaking the words aloud. Startled, he continued, "Are you keeping me here for some reason?"

There was no audible answer. But he had a strong sense that there *was* an answer, just as he had a sense that he was not alone here. "Can you talk?" he asked.

Silence.

He sighed and turned, playing his headlight around the cavern. The light danced back from the blue, translucent ice, glimmering as though *it* were alive. As the beam strayed outward, it picked up the spinning effect again. Clearly this machine was doing *something,* and whatever the hell it was, he would probably be smart to get out of its physical sphere of influence, and then worry about communicating with it afterward. Or better yet, let someone else worry about it.

He felt a vaguely disquieting sense of disapproval, but

no physical resistance, as he took a few unsteady steps away from the device. He approached the boundary where the spinning seemed to begin, and found he had trouble focusing his eyes. He hesitated, then stepped forward. A wave of nausea flushed through him. He staggered, fell— and as he fell, a strange twisting force seized him, *spun* him, and set him gently down on his hands and knees.

Struggling for breath, he looked up and realized that he was facing the alien device again. Gasping, he got back to his feet. Had that really happened? Or had he just been amazingly clumsy?

"Mind if I try again?" he muttered. This time, as he approached the boundary, he closed his eyes to slits—hoping to avoid dizziness. He felt himself falling, and twisting, and landed on his hands and knees again, lightheaded and indignant, facing the machine. He rose, panting, squinting at the object. It showed no reaction. He swept the area again with his light. There had to be some way to get away from it. Everywhere he swung the beam, cavern walls gleamed back at him, moving by in carousel fashion. He turned back to the alien device and hissed, "What do you *want* with me? Am I your prisoner?"

Not prisoner, he thought. Guest.

Where had that thought come from? Stunned, he walked toward the artifact. "Can you talk?" The thing squirmed, black and iridescent in his helmet light. "Can you talk . . . in my thoughts?" he asked. There was no response. But he felt certain that it was aware of him. Perhaps it would react if he touched it.

Perhaps it would kill him if he touched it.

Perhaps he could find something to *throw* at it. That ought to get its attention.

Glancing around, he found a loose chunk of ice, and with a gentle underhand toss, lobbed it toward the machine. It sparkled as it passed through his headlight beam, then dropped toward one of the black globes—and would have hit it, except that it vanished in midair. No flash, no sound. It was just there, then gone.

He decided that it was a good thing that he hadn't touched the machine. On the other hand, he had to get through to it somehow. He picked up another small piece of ice and lobbed it like the first one, this time toward one of the iridescent sections. He missed the machine altogether. One last try: a chunk of ice twirled and tumbled in an arc toward one of the iridescent bubbles . . . and turned to glittering dust before being sucked into the sphere like an indrawn breath.

He waited for something more to happen. Nothing did.

"All right," he muttered. "I guess you don't want to talk."

The wind rose again in his thoughts and whispered: We're learning. We *want* to talk.

He swallowed nervously, fear clamping around his throat. Was *that* his imagination? He didn't think so. Please, he thought, let me get out of this alive. I will never *never* let the fugue carry me away like that again! Just let me get out alive.

We want you to stay alive, he heard the wind say.

He choked, and instinctively reached out with his mind to catch the wind, to make the connection hold, to make it real, like the datanet—and at that moment something erupted from within, not in audible words, but in thoughts that seemed to turn into words:

/// *Help me—I'm trying—* ///

"Jesus!" he cried, grabbing the sides of his helmet. "Who is it? Who is this?"

/// *I am—* ///

whispered the voice from within.

"What?" he croaked. "You are what? The machine? The alien? Is that you talking to me?"

There was a short silence, and a sense of puzzlement. Then:

/// Alien . . . ? ///

"Yes!" he hissed. "Alien. Jesus Christ—what's happening to me?"

/// It's . . . already . . . happened. ///

Already happened? he thought dumbly. He barked, not quite cursing, "You're that thing. *What* are you? What are you here for?"

/// I am . . . quarx. ///

"Uh—?"

The words were starting to form more clearly in his thoughts:

/// I am trying . . .
to talk with you. ///

"Well, I—I can't stay here much longer. Can you understand that? I need to get back to the surface. I'll come back later. To talk. I only have enough power—"

/// I know, ///

whispered the voice.

/// I can . . . help. ///

"What? How?" Bandicut was panting. He was hyperventilating again; he had to slow down. God, it was terrifying, and yet . . . exhilarating! A living alien, talking to him, as if through a neuro! He wondered if he could talk back to it the way he could the datanet. /Can you . . . hear me when I do this?/ he thought, forming the words in his mind with careful deliberation.

/// Yes.
I've been hearing you . . . all along.
It's talking that's . . . difficult. ///

He blinked. /How do you talk to me . . . from way over there? Do you use some kind of . . . transmitter . . . that reaches directly into my brain?/

The answering thought seemed startled.

/// "Over there?"
I'm not, I'm right here. ///

He swallowed. /Where?/

/// In your mind. ///

Well, yes, he thought. But . . .

And then he understood what it was saying to him. /Do you mean . . . are you saying . . . in my . . . /

/// Yes. ///

He froze, trying not to jump to conclusions. /You don't mean in my actual . . . *brain,* do you? You don't mean you're actually *in* my head, do you? Not just connecting, but — ?/

/// Living there?
Yes.
Not physically, as you think of it, but . . .
close enough . . . ///

Bandicut was suddenly dizzy, too dizzy to hear the voice complete its thought. *Not physically,* he thought. And suddenly he knew. It had taken him a while to catch on, but now he understood . . . oh yes, it was like the neurolink, and yes, he was connected; it was like having a memory-resident program alive in his skull, only it was an *alien* mem-res. Not physically there, maybe, but . . . an alien voice in his head. It was different from the neuro, and yet strangely familiar at the same time.

/// Am I—
causing you difficulty? ///

Sarcasm? he thought. But no, it wouldn't understand human sarcasm, would it? It was alien. He let his breath hiss out, not knowing how to answer. "What exactly . . . did you say you were?" he asked suddenly, speaking aloud.

The answer felt muted, almost tentative.

/// Quarx. ///

"Quarx." He swallowed. /Quarx./ He felt like pacing. He paced mentally, framing his words. /We . . . we always wondered . . . who you were. We just knew you were . . . here before us. Here on Triton. A long time ago. *Quarx,* you say./

/// Yes. ///

/I . . . there's a lot I . . . should ask you. That I want to ask you./ He felt clumsy and stupid. What should he be asking?

/// There will be time enough
for all of that. ///

He shook his head. /No, I—I mean I—look, tell me please—/ He drew a breath and asked, almost plaintively, /How the hell did you get into my mind like this?/

The voice seemed to stumble.

/// Well, I . . .
it would be difficult to explain physically.
It was the translator that did it. ///

The translator. He sensed that the voice was referring to the machine in front of him. /This thing?/ He felt an affirmative response. /Is this thing a part of you? Are you a part of it?/ he asked, groping for understanding.

/// No.
The translator is . . . a machine.
I was . . . occupying its space-time, before.
Now I am . . . living . . . with you. ///

With you.

Living.

Bandicut shivered. /I—/ He'd thought he had understood before; he'd thought he could . . . an alien mem-res . . . an enhancement program, like the neurolink; he'd thought he could accept that all right. It was terrifying, yes, but exciting. An alien program. Information. Datapoints. Not . . .

Living.

In my mind.

/// I am alive, yes. ///

He felt himself beginning to hyperventilate again. He couldn't make himself stop. His faceplate began to fog up. He heard the voice whisper,

/// I've been waiting such a LONG time. ///

and somehow that stopped his hyperventilation short. He felt a strange rustling sensation, as if someone were riffling through the pages of his mind, trying to find a connection that was missing. He recalled that he needed to be getting out of this cavern, but the outside world seemed a million miles away now.

/// *I'm sorry if this is . . .*
startling to you. ///

He erupted with a cackle of near-hysterical laughter. /*Startling?* No . . . no . . . not at all./ He gulped. /You aren't . . . living with me to *stay,* are you?/ He clenched his fists, closing his eyes, swallowing, trying not to scream, WHAT DO YOU WANT WITH ME?

/// *I—*
for a while, yes. ///

Bandicut reeled silently.

/// *What do I want?*
I—to get to know you better—
to begin with. ///

/Get to know me,/ he whispered. /Get to know me? Would you mind . . . telling me what the hell you are—?/

/// *Quarx.* ///

/Quarx,/ he repeated. /WHAT DOES THAT MEAN?/

The alien device suddenly flickered, and something appeared in the air off to one side. It looked almost like a hologram—but that wasn't quite right. It was more like a pocket of darkness, and within the darkness, something bright and coruscating and very hard to look at. It was ghostly and frightening, like a glimpse into the heart of a nuclear reaction. He stared at it dumbly for a second, then blinked and yelled, ''Suit!''

Beep.

''Analyze the image in front of me.''

Boop. "*Specify image.*"

''The one right in front of me, damn it! Record it—full spectrum!'' At that moment, the image vanished. Whatever it was, he had scared it away.

Beep. "*Recording. Analysis indicates nitrogen and methane ice at a distance of four and one-half meters.*"

"Not the wall! Didn't you get that other thing, that—"

The quarx interrupted him.

/// That's the best I can— ///

He shifted his attention angrily to the interior of his mind. /What?/ If it had really been the datanet, he would have issued a freeze command, so that he could get a grip on what was happening.

/// You asked . . . what I was.

I tried . . .

I exist in a partial,
you might say . . .
a fractal displacement
from your physical continuum.
But I require an anchor point,
a merger
in this space-time
for coherent survival— ///

/What the hell are you talking about?/ Bandicut whispered, incomprehensible images flickering in his mind.

The voice became more subdued.

/// Sorry.
It is difficult—
the words.
I was trying to show you—
not clear. ///

He struggled to follow, but the images were lost now. Too much was happening, too much all at once. Maybe if you don't think of it as an alien, he thought desperately; think of it as a mem-res, and you'll be able to handle it.

The quarx reacted to his thought.

/// Don't think that I'm just . . . ///

and it hesitated for a moment, apparently sensing his unease.

/// Still . . .
if it helps . . . ///

Bandicut hesitated. What the hell was he supposed to
do now, or think? He might have made humanity's first contact with a living alien, but that didn't mean he wanted a
goddamn alien living in his mind. At least not for very long.
On the other hand, it was an inner voice again, even if it
was different from the neuro. Perhaps while it was here it
would help keep the silence-fugue at bay.

/// I'll try.
I am aware of your . . . difficulty. ///

His thoughts were spinning onward; he didn't respond
to that. There was, of course, the discovery of the alien machine, which he had to report . . .

/// NO!!! ///

He felt a barrier slam down in his mind, as he envisioned
reporting his find. He growled indignantly, "Why shouldn't
I report it?"

/// Because—
of what we have to do. ///

Bandicut's thoughts narrowed. "We—?"

/// For your world, yes.
It's . . . critically important.
I need time to explain to you.
Please. ///

Bandicut grunted. Critically important? He wondered
what that was supposed to mean. At the moment, he
seemed to have no choice, anyway. He hesitated. /Do you
have a name?/ he muttered. /Besides "quarx"?/

The alien seemed to want to say something.

/Well?/

A low, rising squeal began in the front of his head. The
sound shot backward, reverberating in his skull. Abruptly,
it rose to a horrifying shriek, like the sound of a transmission belt shredding. His teeth vibrated. He could not
breathe, or think, or cry out for it to stop. He could only

endure. And suddenly it ceased, leaving him shuddering in silence. /What . . . the hell . . . was that?/ he gasped, barely able to form the words.

The voice sounded puzzled.

/// My name.

Do you wish to hear it again? ///

/Christ, no!/ He shuddered one more time. Before he could recover, he felt a renewed riffling sensation in his mind.

/// You could call me . . . "Charrleeee." ///

"Charlie!" he grunted aloud. Jesus. He snapped inwardly: /Are you making fun of me now?/

/// Fun?

It's the closest . . . approximation I could find.

That you could pronounce. ///

"Great," he whispered. "Charlie. Right?"

/// Charrleeee. ///

He sighed. It could be worse. Better than that horrible shriek. He turned around, clumping in his awkward boots. Hadn't this . . . Charlie . . . told him that it could help him get out of here? They had better get moving, if he was to get out alive.

/// You mean,

if WE are to get out alive. ///

He froze. Yes, he supposed that was what he meant. He blinked suddenly, realizing that something had just changed in his headlight beam. The walls were no longer revolving around him. There was a strange sensation of stillness about the cavern, and he stepped toward the wall for a better look. Maybe now he could try to climb out. Or jump. He might be able to jump high enough in this gravity to reach a handhold near the ceiling.

/// You don't want to do that.

Too risky. ///

/I have to get out of here, damn it!/

/// Yes, but wait. ///

/For what?/

>>> *A better way.* <<<

/What's that supposed to mean?/

There was no immediate answer. But something made him turn back to the alien device, and his heart thumped. The thing was glowing, and the movement of the spherical sections had become quicker and more frantic, or erratic. He felt a chill of uncertainty. /Is that thing going to blow? Christ, I *do* have to get out of here!/

>>> *Wait.* <<<

/But I—/

Before he could complete his thought, he felt a sudden rush of warmth and light, and a spinning wooziness. Then his vision went cottony and white, and he floated up into a dreamy unconsciousness.

3

BEGINNINGS

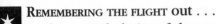 REMEMBERING THE FLIGHT out . . .
In the crystal clarity of the neuro, the planet Neptune floated in deep space with the kind of majesty that only heavenly bodies seemed to possess. She was ghostly and beautiful, a pale blue orb streaked with white storm systems and ringed with faint circles of dust that glinted into visibility only when his thoughts stroked the augmentation driver and brightened the scene to an astral glow. He recalled how the planet looked through the unamped porthole of the ship, cerulean and dim, almost sepulchral, floating like a phantom against the stars; and he felt a powerful rush of gratitude for the vision of the neuro, for the union with the ship's AI that let him experience the approaching planet as a vision of beauty, of wonder.

Bandicut was practically the only person on the shuttle who'd actually enjoyed the long haul out from Ceres Base. While everyone else counted the weeks and months, slowly going stir-crazy as they crossed the endless billions of kilometers, Bandicut had spent hours viewing the approaching planet through neuro-enhanced imagery, and exploring various threads of related information from the datanet.

At this point, near the end of the flight, they were starting to get fairly clear realtime images of their actual destination—the moon Triton, in its crazy, backwards, interloper's orbit around Neptune, well outside the ring system. By fiddling with the image mag, he could enlarge Triton from the small disk that the naked eye saw to a full-sized, three-dimensional body. It was about the same size as Earth's Moon, but there the resemblance ended. Triton was covered with a brownish pink coloration from the darkened methane that coated much of its surface ice. Its countenance bore the scars and craters of a face with a complexion problem. Bandicut could not yet resolve the MINEXFO encampment in the realtime imaging, but he'd glimpsed a few puffs of haze above the areas where he knew the great mining lasers were vaporizing swaths of the surface, exposing veins of metals that lay beneath . . . veins of *alien* metals, exotic alloys that had melted and refrozen eons ago.

It was an exciting prize, those alien alloys that offered the promise of revolutionizing everything from nano-optronics to armored weaponry. And that of course was why human miners were here, at vast expense, with the multinational/multiworld consortium of the Mining Expeditionary Force. Triton had once been a wandering orphan, possibly originating in the solar system, but more likely straying in from the interstellar void. Uncounted millions of years ago, it had passed close to the gas giant Neptune and been captured for eternity. Triton was a moon with an obscure history, but one thing was known for certain: it had hosted a nonhuman civilization at some point in its past. And even if no live aliens (or even dead aliens) had been found, it nevertheless bore a treasure lode of metallic compounds that to date had confounded the ability of human science to reproduce.

As a place to live and work, however, Triton was ranked near the bottom of the list for creature comforts, somewhere between Mercury and Arctic offshore oil platforms on Earth. Triton's surface was one of the coldest naturally occurring spots in the solar system, the mercury hovering at around two hundred forty below zero on the Celsius scale, at midday. The sun was four and a half billion kilometers away, and at its height during Triton's six-Earth-day diurnal period, cast a pallid glow about as bright as a moonlit night on Earth. From the Neptune neighborhood, Earth was over four hours away, even at the lightspeed of laser and maser transmission beams.

Triton in short was a cold, dangerous, and lonely place to be. Bandicut already knew, even before he got there, that he was likely to be asking himself, repeatedly, over the next two years, what the hell he was doing in such a godforsaken corner of the solar system. At the moment, the answer was self-evident, and he hoped he would remember it when the going got difficult. It was a job—and a good chance to use his piloting skills at a time when good spacing jobs were few and far between. Plus it was deep space, which held a special fascination for him, God knew why. And it was a chance, maybe one in a thousand but a chance nevertheless, to be the one to find a *real* artifact of alien technology, not just metallic slag, and maybe even make himself rich with the bonuses.

One other thing he knew: he was going to save up a goodly pile of earnings between now and the year 2166. There weren't too many places to spend it on Triton. So confident was he of his accumulating earnings that he had arranged to channel a full third of it into a trust fund for his only living relative, his niece Dakota Bandicut—nine years old, an orphan, and his favorite person on Earth. The remainder of his earnings, if he lived to collect it, would give him more than enough money for any easily foreseeable needs of his own.

It would be lonely on Triton. But unlike some of his grumbling shipmates, he didn't think he was going to mind the loneliness too much. He was pretty much of a loner anyway, and whenever he got fed up with the work, he could always just immerse himself in the neurolink, which was where he found most of his pleasure anyway. . . .

O

Unfortunately, following his actual arrival on Triton, it hadn't quite worked out that way. . . .

O

```
>
>>>
>>>>>>
>>>>>>>>>>>
>>>>>>>>>>>—<alpha-connect>—>>>>>>>>>>>>>>
>>>
>>>>>
>>>
>>>>>>>>>>>—<full-neural link>—>>>>>>>>>>>
>>>>>>>>>>>>
>>>>>>
>>>
>
```

—<mode shift>—

. . . in the neuro, it was as though he had wings and could change pitch and yaw and roll just by thinking it, maneuvering like a bird with wondrous freedom. It was a skill he'd finely honed; it was the way he'd piloted back in-system, in the Mars and Luna jobs. It was flying the way he loved to fly. But there were certain differences in the equipment and the situation out here, and that was why he was working through the full simulations, to get problems straightened out while he was still on the Triton surface. Except the problems seemed to be getting worse, not better . . .

It was a low, fast surface pass in a light survey ship, the ochre body of Triton filling his view to one side, the full piloting readout directly before him, the scanning-instrument readings to the other side, Neptune a blue reference point behind him at five o'clock. His altitude was reeling down, and he needed to make these course adjustments to a fine degree of accuracy . . . and every maneuver he made seemed to just miss, always a fraction of a second late, and now he had to fire his course outward again to keep from plowing a groove into the moon with his ship, and it was driving him crazy.

/Krackey, is this image-cruncher lagging half a hiccup behind my movements?/

/What's that, Bandie?/ The voice of his coworker and simulation instructor seemed to vibrate in his head, like a bad acoustic speaker. That wasn't right, either; it felt as if there was a bad connection in the neurolink.

/I said, the image processor seems to be lagging. Is that lag going to be real in the survey runs, or is the damn sim computer screwing up?/

Krackey's voice rasped back, /Lagging, you say? Naw, it shouldn't be. Hang on a sec', I'll check. They had a system malfie yesterday, and maybe they didn't get it all flushed out./

/Great./ Bandicut hesitated, half-tempted to just dive into the moon. It was only a sim, after all. Still . . .

/Hang on a sec' longer, Bandie—/

He hung on, orbiting at a safe distance, thinking maybe he ought to just unplug from the thing until this was straightened out. The whole point of running the sim in neuro was to make it totally realistic, just like flying around the rock in realtime. The last thing he wanted to do was rehearse under misleading conditions and practice wrong habits. If they'd put these sims on the shuttle out, he wouldn't have had to be wasting everyone's time with it now that he was on Triton.

There was a crackle of static in his head. He almost grabbed for the abort-cutoff, but then he heard Krackey's voice through the static, saying, /Bandie, the sim-ops guy is on it, he says for you to just hold tight for another minute or two. You want some muzak or something?/

/Shit no, I don't want no muzak, I hate that—/

And then the pain hit him, like a flash of fire across the top of his skull, like a blazing poker—

/**Bandie . . . you okaaaaay . . . ?**/

—and he wanted to scream, but he couldn't even breathe—

/**Bandicooooot, what's wrooooonng—?**/

—and then the voice fled, and Triton and all of the read-outs with it, and the only escape from the pain was by diving into the silence and blackness of unconsciousness

>
>
>
>
>>
>
>>>>>>>>>>>—*<loss of signal>*—>>>>>>>>>>>>>
>
>
>
>>>>>>>>>>>—*<alpha-disconnect>*—>>>>>>>>>>>>>
>
>
—**<mode shift>**—
—**<mode shift>**—
—**<mode shift>**—
—**<mode shift>**—
—**<mode shift>**— . . .

★

For the second time that day, Bandicut awoke from a faint. It took him a few moments to focus his eyes on the icy ground and realize where he was—on Triton, on the surface. Not in a neurosim.

Of course it was not a neurosim. There were no more

neurosims. There was no more neuro. He had been having a terrible nightmare, a dream-memory of something he desperately wanted to forget—the accident, the system malfunction that had fried his neuronal connectors beyond repair, had put him in the hands of incompetent company doctors, ended his piloting career, and left him with recurring silence-fugue. It made him tremble to remember it.

/// Forgive me.

It was . . . helpful . . . to me to see that. ///

/Aaa—!/ He gasped in shock at the voice inside his head. His heart pounded as he remembered who, or what, was speaking to him. An alien. A quarx.

/// Are you injured? ///

He sat up, clutching his helmet. He wanted desperately to rub at his forehead. He wanted to rub at that presence in his mind, peering out through his eyes, taking in the landscape with infuriating eagerness. /You! You're still with me!/ he thought, almost numbly.

/// Yes, of course. ///

He shuddered. Yes, of course. The events of the last hour were slowly coming back to him. /What the hell just happened?/ He'd been trapped underground . . . before all those dreams.

/// We left the cavern. ///

/Yeah. I can see that./ Bandicut peered out toward the horizon and tilted his head back to look at the black Triton sky and the great blue crescent of Neptune. He felt the dreams begin to resurface momentarily, and he shook, waiting for the feeling to pass. He felt bruised and beaten and exhausted. Turning his head, he saw the grounded buggy. He remembered his fall, and thought that it seemed a hundred years ago . . . if indeed it had really happened.

/// It happened. ///

He grunted. At least he was breathing, and apparently unhurt from his fall . . .

If he didn't count the presence of an alien in his mind.

He felt faint as he wondered, ridiculously, how he was going to report this back at base. Somehow that made him tremble again; there was something wrong in that thought.

He grunted again and got up to walk toward the buggy. Just over the horizon, he glimpsed a small recon robot scooting in his direction. It appeared that he had been located. /We aren't going to have privacy for very much longer. Will you tell me how we got out of there?/ He watched the robot bob over a hillock and thought he recognized it.

/// How did it seem to you
that we got out? ///

/What the hell—if I knew, would I have asked? I'm sure I didn't sprout wings and fly!/ He touched the buggy's front fender. The solidity of it was oddly reassuring.

/// I didn't intend . . . sarcasm.
I wondered about your perceptions.
Anyway, it was the translation device
that put us out here. ///

/Translation device?/ His memory flickered like a bad holo. Of course. He had found not just this alien being that was occupying his thoughts; he had found an intact artifact—an alien machine. How could he have forgotten? And the machine itself lay underground, in a cavern just beneath his feet. And as quickly as he thought that, he felt a sharp pang in his thoughts—and remembered when the quarx had stopped him from calling for help. /You're not going to let me report this, are you?/

There was a nervous stirring in his thoughts.

/// I'm sorry. I wish I could.
But it's just not . . . possible, yet. ///

/Not possible. Right./ He thought he sensed the quarx about to speak again, but there was only silence. He thought about prompting the alien to talk, to explain the secrecy—then decided to drop the subject for the moment.

He'd look for his opening to tell someone, when the time was right.

He surveyed the area in front of the buggy, trying to find the spot where he had broken through the ice. There was no indication of any flaw in the surface.

/// *You won't find the break.* ///

/No,/ he admitted, /so how'd your translator lift me out of there?/ He was starting to feel like a pawn, and he didn't like it. It was one thing to be an agent of first contact; it was quite another to be a puppet on a string.

The alien seemed puzzled.

/// *I won't force you to do anything,*
if that's your concern. ///

/It's one of my concerns,/ he answered curtly.

/// *I hope to . . . reassure you.*
And to answer your question:
we weren't lifted.
We were translated . . . spatially.
Do you understand the concept at all? ///

He blinked, eyes unfocused.

/// *Your Einsteinian relativity—* ///

Bandicut interrupted, /You're going to try to explain that by relativity?/

/// *No, that's what I . . .*
it's not covered by your relativity,
is what I meant.
In your terms, I'm not sure how to . . . ///

As the quarx's words trailed off, Bandicut shook his head and scowled at the patch of ice where the hole had briefly existed. He was thinking about the coincidence of that weakness in the ice being there just long enough for him to fall through—then disappearing again. Grunting softly, he turned to see how difficult it would be to free his buggy from the sinkhole that had started this whole episode. He knelt to inspect the undercarriage, and found that the bubble-topped rover was no longer sunk in any sort of slush, but was in fact sitting on top of a nice, hard surface of ice.

He could almost have sworn that he heard the alien clearing its throat.

/// Um, yes—it did that, too. ///

Whatever he might have answered was driven from his thoughts by the bounding arrival, over a hummock, of the robot he had seen a few minutes earlier. It was a gangling but speedy machine, an all-purpose recon-assist unit. It moved like a cross between a grasshopper and a roadrunner.

Its synthesized voice rasped in his helmet comm. "Unit Echo—John Bandicut! Are you unharmed?"

"Suit—comm on," Bandicut grunted. He felt resistance from within, and snapped, /I have to talk to it, damn it!/

/// Uh—okay.

But don't tell it— ///

/Yeah, yeah, yeah./ He frowned, remembering that the robot was undoubtedly here to find out why he had violated the boundaries of the survey zone. He hadn't yet figured out how to explain that away. "Hi there, uh, Napoleon. Er—yeah, I'm okay. I just . . . uh, had a little bit of—" What the hell could he say? Silence-fugue? No way. "—er, navigational trouble. I think I'm all right now. But I'm glad you found me." As the robot stepped closer, seeming to examine him with its gleaming holocam eyes, he felt ridiculously embarrassed. It wasn't as if he had to answer to a stupid robot for his excursion across the STOP HERE line. Did he? Of course, this might be an opportunity to tip someone off to what had happened—

/// Don't. ///

He exhaled in annoyance. /Why the hell *not?*/

/// Because we have something very important
to do. ///

/Like what?/ he snarled. /Conquer my . . . my homeworld?/ It sounded ridiculous, but that was what had popped into his head.

The quarx sounded weary as it answered,

/// John Bandicut,
I have no designs on your homeworld—
none whatsoever. ///

/Then what? Seize control of the base here? Throw us off Triton?/ He wasn't sure where he was getting these ideas, but he really couldn't think of anything else that an alien might want to do that would require secrecy.

/// Not even that.
My mission here is to be helpful, if I can. ///

Bandicut squinted at the robot, thinking that he must be making this robot wonder if something really was wrong. /Well, I have to tell the robot something. If you don't want me to tell it the truth, what excuse do you want me to use? I'm open to suggestions. I'm in enough trouble for being here already./

The alien seemed puzzled.

/// Must you answer
to this simple device? ///

/No, but it's going to send a report back to someone I *will* have to answer to./

/// Then tell it . . .
you had an electrical malfunction. ///

/Are you serious?/ Bandicut snorted. /I can't lie about that! They're going to notice that there's nothing wrong with the buggy, when I get back./ As he spoke to the quarx, he was aware of the robot staring back at him, and for an instant he had the humiliating thought that he was moving his lips as he subvocalized to the alien.

/// You won't . . . lie.
Tell it
you had an electrical malfunction. ///

He grumbled to himself for a moment, then spoke aloud. "Napoleon, I'm glad you came along. I had a bit of an . . . electrical problem. Maybe you can help." Wincing at the transparent phoniness of his statement, he cleared his throat.

/// *You already fixed the problem.* ///

"What?" /I mean, what?/

The robot eased forward, a small display of red lights winking behind its eyes. "John Bandicut, are you certain that you are all right?"

"Uh, yeah. Why do you ask?" He coughed and moved nervously toward the driver's seat of the buggy.

The synthesized voice sounded almost chiding. "You sound . . . anxious. Have you had any unusual . . . physiological symptoms? Perhaps I should drive the rover in for you."

"What physiological symptoms? What the hell are you talking about, Nappy?" He felt his voice quavering.

The robot extended a slender tool-arm toward him, as though in empathy. He knew it was just programming, but for an instant, he felt as if the robot really did want to reach out to him. He'd worked with Napoleon from time to time, and the robots did maintain memories of individual human workers. "John Bandicut," it said, "may I suggest that you allow me to check your suit and rover for proper function?"

Bandicut drew a breath. /Well?/

/// *I have no objection.* ///

He shrugged. "Okay, Nappy. But my reserves are getting a little low, so snap it up."

The robot inserted a small probe into a jack located at belly-button level on Bandicut's suit. "You have a damaged antenna, and your power reserves are below twenty percent," it remarked. "But your life support is within acceptable limits."

/// *Put your hand on the robot,* ///

the alien said urgently.

/Huh?/

/// *Please.* ///

Bandicut shrugged and placed his right palm on the top

of the robot's vision module. He felt a slight warmth in his hand, and Napoleon quivered a little and froze in place. Bandicut was aware of *something* passing between him and the robot, something like . . . thought . . . or perhaps it was just fleeting electrical impulses.

/// *That's fine.*
You can take your hand away. ///

He did so, and Napoleon suddenly resumed its activity. It withdrew its probe from the navel of Bandicut's suit, and turned to the rover. Lifting the cowling with a quick, smooth movement (something that Bandicut himself never could seem to do), it visually inspected the rover's electrical and mechanical components. Jacking in its probe, it said, "The rover's drive systems test satisfactory. Although . . ." The robot hesitated.

"Although what?" Bandicut said suspiciously.

"There appear to be certain anomalies in the system. I am unsure of their nature." The robot extended its tool-arm into the power compartment. Bandicut couldn't quite see what it was doing, but he thought he glimpsed some electrical-arc flashes. Before he could move to look, Napoleon unplugged its probe and closed the cowling. "I will recommend a thorough check when we return to base. With your permission, I will ride along and monitor."

Bandicut squinted at the robot, wondering what had just happened. Finally he shrugged. "Okay—hop aboard."

The robot clamped four of its appendages to the side of the rover and hoisted itself off the ground, pivoting its center of gravity in close to the cowling. It plugged into another jack and adjusted its position like a strange monkey perched on the side of the rover's power compartment. "Whenever you're ready, John Bandicut. Shall I call in for you?"

Bandicut scowled and climbed back aboard. "Never mind. I'll do it from here." He reconnected himself to the rover's life support, then settled into position to drive.

/Mind if I take a nav fix?/ he asked the quarx. /So we can locate this spot again?/

/// *Not necessary,* ///

the quarx answered calmly.

/// *Your nav's out, anyway.* ///

Bandicut nodded slowly. /If you say so./ He switched on the power. The nav, as promised, was indeed out. He shrugged, nudged the joystick, and drove off in a sweeping turn, the robot bobbing gently up and down on the fender.

★

As they approached the STOP HERE line, from the wrong side, Bandicut realized that the quarx had been quiet for a time. He found himself wondering something: why didn't he feel more upset, or at least more *peculiar,* about the presence of the alien being in his mind? Any ordinary human would be nearly insane with fear, indignation, and bewilderment. He was plenty confused, and indignant— but he was not yet over the edge into madness, and he wondered why. He felt that sensation of a wind in his thoughts for a moment, and then the alien stirred and spoke.

/// *I had hopes*
that you would be able to . . .
accept . . . my presence better than most.
I sensed a certain . . . readiness. ///

Bandicut recalled his mental state when he had driven out here, just before he had fallen into the cavern. The silence-fugue. It was caused, not by any fundamental disorder in his psychological makeup—at least he didn't think so, not that he really trusted the doctors here on Triton to know—but by the damage to his neuroconnectors, coupled with the *absence* of the link, which he had grown to require, like oxygen or fuel.

The alien had seen that vacancy and taken advantage of it.

/// *Let's say rather that*
your need *made you a more* capable *candidate*
for my presence. ///

/You make it sound like an honor that I was out of my mind with silence-fugue./

/// Not the silence-fugue.
But your desire and need for
this kind of connection. ///

He drove thoughtfully for another few moments. /What will happen if I flip off into fugue-state again? Will it be as crazy for you as it is for me?/

The alien was silent, apparently thinking.

/// I don't know, ///

it said at last.

/// But if I can help you out of it,
I will. ///

Huh, he thought, but not directly to the alien. He wanted to come back with some sort of snappish response, but the alien's answer actually seemed reasonable, and possibly even honest.

The quarx offered,

/// You know,
it might make things more comfortable
if you would think of me as "Charlie"
—instead of "the alien." ///

Bandicut grunted and expelled his breath.

/// Just a suggestion. ///

He grunted again. He was driving faster now; he was coming into an area that he knew well. The robot was bobbing in silence on the side of the buggy, apparently content to listen to the motors and whatnot, and leave him alone. /*Charlie*,/ he thought, trying it out for feel. To his surprise, it felt okay.

A short time later, he said, /Charlie. Seeing as how we're going to be so all-fired familiar with each other—/

/// Yes? ///

/—would you mind telling me, in thirty words or less, where you're from and what it is you want with me?/

There was a brief hesitation; he thought he sensed words at the tip of his mental tongue.

/// There's no . . . short answer . . . to either question,
unfortunately, ///

the quarx murmured at last.

/All right, then—give me the long answer./

The wind riffled in his thoughts.

/// I'll try.
Can you listen and drive at the same time? ///

/I'll try,/ he said sarcastically, steering along a winding path that climbed a low ridge.

/// Okay. ///

There was a pause. Then the quarx began,

/// As for where I'm from,
that's a long story
and I sense that it is not uppermost
in your thoughts.
With your permission, I will begin with
the second question— ///

/Yes, yes, go on./

/// Thank you.
First I must tell you that I am, in truth,
as much at the mercy of fate,
destiny,
external direction,
whatever you wish to call it,
as you. ///

/Mm./ Bandicut squinted, steering around a tight curve at a trifle too high a speed.

/// The translator and I work together.
Much of what I do comes from its knowledge.
Its direction, if you will. ///

/Mm?/ Bandicut frowned, slowing a little. He didn't want Napoleon to record that he was operating at unsafe speeds.

/// And it is the translator that informs me
of the need for action
—possibly drastic action—
for which I will need human assistance. ///
/Yeah? Assistance to do what?/
/// Assistance to, er— ///
/What?/ Bandicut demanded. /For God's sake, just spit it
out!/ He sped up again in irritation.
/// Okay.
Assistance to . . . save your Earth
from destruction. ///
Bandicut veered off the edge of the path.

4

RETURN TO BASE

THE ROVER HEELED over sharply as the wheels dipped to the left. *"Mokin' foke!"* he yelled, struggling to keep control of the joystick as he bounced sideways, banging his helmet against the canopy. In Earth gravity, he probably would have rolled over; but he had just enough float to keep it under control while he slowed down and steered the rover back up onto the path. Then he braked to a halt and sighed. /All right, goddammit. Now what did you just say?/

    /// I'm . . . sorry if I startled you. ///

/*Sorry?* I don't give mokin' foke whether you're *sorry.*/ Bandicut took a deep breath. /Did you, or did you not, just say, 'Save the Earth from destruction'? Am I supposed to believe that? Or was it some kind of joke?/ He blinked, wanting to stare at the alien. Since that was impossible, he gazed instead at Napoleon, which was swiveling its robot head to fix him with an inquisitive stare of its own.

/// Yes.
I had sensed that it might . . . startle you.
That's why I asked
if you could drive and listen— ///

/Never mind that dingo shit. Just tell me what the

fr'deek you *meant.*/ He gave the robot a wave, hoping that
the metal creature would refrain from asking questions.

/// *Well . . . it's very complex,*
and I don't have all the information yet.
That's why I need time— ///

Bandicut grunted harshly. If he could have seared the
quarx with a glare, he would have. He was aware of Napoleon trying to raise him on the comm. Exhaling loudly, he
put the rover back into forward motion. The robot swiveled
its head worriedly. "Suit—comm on. Nappy—ah—I'm okay
here," he called.

The robot looked back. "Are you certain, John Bandicut?"

"I'm certain. Comm off." /Now *tell* me./

He sensed an awkwardness in the answer.

/// *It's . . . an approaching cosmological hazard.*
Look—I think we should wait
until we're someplace where we can talk.
The danger's coming soon,
but not that *soon.* ///

Cosmological hazard? Coming soon . . . ? /Listen, damn
it—/

/// *I don't mean to evade your question.*
But we don't want to draw attention
to ourselves, do we?
What's this new escort coming our way? ///

/Escort?/ He suddenly noticed several other robots of
various configurations moving along the top of the ridge. As
the buggy crested the ridge, the robots fell into formation
flanking him, apparently for the purpose of accompanying
him back to base.

He cursed silently. /All right, I'll play along—for now.
But as soon as we're alone, you talk. *Comprende?*/

/// *Com . . . prendo,* ///

the alien croaked.

Scowling, Bandicut switched on the panel comm and

squeezed the mike switch. It was time he called in and let base camp know he was alive. He heard a blast of static, which wasn't encouraging—but he transmitted anyway. "Base Camp Exo-op, Unit Echo. Base Camp, Unit Echo. Do you read?" He was answered with more static. What was going on? he wondered. His suit antenna was broken, but not the buggy's. He tried again. "Base Camp, Echo. Anyone, this is Bandicut. Does anyone read me? Any station?"

The northern mining battery was just coming into view over the horizon. Base Camp was about a kilometer beyond it. The main surface-stripping laser was inactive at the moment. He saw one of the big crawlers moving over the beam-spread area, and assumed that it was safe to proceed, even in the absence of radio contact. He kept trying the comm, but the closest he came to actual contact was, faintly through the static, a voice saying, ". . . GOT HIM IN SIGHT, HEADING INBOUND FROM WENDY." Eventually he gave up and just kept driving. It wasn't worth worrying about now; he was almost there.

/// *I did that to help you.* ///

/Huh?/

/// *The electrical . . . malfie.* ///

He squinted through the windshield, an uneasy clarity coming to him. The robot in the power compartment. The flashes. /Oh./

/// *Remember that when you get in.* ///
/// *An electrical malfie.* ///

He let out his breath and didn't answer.

With the exception of Napoleon bouncing on his front fender, the robot escort peeled away as he rolled into the maintenance shed. The glare of lights inside threw off his visor-augment for a moment, and he squinted as he followed a shop mech, directing him to drive straight into the service airlock for the shirtsleeve repair section. He waited as air hissed into the airlock chamber. Once he was through, he shut down the power and pulled his helmet off with a sigh of relief. He felt as if he'd been locked inside it for days.

Climbing out, helmet cradled under his right arm, he called out to the burly repair crew chief, who was ambling over with a scowl. "Hi, Pacho. How's business?"

Pacho Rawlins rarely smiled, and he didn't now. "What the fuck's going on, Bandicoot? Ops says for you to get your ass upstairs as soon as you get in. Sounds like they want to chew your butt up. What'd you do this time?" Rawlins swatted Napoleon off the fender and opened the main cowling with a jerk.

/// An electrical malfie. ///

"I had . . . an electrical malfie," Bandicut said, flushing. Rawlins squinted at him and with a shake of his head bent to peer into the buggy's power compartment. "It took out my nav and my comm and—"

"Christ, Bandicut!" Rawlins yelled. "What did you *do* to this thing?"

"What do you mean?" Nervously, Bandicut leaned to see what the chief had found.

"Malfie? Hell, you fried half the goddamn compartment! What'd you do, drive in front of a goddamn laser?"

Bandicut had trouble drawing a breath. The power compartment did, indeed, look fried. One cable was completely melted; many others were scorched. /You did this?/ he whispered to Charlie. He could not imagine what had kept the thing running at all. And he had been depending on it for life support!

/// The robot did it.
I made sure it didn't touch the life support. ///

Bandicut shook his head. "Ah," he mumbled to the chief, "I'm not really sure what happened, Pacho. I didn't do anything except limp home after it happened—and I was damn lucky. Can you take care of it okay?"

Rawlins glared. "Can I take *care* of it?" He shook his

head, walking away. "Jesus Aloysius Christ!" When he turned back and saw Bandicut still staring at him, he said, "What are you doing still here? Get your ass over to ops like they said, will you? I don't want to get blamed for that, too."

Bandicut shrugged and left the maintenance area. He was just as happy not to have to explain any more to Rawlins, and he didn't speak to either of the other survey drivers that he passed. Returning to the ready room, he showered and dressed in his station casuals. He felt very strange . . . almost with an absence of emotion, as if a whole reservoir of bewilderment and anxiety were stoppered up inside him, waiting for the most awkward moment to erupt. He was sure it was at least partly because he was on his way to ops; but it was a coldly disturbing sensation nonetheless, and he wondered if he were building up to another silence-fugue. He didn't know what he would do if that happened. He wasn't planning to tell anyone about the earlier episode, unless absolutely forced to. A disturbance of that magnitude could put him off the active list altogether.

The quarx stirred from its silence.

/// Correct me if I misunderstand, please.
Wasn't your fugue caused by an injury
resulting from company equipment malfunction? ///

He hesitated, his shirt half snugged up the front. /Yeah. But so what?/ He willed his fingers to continue working, but it was like making them move through molasses. Charlie had touched upon an extremely raw nerve.

/// Then . . . if I might ask . . .
shouldn't the company be . . . responsible?
Legally? ///

He glared inwardly at the quarx. /What, you're an expert in our law?/

/// Well . . .
I have picked up some information
over the years. ///

/And just how have you done that?/
/// TV and radio, mostly. ///

"TV!" Bandicut yelled, slamming his locker shut. He looked around, red faced—hoping no one had heard him. Fortunately, the locker room was empty. /What the hell do you know about TV?/ he asked in an inner whisper.

/// Well, you know—
your people broadcast it into space
for a good many of your years. ///

Bandicut squinted, and finally laughed bitterly. /I see. Well, Charlie—I got news for you. TV don't exactly always get it right. We're a long way from the law out here. A *lonnnng* way./ He clamped his jaw. He didn't want to think about it any further . . . think about what the company owed him, about the loss of the neuro and the botched effort to fix it.

/// A long way from the law—? ///
the quarx mused.

/// You mean, like in the Old West? ///

/Huh? What are you talking about?/ Bandicut shook his head, feeling as though he had skipped a beat. /The Old West? You mean, the *American* Old West?/

• */// Right.*
Outlaws and sheriffs.
Like on TV. ///

Bandicut rolled his eyes up, and for the first time today, laughed out loud in genuine amusement. /*Christ,* Charlie— give me a break! Now, let's go!/ He straightened his collar and headed out into the corridor with brisk, floating strides, as the quarx muttered to itself in quiet puzzlement.

*

Things seemed pretty subdued in the ops center when he walked in. If any excitement had been generated by his disappearance, it seemed to have died down by now. Two of the mining dispatchers glanced his way in momentary curiosity, but he just nodded back with his very best expression of unconcern, and they didn't give him a second glance. Only Georgia Patwell, who had apparently just taken over the exo-op comm seat, flashed him a brief, quizzical smile before turning her attention back to her console. It would have been nice if he could have reported to her, but there would be no such luck.

Lonnie Stelnik was hunkered down in the back of the ops room, drinking coffee and poring over sector reports. He was tall and lanky, with vulturous eyes, a beak-shaped nose, and an expression that discouraged conversation. When Stelnik looked up, the expression changed from boredom to condescension. As the exo-op who'd been on duty, he was Bandicut's super for the work shift and therefore the one to whom Bandicut had to explain himself.

/// You don't like this man? ///

/No./ Bandicut nodded to Stelnik.

/// May I ask . . . why not? ///

/Let's just say he's not afraid to step on people's necks to get to the top./

/// ??? ///

"Bandicut." Stelnik crossed his arms over his chest. "What the hell happened out there? You vanished without a word. And we interrupted a lot of work to go looking for you. Then here you come, riding in like a knight from battle."

"What, would you rather I hadn't made it back?" Bandicut snapped. "I had an equipment malfunction!" Great, he thought, it takes exactly ten seconds to blow up at this jerk. Gotta keep a lid on it.

Stelnik shrugged. "We sent out the robots, didn't we? Now, do you mind telling me what you were doing way out past position Wendy?" Stelnik leaned back, stretching out while peering down his nose at Bandicut. His eyes glinted. "Plus, I've got this report here from Rawlins in maintenance, saying you did some *serious* damage to your rover.

You want to tell me about it? Jackson's not gonna like this, you know.''

Bandicut felt a second flash of irritation. *"I didn't do anything to the rover. Don't blame me for equipment failures, all right?"* He swallowed at the half-truth.

Stelnik shrugged, unfolded his arms, and flicked on a holoscreen. "Okay, you can give me the whole story in a second. You can tell Cole at the same time."

Bandicut groaned inwardly.

/// What's wrong? Who's Cole? ///

/Cole Jackson. Director of Survey Operations./

/// You don't like him, either? ///

/Let's just say, between Stelnik and Jackson, it's hard to say who's the more self-serving. Cole's going to be mad as hell, because we screwed up his nice, neat work charts./

The quarx seemed to twitch nervously.

/// You aren't going to try to tell them
about me, are you? ///

/These guys? Not on my deathbed. If I turn you in, it'll be to somebody I trust a lot more than these two./ That answer did not entirely soothe the quarx, he realized. He shrugged inwardly. /I hope you've thought of a good explanation for that damage to the electronics./

/// Uh . . . working on it . . . ///

Bandicut cleared his throat. "Listen, you mind if I sit?" It wasn't really necessary, in one-thirteenth Earth gravity, but he wanted to call Stelnik on his bad manners.

With an annoyed look, Stelnik twisted around and found a short stool under the counter, which he hauled out for Bandicut to perch on. Meanwhile, a woman's face had appeared in the holoscreen. "Janie—get me Jackson, will you?" Stelnik said. He tapped his fingers on the table until the screen blinked and a middle-aged man's face appeared, wearing old-fashioned eyeglasses. "Cole," said Stelnik, "I've got Bandicut here with me."

"So I see," said the face in the screen.

"He was just about to tell me how he fried the electronics in that rover. You got the report, right?"

"I did. I must say, John—I hope you have a good explanation." Jackson peered out of the holoscreen, stroking the underside of his chin with his fingertips.

Bandicut cleared his throat. "Well, I—"

"It says here that you were out of the approved sector, as well," Jackson said sharply. Stelnik, his eyes shifting back and forth between Bandicut and the screen, barely concealed a smirk. Was he hoping to add the firing of a negligent driver to his record of tough-minded management?

Bandicut stirred and tried to think fast. "Well, as I said, I had an electrical malfie. I was just telling Lonnie here, I don't know exactly what went wrong. But the first thing that went was my nav. I missed the markers—and I, uh, don't know that particular stretch out there as well as some of the others." That last part, at least, was true.

"Nav, huh?" Jackson did not look entirely convinced.

"Nav and comm." He was thinking frantically now. "Something crisped itself in the electrical system, and eventually stopped me altogether for a while. And I, uh, just had to patch it together as best I could to get home. Napoleon came along right after I got the thing running again." He felt his face hot with anxiety as he struggled to sound convincing.

/// You're doing fine. ///
/I'm a lousy liar. I don't like lying. Why am I doing this?/
/// Because if you tell people about me,
our chances of success will diminish markedly. ///
/Success?/
/// Saving the Earth.
I promise, I'll explain later. ///

Bandicut sighed, not replying. Neither Jackson nor Stelnik had responded to his explanation. Stelnik's gaze was slanted down his nose again; Jackson looked worried, as though he might have to log something inexplicable on his reports, and how would that look on his job review? It was Jackson who spoke first. "The report from Pacho Rawlins called it the most . . . *unusual* . . . malfunction he'd ever seen."

Stelnik cackled and rocked forward. "That wasn't the way he phrased it in the report *I* saw."

"Well, *weird* might have been the word he used," Jackson said.

"*Fucked* was the word he used, Cole. He said it was the most *fucked* power compartment he'd ever laid eyes on."

Jackson adjusted his eyeglasses. "Whatever. There's certainly no need to repeat Mr. Rawlins's vulgarity." His gaze shifted. "In any case—John, what can you tell us about that?"

Stelnik rubbed his nose.

Bandicut thought hard, and a possible explanation welled up in his mind. "I'm hardly an expert, Cole, but I figure it might be that some of those components, like that cable that broke loose that I had to arc-weld back together"—he couldn't believe he was saying this—"weren't quite as cryo-ready as they were supposed to be. You know, we have had trouble with that sort of thing before."

Stelnik snorted, looking away. But Jackson squinted as he met Bandicut's gaze in the screen. "Well . . ." he said after a moment, "it's true, we have had our fair share of low-temperature problems."

And if that were the explanation, it would make the work audit a lot simpler, wouldn't it? Bandicut thought, waiting for Jackson to bite. He could see Jackson trying to decide whether it was sufficiently credible for *his* superiors to accept.

"I don't recall the robot's diagnostic report saying anything about cryo-failure," Stelnik said, making a sucking noise with his lips. "I'm not saying it's impossible, Bandicoot, but—"

"But what? I had the thing running again by the time the

robot got there." Bandicut shook his head in exaggerated disgust and hissed silently to the quarx, /What is Napoleon going to report? If it says that *it* fried the circuits, that won't square with what I'm claiming!/

/// Napoleon has no memory of what it did.
I took care of that already.
It's a very simple machine, very easy to reprogram.
We're okay, I think. ///

/You *think?*/ Bandicut cleared his throat again. "Anyway, Napoleon didn't run his diags on it until I'd fixed it already. I mean, as much as I was able to." He held out his open hands as if to rest his case.

Jackson peered out of the holoscreen. "John, the robot's name is Recon Thirty-nine, not Napoleon. Use nicknames in the field, if you must, but please—when we're trying to get our information straight—"

Bandicut caught himself about to roll his eyes in exasperation. "Recon Thirty-nine. Right, that's what I meant."

"Well . . ." Jackson said with a shrug. "It seems as though we might have to credit you with a field repair." Stelnik's eyes bulged, but before he could interject, Jackson continued, "Nevertheless, until we complete an investigation, I think we'll have to reassign you from survey to mining ops. As a temporary measure, just so there are no questions. Fair enough?"

Stelnik relaxed and smiled faintly.

Bandicut swallowed. Mining ops. Great. Bad enough he'd been demoted from piloting because they'd fried his neuros; now he was going to be dropped from survey driving and put in the mines. He cleared his throat. "You're saying, just until we have a report, right? This isn't some kind of demotion, is it?"

"John, if the report puts you in the clear, we'll have you back out there as fast as we can," Jackson promised. "Lonnie, you'll forward John's written report to me ASAP, won't you?"

"Yeah, roger wilco," Stelnik said.

Jackson peered at him for a moment, as though trying to decide if he were being sarcastic; then the screen went blank. Stelnik grunted and swung a keypad terminal around to Bandicut. "Type, please. If you don't mind," he said. No question this time; he was being sarcastic.

Bandicut nodded and poised his fingers over the keypad. He looked at Stelnik, who was continuing to stare at him, and said, "You can be the first to read it when I'm done, okay?"

Stelnik shrugged and wandered away. Georgia, working the exo-ops communications, barely concealed her irritation as he hovered over her shoulder. Nevertheless, she caught Bandicut's eye and winked in sympathy.

Bandicut typed a cryptic, fictional account of events, thinking the whole time that he had never before lied on an official form, and he didn't like starting now. He stared at what he had written.

/// Looks good.
That should jibe with the robot's diagnostic.
Will they buy it? ///

/How the hell should I know? Do you mind if I just add, "P.S. Discovered alien artifact and living alien"? It would make me rich, you know. We could retire to Costa Rica./

There was a sound like a sigh in his mind.

/// If you file what you have now,
will it be possible for us to go somewhere
and talk quietly? ///

/I guess so./

/// Then . . . may we do that, please? ///

Bandicut scowled, hesitated, and pressed FILE. He caught Stelnik's eye, hooked a thumb at the terminal, and left the ops center without another word.

5

SOME ANSWERS

THE DORM ROOM, thankfully, was empty. Crawling into his bunk, Bandicut pulled the curtain flap closed around him for privacy from the other five bunks. Lying back, he drew a deep breath and sighed, closing his eyes to a sudden, overwhelming weariness. He had a thousand questions to ask the quarx; but really, for just one moment, all he wanted to do was rest his eyes and his mind.

It was impossible, of course. Visions of the ice cavern rose in his thoughts like ghosts haunting him even in the privacy of his own mind. And not just the cavern: the artifact danced before him like a jeering clown, its spheres whirling and eyes winking. /Jesus!/ He sat up abruptly, bouncing to the ceiling of his bunk, blinking his eyes in the near-darkness.

　　　/// I'm not Jesus. I'm Char— ///

/I *know* you're not Jesus!/ he snapped. /It's just a fucking figure of speech, okay?/ He sank back again groaning, feeling that he was floating, even though he was motionless in his bunk.

　　　/// Oh. ///

The quarx seemed puzzled.

/// You seemed disoriented and confused.
I thought maybe you thought . . .
Never mind.
Do you want to talk? ///

Bandicut drew a deep, slow breath. The darkness was crowding in around him, making him suddenly, extremely nervous. He knew what that meant: he needed the neuro, badly. He was on his way into another silence-fugue. /Charlie!/ he whispered urgently. The darkness was crowding closer still, and he heard the distant muttering of unreal voices . . .

/// What is it?
Are you in distress? ///

/Uh . . . oh damn, I need the neuro . . . if only I could link into something . . . can you, can you stop this—*ohhhhhh, jeeez*—/

Before his outcry was finished, everything around him changed with a flash . . .

```
>
  >>>
    >>>>>>
      >>>>>>>>>>>>
    >>>>>>>>>>>—<alpha-connect>—>>>>>>
      >>>>>>>>>>>>>>>>>>>>>>>>>>>>>>>>>>>>>>
    >>>>>>>>>—<full-neural link>—>>>>>
      >>>>>>>>>>>>>>
    >>>>>>
  >>>
>—<mode shift>—
```

It was like a holo-image flicking on, transforming the darkness into an array of images: information sources, pulsing and waiting. He gasped, heart pounding. He had just flipped over from impending fugue to . . . data-connect! But how? And to what?

/Is this better?/ asked the quarx, from somewhere

within the link. Its voice sounded different, like another human in the neuro.

He could not speak. His heart thundered with joy. He was trembling. He hadn't really imagined that it was possible, hadn't dreamed—

/Take it easy now. It's not—/

/You connected me! You did it! Jesus, it's—it's—/

/John, listen to me!/

The array twinkled around him like a series of gleaming panels, beckoning his inquiries in the dark. He reached out with a tentative finger of thought and—

/It's NOT WHAT YOU THINK!/

—touched an unyielding, unliving surface. There was no connection here, no source, no pulse; it was just an illusion.

/John, don't flip over into fugue—it's—/

/Nothing! It's nothing!/

The quarx was struggling for words. /It's a . . . stage set, John!/

/What? *Stage set?*/ His frustration rose like a cloud of toxic smoke in the image. /A stage set for *what?*/

/I had to act fast. You were slipping away, and this was the best I could do. It was the best I could do!/

/Best you could do!/ he moaned. /It's a fake!/ A crushing depression was settling around him as he realized the full emptiness of the illusion . . .

/Look—give me a moment, John! Let me see if I can make it real! Hold on a moment longer. Try it . . . wait! . . . *now.*/

One of the data-connect panel-images was pulsing bright emerald, against an aura of sunset red. Bandicut's anger twisted around him and finally blew away, leaving him breathless but clearheaded. He suddenly realized what the quarx was trying to tell him. The illusion had short-circuited the fugue; and that blinking light was the one connection that the quarx could make for him, without his neurolink. It was a connection to the quarx. Alien as datanet.

/Link in and ask me questions,/ the quarx said softly.

Nodding to himself, swallowing, feeling a little ashamed for his anger, and wanting desperately for this to be more than he thought it possibly could be, he reached out with his thought toward the pulsing panel, and he plugged in, and his remaining outward senses fell away as he was fully enclosed by darkness, but a darkness filled with energy . . .

—<mode-level shift>—

/Are you here?/ he whispered in astonishment.

>> **Ask me what you want to know.** >>

It was the quarx's voice, but altered . . . deeper and more resonant, exactly like an information-source replying through the datanet.

He sighed with unexpected pleasure, and a tremendous feeling of need welled up and then as quickly ebbed away. Dizzily, he whispered, /I want to know where you came from and why. And I want to know exactly what you want of me./

>> **I shall try. Where would you like me to begin?** >>

He shrugged mentally. /At the beginning, I guess./

>> **Of time? I wasn't there.** >>

He began to retort angrily, then realized that the quarx was attempting humor, attempting to lighten things up; and despite himself, he chuckled a little. /All right, you can start later than that. Let's stick to your personal lifetime. Unless, of course, you're *really* long-lived, in which case, you can start by telling what you want with me, and work backwards./

There was a moment of uneasy silence.

>> I'm . . . no . . . not long-lived, certainly not in the way you're thinking. It's true I was . . . in a sense . . . alive, millions of years ago, but that's . . . well . . . because I was in stasis in the translator . . . >>

Bandicut tried to follow that, frowning. /You're not long-lived, but you were alive—in a sense—a million years ago?/

>> Yes, but the millions of years don't count, you see, because of the stasis . . . whereas, to understand a quarxian life cycle, the first thing you need to ask is . . . >>

Bandicut felt himself sliding toward mental quicksand, and interrupted, /All right, wait! How about if you explain all that later./ He paused, sensing the quarx's discomfiture at the interruption. /Let's start with the present, and this "mission" of yours. What is it you're planning to do here? What is this about Earth and some sort of danger?/

The quarx hesitated, as though uncomfortable with the question. Bandicut began to grow impatient, but before he could ask why, the quarx finally spoke.

>> You see . . . that's difficult to explain fully just now, because I don't have all of the information yet. The first thing I must do is gather additional data for the translator to process . . . >>

/Gather data?/ Bandicut asked suspiciously, visions of alien invasions dancing in his head.

>> No invasions, I assure you. Not from us, anyway. There may, indeed, be something heading for your home planet; but, I believe, it's more in the nature of cosmic debris—and it is my job, and the translator's, to identify that hazard and act to prevent it from striking. With your help, of course . . . >>

/Of course,/ Bandicut muttered. /What sort of help? And what kind of debris are we talking about?/

>> Well . . . I can't give you the specifics on the debris until we have the rest of that data. I can *guess,* but— >>

/*Guess?*/ Bandicut felt a rush of anger. /Quit bullshitting me, Charlie, or I'm going to go to our company quack, Dr. Switzer, and have him cut you out with a knife!/

He immediately sensed the quarx's affront.

>> I'm not "bullshitting" you, and I thought you understood that I have no physical presence as you think of it, so your doctor's knife could only harm you, not me. >>

Bandicut sighed in annoyance. /Look, that was just another figure of speech, okay? Now, do you want to continue?/

>> Oh. Very well. Here is what I was given: a picture of small, orbital-dynamical shifts somewhere in your solar system, leading to the potential hazard. I suspect it's some sort of sizable interplanetary rubble. Listen, John, you must understand that I'm not . . . "sitting in the left-hand seat" on this one, as you pilot-types would say. So I can't— >>

/Then who *is* sitting in the left-hand seat?/ Bandicut interrupted.

>> The translator. And once it has the data it needs to positively identify the danger . . . it will pass that information on to me. And I'll pass it on to you. >>

Bandicut thought he sensed a certain hesitation in the quarx's voice. /Wait just a minute,/ he said. /Who controls the translator? You do, right?/

>> Me? *Hardly* . . . >>

Bandicut felt dizzy, and he sensed an eruption of troubled feelings in the quarx. /You mean there's someone else here? Damn it, I knew it—/

>> **John, *no*. It's not what you're thinking. It's just the translator and me, and the translator is just a machine. But it's . . . sent by others who are, I assure you, very far away. And I've never known it to attempt anything that wasn't . . . helpful to those it visited. >>**

It seemed to Bandicut that the quarx was more than a little hesitant when it spoke about the translator. He wondered why. /Well, that doesn't sound like such a big deal— identifying some space rubble,/ he said cautiously. /But I have to say, you don't sound entirely convinced about it yourself./

>> **What? No, no—the translator is trustworthy. But it's not . . . always easy . . . to do what it wants, is the problem. Look, would it help if I filled you in with some background? >>**

/Isn't that what I've been asking for?/

>> **I thought you . . . never mind. Just watch, and listen . . . >>**

—<mode-level shift>— . . .

✳

The information swirled by like a churning white-water rapids, and it seemed that all he could do was sample here and there, and file for future analysis. But that was difficult; perhaps he would be better off just jumping in and riding downstream with the flow . . .

It was millions of years ago, just as human science had surmised, that an orphaned body later to be named Triton had fallen into the gravitational influence of the solar system. Charlie and his translator were aboard, though the quarx was in stasis-sleep, and would remain that way for millennia yet to come, until awakened by the translator. But the translator never slept. It probed ceaselessly, monitoring the inner solar system and the evolution of sentient life on the third planet, unmistakably marked by first gradual—then abrupt—transformations of its biosphere. When there were visible events to be observed, the translator recorded them, from volcanoes to atomic explosions to the migrations of small vessels out of the atmosphere. It studied events of all kinds, whether apparently significant or not, and in its own methodical way, drew conclusions about the events it had studied.

Much of what Charlie knew, he had learned directly from the translator. Since his awakening, he had viewed years of reruns of Earth television, all recorded by the translator in that window of time when TV signals had been broadcast into space, before laser and opfiber transmission had mostly ended the free show. He owed much of his knowledge of human culture to such broadcasts.

He'd also gleaned hints of what it was he was doing here, what purpose he was intended to serve. Bandicut could only register astonishment: how could the quarx not know his own mission? But it was not his first, far from it, and he had yet to fully understand a mission prior to undertaking it.

The other thing that astonished Bandicut, as he caught all of this in a great swirling stream, was that the quarx really didn't know how the translator performed many of the feats in which the quarx himself was a participant. Surely, if he'd been alive in the translator for millions of years, didn't he *have* to know how it worked? No no no, whispered a quarxly voice, almost lost in the undercurrent. I'm not the master of that science. The quarx knew how to *use* the translator, but it was not actually his machine, not a quarxly machine at all.

But where . . . how . . . had Charlie come to be in such a time and place . . . ?

—shift—

The images changed like a whirlpool yawning. There were glimpses of dozens of worlds, dozens of hosts in quarxly lives past . . . it was like a flickering of holocards . . . and then the image settled, and filled with the sounds and impressions of other beings, alien beings, living on this very moon. The beings who had left the metal deposits? Their footsteps echoed around the translator, their voices and activities an incomprehensible murmur. For an instant Bandicut thought, with a flash of alarm, that they were here on Triton *now—*

—and then he realized that this scene was far, far in the past, long before Triton had ever come to the solar system. It was the moon as it had been, not just in the past, but so *deep* in the past that primitive life had scarcely yet evolved on Earth. This was Triton eons ago, in another star system, another reality.

It was Triton at war.

In frightening silence, he watched as long plumes of light splashed languidly across the ruined landscape of a nearby planetary body, the mother world. He was aware that the light beams came from the surface of Triton, and they were no mining lasers. They were weapons, terrible weapons, and they were raining devastation upon their homeworld. The plumes of destruction flowed and surged over the planet's surface like tides, and the civilization beneath them crumbled, melted, evaporated.

Nor was the conflict confined to the planet's surface: battle raged in space, as well—between the planet and its moon, and on the surface of the moon. Spaceships tumbled past one another, lancing each other into debris. Streams of fire swept over the surface of the moon, boiling away its atmosphere and reducing miracles of technology to molten slag. The footsteps were gone now; it all happened in silence. But he imagined that he could hear the screams of dying beings echoing across the emptiness of space.

There was no escape, none at all—except down into the buried, shielded translator, the place from which the quarx had first emerged in his failed, futile effort to prevent this tragedy from happening. Though damaged and unable to escape, the translator could probably survive the dark and the cold to come, if it could just survive this last terrible onslaught of violence. The quarx was now slipping downward through the deep darkness of ice, into the machine that might bear him through eons, and perhaps an eternity, of silent exile. He felt, but only distantly, the final tremendous explosions that vaporized the last living beings on the surface and hurled the moon out of orbit, out of its star system, and into the somber and lonely silence of interstellar space. With those explosions had come the final, bitter end to this war, and to the last of those who had fought it.

The quarx drifted off into a timeless, dreamless stasis-sleep. His final thoughts were darkened with grief. Where he was bound now, he had no idea. But he knew it could take longer than the lifetime of his own race to reach his next destination. And while he slept, the translator repaired itself. Would he ever see another quarx? All he really knew for certain was that his life had changed forever, yet again.

Bandicut's whisper was a part of the blurred datastream. *My God, is this your memory? Did you really live through this? Were those your people who died?*

Not my people, no. For a time, yes, but not anymore . . . that time was past . . .

—shift—

The battle images spun swirling away, the whirlpool of memory displaced by new images of Triton in orbit around the cold, cerulean planet Neptune. The heat of its capture had melted most of the moon, causing all the stone and metal in its crust to sink to the core; but some of that energy had been harnessed by the translator, and it, with some of the metal remnants of the alien civilization, had erupted back upward to the surface in a great convective flow as Triton cooled.

With awakening, for the quarx, there was a sense that certain memories were faded or perhaps had been lost, that some very important work had gone unfinished, that some failure had to be rectified, some wrong atoned for, some need fulfilled. There was a reverberating memory that this was how it *always* felt to awaken.

The quarx felt a deep loneliness and longing, but also a sudden new urgency. Here was a new place and time, a new solar system, a new race called "humanity" that had come into being while he had slept. And humanity had found its way to Triton, and would soon discover the translator. Who were they, these humans—and were they dangerous? Would one of them make a suitable host and companion? *Were they dangerous?* Why had the translator waited so long to wake him? It had served him well, and protected him—but it was not *life* to be trapped in that machine forever. How he longed to be free of its bonds—to grow, to taste again the reality of life with another!

But it was not to be easy; there was something that had to be done here—a matter of life and death, not just for him, but for the beings of this solar system. He did not know yet what it was, but he knew that that was why he had been awakened, and he knew that it would be risky and costly, because it always was. He had much to learn, and quickly.

With the help of the translator, he listened to humanity and came to know their languages and some of their ways. He watched their entertainment and studied their history through what he could capture of their datanet. He struggled to get to know a race that sometimes made him shudder with fear.

Fear . . . ?

They were a dangerous species, humanity. Of course, most sentient species were; and with that thought came another shudder.

Do you fear *all* sentient species? whispered Bandicut.

Watch the datastream, you're missing too much, was the whispered answer.

The quarx still had much to learn, even as he paid particular attention to a survey pilot named Bandicut who was stumbling along in a rare but promising condition known as silence-fugue, toward a potential meeting. The translator hinted that time was probably growing short, and this person seemed the most promising of an uncertain lot . . .

—<mode-level shift>—

The datastream changed, and most of it diverted away, while a single, bright connection remained.

/Are you saying that you deliberately—/

>> I didn't say that. >>

/—drew me in—?/

>> I didn't say that exactly. >>

/But you knew a lot about me already, and you sure as hell opened the ground under my feet!/

>> Well . . . yes . . . >>

/So you knew I was coming?/

>> I sensed . . . yes . . . when I am in the translator, it enables me a certain degree of . . . what you would probably call telepathic scanning. It is nothing like the intimate contact that we have now. It is more like a . . . radar sweep. >>

/Radar sweep? And are you still doing this? Are you probing the other people here?/

>> I can't, not outside of the translator. Except in a limited way, when you physically touch someone, or something. >>

Bandicut remembered Napoleon. /Like the robot, you mean?/

>> Yes. >>

Bandicut was silent for a time, trying to absorb all that the quarx had told him. /Charlie,/ he said finally, /are you trying to say that you spend your life traveling around the galaxy trying to bail civilizations out of trouble? Because that's what it sounds like . . . /

>> Well, yes—I mean, no! Not always whole civilizations . . . >>

Bandicut blinked. /Good God, but you mean it's true? Is that what you do? It sounds like . . . I mean, don't you . . . have a life of your *own* to live?/ He swallowed, and realized that a shadow of grief seemed to have come across Charlie with his words. /I'm sorry, look, I didn't mean . . . if I said something . . . /

The quarx spoke, but as though from a great distance.

>> It's not . . . so bad, really. It has its own rewards, you know. >>

/Charlie—/ He hesitated, and after a moment, the quarx drew back toward him, speaking softly.

>> It is true that I am on a . . . journey, John Bandicut. And that I don't always know where I am going, or for what purpose. Or whether I will ever return . . . to my own kind. Or even if they are— >>

The quarx paused. /What?/ Bandicut asked. /Alive, or something?/

>> Yes. >>

/Jesus . . . I'm sorry. I didn't mean to—/

>> It's been a *long* journey, John. I've seen more than one civilization fall, and I've seen some saved,

**and the latter way is better. I'd like to help save yours,
if I can. >>**

Bandicut was silent. They had to save the Earth, the
quarx had said. And he wanted Bandicut's help. /You want
to, uh, tell me a little more about that?/ he asked at last.

**>> I'll try. Let's start with a question. How much do
you know about chaos? >>**

/How do you mean? Randomness, disorder, entropy?/

>> No, I mean the *science* of chaos. >>

/Oh. Not too much. What *should* I know about it?/

—<mode-level shift>—

The explanation came in streams and waves, curling
around him like breakers rolling in upon a shore . . .

The dynamical theories of chaos were the only practical
means of describing many kinds of natural events, of il-
luminating past and present patterns, and of predicting
future patterns of similar events. Among the subjects
described by chaos theory were fluid turbulence, atmos-
pheric weather patterns, the movements of particles, of individual lives, of planetary bodies in orbit . . . and even the
social forces that swirled through crisis upon crisis in the
history of any civilization, including Earth's. It was the last
two of these subjects that had drawn the sharpest attention
of the translator.

It was the study of the chaotic patterns of orbital resonance in the solar system that made the translator suspect,
long ago, that the Earth might one day be in trouble.

How's that? whispered Bandicut.

Let the stream carry you, and just try to follow, murmured the quarx.

The human science of chaos was far too immature, even
in its second century of organized existence, to adequately

analyze the appropriate data; and even the translator, with its vastly more powerful chaos-calculator, was still working furiously, refining and analyzing, drawing together vague and shadowy possibilities into a picture that soon would make clear exactly what would go wrong, and where . . . and what must be done . . .

Charlie . . . ? I'm not . . .

Take an example, murmured the quarx. Motions of particles in a cloud of smoke—or in the rings around a planet, a planet such as Neptune, or Saturn. All the particles followed known physical laws of motion. But the motions were too hopelessly complex, viewed from a perspective of close detail, for predictions of any individual particle's motion to be useful. The tiniest perturbation of an orbit in one place could cause a drastic change in a particle's path elsewhere; and every particle exerted some degree of force on every other particle, so if you were trying to predict a particle's path with any precision, taking into account the millions of moving bodies and fluctuating conditions . . .

It was impossible—unless you employed truly *advanced* chaos dynamics, such as the calculations used by the translator. And even then, working out general patterns of orbital resonance and the stability and instability of orbits was one thing, but the raw-data requirement for tracking where one *individual* particle might get flung out of its orbit like a bullet was truly staggering, and best represented this way:

An image flicked into existence, showing a series of hollow, transparent, concentric tori, colored various shades of green, blue, orange, and red. Waves of distortion began rippling through the donuts, and then kinks appeared as resonant instabilities, and then the tori opened up like onion shells and twisted like bizarre Möbius strips, and shredded into four-dimensional ferns . . .

I am not following this, not at all—

—<mode-level shift>—

The image vanished, and Bandicut let out a long breath. /Now, that sure was helpful./ He sensed frustration coming from the quarx.

>> I don't expect you to follow the actual math, John. But I was trying to let you see the general outline of the problem, and the solution process. The translator, to put it *very* simply, is making n-dimensional phase-space analyses of the movements of objects in your solar system . . . >>

/That's putting it simply—?/ Bandicut asked, but the quarx continued without missing a beat.

>> . . . including those at the outer periphery, not just in the Kuiper Belt, but in what you call the Oort Cloud . . . >>

/Kuiper Belt? Oort Cloud? There's nothing but empty space there, and a few zillion comets./

>> Precisely. Plus some dark planets which you haven't discovered yet. Your science is not yet tracking the large-scale movements of those bodies, or their gravitational effects on each other. Nevertheless, the translator is mapping the resonant attractor patterns that emerge over time, in an effort to mark the probable locations of future events. And now it needs the specific transient identifiers to locate— >>

/Would you explain this in *English,* please?/

>> I'm trying, I really am. It's a question in one sense of identifying the largest-scale meta-attractions, and then using that as a focusing device to scale down to— >>

/Fucking A, Charlie, if you can't explain it, can you just cut to the conclusion?/

>> I . . . yes, if you wish. The conclusion is that something's very likely to hit the Earth, something big, and I'm not sure yet what it is, and I need your help to find out. >>

Bandicut remained silent and puzzled for a little while. /Oh. That's more or less what you said in the first place, isn't it? But listen, then . . . why insist upon secrecy?/

There was a sigh, before the quarx answered.

>> That's another part of the chaos analysis: the sociopolitical attractors. The translator says that time is too short, and if we go public, we'll set up turbulences that may delay our acting until it's too late. >>

Bandicut frowned. Before he could think of a reply, the quarx whispered one more thing.

>> I'm putting a pretty heavy burden on you, I know. But there's one more thing here that you ought to know, too. >>

/Which is—?/

>> Uh—well, you see . . . there's a good possibility that I might not live long enough to see this to its proper—*oh, hell's bells! NOW what's happening—?* >>

He was interrupted by a hash of static.

6

NEUROLINK

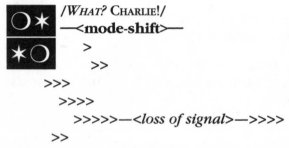

/*WHAT?* CHARLIE!/
—<mode-shift>—
>
>>
>>>
>>>>
>>>>>—<*loss of signal*>—>>>>
>>

He couldn't hear the quarx over the static. There was some sort of jostling going on, but he couldn't tell if it was within the data-connection, or on the outside.

The static faded, but there was still some sort of scratchy interference, like a malfunctioning neurolink junction, or an audio speaker distorting a human voice. For a moment, he felt a rush of panic. Was this going to be another devastating breakdown, only without the neuro? It had seemed safe enough . . . but now the data-connection was disintegrating, and all of Charlie's explanatory images had turned to snow. The interference persisted a moment longer, before

>>
>>>>
>>>>>—<*alpha-disconnect*>—>>>>

>>>
  >>
 >

was followed by a stunning silence. The silence was broken only by the jangling of his nerves and the slow return of his external senses.

/Charlie? Are you still there?/

The quarx stirred.

/// I'm here, but so is someone else!
Open your eyes, John!
Open your eyes! ///

What the hell was Charlie talking about? Was someone else trying to get access to his thoughts? Suddenly he realized that the quarx was speaking literally. His eyelids flicked open, and in the gloom of his bunk, he saw the privacy-curtain dimpling inward with rhythmic beats. Someone was whacking on it from the outside. He heard a muffled voice. "Bandie! You in there? Hey, Bandie!"

/// Who is it? ///

Bandicut groaned. /I think I know. I'd better answer./

/// Don't tell them about me! ///

/Gimme a break, will you?/ He opened the curtain a few inches and peered out into the glare of the room light. "What d'ya want, Krackey?" he grunted.

His roommate, Gordon Kracking, was pacing back and forth in front of their stacked bunks, waving his arms in obvious distress. Bandicut sighed. Krackey was arguably one of the brightest individuals in the entire Triton operation—and also one of the most ungainly, with angular bones and an owlish haircut; and whenever he was really worked up about something, all of that mental power somehow transformed him into a sight that reminded Bandicut of a crippled duck trying to fly.

/// Who is this? ///

the quarx asked.

/My friend,/ Bandicut sighed. /Don't mind him, he's a bit of a goak./

/// Goak—? ///

"Bandie!" Kracking cried. "I knew you were in there!"

"Yeah, Krackey, you got me on that one. Now make a little room, will you?" Bandicut pushed the curtain open and swung his feet out over the edge of the bunk. At the same time, he sat up, banging his head on the bunk above him. *"Ow!"* He cursed quietly. Three months in this place and he was still banging his goddamn head on that goddamn bunk.

Krackey greeted him like a long-lost brother. "Bandie! What happened out there, man? We were afraid you were a goner!"

Bandicut squinted back at him from the bunk. His head was still foggy with the things Charlie had been saying, and he was trying to remember what it was they had been talking about at the very end, before the interruption. He felt as if he had awakened from a dream, and the threads of it were slipping away, even as he tried to fix them in his memory. But it was too late; they were gone. "What are you talking about?" he rasped finally.

Krackey cocked his head, eyes blazing. He had one blue and one green eye, like a cat. "Bandie, everyone knows about it—how you fried your buggy and would be frozen stiff out there if Genghis hadn't come along and gotten you running again. What were you doing in the laser area anyway?"

Bandicut let out an annoyed breath. "Who said I was in the laser area?"

"That's what I heard," said Krackey. "I don't know who said it first."

"What else did they say—that I went into orbit? Look, *I* didn't fry anything—and it wasn't Genghis, it was Napoleon. And he didn't fix it, he just hopped a ride back to save his lazy, robot ass the walk home."

Krackey was shaking his head. "Bandie, that's not the way people are saying it. Look, man—I trust you, you know that. If you want me to set the record straight for you—"

Bandicut sighed as he slid down from his bunk. "All right, Krackey. Yeah, I guess I can tell you. What really happened is that I met an alien out there, and was lucky to get back without being dissected alive."

/// What are you doing!!! ///

Krackey looked hurt as Bandicut walked past him. "Come on, John—I'll keep it quiet if you want me to. But what really happened? I heard Jackson was fit to be tied."

"I just told you."

/// John, you PROMISED! ///

He ignored the quarx. "Look, Jackson should be put out of his misery, for all of our sakes. I didn't do anything that—" He sighed. "Ah, never mind. You wouldn't believe me anyway. No one else does." He traipsed into the lav, with Krackey following. /Don't worry, Charlie. You don't think he'd actually *believe* me, do you?/

"Come on, Bandie!" Krackey wailed.

/// Will he? ///

/Not a chance./ Peering into the sink mirror at his angular, unshaven face and his copper-green eyes, he thought, Do I *look* possessed? Are you in there, Charlie, in those eyes? Sighing, he shook his head and glanced back at his friend. "Krack, if you don't want to believe me, you can read all about it on the board newsies. They won't have it right, either—but at least it'll be official."

"Bandicoot, give me a break! Why'd they demote you to mining ops? *Something* must have happened!" Krackey couldn't bear mysteries like this, and he was staring at Bandicut imploringly. Suddenly his eyes widened and understanding seemed to dawn. "Bandie!" He lowered his voice. "You didn't have one of those damn fugues, did you?"

Bandicut nearly froze, but forced himself to bend to wash his hands and face. He dried himself and said in a low voice, through the towel, "Now, Krackey—if that's what had happened, they'd have me in the funny room already, wouldn't they?" He peered up at his friend and was greeted with a sober gaze. He *had* had a fugue, Krackey was realizing. "Look," Bandicut said quietly, "I'd appreciate it if we could drop the subject for a while. You can just tell people that it was all blown out of proportion. Really—I had a malfie, but I fixed it, and nothing happened. Okay?"

Krackey nodded slowly. "Okay, Bandie." He hesitated, scratching the back of his neck. "But listen—let me know if it happens again, will you? You can't let this keep happening. If it does, like it or not, you're going to have to see the docs."

Bandicut snorted.

"I mean it, Bandie."

"Yeah," Bandicut sighed. "I will. Okay?" He waited until Krackey nodded, then he returned to zip up his bunk curtain, and he left the dorm without another word.

He wasn't going to be able to just waltz around the base pretending nothing had happened, he soon realized. He went to the cafeteria for an early supper, and by the time he'd finished eating, three different people had stopped to ask him what had happened out on the plain—the unspoken gist being, are you still employed here, and are you planning to do anything else that will screw up the works for the rest of us? He answered the questions casually but tersely, and by the third time, he was starting to feel pretty peeved.

                    /// *You aren't going to tell anyone else*
                        that you met an alien,
                            are you? ///
Charlie asked worriedly.

"You haven't heard me tell anyone, have you?" he snapped. Realizing that he had just spoken aloud, he glanced around self-consciously, grateful that the room was mostly empty. Careful! he thought. It was easy enough to direct his thoughts inward, while maintaining outward silence, as long as he thought of it in terms of neuro-connect. The trouble was that that state of mind tended to leave him with a blank and rather stupid expression on his face, and that didn't seem like a very helpful camouflage.

The quarx persisted.

/// When you told Krackey before . . . about me.
Was that a joke? ///

He shrugged. /Ha ha./

/// I'm serious! ///

/Yeah, okay. Yes, it was a joke./ He finished his tempeh-and-tomato sandwich and began picking at the custard dessert.

/// Well . . . was it a joke on me,
or on Krackey? ///

Bandicut stared at the wall, knowing he had a dumb expression on his face, but unable to help it. /I'll leave that for you to figure out,/ he said. /Jeez, Charlie, I thought you said you'd learned all about us by watching TV. You sound like a raw recruit! What kind of an invader are you?/

/// I'm not any kind of an invader! ///

/Hah! Gotcha./

/// Oh.
That was another joke.
Like on TV.
Right? ///

Before he could think of a response, Bandicut heard a sudden rush of laughter in his mind, like a gust of wind blowing open a door. He almost choked on his custard. /What was *that* for?/ he grunted in bewilderment.

/// Laughtrack.
Isn't that how jokes are answered,
on TV? ///

Bandicut shook his head in bewilderment. /What *are* you talking about? I've never even heard of such a thing./

/// No? Really? ///

/I think you're operating with some rather quaint and outmoded ideas, Charlie. Maybe we should sit and watch the holo for a few days, and just let you catch up./ Bandicut rose from the table and hooked a thumb at the busrobot, pointing to his dirty dishes on the table. The robot twitched slightly; he could have sworn that it shrugged and looked away from him. Shaking his head, he loped out of the cafeteria, moving along an empty third-level corridor.

/// Were you serious about watching TV?
I don't think we can afford the time— ///

/I was most certainly *not* serious. Look, Charlie—if you don't mind, I'd like to cut the crap here and start understanding what's happening to my life./

/// I think that's wise. ///

Bandicut nodded and stopped to peer out one of the corridor windows, with a view toward the main surface mining area. A cloud of vapor was rising from beyond the intervening building structures; the lasers were back in operation, burning away ices and rock in search of embedded metals. The metals of a civilization from another star system, another eon . . . a civilization destroyed by war. The images that the quarx had shared with him rose again in his mind. It occurred to him that he was the only human being alive who knew the actual source and history of those metals.

He felt a sudden, deep sadness in his heart, and realized that Charlie was also seeing those images again, and grieving for what had been. /I'm sorry, Charlie./

The quarx stirred uneasily, and changed the subject.

/// I guess I still have some things
to explain to you. ///

/I haven't forgotten. But your "mission" isn't the only thing I have to think about. I need to go check the system boards and see what sort of reassignment they've given me. Just because I've been given a mission to save the Earth doesn't mean I don't still have a job to do here. Unless you decide our mission is urgent enough to let me talk . . ./

The quarx spoke up hastily.

/// No.
We can always go public, if the situation warrants.
*But we can't then go un*public,*
if you follow. ///

/Yes, well . . ./ Bandicut turned to continue down the corridor.

"John!" he heard, from behind him. It was a woman's voice. He turned and saw Georgia Patwell from ops coming his way with a relaxed, loping, long-legged stride that seemed to fit perfectly with the low gravity. She was accompanied by another woman, about six inches shorter, who was moving with a more energetic gait. Bandicut recognized the other woman from the exoarchaeology group down in the basement.

"Hi," he said, hoping he wouldn't be asked one more time what he'd done wrong.

"Bandie, I thought you were going to give Stelnik hives today, when you dropped out of contact," Georgia said, gliding to a stop with a grin. "I know I shouldn't, but I have to give you credit. That was great."

"Uh—thanks."

"You're all right, though, aren't you?" She suddenly looked concerned. "I read your report. I don't know where everyone else is getting their ideas, but it sounds as if they're trying to elect you sacrificial lamb of the week."

"I, uh—"

"You know my friend, don't you?" Georgia turned slightly to include the other woman in the conversation. "Julie Stone, from exoarch? John Bandicut, survey ops?"

Bandicut gulped and nodded, trying to smile. "I, uh—yes, I think we've met—"

Julie offered a hand to shake. "In the rec area. I've seen you playing Einey Steiney, but I don't think we've been introduced." Her face flashed with a quick smile, then became inscrutable. She was pretty, Bandicut thought, with short brown hair and blue eyes; and she was probably thinking to herself, so this is the goak who fried his neuros, and then fried a rover for good measure and held up half the station's operations for a couple of hours. Good one to stay away from, she was probably thinking.

He felt a sudden temptation to introduce Charlie to the two women, then felt his face flush as he realized he was still shaking her hand. "Nice to meet you," he croaked, letting go.

"I guess you had kind of a tough day," Julie offered. "Georgia was just telling me about it."

Great, Bandicut groaned inwardly. He took a breath and nodded. "It wasn't one of my better days. I was just on my way to . . . see where I've been reassigned."

"Well, good luck," said Julie.

"Hang in there, Bandie," Georgia said, patting him on the arm as she continued on her way with Julie.

Thanks, Bandicut whispered silently. He sighed and followed the women, but slowly, allowing them to disappear through the bulkhead doors ahead of him.

/// You seemed rather
ill at ease with those women, ///
the quarx noted.

Bandicut shrugged. /Not with Georgia. She's easy to be friends with. She's married, of course, which is probably why. No threat, you know. But the other one—/ He hesitated.

/// Julie?
Didn't she fit your idea of . . .
friendliness? ///
/Uh-huh. That's why I was . . . well. I always expect the worst, somehow, when I meet a woman I like. I always figure something will go wrong, that they'll wind up . . . not . . . I don't know why./

/// Hm. ///

/What do you mean, "Hm"? You aren't going to start psychoanalyzing me, are you?/

/// Well, no, but . . . I just wondered . . .
is this the way you always relate
to women? ///

Bandicut stopped at another window and pressed his fingers to the supertherm glass. Just on the other side of that pane was a rarefied atmosphere at a temperature much closer to absolute zero than to the temperature inside which was keeping him alive. Sometimes it was a distraction to think about things like that, but right now he found that it focused his thoughts remarkably. /I don't really *have* many relationships with women, Charlie, except for a few . . . friends . . . like Georgia./

The quarx was silent for a moment.

/// Didn't I glimpse
something about a . . . niece? ///

/Dakota? Well, yes—she was orphaned when the rest of my family was killed in the Chunnel. But Charlie, she's just a girl, plus she's related. That's hardly the same thing./

/// But you're
sending her some of your earnings? ///

Bandicut shrugged. /Big deal. I couldn't let her depend on my sister-in-law's family, could I?/

/// Um . . . ///

/She's a nice kid, Dakota. I want her to have a chance when she gets older./ Bandicut turned away from the window with a sigh. /I gotta go see where I'm posted for work tomorrow. Want to come?/ He started back down the corridor, passing several people and not meeting their eyes.

/// Ho ho.
John, I have an idea.
Is there anything you have to be doing
right now? ///

/Besides checking the postings? I guess not./ He thought of the sleep he was going to need if he was posted to mining work tomorrow. /Except—/

/// You can sleep later.
I think you'll like this idea. ///

/I'm listening./

/// Good.
Is there someplace we can go,
where if you still had your neuro,
you'd be able to connect to the datanet? ///

Bandicut walked a little more briskly. /I guess so. Why?/

/// There's something I'd like to try.
I might be able to improve
on what we did a while ago. ///

/You're going to try to plug me in?/ Bandicut felt his pulse rate increase. /Well—there are the operations centers, but we couldn't just walk in and use them. Anyway, *I* can't just plug in—or even pretend to—without people noticing. Charlie, everyone knows I lost my neuro!/

/// Isn't there someplace private? ///

/I suppose we could use the rec center. That wouldn't give us full datanet access, but we could reach some of the public info services. We could use a booth, and nobody would know if we were connecting direct, or by screen./

/// Sounds perfect.
Let's go. ///

✶

From the smell of the rec center, someone had thrown a party here recently, with liberal amounts of locally fermented, hydroponic-grain beverages. By now, the dep-heads had probably plastered the system board with notices warning against any future such occurrences. Bandicut wrinkled his nose against the stale beer smell and found an empty booth. He didn't give a damn what management thought, as long as they didn't try to associate him with it.

/Here we go,/ he said, locking the booth door and sliding into the console seat. /This is where people come when they want to send or receive messages from in-system. They expect people to be looking for privacy here. But we aren't going to get the higher functions./

/// We'll see. ///

He raised his eyebrows, but didn't ask what the quarx meant. /How do you want to do this? First I need to check the postings. I can do that from here./ He poked at the screen controls and brought up the newest notices and job listings. He noted that a brief summary of his mishap was posted, with a warning that until an investigation was completed, all rover electrical systems should be regarded as susceptible to possible cryo-failure. /They bought it,/ he muttered in disbelief. He checked the job postings and cursed. He was to report to mining ops for the early shift the next day. /They didn't buy it that much./ With a sigh, he flicked off the screen. He didn't even want to read the newsies of his accident, knowing how much the local amateur newsie reporters took from the rumor mills.

/What do you want me to do?/ he asked the quarx.

/// Put the 'trodes on your head. ///

/Charlie, they took my implants out. There's nothing for the 'trodes to connect to./

/// Leave that to me. ///

He reached for the headset and hesitated, hands holding the set in midair. /Are you sure you know what you're doing? If this goes wrong . . ./

/// It might not work.
But I don't think there's any danger. ///

Though he found this less than wholly reassuring, Bandicut positioned the neural set over his temples. The inductance electrodes pressed firmly against the spots on either side where he had once had receptor plates implanted under his skin. The contact made him acutely aware of the emptiness, the lack of what had once felt as important to him as his eyes, or his hands.

/// Okay, I need to make some adjustments.
Try to keep your thoughts still. ///

He tried. He pushed away a fleeting rush of excitement at the thought that the quarx might actually be able to work a miracle here. He thought of the medical labs; he thought of the wrecked buggy; he thought of sleep; he thought of a pink elephant. He thought of how miserable he was going to feel if he got his hopes up for this and then nothing happened.

/// Hush, John.
Wait . . . maybe I can help. ///

He felt something like a warm, soft rain in his mind and felt the thoughts melt away, leaving him relaxed and expectant. The quarx must have done something to give him soothing alpha-wave relaxation. It was blissful.

There was a brief rush of static, and then he fell off the edge of a cliff into a deep, long, weightless fall . . .

```
>
   >>>
     >>>>>>
       >>>>>>>>>>>
>>>>>>>>>>>>>>>>>>>—<alpha-connect>—>>>>>
       >>>>>>>>>>>>>>>>>>>>>>>>>>>>>>>>>
>>>>>>>>>>>>>>>>>>>—<full-neural link>—>>>>
       >>>>>>>>>>>>
     >>>>>>
   >>>
>
```
—<mode shift>—

Lights sparkled around him, like a fishing net encrusted with diamonds, flung against a night sky. Each light burned with possibility, with connectedness and energy. His heart leaped. The linkup was a little rough, but . . . this was pre-cisely what he had been hoping for . . . if it was real.

Charlie cut in.

/// It is real.

Is this the datanet we should be looking for? ///

/Charlie—this shouldn't be possible! Not without the neuros! How did you do it?/

/// Oh, it was just
a matter of making certain cross-connections
in the neuronal structure— ///

/You mean, altering my *brain*?/

/// Well, no.
I mean, not—well, no.
I mean using MY quasi-neuronal capacities
to bridge the missing elements
in YOUR neuronal system.
I merely altered certain characteristics
of the space-time matrix around your neurons.
It's basically how
I talk to you, anyway. ///

/Ah,/ he thought dizzily. /That was another thing I'd been meaning to ask you about./

/// Now you know.
But let's not get bogged down in technical details.
We have a lot to do,
now that we're tuned in and turned on,
as your people like to say. ///

/I've never said that—/

/// Fucking figure of speech, okay? ///

Bandicut blinked, then laughed out loud. /Charlie! You just made a joke! Did you know you just made a joke?/

/// Ha ha.
I think we should get busy here.
I see a lot going on,
and I think we should explore it.

Let's tie into some of those glittering bangles
and see what there is to see.
Are you with me? ///
/Where else would I be?/
A tendril of light leaped out and linked him, sizzling, to one, then two, then three of the pulsing nexi of data.

7

DATANET

>> . . . CERES EXCHANGE down 23 points in final trading. Following are highlighted prices (Euroyen): . . . . . Asteroid Aggregate, 75.73. . . . . . . Boeing-Ford Pressure Hulls, 64.94. . . . . . Ceres-Mars Express, 57.60 . . . >>

Stock quotes? They were flying by in a blur. Directly above and below it were other streams of data, just as blinding. He blinked his attention back to the quotes:

>> . . . Sanyo Mining & Extraction, 83.25 . . . Sirtus Astronics, 54.76 . . . SemiOps Systems, 93.44 . . . >>

He jerked his attention away. What the hell did he care about stock prices? And why would Charlie care?

The quarx spoke from his accustomed position in the center of Bandicut's consciousness.

/// I don't know if it's relevant.
But it is interesting. ///

One of the other channels was a political digest service. News capsules were streaming past:

>> . . . Secretary of the New England Nations denied Vatican assertions that recent state-sponsored ordinations of women were intended to subvert the

authority of the Papacy. Observers noted significant contradictions, however . . .

>> . . . third attempt on the life of Renaldo Pelliquez, CEO of the Caribbean Coalition, thwarted when an eleven-year-old street hawker noticed a suspicious vehicle in the central plaza of Ponce, Puerto Rico . . .

>> . . . New efforts to open North China to world trade received a setback when . . . >>

He could only snatch a sentence or two at a time; it was like trying to drink from a fire hose. He lurched from the political channel into another, a geyser of musical/video entertainment. It was compressed, accelerated, impossible to track.

/// Ride with it, John.
Go with the flow. ///

/Go with the flow? I can't keep up with this!/

/// Your baud rate was a little low,
so I increased it,
to get as much data as possible. ///

He tried, but it was impossible to keep up with the flow—or to back away from it. /I can't do it, Charlie! You're drowning me!/

/// Okay, wait—
let's try a different perspective . . . ///

The riptide of data dropped away abruptly, so that he seemed to be looking down over the datastreams from a great height. He gasped for breath. Everything was changed: the data were a topography, a smooth blur of broad brushstrokes, a swirling of smoke, the individual datapoints no more visible than the molecules of water in Niagara Falls. It was easier to watch now, but he couldn't quite see the point of it.

/// Watch this. ///

He blinked, and it changed again: the viewpoint flicking

wider, then wider again. He saw a hundred more channels of fluid movement, on a vast scale, as if he were floating high above a carved and runneled plain, watching fluvial motion as the gods might watch it. He was reminded of fractal imagery in which certain geometric qualities persisted even through repeated changes of scale. It was an orchestrated image of turbulence, chaotic beyond his comprehension.

/// Precisely.
Fascinating, isn't it? ///

/Yes, I suppose so—but what good is it? I thought you wanted information about—/ He paused and thought a moment. /Actually, what *did* you want information about?/

/// For now, exactly what you're seeing.
The details are still entrained in the raw data,
but we don't need them just now. ///

/We don't? Why not?/

The quarx coughed delicately.

/// By "we," actually,
I meant the translator and I. ///

Bandicut felt strangely let down. /Oh. You mean, I wouldn't be able to understand it even if you told me?/

/// I meant no offense, John.
Remember, we talked about dynamical chaos
and ways of analyzing it? ///

Bandicut strained to remember. They'd gotten interrupted, and he hadn't quite been following it to begin with.

/// Well,
this information can be translated
into a harmonic resonance
that will ultimately,
through various cycles of analysis,
move us toward that answer you wanted. ///

Bandicut remained mute with incomprehension.

/// About what's going to hit the Earth?
And what to do about it? ///

/Ah. That./ Bandicut watched the strange graphical display with an uneasy feeling of disconnectedness. Whatever information was contained in there was going to remain completely incomprehensible, unless Charlie did something to explain it.

/// *John? Are you listening?*
I'm trying to help.
Do you hear that musical activity? ///

He listened. In the background there was indeed a deep, thrumming harmonic rhythm, which he supposed could be called music. /Yes./

/// *Well, that's the* sound *of the turbulence,*
filtered and partially transformed.
To me, it's still mostly incomprehensible.
But the translator can actually turn this
into useful attractor-equations. ///

Bandicut felt a great ringing emptiness where his understanding was supposed to be. Still, he had to try. /You mean . . . to predict broad changes in . . . patterns of . . . ?/ His voice trailed off.

/// *Not exactly.*
I mean, that can be done, yes.
But what we really want
is to derive actual detail *from this—* ///

Detail? /How's that?/ Bandicut croaked.

/// *—though Heaven forbid*
you should ask me how. ///

He blinked, and felt an involuntary snarl rising in his throat. /I *am* asking you!/

/// *Well, I acknowledge the question.*
But it's all in the translator's core programs,
which I did not create,
and only partially understand.
As I explained before,
I am neither the owner,
nor the designer,

nor the master,
of the translator.
I am merely paired up with it. ///

Bandicut absorbed that with some incredulity, but the quarx continued without pause.

/// Anyway, we're getting good data here,
but I need a way to channel it to the translator. ///

/Is that a problem? I thought you had everything locked in. I thought you had our TV and our datanet and all that shit./

/// Well, yes.
We had all that . . . shit . . .
as you so finely put it. ///

Bandicut frowned. /You mean, you don't now?/

/// Sadly, no.
The TV was the first to go,
when they stopped using open broadcasts. ///

/So you missed out on a lot of good programming, huh? What about the datanet? You seem to know it pretty well./

/// That's on a tightline from stations in-system,
just like TV now. ///

Bandicut was still puzzled. /So, can't you pick up the laser beam?/

/// Well, we could.
But when you put your base here,
we had to move ourselves underground,
out of sight.
That meant modulating through the ice,
which was okay—until your mining ops
started blanketing the surface with smog deposition.
Now we can only pick up local transmissions,
and even that's difficult. ///

/But wait—you knew *I* was coming along toward your little cavern, didn't you? How'd you know that?/

/// Altogether different matter.
That was my direct sensing.

I felt your presence and state of mind.
But as for monitoring general activity
throughout the solar system—
that's been hard. ///

/My apologies,/ Bandicut said, not even sure why he felt the impulse to be sarcastic.

Charlie appeared not to notice.

/// Thanks to your help,
this is the best datastream we've had in years. ///

/Uh-huh. So now that you've got it, what are you going to do with it? How are you going to get it to the translator?/

/// I'm not sure, actually.
But I can hold quite a lot in memory,
while we figure out a way. ///

/We?/

/// You and I.
If you come up with a good idea,
don't think I won't listen to it. ///

Bandicut nodded to himself, unsure whether to be flattered or not.

/// Hey—look at that signal over there! ///

He felt a sudden slowdown in the transmission speed. The fractal-landscape dropped away, and an image-panel flipped up into view. It held the face of a man, who looked directly into Bandicut's eyes. A voice boomed into Bandicut's head like a bass drum:

>> "SEE HOW MUCH FASTER YOU CAN TRANS-LOAD THAT ALL-IMPORTANT DATACACHE WHEN YOU OPEN AN ACCOUNT WITH *PLANETVIEW ON-LINE SYSTEMS!*

>> "FOR A LOW-COST DEMONSTRATION, ALL YOU HAVE TO DO IS SAY *'OKAY—I'LL TRY!'*

>> "OUR INSTANT-EXCHANGE SYSTEM WILL OPEN A TEMPORARY ACCOUNT FOR YOU WITHOUT SIG-NAL DELAY—EVEN IF YOU'RE CALLING FROM ONE

OF OUR DISTANT PLANETARY OUTPOSTS. GIVE US A
TRY NOW!" >>

/// *Hey, let's do it,* ///
the quarx urged.

/Why? It'd take eight hours for our request to bounce to
Earth and back—/

/// *No, no,*
they've got it in terminal memory.
We can get on right away.
Let's do it. ///

/That all depends on whether I have the credit for whatever you have in mind,/ Bandicut answered cautiously,
tempted despite himself.

/// *They said it's low cost,* ///
the quarx pointed out.

The salesman nodded and jabbed his finger at Bandicut.

>> **"Your friend has the right idea, sir! There's ab-**
solutely no risk. You'll have your account at once,
and if you're not one hundred percent satisfied, we'll
cancel with no further obliga—" >>

/All right, all right,/ Bandicut groaned.

>> **"All you have to do is say—"** >>

/I'll try it now!/ Bandicut growled, hoping to cut off the
sales pitch.

/// *No, no—you're supposed to say—* ///

>> **"Close enough."** >>

The salesman winked and vanished, and in his place a
large menu of options appeared, floating in space. Blinking
at the top were the words:

<< **ACCOUNT NOW ACTIVE!** >>
<< **The more you use it, the cheaper it becomes!** >>

/Sure,/ Bandicut muttered. He sensed Charlie stirring eagerly. /So what do you want to do with this?/

/// May I? ///

He nodded and a flash of light stabbed out and touched a point on the menu index. Faster than he could follow, a submenu blinked on, and another light stabbed, calling up a third menu, then a fourth. Each time, the quarx made its choice before Bandicut could read the menu. Something to do with astronomical data . . .

/// Ah, here we are! ///

Pages of letters and numbers began swarming past at a dizzying rate. Bandicut blinked, trying to follow. It looked familiar. It *was* familiar; it was a table of data on the positions and movements of astronomical bodies.

/Is that an ephemeris?/ he protested. /Charlie, you could have gotten that stuff from the station library! It wouldn't have cost a cent!/

For a few moments there was no answer, as the data spun past at a rate too fast to follow. Then the quarx answered softly,

/// Library? Oh . . . ///

Bandicut sighed and watched the flow, not as individual datapoints, but as a flowing stream. The effort was giving him a headache. /Say, Charlie—/

The quarx sounded subdued.

/// Are you angry? ///

/I should be. But I'm wondering something. This obviously isn't being transmitted from off Triton. So how are they getting it to us so fast? I mean, it's one thing to have a sign-up module here in terminal memory, but they can't have their whole damn database loaded up to Triton!/

/// Hmm . . . good question.
Give me a moment to check something. ///

At that instant, the datastream ended, and a message scrolled across Bandicut's vision:

>> You have received all of the data available at your present location. For a more in-depth output,

please note your request now, and you will be notified when the additional information has been transmitted from our core systems in Earth orbit. Please remember: even Planetview can't violate the speed of light, hard though we may try. But no one can fulfill your request faster than PLANETVIEW! >>

/// We'd like the full, updated ephemeris—
including all comets and asteroids.
Okay? ///

The question seemed to be directed at Bandicut; but without waiting for his reply, a beam of light flashed out and made the request.

>> Thank you. From Triton, your request will take a minimum of eight hours to fulfill. Thank you for using— >>

/Would you cut that damn thing off, please?/

The sound dropped to a whisper.

/So tell me. Where'd they get that ephemeris you just filed away?/

/// Actually . . .
er . . . I'm sorry, John . . .
I didn't realize . . . ///

/What?/

The quarx's voice was apologetic.

/// Well, from the datapath . . .
um . . . it looks like they fed it to us from,
uh, the station library. ///

There was a long silence, before Bandicut murmured, /You're telling me we just paid them through the nose to tap our own station library and feed it right back to us?/

/// Um . . .
I guess I owe you one, John.
Was it very expensive? ///

He exhaled noisily. /Let's check the charges. There it is. *Ho-ly smokes!/*

The quarx cringed. It felt to Bandicut as if his brain were wrinkling.

/// Is it that bad?
Or are you joking again? ///

He held out for a moment longer, before releasing the tension with a chuckle. /Aw, I guess I can afford it okay. It'll cost me a coupla' beers, though./

/// Good.
I mean . . . I'm sorry.
But anyway, you can't take it with you—
right? ///

Bandicut stared at a point in the dataspace where he imagined a quarx might be floating. /Now what exactly did you mean by that? Was that a figure of speech, or are you planning to take me somewhere?/

Charlie seemed nonplussed.

/// Nothing!
Fucking figure of speech! ///

A raucous laugh came up, Charlie's "laughtrack" covering up his embarrassment, rather poorly.

Bandicut made a mental cutting-of-the-throat gesture. He was rewarded with silence. /Are we done now? Can we get the hell out of this con operation?/

The answering voice was very small.

/// Okay. ///

The Planetview menus vanished. Bandicut was about to disconnect from the datanet as a whole, when he felt something like a hand touching him, lightly restraining him.

/// Just one more thing?
Please? ///

He sighed tolerantly. /What this time?/

/// Something I just thought of. ///

In the dark of the silenced datanet, a beam of light flicked out, triggering something he couldn't quite see.

Before he could even ask, he felt a series of reactions cascading through the dataspace around him, dominoes falling through the silence and the dark. Though he couldn't quite follow what was happening, he had an uncomfortable suspicion that Charlie was somehow altering some of the fixed parameters of the datanet connection. He thought he heard an alarm sounding somewhere just at the edge of the system, but it fell silent so quickly that he wasn't actually sure he had heard it.

/// I hope no one else heard it, either. ///
/What are you doing?/
/// Hold on—
I've just about got the uplink
to the orbital station . . . ///
/WHAT?/
/// Now, if I can just defocus
their downlink beam by a hair . . . ///

Suddenly, without actually seeing the quarx's actions, he had a shockingly clear view of its results. He felt a dizzying buzz, datastreams flowing through his brain faster even than before, flashing through some jury-rigged linkage in the base's dataflow system, beaming up to the support station in orbit above Triton and flashing back down in a slightly widened and misaligned signal beam . . . a beam that just grazed the terrain where Bandicut and his rover had meandered.

A beam that at this moment was no doubt being monitored by an alien machine in a subterranean cavern.

/CHARLIE!/

/// Almost done.
A few more seconds . . .
there.
Off.
Signal back to normal— ///
/Charlie!/ he whispered dizzily.

*/// —no essential communications interrupted,
just a brief anomaly in the transmission,
and if anybody traces it
they'll just wonder how the hell some ancient TV
program
called "Father Knows Best"
got interposed over routine telemetry.
And why so much static.
Heh, heh. ///*

Bandicut was weak with horror, with awe, with astonishment. /Jesus mokin' fokin' Christ, Charlie!/ he whispered, when he had regained the ability to speak. /Did you actually get all that data transmitted to your wondermachine?/

*/// I think so.
As for whether it was received and understood,
I don't know yet.
But as they say,
you have to make hay while the sun shines.
Thanks for the help, pardner. ///*

For a moment, Bandicut could not think of how to respond. Make hay while the sun shines? What the hell did that mean? He felt a sudden, draining self-doubt. Had he just betrayed his race to a clever alien invader . . . or taken the first step toward saving Earth?

/// John—it's going to be okay. ///

It wasn't as if he was used to this sort of thing, even in neurolink. He just had no idea what to think, or say.

/// We can leave now, if you want, ///
said the quarx softly.

*/// I believe
you wanted to get some sleep? ///*

8

MINING OPS

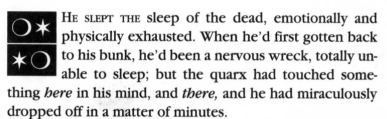HE SLEPT THE sleep of the dead, emotionally and physically exhausted. When he'd first gotten back to his bunk, he'd been a nervous wreck, totally unable to sleep; but the quarx had touched something *here* in his mind, and *there,* and he had miraculously dropped off in a matter of minutes.

At some point during the night, he became aware of dreaming. He did not wake, but felt a profound inner certainty that came to life even in the depths of sleep. The dream was alien and at times alarming: images of ghostly lights drifting in darkness, and rushing toward him at great speed before expanding and turning inside out, with a bewildering series of flashes, and an abrupt twisting of the darkness. He felt that this was something more than just images of lights—that it was space-time itself twisting and devouring its own tail, that it was some quarxly transformation or journey, and he found himself unaccountably frightened and lonely . . .

And as that dream image flickered away, he glimpsed a creature like a slender tree trunk swaying in the wind, and he recognized it as one of the Fffff'tink. He knew that his quarx, or at least a quarx very *like* the quarx he knew, had lived in its mind for a very long time, during which the Fffff'tink endured solar flares, earthquakes, and opposition from its own fellows as it struggled to help move a remnant of its people into space, to escape a dying world. And during that time, the quarx died several times; and in the end, when the Fffff'tink died, releasing it, the quarx never learned for certain whether the Fffff'tink civilization had survived or not . . .

✴

Base-morning came all too soon. Bandicut awoke to a chirruping alarm-clock sound and rolled over, remembering with a shiver the dreams, and then the presence of the quarx in his mind; and for a moment, he wanted to ask, do all of your hosts die in terrible catastrophes, but before he could form the words, he fell asleep again.

The next time he awoke, it was to a brash bugle call in his head, blatting a musical reveille.

/// GOOD MAWWWNIN', TRITONNNN! ///

He groaned, pushing himself up on one elbow. "What the kr'deekin' hell—?" And then he realized the source, and his vision turned red, even in the darkness of the bunk. /Charlie, what are you—/

/// It's from an old movie!
Just trying to help you start the day right! ///

/Well, DON'T!/ He practically screamed the words out loud.

/// Sorry . . . I guess I didn't— ///

/No, you didn't. I do *not* like to be awakened that way. Ever. I do not have a sense of humor in the morning./ Bandicut sank back and ran his hand through his hair, blinking in an effort to come fully awake.

/// I really didn't mean to— ///

/Never mind. Just let me wake up, okay? God, were those your memories I was dreaming?/ The dream images clung to him like cobwebs, vague but troubling.

/// Probably.
I was . . . dreaming . . . myself.
Was it . . . the Fffff'tink? ///

The quarx's voice was muted, and seemed sad.

He sighed, nodding, and rolled back up on one elbow. /Hell of an autobiography you could write, man./ He was answered by silence, which was perhaps just as well. For a little while, he thought, he would like to hear just one voice in his head. He yanked his privacy-curtain aside and slid down from his bunk. He made no effort to greet the others who were emerging from their cubbies, but went straight into the shower with his wash kit. By the time he came out, somewhat more awake, he saw that Krackey was up. He greeted his friend with a grunt.

"Mining ops today?" Krackey murmured sympathetically.

He nodded and shrugged on his jumpsuit. Krackey seemed to recognize his need for quiet this morning, for which he was grateful.

Not everyone else was so respectful. "Bandicoot!" called Mick Eddison, a tall, whiplike, moodily dispositioned man who worked in the deep mines. "I hear you're coming down to join us in some real hands-on work today. You going to be one of the guys for a change?"

Bandicut sighed, realizing that there was no hope of avoiding this sort of needling. "Well, Eddie—since you asked—I heard you guys weren't doing too well down there. Not enough brains, is the way Cole Jackson put it to me. So I offered to come help you out."

Eddison glared at him, but several of the others guffawed at Eddison's expense and snapped their towels at him until he shouted, "Keep that up, and I'm gonna put someone's kreekin' *head* through that wall!" That brought some thumping from the opposite side of the wall. Bandicut left to go to breakfast, shaking his head in amused exasperation.

/// Are they always so . . . crude? ///
Charlie wondered on the way to the cafeteria.

/Hah! Charlie, my friend, this is the working man's world,/ Bandicut answered. /We don't exactly run what you would call a highbrow operation here./

/// Apparently not.
May I ask: why do they call you Bandicoot? ///

Bandicut took his place in the food service line. /It's just a dumb nickname they gave me. It's an animal—either a rat or a marsupial, depending on whether you're talking India or Australia. I looked it up. They're both pretty ugly critters./

/// Oh. I think I see.
Would you like me to call you Bandicoot also? ///

/Try it and you'll be one dead mokin' goak,/ Bandicut threatened cheerfully. /Bad enough I have to put up with it from these cretins. From you I expect respect./

Charlie hesitated.

/// Oh. Now I think I see. ///

Bandicut slid a plate of cultured eggs onto his tray, along with some toast and a cup of roastamoke, and looked for a quiet place to sit. He knew he wouldn't get through breakfast without more ribbing from his coworkers, but most of it turned out to be good-natured. He was finally starting to feel almost good—except for a busrobot that was chittering annoyingly at him as he dumped his own breakfast tray—when Eddison walked in and asked loudly, "So whose team are they putting you on, Bandicoot? Whose equipment gets fried today?"

Bandicut handed his empty tray to the robot to shut it up. "Well, now I guess that's up to Herb, isn't it?" he said mildly. "If we're both lucky, it won't be yours."

/// Who's Herb? ///

Charlie asked, preventing him from hearing Eddison's reply over the muttering of laughter, which was probably just as well.

/Herb Massengale. The mining supervisor./

/// *You don't sound happy.* ///

Bandicut followed the general movement of workers down the corridor. /I think, if I had a choice, I'd rather work with Lonnie Stelnik,/ he said.

/// *My.*

Are all of your supervisors so unpleasant? ///

Bandicut chuckled. /Well, now, haven't you just put your finger on it. Lemme put it this way. Lonnie Stelnik's self-centered and ambitious, but at least he's no dummy. Cole Jackson's different—he's a cowardly rule-worshiper— but give him his due, he's not dumb, either. But Herb Massengale? Well, you'll see./

Charlie seemed thoughtful.

/Why so quiet, suddenly? Are you wondering why you aliens ever bothered listing humanity on the roll call of sentient species?/ he asked. When there was no answer, he added, /We *are* on the rolls, aren't we? Of sentient species?/

/// *Mmm.* ///

/What the hell does *that* mean? Oh, I get it—that was a joke, right?/

Charlie seemed to clear his quarxian throat.

/// *Sort of.*

But the truth is,
I'm wondering about the people in authority here.
Their character . . . well, we must take it into account,
when we make our plans. ///

/Ah./ Bandicut grunted. /I wish I could offer you more encouragement on that score./ He followed a group of men toward the ready room, but paused when he heard Gordon Kracking's voice behind him in the corridor.

"Bandie—didn't you look at the postings this morning?"

He turned around. "No, I looked last night. Why?"

Krackey caught up with him. "You're not supposed to

be here. You're supposed to be upstairs for a hearing on your accident.''

"You're sure?"

"Sure I'm sure. I work on the system board, don't I?"

Bandicut grinned. "Reprieve! Thanks, Krackey." He turned and started back the other way, heading for the pole up.

✳

He ascended the pole with a few easy arm-over-arm pulls and stepped off on the third and top floor of the station. The briefing room was just past Cole Jackson's office, near the station commander's. He could hear Jackson's voice, and Lonnie Stelnik's. What fun, he thought. /Charlie, if they start grilling me, be ready with some good answers, all right?/

/// I'll do my best. ///

"There he is!" said Stelnik, as Bandicut walked into the cramped conference room. The station commander's administrative assistant, a thin Chinese woman named Li Chang, was there also.

"You might have let a guy know," Bandicut said, taking a seat. "As of last night, you had me slated for the mines this morning."

Cole Jackson pushed up his eyeglasses and smiled. "Don't worry, John. We'll get you right back down there. But first we'd like you to look over your report and tell us if there's anything you'd like to add or change." He pushed his glasses up his nose again and handed Bandicut a hard copy of his report.

Bandicut glanced at the paper. "Has Pacho found the problem yet?"

Stelnik snorted. Jackson answered, "Mr. Rawlins has not yet determined the cause of the malfunction, no. In fact, he admits to being rather puzzled." Jackson glanced at Stelnik as though expecting a vulgar characterization. When none was forthcoming, he continued, "Therefore, John, it's especially important that you search your memory for *anything* that could illuminate the cause of the incident. We're holding up the survey for the time being, but we can't do that forever."

Bandicut nodded, and frowned down at his report. /For a pack of lies, it looks pretty reasonable,/ he muttered to the quarx. He swallowed, trying to maintain a normal expression. "No, I wish I could help you, but I think this really about covers it," he said. /Give or take an alien or two./

/// Only one. ///

"Take your time, John. This is important."

"Well, yes, but—"

"Let me emphasize," Jackson said, with a sideways glance at Chang, who would be reporting to the station commander. "We have certain quotas to fulfill—"

"You can't put quotas on finding alien metal deposits," Bandicut pointed out.

"Perhaps not. But we have quotas on volume and tonnage to be processed, and it is *very important* that we meet those quotas," Jackson said, somewhat more sternly than was necessary. "This is not a game! We are here at enormous expense to the MINEXFO consortium, and there are important products to be developed from our findings. It is crucial that we demonstrate progress. There are consortium shareholders to satisfy, and potential competitors who might want to replace us here. I just want to make sure you understand that, John."

"I understand it," Bandicut said testily. "I'm ready to go back out as soon as you fix my rover."

Jackson sat back, pressing his hands together in front of his face. After studying Bandicut for a moment, he nodded, with another glance at Chang, who had not said a word and looked as though she did not intend to. "Very well. But we cannot do so until we are certain we have established safe working conditions." He cleared his throat noisily. "Well, then, if we might go through this report, we will try to clarify any points of confusion. Lonnie, would you like to take it from that angle?''

Stelnik's eyes glinted as he sat forward and said, "Indeed. John, tell me—with reference to your report of lost communications and navigation—what was your first indication of trouble yesterday?"

Bandicut took a breath. /What did you tell that robot?/ he whispered silently.

*/// A voltage spike,
scrambling the nav settings . . . ///*

He caught himself in the act of nodding to the quarx, and let the movement continue as a nod to Stelnik. "Well, Lonnie—I was just out of visual range of marker Wendy when I saw a fluctuation in the nav. I suspected a voltage spike. But the comm dropped out before I could call in . . .''

If his listeners were forming opinions, he could not discern it on their faces as he continued spinning his tale.

⊠

"Thank you, John. We'll be in touch as the investigation proceeds, and we'll call you back if we have further questions. You can report to mining ops now."

"Right. See you around, Cole. Lonnie."

The quarx spoke softly as he slid back down the pole to the first level.

/// What was the purpose of that meeting, John? ///

Bandicut stepped off and walked toward the ready room for the second time that morning. /Charlie, you've just witnessed modern management at its best. What you saw was a careful effort by Jackson to make sure that he and the company are covered, if any questions arise—either about safety or productivity./

/// Uh-huh. ///

/Plus, Lonnie was probably hoping to catch me in a lie, because that would prove how sharp he is./

The quarx didn't sound happy.

/// Uh-huh. Anything else? ///

He reached the ready room. /Plus, let's give them credit. I suppose they really *were* trying to figure out what the hell happened./ He let out a long breath. /And I have to say, my quarxian friend, that the hypocrisy of all this has not escaped me. I do not feel too wonderful about having, yet again, lied through my teeth./

Charlie was silent a moment, but Bandicut could feel the mental tension building. When Charlie answered, it was in a very soft voice in the center of his consciousness.

/// I do understand, John Bandicut.
I share your ethical misgivings. ///

/You do?/

/// Yes, but I am afraid I must say, as well . . .
that meeting did not give me reason to feel
that we would dare entrust our secret
to those individuals. ///

Bandicut nodded, his vision clouding as he realized what the quarx was saying. They were not going to be sharing their secret with *anyone,* anytime soon. But neither could he muster any good reason to disagree.

"BANDICUT! Get the hell over here!" Herbert Massengale was standing in the doorway to his office, clipboard in hand. As Bandicut approached, Massengale glared at him. "I just got the bad news, Bandicut. You're on my team."

"So I'm told."

"Now, what the fokin' moke am I supposed to do with a nine-pin-head goak who don't even got his pins anymore?" Massengale rapped his knuckles on the clipboard in disgust.

/// What's he talking about?
What's a nine-pin-head goak? ///

/It's an, er, "affectionate" nickname for neurojackers./

/// Affectionate? ///

/Well . . . no. See, he doesn't neurolink himself, and he hates the guts of anyone who does./

/// That doesn't seem reasonable. ///

/What's reasonable got to do with it?/

"What are you grinnin' about?" Massengale growled. "You look like you're plugged into a mokin' computer right now. Are you gonna go zombie on me before you even start?"

Bandicut felt his face redden. He was going to have to learn to talk to Charlie without looking like an idiot. "Herb, if there's something you have for me to do, maybe we could just get on with it," he said, straining for politeness.

Massengale stared at him as if Bandicut had just done something to his nice clean windshield. "Yeahhhhh. We're shorthanded on the crawlers. Report to Bronson on number three." Without waiting for an answer, Massengale strolled away.

Bandicut curled his lip downward. It was more or less what he had expected. He knew nothing about crawler operations. If he were lucky, he would merely get in the way, instead of becoming an active hazard to the operation.

Shaking his head, he reported to the equipment window and signed out an outdoor exposure suit. When he had finished gearing up—and it had been a long time since he'd checked a suit so carefully—he went outside through the pressure lock, looking for Crawler Three and Bronson. He peered about the vast unroofed crawler bay, trying to figure out where he was supposed to be. Two of the huge mining machines had already pulled out of their docking bays and were lumbering off toward the work fields, amber beacons rotating in the perpetual night of the Triton sky. About a hundred meters down the docking bay, he spotted a faded, dusty numeral 3 on another crawler. As he set off toward it with a loping stride, its beacons flicked on, glaring in his face. He hurried, calling out on the comm. "Bronson!"

The crawler chief was halfway up a ladder on the transom of the enormous machine, one hand raised to wave the driver on. He turned his helmeted head and lowered his hand. Bandicut could just make out a frown through the faceplate. Bronson's voice moaned with an exaggerated, aggrieved tone through the background chatter on the comm. "What the—Bandicut! Now don't tell me that asshole Herb sent you out to work with *me!*"

Bandicut halted at the base of the crawler and looked up with a grin. "Can I quote you to the boss on that? Especially the asshole part?"

Bronson snorted, white eyes gleaming through the visor from an almost invisible black-skinned face. "Lissen—*I'm* the mokin' boss out here, and unless you wanna try mind-meldin' with some a' that rock out there, I suggest you shut up and get your tailpipe up in that hold. So how ya' doin', anyway, Bandie?"

"Okay. What am I supposed to *do* here?"

"Oh, whatever my man Jake tells you," Bronson drawled. "Now, get your tail up there. We're late already."

Bandicut gave Bronson a jaunty salute and grabbed a ladder up to the work cabin. As he climbed, he saw Bronson mounting the ladder to the roof of the crawler and heard him drawl: "Get 'er movin', Fitznell." The massive machine rumbled for an instant, then lurched forward, just as Bandicut was ducking through the cabin threshold. He lost his balance momentarily, slamming his left shoulder into the bulkhead. Grabbing the handrail with a curse, he heaved himself the rest of the way in and pulled the door closed behind him.

The inside of the crawler looked more like a small, machine-filled factory than a vehicle—except that it was in jerky motion. He was on a narrow platform that connected to a series of catwalks spanning the interior. A suited man was standing at a forward control panel. He turned, saw Bandicut, and waved him over. Bandicut threaded his way forward, ducking to avoid cables and pipes. Below him on his left, two mining drones hung in their cradles like enormous crabs waiting to go scuttling over the mine bed. Farther to the left, he vaguely recognized the shadowy bulk of the power reactor and ore processor.

/// I gather
you're not too familiar with this equipment. ///

/Nah, I was shown around one of these things when I first arrived on Triton, but I haven't had any reason to be inside one since./ He finally reached the man at the control panel. It was Jake Looks-Over, a part Amerind whom he knew from games of EineySteiney in the rec lounge. "Hi, Jake. What can I do here?"

Jake grinned behind his faceplate, eyes bright against a burnished face. "Hey, Bandie! That depends, I guess. You just along for the ride, or did they send you in from the frontier to find out what real work is like?"

Bandicut grabbed another handhold. "I was hoping I wouldn't *have* to do any real work. From what I hear, you guys need more brains than brawn out here."

Jake raised one eyebrow toward a monitor on the control board, where a woman's helmeted face was visible. "You hear that, Amy? John Bandicut's here to give us the benefit of his brains. Someone must've squealed on us."

The woman's face jounced with the vibration. Bandicut realized that she was driving the crawler. "Haven't I been threatening all along to squeal on you guys?" she said. Bandicut could just see the landscape moving outside the cockpit, past her head.

"Fitznell, whose side are you on, anyway?" Jake protested.

"You guys *must* be hard up if you want me out here helping you," Bandicut said. "But that's what they tell me to do, so I do it."

Jake nodded. "Well, we can put you to work driving a miner. An ace pilot like you ought to be able to handle some drones, right?"

"That depends. How hard is it?"

Jake grinned without answering.

Bandicut peered at the external monitors. The crawler was rumbling down a long access road out of the main camp. Soon it would begin descending into a vast depression a kilometer or so to the west. The mining area was ringed with lights that glared and shifted surreally in the monitors.

"We'll be there in five minutes," Jake said. "You can stash your lunch in that locker."

"Lunch?" Bandicut croaked.

"No one told you to bring a lunch? Hoo boy, you're going to be one hungry customer by the time we're done here." Jake shook his head. "Well, never mind. You want to go up and have a look from the cab before we strap you in? That okay, Amy?"

"Sure," said the driver.

Jake hooked a thumb toward a ladder on his left. Bandicut mounted the ladder, glancing nervously to see where he would fall if he slipped. The sight of the vibrating machinery caused him to tighten his grip on the handholds. He caught a handle at the top, a hatch slid open, and he climbed up into the back of the cab.

Amy Fitznell's helmeted head bobbed as she drove. She glanced up into the overhead mirror, her visor shifting in the polished glass. "Hi, Bandie. Have a seat and take a look around."

Bandicut slid into the right-hand seat and peered out the forward window. In the perpetual Triton gloom, the crawler and roadway lights combined to make an eerie highway landscape. Two crawlers ahead were turning off into various sectors. "Which one we going to?" he asked.

"Northwest sector." Fitznell, scanning the instruments and monitors, looked every bit as busy as a pilot. Bandicut felt a little envious; he wondered what it felt like to drive one of these monsters. "Eat your heart out," she murmured, as though reading his mind. "Mine's bigger than yours."

Bandicut laughed.

/// What's that mean? ///

/Never mind. Too hard to explain./

"Better go back and let Jake get you squared away," Fitznell said.

"Okay, thanks for the look." Bandicut exited the way he had come.

As he stepped off the ladder onto the work platform, Jake pointed to one of the mining drones hanging in the cradles. "Bandie, I'm putting you on drones three and four there. Think you can handle 'em?"

Bandicut grimaced. "You sure you want me to run those things? I don't know the first thing about it."

"Don't worry, I'll check you out." Jake pressed several switches, then spoke again in a fast rattle. "Okay, now listen. You're gonna be riding the drones on the inside track. It'll be easier at the start, 'cause I'll be tracking the outer walls on the first pass. But when we get tight on the inside, you'll have to watch your step. Okay? Go get yourself strapped into that jump seat."

Bandicut peered to his right and spotted the jump seat folded into the crawler's outer wall. "Get going," Jake said. "We'll be on station in a minute." Bandicut made his way along the catwalk, pulled the seat down, and turned to sit, facing back toward Jake. "Strap up and plug in your comm," Jake instructed.

Bandicut found the straps and, with some difficulty, got them buckled and adjusted. "When was this setup designed?" he muttered. "Last century?"

"As a matter of fact . . . yes, I think so," Jake said. "Plug in your comm."

He located the jack and did so, and Jake's voice became slightly clearer in his ears.

"See that control board on your right? Lift it into position in front of you."

Bandicut groped and found the board hanging vertically

against the wall. He yanked. Nothing. He groped for the release. The board jerked up suddenly and swung into his lap. He grunted and lifted the cover. He found a display board and a worn-looking key and joy pad. "Now what do I do?"

"Click off the safety and press the ENGAGE button."

"What the hell, Jake, half these labels are worn off!"

"I know. It's on the right."

Muttering, Bandicut found the button. The wall behind him suddenly jerked and turned, and he spun out, seat and board and all, and found himself hanging out over the right side of the lumbering crawler. The ground sped by beneath him, blurring with the shifting of the light-augment in his helmet. He swayed dizzily against his safety harness, feeling utterly naked in the seat as the crawler heaved over a large bump in the roadway. He caught the gurgling sound rising in his throat, but his hands tightened on the control board as it flexed up and down on its extended support. In his helmet was a cackling of merriment.

" 'Kay, Bandie, you're doin' great!" Jake called. "Don't hang on so tight you break the thing off! Just hook your feet in those stirrups and pretend you're riding a horse."

Riding a horse? Bandicut thought dimly, and shouted, "I don't know how to ride a goddamn—"

/// Yee-hahhhh!
Grab those reins! ///

The quarx's voice cut through the din like a cleaver.

/What—?/

/// Like this, John! ///

For an instant, his vision was overlaid with a scratchy image of two men riding horses, and whooping, and shooting handguns into the air. They were pounding along a dusty dirt road at a frightful speed.

/// That's how you ride a horse! ///

/Charlie, you idiot! That's goddamn Hollywood! It's not real! Get it off!/

/// Sorry . . . I just thought . . . ///

The image vanished.

"Just relax and ride with the bounces," Jake was calling. After a moment he added, "How you doin' out there?"

Bandicut finally got his feet hooked into the stirrups.

"How's he doin'? He's doin' like a dink!" chortled someone—Bronson, he realized. Peering around, he spotted the boss in the observer seat way up on top of the crawler, peering down over the side. Bronson was shaking with laughter. "Hang in there, Bandicoot!" he called.

"Take a look at your board," Jake said. "Don't touch anything, just look for the row labeled DEPLOY, with some numbers."

Bandicut squinted, trying to read the labels against the jerky movement. "Okay," he said finally. "Now what?"

Before Jake could answer, the crawler slowed and began a sweeping turn. Bandicut looked up and saw walls of carved ice, mottled with stone, rising alongside the roadway. Suddenly the walls opened out, and the crawler slowed even more. Bandicut gazed out over an expanse of scarred land, depressed below the surrounding terrain. They had arrived on station.

"Now," Jake continued, "get ready to deploy. You're gonna use those controls to guide the drones. Just like driving a buggy. Switch on your field monitors."

Bandicut fiddled a bit, and a display came on, giving him a split screen, both showing him the inside of the crawler. Nose cameras on the mining drones, probably. "Jake," he muttered, "you haven't forgotten that I have *no* bleeking idea what I'm doing?"

"Hey, you think any of us knew what we were doing the first time we hung our fannies out there?"

Fitznell snorted from the cab. "Do any of you know what you're doing *now*?"

"If you morons would knock it off and *deploy,*" called Bronson.

"Rog'—"

"Deploying," said Jake.

Bandicut felt a new rumble behind his back, which he presumed was the opposite-side station swinging out with Jake on board. A few moments later he felt a lower and deeper rumble and the movement of heavy hydraulics. "Bandie," he heard, "deploy number four first, then number three."

"Just press—?"

"Yup."

He felt an almost surreal sense of uninvolvement as he placed his finger on the button. Glancing up at the blue scythe of Neptune, he thought of Earth so far away he couldn't even see it; and he shook his head in sudden bewilderment. What in God's name was he doing here? Out across the scarred landscape, he saw two puffs of condensing vapor, barely illuminated by red laser light. Then he saw the recon robots responsible for the puffs, and he realized that they were sending probing beams into the ice and sending the telemetry to the crawler's computer. He realized with a pang that he would feel a lot more confident if he were linked into that computer, neuron to neuron, instead of hanging out here with his eyeballs and a couple of joysticks.

"Let's get going," Bronson called.

"Bandie, do it," said Jake.

Bandicut pressed the button. His seat shuddered as the side of the crawler opened up and disgorged a drone, its dusty position lights glowing red, like some sort of large, demonic cockroach. The drone veered a little, then matched speeds with the mother cockroach. A green light blinked on under Bandicut's hand. On his monitor, he saw a drone's-eye view of the ground streaming past. An amber light strobed. "It's down!"

"Press the key marked AUTOTRACK," Jake continued.

He squinted anxiously. *What* key marked AUTOTRACK?"

"Top row of keys—"

"You mean where *all* the labels are worn off?"

"Third key from the right," Jake said, unperturbed.

Bandicut pressed the key. The amber light went green. He peered down and saw the drone moving away from the crawler, taking up a parallel course about five meters to the right. A thick umbilical dipped and swayed across the intervening space. It must be working right, he thought. He hadn't heard anyone yell yet.

"Deploy number three."

He pressed the button. A new rumbling announced the ejection of a second drone. He wasted no time in putting that one on automatic, and soon the two drones were flanking each other, with number four trailing behind and to the outside, forming a perfect half of a *V* with the crawler.

"Are we dragging now?" he asked.

"Naw," Jake answered. "Bronson'll give us the word. How we doin', Chester?"

"Hold on to your mokin' drawers," Bronson drawled. "Almost there." Bandicut glanced up and saw the boss bobbing atop the crawler, his helmet gleaming in the running lights. "Get ready to drop in about ten seconds."

Jake's voice cut in, "Bandie, on his call, press the next button to the left."

"Drop 'em *now,*" Bronson said.

Bandicut jabbed the button and waited for something to happen. He felt nothing, but in the monitors, the head-on views shrank and new split-screen images appeared; and he glimpsed mining lasers burrowing into the surface and saw confusing images of surface materials churning and being separated inside the drones. Glancing back at the actual drones, he saw light flickering beneath them; and emerging from behind them were twin clouds of vapor and dust.

"Hey Bandicoot, you're a miner now!" Jake called.

He watched, nodding, as the two drones under his command churned their way through Triton's surface like two moles burrowing for metallic remnants of an eons-old civilization.

9

DOWNLOAD

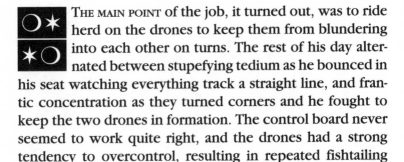The MAIN POINT of the job, it turned out, was to ride herd on the drones to keep them from blundering into each other on turns. The rest of his day alternated between stupefying tedium as he bounced in his seat watching everything track a straight line, and frantic concentration as they turned corners and he fought to keep the two drones in formation. The control board never seemed to work quite right, and the drones had a strong tendency to overcontrol, resulting in repeated fishtailing and skidding.

The effort gave him a thumping headache, and it didn't help that his every mistake was accompanied by whoops and snorts from the top of the crawler. He half suspected Fitznell of racing around the corners to see how much he could take without demolishing the drones. And he wondered at Jake's claim, when he asked why the computer didn't handle the turns, that the control module had failed so many times that they'd simply given up on it and gone to manual control.

By the end of the day, he was tense and exhausted—and ravenously hungry, even though Jake and Amy had shared their lunches with him. As they started back to base, Charlie broke a long silence to ask Bandicut if he was okay. Yes,

Bandicut grunted silently, making it perfectly clear that he was in no mood for conversation. Charlie took the hint and disappeared again.

Back at the base, Jake and Amy congratulated him on surviving their hazing, and invited him for a beer after dinner. Bandicut squinted in thought, then shook his head with a sigh. "I just want to eat and go straight to bed. Rain check?"

"Sure," Jake said. "Tomorrow, you'll sail through it like the wind."

"Like the wind. Sure," Bandicut muttered sardonically. With a wave, he jumped off the ladder from the crawler and strode off to the showers.

In no time at all, his alarm was trilling in his ear. He rolled over in his bunk and groaned, realizing that it was time to start the cycle all over again. /Charlie, I hope you're getting used to this. It looks like I'm gonna be doing it for a while—especially if Jackson doesn't hurry up and clear me back to survey duty./

> /// Well, if you can survive it,
>   I guess I can, too. ///

the quarx answered. But Bandicut could tell Charlie was chafing at the delay. He wanted to get back to his translator, and he couldn't do that as long as Bandicut was stuck in mining ops.

His coworkers took it easier on him the second day, and by evening Bandicut was ready for some diversion. After supper, he went with Jake to the rec lounge for a beer and a few games of EineySteiney pool. The game was played on a continuously curved, charcoal gray, three-dimensional holographic surface, with gravity wells for pockets and variable slopes for orbiting bank shots. The programming today had the balls labeled after the planets of the solar system. Charlie perked up after the opening shot, as they watched the variously colored balls flash and spin away from the center of the table. One ball, golden Mercury, spun into the end well, while the others looped around, coasting over hills and ridges until they finally came to rest in the valleys.

/// Mind if I play with you? ///

Charlie asked as Bandicut bent to take a shot, sighting along his cue wand.

/Eh?/ Bandicut paused, eyeing a shot on mirror-surfaced Venus. /You know how to play pool?/

/// I'm learning. ///

/On my time, you want to learn?/

/// I'm pretty good at orbital dynamics.
This looks like a fairly easy set of parameters. ///

/Easy, huh?/ Bandicut let his breath out, aware of Jake and several spectators waiting. /Okay, this shot's yours./

He was half expecting the quarx to take control of his limbs. Instead he felt a gentle pressure guiding the position of his right arm as he lined up the wand with the white cue ball. He squeezed the trigger, and a laser pulse struck the cue ball, which spun up and over a rise and clicked satisfyingly into silvery Venus. Knocked out of its valley, Venus rebounded from the side rail, crested a rise, and spiraled with quickening orbits into a gravity-well pocket.

"Ho, Bandie—you been practicin', man?" Jake raised his wand in salute.

"Nah, just a little innate talent I been holding back till now." Bandicut straightened up with a grin and circled the table, looking for his next shot. /Nice work there, partner./

/// Thanks.
Let's try that translucent green-and-blue ball.
Is that Earth? ///

Bandicut nodded, then realized that he had done so in front of Jake and the others, as well. Everyone was watching him—including, he realized, that moxy-looking woman from exoarch, Julie Stone. Perhaps he had looked as though he were carefully studying the layout of the table, nodding to himself. He tried to keep his expression natural, and knew that he was probably screwing his face up more than ever. "Concentrate," he murmured as he bent over the table. "Earth in the end well."

/// All the way down the table?
There are three ridges in between. ///
/Let's do it./

The laser flashed, and the cue ball flew up off the table's surface, came back down on the far side of the target ball, then bounced out of play and dissolved in midair with a musical chuckle. Bandicut straightened up, sighing.

"Man, I wish I had some of your in-nate talent," Jake said, laughing as he moved around the table, waiting for a new cue ball to appear.

"Yeah, well, that's the thing about talent," Bandicut muttered, trying not to look as though he'd noticed Julie's presence. He inadvertently caught her eye, and a grin flashed on her face. "Sometimes raw talent is just, uh, hard to control . . . you know?"

"Yeah, I know. Oh, yeah," Jake said, sighting his shot and zapping the Earth in a quick loop around the upper curve of the table and down into a well. It whirred resoundingly as it spiraled in. He looked up and grinned.

Bandicut nodded graciously. /So, uh, how come we missed that shot, anyway?/

/// I'm still on the learning curve, okay?
Were you born knowing how to play the game? ///
/Okay, okay—don't get sore./

/// I'm not sore.
But we're going to win this game.
You want to impress Julie, don't you? ///

Bandicut flushed, and avoided looking at Julie. He turned back as Jake easily knocked Mars, Jupiter, and Saturn into wells. /We won't have the chance, if Jake doesn't start missing some shots./

The cue ball danced, and Uranus, pale green with silver crescents, spun around a well and back up over a ridge to come to rest in a valley. Jake took a swig from his beer. "All yours, John."

"Do it, Bandie." That was Amy Fitznell, who had just walked up carrying a drink that glowed neon pink under the rec lounge lights. "Make him suffer for the way he's abused you for the last two days." She winked at Jake.

"Okay. This one's for you." Bandicut caught Julie's eye by accident, caught a seemingly bashful smile, and grinned to himself. He sighted along the wand, measured the angles, and squeezed. The laser pulsed, the balls clicked, and not just Uranus but mirror-black Pluto spun into pockets.

"Ah, too bad!" Jake said, with an obvious mixture of glee at the premature sinking of Pluto and admiration for the physics of the shot.

Bandicut shook his head ruefully. "Sorry, Amy. I tried to get him for you."

/// What happened? ///

/I lost the game. You have to sink Pluto last./

/// Oh. Sorry!

I thought it was a pretty clever shot. ///

/It was a clever shot. It just cost me the game, that's all./

" 'Nother game, Bandie?" Jake asked, pressing RESET.

Bandicut drew a breath. Julie was just standing there, and looked as though she might like some company. On the other hand, what was he going to say? He wasn't used to having company in his head when he approached women. "I dunno. Anyone waiting to get in for a game?" He held up the wand.

/// Say, John—this game reminds me.

There's something we need to do. ///

/What's that? I want to say hi to Julie./

/// Well . . . yes, but . . . ///

Amy took the wand with a predatory smile and accepted Jake's challenge for the next game. Bandicut moved around the table toward Julie.

/// John? ///

She tipped her head at his approach, bright blue eyes flashing. "Hi, there. Nice couple of shots. How are you?" She sipped what looked like a glass of tomato juice.

"Fine. Just fine," he murmured, trying to rid his mind of Charlie so he wouldn't be staring at her like a first-class idiot. "How are, uh—how are you? How's Georgia?" What a goak. Ask about her, not about her friend. "How's . . . exoarch? Anything interesting turning up?"

/// Is this how you approach women?
This seems . . . awkward. ///

/Shut the hell up./ Bandicut grinned, willing Charlie to be gone.

Julie's smile dazzled him. "Oh, we're just fine. If we find any aliens or alien relics, I assure you, you'll hear about it!" She laughed. "It's not as if the company has us here because they expect us to find anything." She shook her head and took another sip of juice.

"Right—uh—sop to the environmental lobby. Isn't that what everyone says?" Great. Now you've insulted her. "I suppose you get tired of hearing that," he added quickly.

"Yuh. Both counts." She shrugged. "But it's not as if we aren't trying. We're going over all the orbital scans, all wavelengths, looking for that one clue that'll lead us to the find." He must have been looking at her stupidly, because she cocked her head with a quizzical expression. "I mean, if there's all this metal residue, there must be something intact *somewhere* on Triton, don't you think? Even if it's hundreds of meters below the surface?"

Bandicut coughed. "Yes. Yes, I suppose that's a . . . good bet."

/// John, be careful. ///

He felt his head bobbing. This was leading in a danger-ous direction, and he had no idea how to back out of it. He just wanted to talk to Julie, not spill everything he knew about aliens.

/// John—listen, please.
We really need to go collect our data . . . ///
/What data . . . ?/

"Well, I think so," Julie said, turning to look around the lounge. She waved at some people on the far side. "I see some of my cohorts have arrived. I promised I'd meet them. Would you like to come join us?"

"I, uh—"

/// John, that information could be vital.
We've got to have it. ///

"It's okay. No pressure," she said, laughing easily.

He forced a smile. "Maybe another time? I'd like to. But I'm pretty tired tonight. It's been . . . a hard couple of days. I think I'm just going to check the board postings and then go to bed."

Julie's eyes flashed penetratingly. "Okay. Nice to see you, though—okay?" Without waiting for him to stutter an answer, she waved and left to join her friends.

/Auuuggghh./ His pulse was pounding as he watched her leave. /Maybe I should have gone with her./

/// John— ///
/What were you trying to say, a minute ago?/
/// Can we go to the comm booth? ///

/It's hard enough, without trying to listen to you on the inside, at the same time./ His pulse was still pounding.

/// John—can we go to the comm booth?
Please? ///

He let out a breath. /Yeah. Let's go./

✳

>>>>>>>>>>>>
>>>>>>
>>>
>
—<mode shift>—

A burst of fireworks expanded in his vision, then crystallized into a network, which hung against darkness for a heartstopping instant—then drained like rivulets of glowing water toward him, into his vision, his eyes, his brain, his consciousness . . .

>> **Thank you for choosing Planetview Systems as your all-hour information service. We have researched and placed in cache the information that you requested during your last session. Would you like to downlink the data at this time?** >>

Now what the hell was that all about? Bandicut thought. Of course: Charlie had signed him onto Planetview and requested a complete, full-volume, updated ephemeris. /That the stuff you want?/ he asked.

/// *Yes.*
Please give me a moment
while I prepare a storage area for it. ///

/You can use my personal safe-zone here in the datanet, if you want./

/// *No, this is better.*
I'm setting up a cache file in your brain . . . ///

/Huh?/

/// *Go ahead.*
Take the downlink. ///

/Hey, I don't want this stuff cluttering up my long-term memory!/

/// *It won't.*
You won't even miss the storage space.
YES, WE'D LIKE THE DOWNLINK. ///

Bandicut sputtered in protest, but the Planetview prompter had heard the quarx's voice.

>> **Prepare your cache and signal when ready . . .** >>

He took a breath, but the quarx beat him to it.

/// *Ready.* ///

>> **Cometary listings updated 2164MAR, code sequence: R.A. (H,M,S); DEC. (D,M,S); TYP; MAG; DIS; PHAS; A.VEL.; . . . >>**

Numbers and characters began flowing past with dizzying speed. For the first few seconds, he tried to make sense of it, but it was like trying to seine Niagara Falls. He couldn't feel it going into his brain; he wondered if only the quarx would be able to retrieve it.

/// John, you worry too much.
Relax and let me take care of it. ///
/Okay,/ he sighed.

The dataflow rumbled on, a torrential waterfall beneath the surface of his consciousness. . . .

✳

>> **Download complete. Do you require further information? Please check our menu for exciting new services—>>**

/Bye!/ Bandicut barked, and the prompt vanished. They were out of Planetview Systems, but the datanet still gleamed around them like the ice of Charlie's cavern. /You didn't want anything else, did you?/

The quarx seemed lost in thought.

/Charlie?/

/// Sorry.
No, I think that's all I wanted
from Planetview.
I was just wondering
how to get this data to the translator. ///
Bandicut shrugged helplessly.

/// I could repeat what I did last time,
but it's much longer.
There's a greater risk of detection.
In person would be a lot better. ///
/Well,/ Bandicut said, /I don't know how soon I'll have any chance of going out on another survey run. And even

then, I won't exactly be free to just wander out to your cavern./

> /// *I think I can help you manage that last part.*
> *The question, though, is—should we wait?*
> *I think, for now—yes.* ///

/Are we done here?/

> /// *Yes.* ///

Bandicut nodded and peered at the spangles of light that formed the datanet. Another time, if he were less tired, he would like to peruse them further. /Okay,/ he said, and touched the connection with his thought, and let the sensation of the disconnect cascade like cooling water through his brain.

10

MEMORY DEATH

HE DREAMED VIVIDLY that night, but of his own past, not Charlie's. He dreamed of his parents and his brother Joe, and Megan, before they were killed in the collapse of the EuroChunnel; he dreamed of them the last time he saw them, saying good-bye in St. Louis after Joe and Megan had dropped Dakota off with Megan's parents. The four of them were heading for a grownups-only holiday in London and Paris, while John was about to catch a flight to Bogotá, Colombia, and the railgun launcher. He was bound for a tour of duty in space, and his family was bound for death. But they didn't know that then.

He dreamed of Dakota at the funeral, bewildered and trembling, hugging him briefly but too shaken to say much of anything. But her eyes, those green Bandicut-child eyes, caught his just long enough to seem to make a silent plea. Begging him to take her to space. If not now, then soon. She'd always been a space nut, always asked him about his work every chance she got. It was out of the question, of course; at nine, she was much too young, and what would she do at L5 anyway? Megan's parents were Dakota's legal guardians now, and they didn't think too highly of space work, and even if he didn't think that highly of *them*, there was nothing he could do to change it.

Then the dream changed, and he was floating through a wispy, star-filled nebula, speeding to catch up with someone from whom he'd gotten separated, but he couldn't quite picture who it was. . . .

✳

The third day out on the crawlers was little different from the second, except that Charlie seemed troubled as they rode around and around the track, each pass carving a little deeper into the surface of the moon. It was clear that Charlie was fretting about the time that was slipping by, with no hope in sight for a return to his cavern and the translator.

Bandicut, bouncing in his jump seat under the baleful eye of Neptune, was too preoccupied with his own boredom to be of much help. He liked his coworkers but loathed the repetitiveness of the job; it was so deadening that he found it hard to muster concern for Charlie's problem, even though it theoretically concerned him deeply: it was only the safety of the entire Earth. It was just too theoretical. But his boredom was real and palpable.

/// *We might have to steal a rover*
to go back, ///

Charlie murmured, sounding as though he were talking more to himself than to his host.

/Fat chance of that,/ Bandicut muttered, fishtailing the drones around a tight, inner corner.

/// *You've got to help me get out there.* ///

/Let's talk about it later, okay?/ The truth was, even if his heart had been in it at the moment, Bandicut could have offered only limited reassurance, since there was no way of knowing how long his superiors would take to write off the accident and send him back out on survey duty.

/// *Yeah . . . later . . .* ///

the quarx whispered, stirring listlessly.

/Hey, you okay there?/ Bandicut asked, squinting back at the churning drones as the course straightened out.

There was no answer.

★

It was only as they were arriving back at base that he realized that Charlie was not just worried; he was unwell.
There were occasional flutters of distress that made Bandicut shiver, and once or twice he had dream-flashes of
quarxian memory: flickering glimpses of alien beings, alien
worlds, and feelings of grieving over some undefinable loss.

"You okay there, Bandie?" Jake asked, turning from his
locker. The Amerind zipped up his casual jumpsuit.
"You're looking a little green."

Bandicut rose from the bench where he'd been sitting
and pulled on his own suit. "Yeah—fine, Jake. Fine. See you
later, okay?"

Jake peered at him. "Okay. But you look like you should
get some rest."

Bandicut nodded and waited for Jake to leave. /You
okay, Charlie?/ he asked again, and this time the quarx answered, but only after he'd started down the corridor toward the cafeteria.

> /// John, is there some place . . .
> where we can be in private,
> and not be interrupted? ///

He sensed a great exertion. /Well, yeah, I guess. What's
wrong? Can I get some supper first?/

The quarx whispered,

> /// John, I may have . . . miscalculated . . .
> please, no delay. ///

/We could lock ourselves into one of the VR rooms. It's
plenty private there./

> /// Yes . . . ///

He walked quickly to the lounge and checked the VR
occupancy board. One room was available and he ducked
in, securing the door behind him. /Okay, we're alone.
What's wrong, guy? Are you all right?/

The quarx seemed to perk up a little in the new surroundings.

/// I'm . . . okay for the moment, I think.
What is this place? ///

/It's a virtual reality room. I thought you watched a lot of TV. Don't you know a VR setup when you see one?/ He opened a panel and showed Charlie where the visor, vest, gloves, and shoes were kept.

/// Old TV. It didn't show anything like this.
You're sure it's private here? ///

/It's about the most private place on Triton. People are expected to talk to themselves and generally act weird in here, because it's all make-believe once you turn on the holos and the feedback gear. That's the whole point./

/// Good. That's good.
Very good. ///

Puzzled, Bandicut said, /So do you want me to put this stuff on, so you can see how it works?/

/// Yeah . . . uh, sure. ///

He began putting on the shoes and gloves, and realized that this was all wrong. The quarx had needed to talk. /Charlie, hold it—this VR stuff can wait. Tell me what's wrong./

The quarx shivered.

/// It's . . . okay, John.
It's just that . . .
Well, I think I'm getting ready to die. ///

Bandicut felt a sharp pain across his chest as he tensed. His hands froze, the gloves halfway on. /What?/

/// You remember, I told you . . . ///

He remembered, the quarx had started to tell him once, something about how he might die at some point in the future. The conversation had been interrupted. But it hadn't seemed very real then, anyway, or at least he hadn't known Charlie so well then. /You started, but you didn't finish. What is this, Charlie?/

/// I'm sorry, John—
I'd wanted to prepare you better. ///

/But . . . when? *Why?*/ Somehow, he'd known from the dreams that death came to the quarx in ways that were going to be difficult for him to comprehend. /Charlie?/

/// I'm . . . not sure when.
But soon, I think. ///

Bandicut swallowed, suddenly dizzy. /What do you want me to do? What should I expect?/ He felt a strange mixture of fear and urgency and . . . something almost like relief. He was ashamed of the relief. He knew there was a lot at stake. Not just the quarx, or him. Earth, maybe.

/// There's nothing you can do
about my dying.
And don't . . . be concerned about your feelings.
They're perfectly natural,
I think. ///

/How the hell would you know?/ Bandicut cried. /Charlie, what about . . . what about . . . *everything?* Your mission? And the translator?/

/// You'll have to carry on.
There will be . . . another.
But I must brief you.
You must . . . get the data to the translator. ///

Bandicut swallowed. /Charlie, I don't want you to die./ He felt a sudden surge of empathy from the quarx.

/// I'm glad, John.
But look—we're getting all morbid.
I don't want to get morbid.
Please—
how about showing me something on that . . .
VR thing. ///

Bandicut drew a sharp breath. /Are you serious? Now?/

/// Please . . .
something peaceful.
I'd like to see Earth.
Are there any Earth scenes? ///

Bandicut read the selections. /Okay,/ he whispered, and

made a choice. The room vanished, and the sound of a gentle surf filled his ears, and a brightening light overhead turned into a beaming midday sun. He was standing on a beach, looking out over an expanse of sea. After a moment, he murmured, "VR Control—give me late afternoon. Sunset." The sun faded from overhead and reappeared, enormous and crimson over the ocean. The bottom edge of the sun's disk touched the water, flattening outward in a rippling reflection. /How's this?/ he asked, stepping to the water's edge.

> /// *John, it's . . . breathtaking.* ///

There was a deep wistfulness in the quarx's voice. Bandicut wondered if it were making him homesick. He felt a momentary dizziness, and suddenly felt himself hurtling headlong through space, through flickering light, tumbling and turning himself inside out. Then the feeling went away, and he was standing by the seashore again, swaying a little. He took a deep breath. Was Charlie reliving his life? Bandicut knelt and ran his hand through the sand. /Was your . . . world . . . anything like this?/

Charlie hesitated.

> /// *I don't think so. No.* ///

Bandicut gazed up into the setting sun. /What *was* your world like?/

The answer came in a whisper.

> /// *I wish I . . . could remember.*
> *John, we must talk now.* ///

/Yes./ Bandicut frowned, wondering, how long had it been since the quarx had seen his own world? A million years? A hundred million? Did he even *have* a world of his own? /You must brief me,/ he whispered.

> /// *John.*
> *You will not be . . . alone.*
> *Expect another.*
> *But you must be prepared to . . .*
> *take responsibility.* ///

Responsibility? He swallowed, thinking—the Earth is in danger from some cosmic collision, and I'm supposed to take responsibility? This is madness . . . madness . . .

/// John, the data that you hold in your mind— ///

/Data?/ Yes yes, of course, the ephemeris.

*/// I have marked its location so that
I . . . your new companion . . .
will be able to give it to the translator.
It must reach the translator! ///*

/Right,/ he whispered. He didn't know what else to say. He couldn't quite believe this was happening. Another . . . new companion . . . what the hell did that mean?

*/// And John, you must remember . . .
EineySteiney pool! ///*

/What—?/

*/// Remember it.
It's the most important thing.
That, and the data. ///*

/Okay,/ he whispered, bewildered. /Charlie—what did you mean when you said there would be . . . another? Another what? Another quarx?/

He felt a sudden physical weakness, and almost doubled over.

/// Aw jeez, Bart—it's gettin' all fuzzy, ///
the quarx groaned abruptly.

/Charlie? What are you doing? What are you talking about?/

*/// Yeah, real fuzzy-like.
Kinda' . . . misty 'round the edges. ///*
The quarx was speaking in a drawl, some kind of goddamn phony western accent, probably from those goddamn old TV shows. Charlie *loved* that shit, he thought.

*/// Ahhhh, jeez, Bart—
the pain! ///*

/Stop!/ he said. He was starting to become angry. /What the hell do you think you're doing—?/

/// I'm not gonna make it, old buddy— ///
/Stop it, damn you!/
The quarx gasped,
/// Let me—go out in style—John— ///
/NO, damn it!/
/// I'm not gonna make it.
I think this may be it . . . ///
Bandicut felt a sharp sinking feeling in his chest. /God-
damnit, don't pull this shit on me! Charlie!/
/// It's such a beautiful view—
I just wish I could . . . aaahhhhhhhh . . . ///
There was a gasping sound, then silence. Bandicut
scowled, looking around the beach, as though he would
find the quarx there. /Charlie? *Charlie? Goddamnit—!*/
There was no answer, no stir of presence.
Bandicut was stunned into sudden silence. Was he
gone, then? Was Charlie gone—the only alien in the solar
system? Bandicut didn't know what to think. He felt a pro-
found confusion, and fear.
Three heartbeats later, he heard a soft chuckle.
/// Gotcha. ///
For ten more heartbeats, he couldn't speak. When he
did, it was with barely controlled rage. /You *asshole.* You
are a total asshole. Do you know that? Was that supposed to
be some kind of *joke? WAS IT?*/
The quarx whispered hoarsely,
/// I'm . . . sorry.
I just thought, it's my last chance . . .
I'm awfully mokin' sorry. ///
/*Sorry?* That was the dumbest-ass stunt I've ever seen!
Sorry! Christ, I thought you were really gone!/ Bandicut
picked up a handful of sand and flung it into the ocean.
/*Christ,* Charlie!/
/// I really am . . . sorry.
I don't want to go, I don't want to die, but
I thought this might— ///

/Asshole!/

/// —*make it a little easier*— ///

Bandicut let another handful of sand run through his fingers. He felt as if his thoughts were melting into the ocean along with that great crimson sun. /Lamebrained dingo-shit is what it was, Charlie./

/// *I'm sorry . . . Bandie.* ///

He looked up into the sky, squinting. /Did I give you permission to call me that?/ he whispered, swallowing.

There was no real answer, just a soft, distant sigh somewhere in the back of his mind. He felt suddenly drained of energy, as if something had gone out of him. He heard, or imagined that he heard, a single whispered word: *Bye.*

/Charlie?/ The quarx didn't answer, and he started to get angry all over again. He got up and walked along the beach, waiting for the quarx to reappear. "Charlie?" he called aloud. "Don't you have to finish briefing me?"

There was still no answer. He stepped to the edge of the water, then into the water, and felt the cool sea wash over his feet. The sunset was gorgeous, a flattened glowing orb settling into the ocean. "That's something I really miss, from Earth," he murmured. "I'm sorry I yelled at you. I shouldn't have gotten so sore. Charlie? You there?" /*Charlie, DAMN IT, answer me!*/

In the silence that followed, he grew increasingly anxious. He felt none of the inner rustlings that marked Charlie's presence. /Charlie?/ he whispered, pleading. /Are you still there—somewhere?/

And that was when he knew . . . Charlie had whispered his farewell, and meant it. He was gone. Bandicut turned and walked the other way along the water's edge. It hurt to take a breath in, and to let it out. He blew through his clenched fist and thought: I don't even know if I should be happy or sad. Maybe it's not the worst thing in the world for him to be gone. Maybe, for him, it's a blessing. But . . .

/Damn you, you never even told me where you were from—or about your people, or—/

It just all seemed . . . not just sad, but *inappropriate,* somehow. It shouldn't end this way. Not the first alien contact for all of humanity. No one else even knew about it. He had been the sole point of contact with the race of quarx. And now Charlie was gone.

Bandicut sat down on the sand, trying to swallow. It wasn't just the loss of an alien contact. It was the loss of a . . . friend. He stared across the vast expanse of ocean at the fiery red orb, until the intensity of the glow began to hurt his eyes, and only after a few minutes did he begin to wipe at the streaming tears that were blurring his vision of the setting sun.

11

CHARLIE?

HE REMAINED WHERE he was until the holographic sun had sunk beneath the horizon and the sky had begun to darken. Finally he told the VR room to switch itself off, and he hung the sensory gear in the closet. Still, though, he lingered before leaving the room. He had no idea what to do with himself now. He was exhausted physically and emotionally, but sleep was out of the question; so was eating. He knew he ought to think through the implications of what Charlie had said at the end: that he had to take responsibility, that there would be "another," that he needed to get the data to the translator. EineySteiney. But he couldn't; he just couldn't think about all that now.

He left the room finally and found himself walking down the corridor toward the gym and the centrifuge room. Maybe that would be the best antidote: to put in some pounding physical exercise and just utterly drain himself. There was no doubt he needed the exercise. Maybe it would help him get his mind off Charlie.

The late Charlie.

When he got to the gym, he had to wait for a chance in the 'fuge room. He spent the time warming up on the lever-benches, doing shoulder stretches and waist flexes. He was aware of the desk scanner-robot peering his way from time to time and began, ridiculously, to feel self-conscious. He wondered if his inner distress was showing clearly enough on his face for even a robot to see it. Flushing, he stepped up his pace of exercise. If he had to look distressed, by God, it was going to be because he was pushing himself. He didn't need anyone nosing around asking what was wrong.

Sweat beading on his forehead, he still could not keep from spinning his mental wheels, trying to think what to do next. He couldn't keep his experience with the quarx a secret forever. If he was supposed to be taking responsibility, then he had to make decisions. Ultimately, this was something the world needed to know about: the first living contact with an alien intelligence. Maybe someone who was smarter than he was could figure out why the Earth was in danger. But whom could he tell, and with what for evidence—unless he led a search party back to the cavern and the translator?

But to do that, he would have to tell Cole Jackson. The man would never believe him; and even if he did, Jackson would only look for some way to grab the credit, the way he did when that stranded *Time-Life* photographer was rescued two months ago—when he took a commendation "on behalf of" the two men who'd acted, while he'd stood around scratching his ass, making plans. Bandicut could imagine Jackson's pleasure in taking credit for alien contact.

But whom else could he tell? Despite the fact that they were here on Triton to dig alien metals out of the ground, there was no department assigned the job of dealing with *living* aliens. That might be stupid, but there it was.

That seemed to leave two other choices. There was Dr. Switzer, who would probably find nothing in Bandicut's mind except psychosis; and there was the tiny exoarchaeology group, where Julie Stone worked. He felt a certain appeal in giving the science people a chance before the marketing people took over. But exoarch wasn't part of MINEXFO, and it would not be viewed favorably for him to tell exoarch instead of going through company channels. In any event, he had a hunch—Julie notwithstanding—that exoarch would think he was as crazy as a loon, just like everyone else. He knew if the situation were reversed, *he* wouldn't believe a story like his, not for a moment.

He puffed, straining against the levers.

"Mr. Bandicut!" said a synthesized voice. "Do you wish to use the centrifuge or not? There are others waiting."

"Huh?" He sat up on the leverbench and peered toward the front desk. The scanner-robot was staring unblinking in his direction. "Okay. I'm going," he grunted, wiping his forehead on his sleeve. He extricated himself from the leverpress and went through the sliding door into the 'fuge room.

The centrifuge room rotated around the gym like a gigantic, inward-banked angel food cake. Bandicut paused on the wide, stationary inner track, then stepped out across the red, orange, and yellow transition bands, staggering a little as his weight increased by increments, each ring outward moving faster than the one before. He made his way to the green outer ring, which held the main .8-gee running track and an assortment of high-gee exercisers strung along its outer circumference.

Taking a few deep breaths, he jogged up to speed, finding a gap among the other runners. The sensation of revolving was disconcerting at first, as he whizzed past a couple of people on the slower, inner bands. But he adjusted quickly, and began a steady, mindless pace, pounding his way around the track. He didn't speak to anyone, and didn't bother to count laps or keep track of his speed. The monitor on his wrist would let him know if he was about to keel over—if his knees didn't buckle under first.

It wasn't long before the burning in his lungs told him that he had become far too lax in his exercising; he needed to do this more often. He tried to empty his mind, except for the physical ache. But inevitably his thoughts drifted back to Charlie, and to how he might locate Charlie's translator and produce it as evidence of his discovery.

Please don't tell anyone.

He stumbled, lost his balance with the Coriolis veering, and rolled off the track to the outside. Had he just heard a voice—a tiny whisper? He thought it had sounded like the voice of Charlie. More likely, it was his memory of the quarx's voice. His monitor was beeping furiously, his heart pounding. He grabbed for the mute switch on his wrist, and he searched frantically in his mind. /*Charlie?*/ he whispered. It took all of his self-control not to call the quarx's name aloud.

The only answer was the pounding of his pulse in his eardrums. He dragged for breath in the heavy gravity. It must have been the strain, the lightheadedness from running. He had imagined the sound.

"Hey—you okay there?" One of the other runners was bending down next to him.

"I, uh—" he croaked, wheezing in another breath.

The runner put his hands on his hips, catching his own breath. "Whooeee. I thought mebbe you were having some—"

"No—" Bandicut panted, waving the other man on. "I'm fine. Just a little . . . winded."

" 'Kay. See ya." The runner jogged off again.

Bandicut sat back on the padded sidestrip, watching the stream of workers jog past. His heart rate was coming down slowly. /Charlie?/ he whispered. /Did you plant that memory?/

He thought he heard a high keening sound, like his sinuses depressurizing; then it was gone. Maybe it *was* his sinuses depressurizing. He felt no presence of a quarx. He sighed and cursed and got to his feet. Maybe it was time he went to bed, after all.

★

Stretching out in the privacy of his bunk, he knew that he was not going to be able to sleep yet. He pulled his note-book out of the cubby beside his head and, resting on one elbow, jacked it into the wall. He wanted to check the system board to see if Jackson and the department had left him any messages about their investigation. They had: Jackson wanted to know if he had *heard* anything in the rover before the nav and comm went out on him. He typed a short reply: *No.* He sent a separate query asking when they anticipated putting him back on survey duty. It was not that he had even the slightest idea what he would do when they put him back out there. But some of the posts on the general-comments board were from miners offering their services for survey driving, and it worried him that someone else wandering around in his territory might stumble into Charlie's cavern.

The little screen seemed to glow back at him like a living thing on his bunk. He paused in his browsing of messages. There was really very little that he was interested in here; he was just postponing sleep. He was also, he realized, extremely tired. If nothing else, that made a fertile ground for silence-fugue. That was the last thing he wanted to deal with now. He unplugged the unit, stashed it in the cubby, and lay back, closing his eyes.

Sleep did not come easily. He seemed surrounded by irritating noises, sounds he ordinarily did not notice at all: the voices of men coming and going in the dorm rooms, even the adjoining rooms; the sounds of plumbing in the can, ten meters away; even someone's holovid, in this dorm room or another. It was certainly strange for him to be hearing all of these things through his privacy curtain, which ordinarily screened out all but the loudest sounds. But he was too tired, too groggy, and too depressed to think anything more about it than how annoying it was.

Even his own heartbeat seemed to thunder in his ears.

He felt as though all of his senses, both inner and outer, were afire—as though Charlie, in his departure, had somehow flayed his nerve endings so that he would forever be adrift in a sea of noise, fretfulness, and chaos. /Damn you, Charlie, for leaving like that . . ./

His thoughts seemed to drift away like whispers on the wind, *Damn you, Charlie . . . damn you, Charlie . . .* and then it was gone, like the sound of a dream passing in the night. He thought he heard an answering whisper, *Who is Charlie?* and he blinked his eyes in the dark and searched his mind, and wondered: indeed, who was Charlie? And why did he come to me, and then leave before his work— our work—was done? And will I be hearing voices in my imagination for the rest of my life?

And he felt a creeping sense of inevitability wash over him, saying, yes, you will . . . as he drifted off to sleep at last.

★

It seemed only an instant later when he was startled awake by a gurgling sound:

/// *Where the . . . (glurrrk) . . . am I?* ///

He heaved himself up on one elbow, staring into the near-total darkness of his bunk alcove. The tiny red clock readout provided the only light, glowing blood red as it floated in space beside him, telling him that it was 0447, the middle of the night. What the hell had awakened him? "Charlie?" he called out softly.

For a moment, through his grogginess, he felt the weight of his own stupidity. What was he doing, calling out aloud to a dead alien? But he was certain he had heard something.

There was another gurgling sound, like a clogged drain. He strained to hear. Was it coming from outside? From the lavatory? No . . .

He wondered if he were going out of his mind. Silence-fugue? It didn't feel like it, but . . . voices in the night? Probably just a dream, for God's sake. Was he losing the ability to

distinguish between dream and reality? Was it that hard, losing Charlie?

/// Char-leee? ///

Bandicut froze. That was a definite voice.

*/// Was that . . .
what you called—? ///*

/Charlie!/ he screamed. He was suddenly gasping again,
overwhelmed by a need to drag air into his lungs. /Charlie,
is that you?/

/// I'm—not sure— ///

/Charliiiiie! What are you doing to me, damn you?/ He
fell back on his pillow, holding his head in both hands.
/Furgin' hell, is this some kind of—/

He was interrupted by a stronger voice:

*/// Please—
please stop shouting, sir!
I must know—who you are— ///*

Bandicut gasped breathlessly. Suddenly he realized that
he felt a multiple bewilderment—his own, and someone
else's—someone in his head.

He sat up again, dizzily. /Charlie? Is it really you? Or—/

Time seemed suspended, through a long moment of uncertainty. Then a very soft, tentative voice said:

*/// Charlie . . . ?
Perhaps . . . you could call me that. ///*

Bandicut felt a cold chill run down his back.

*/// Your name is . . . Bandicut.
Yes? ///*

/Yes,/ he whispered. /But who—?/

*/// I think I . . .
have memories of you,
John Bandicut. ///*

Bandicut felt as if he were spinning in a centrifuge out of
control, his mind staggering from unrelenting Coriolis veering. He lay back down.

/// Can you tell me please
. . . what happened? ///

/What *happened?* You *died!* Last night!/ He felt his bewilderment rippling back upon itself. His thoughts flashed involuntarily back to Charlie's death—reviewing the events as if in blazing holo. It was a disturbing, disorienting review—the death, and its emotional and physical effects. But there was a quarx in his head again. Was it really Charlie?

/// Something . . . else . . . happened. ///

Bandicut lay helpless as the thing in his mind struggled to sort its way through the facts. /What else happened?/ Bandicut whispered.

/// Not just . . . death. ///

/No—?/

/// —Something—

·

—quarx—

·

—I—

·

. . . ///

It seemed to run out of words.

Bandicut whispered, /Please—just tell me—are you the Charlie I knew?/

There was another long hesitation.

/// I . . . am uncertain . . . ///

/But—/

/// ·

·

·

< quarx >

·

<< die >>

·

·

???

.

.

< quarx >

.

.

<<< reborn >>>

.

.

.

—I—

.

.

< uncertain >

.

.

< remembering >

.

.

—you—

.

.

—once knew—

.

—a Charlie?—

.
///

Bandicut struggled to keep from crying out his intense
. . . he didn't even know what the emotion was, just that it
was building like a scream that wanted to get out, but
couldn't because a weight was sitting on top of it. He felt
his breath rush in and out, and behind his closed eyelids,
lights were flashing and he felt as if he were falling . . .

/// What—?

.

What is this?

.

Stop!

.

STO-O-O-P-P-P-P! ///

He felt himself jerked back to stillness, abruptly, as though a band of steel had clamped down upon his brain. He gasped, dizzily. /You . . . used to do that a lot more . . . gently,/ he wheezed.

/// ??? ///

He gulped. /Silence-fugue. It . . . hits me . . . and it's all I can do to . . . keep my head on straight until it passes. But you found a way to—/

/// I—? ///

/You. Before you—/ he choked on the word /—*died!*/ Bandicut felt himself suddenly burning with rage. /Before you started moking with my mind!/

/// —I— ///

the creature gasped at his rage

/// —*did nothing*— ///

/Then—/ Bandicut whispered raggedly, /please tell me—who are you? And where is Charlie?/

The quarx seemed stunned.

/// .

.

Charlie

.

.

transformed

.

.

I am

.

.

I am not

.

.

you may call me

.

.

Charlie

.

. ///

Bandicut's heart pounded.
/// You still don't . . . ? ///
No. I don't understand. Or maybe I do. He felt a power-ful sensation of wheels shifting and spinning in his mind.
/// Charlie died—? ///
whispered the quarx.
/Yes./
/// I am of the . . . ashes? ///
Bandicut stared into the darkness.
/// Now do you . . . ? ///
/Yes,/ he whispered. /I think I do now./

12

CHARLIE-TWO

 WHEN THE ALARM chimed, he rolled out of his bunk with a groan. Although he'd eventually sunk into a muddled slumber, he did not feel rested in the least. He considered calling in sick, but he didn't want to have to concoct reasons. Vague claims of insomnia were unlikely to cut much mustard with Dr. Switzer.

He grabbed something to eat in the cafeteria and headed for the ready room.

/// What is planned for today? ///
asked the quarx. Charlie—the new Charlie—had awakened somewhat clearer-headed, or at least more articulate, than he had been in the middle of the night.

/I have to go to work,/ Bandicut answered curtly, trying to brush the question off. He hauled his suit out of the locker. They had a lot to talk about, but now was hardly the time—and truthfully, he hadn't much stomach for it. He wanted to pretend that Charlie-One was still with him, pretend that last night hadn't happened.

/// He . . . we . . .
did not mean for it to be
disruptive.
It's unlikely that he **wanted** *to die,*
you know. ///

Bandicut grunted, hauling the bulky mining suit up over his shoulders. The last of the other workers had just disappeared out the airlock. /No, I suppose not./ And how am I going to get through this day? he wondered. By pretending everything is okay? By doing nothing that will take me even remotely closer to understanding—much less accomplishing—Charlie's and my mission? /Do you—/ he whispered, /know what Charlie knew? Do you remember what we talked about? Our . . . purpose?/

The answering voice sounded apologetic.

/// I'm not . . . entirely sure.
Some. Not all. ///

/Then he's really gone? Charlie? Part of him, anyway?/

/// I am sorry.
Was he . . . a good friend? ///

Bandicut sighed and didn't answer for a while, as he wrestled with the last fittings on his suit. /Nah,/ he whispered at last. /Would a good friend have done something like that to me?/ Without waiting for an answer, he clamped his visor closed and hurried off to the airlock.

∗

/// It is not
that I remember nothing. ///

the quarx said, rather severely it seemed, as the air whispered out of the airlock.

/// But rather that I need
to consolidate
pieces of my memory. ///

Bandicut had noticed that this version of Charlie seemed to have a starchier disposition than the first Charlie's. /Pieces of your memory? Is that going to take a long time? I wish you'd explain to me *how* you appeared out of the little pieces that Charlie left behind./

The quarx seemed to be groping for words.

/// How?
I don't know.

I didn't . . . exactly appear out of his pieces.
I am him—
just not entirely.
There is an oblique recurrency
in our . . . life cycle. ///

Bandicut was watching the pressure readout in irritation. /What are you saying, you don't really die?/

The quarx sounded offended.

/// We certainly do *die.*
Perhaps, though, the term "death" is misleading,
in your language.
There is a continuation, and an alteration
in our— ///

His voice dropped to a wordless, gravelly moan, which pitched up and down like waves on an ocean. He paused, apparently deciding that he could not find the right word.

/// I'm afraid
your language doesn't quite suffice— ///

/Hey!/ Bandicut snapped. /I'm so mokin' sorry our language can't handle the reproductive cycle of mokin' quarxes!/ He checked the last settings on his life support and savagely punched the airlock exit button.

/// I didn't mean . . .
actually I think you mean "quarx,"
rather than "quarxes";
I believe that's truer to the spirit of both
singular and plural . . . ///

Bandicut ignored him and bounded with shallow, jogging leaps toward the crawler bay.

★

Crawler Three was powering up as he reached the docking bay. He yelled to Bronson, hanging off the stern ladder. "Hold up!"

Bronson waved him away. "Go see Massengale!" he called, his voice scratchy through the comm. "You've been reassigned!"

Bandicut peered up at the crawler boss. *"What?* Why?"

Bronson's grinning eyes were just visible behind his visor. "I dunno. Prob'ly didn't like you learnin' your job here so fast. Hell, he's prob'ly disappointed you didn't fall off an' kill your damn self."

"Yeah," Bandicut muttered. "Okay, see you around." Scowling, he turned back toward the airlock.

"Hey, Bandicoot."

He swiveled back. "Yeah?"

Bronson's grin was wide. "You did okay here, for an outa-work survey jock. Take it easy, y'hear?" He waved and clambered up the ladder to the top of the crawler. Bandicut stared after him for a moment, then shook his head and walked at a leisurely pace back toward the ready room.

/// Is this what you would term
. . . a setback? ///

the quarx asked.

He shrugged. /Damn near everything I've been doing has been a setback, if you're talking about our "mission." Do you remember the last few days of work—what we've been doing? Charlie seemed to think he was learning something from it, though I'll be joogered if I know what./

/// I remember those days . . .
only vaguely. ///

/Well, do you remember Herb Massengale?/

/// Um . . .
wasn't he . . . some kind of . . . asshole?
Is that the correct word? ///

Bandicut laughed out loud and punched the airlock control. /Okay, Charlie! There *is* some of you in there, after all!/ He stepped into the pressurized room. Before unsuiting, he plugged his helmet comm into a wall jack and paged Herb Massengale.

The voice that answered was flat and unpleasant. "That you, Bandicut?"

"Yeah, it's me. I'm in the ready room. Bronson said you wanted to talk to me."

"Get out of your suit and come to my office."

"Why didn't you tell me *before* I got suited up?"

"When you're in charge, you can ask the questions."

"I see." *Jerk.* "I'll be there in a little while."

"Make it snappy, Bandicut."

/// *This man doesn't like you,*
does he? ///

Charlie noted in a concerned tone.

He didn't bother to answer, but yanked his comm plug out of the wall jack and started unzipping his pressure suit.

/// *I suspect that he's . . . baiting you.*
Is that it? ///

Bandicut nodded silently, darkly. He had a feeling that he knew what Massengale had in mind for him. And he was going to like it even less than the crawlers.

✳

Massengale didn't look up from his desk. "What took you so long?"

"I could have been here an hour ago," Bandicut said evenly, "if you hadn't—" He paused and shrugged.

Massengale drew a nostril-flaring breath and lifted his gaze to stare at Bandicut. "Siddown." He jerked his thumb at a bench against the wall.

/// *What a shithead.* ///

Bandicut snorted, trying not to laugh.

Massengale's eyes narrowed. "Problem?"

Bandicut shook his head silently, turning away to walk to the bench. /Stuff it, Charlie, until we get out of here./

/// *Even if he is a—?* ///

/Yes. *Especially* because that's what he is. Anyway, how'd did you get to be so good with the cuss words, all of a sudden?/

/// *I'm exploring*
prememories of your culture.

Such expressions are common among your class,
are they not? ///

Bandicut had to agree that they were. But he was aware
that Massengale was watching him suspiciously. To camouflage the blank gaze that had undoubtedly come over him,
he rubbed the side of his jaw as though smoothing out a
facial tic. "So," he murmured. "I assume you have some
other work for me?"

"Yeah," Massengale said. "I thought maybe you'd been
loafing out there on the crawlers long enough, and it was
time for you to earn your keep. Since your own department
hasn't seen fit to ask for you back . . ." He paused to ap-
praise the effect of his words, but Bandicut returned his
gaze expressionlessly. Massengale shrugged. "I need you in
Shaft Three. I got men out with injuries, and they're shorthanded."

"I don't know squat about deep mine work," Bandicut
pointed out.

Massengale chuckled. "So what else is new?" Bandicut
flushed. "They'll show you what you need to know. Just
don't screw anything up this time." Massengale stared at
him for a moment longer, and Bandicut could almost hear
his thought: *We don't need any goddamn neurojack fair-*
ies down there, either, so whatever that look is on your
face, wipe it off. But all Massengale actually said was,
"There's a supply van going out in twenty minutes. That
oughta give you enough time to grab a suit." Massengale's
lips curled into a faint smile.

/*That oughta give you enough time,*/ Bandicut mimicked, as he returned to the storeroom to check out a deep-
mine suit. /I'd love to drop that guy down one of his own
mine shafts./

/// In this gravity,
would he not fall slowly?
I wonder if that would create
the result you desire. ///

/It was a rhetorical comment./ The first Charlie would have understood that, damn it. But Bandicut didn't have time to talk about it, and he didn't *want* to have to explain things to this quarx. The storeroom robot was handing him the components of his suit, and he didn't plan to step out of the ready room without thoroughly inspecting the pieces that would separate his hide from near vacuum. It was another thirty minutes before he was exiting through the airlock in search of the supply van.

/// What's different about this suit? ///
Charlie asked, as he strode down the departure dock.

/A few more lights, more air, more protection against cave-in crushing,/ Bandicut murmured.

/// I see.
Cave-in crushing . . . ? ///

/Don't worry, it rarely happens./ Bandicut peered around, and finally spotted the van in the glare of the floodlights. Two suited men were walking around outside it. /At least, I hope that's true./

Charlie considered that for a long moment.

/// Do I understand that as
. . . humor? ///

/Ha ha ha./ Bandicut waved to the apparent driver of the van. He was answered by a gesture to hurry up and get in.

Charlie was quiet as Bandicut settled into the back of the vehicle and hooked his wrists into the restraints. The van jerked into motion, and he watched in silence as they pulled out of the docks and drove to the south, away from the surface mines, toward Shaft Three.

The ride was a short one. But Bandicut had a terrible sense of traveling a long way from where he wanted to go. A long way from Charlie-One's cavern, a long way from the translator. A long way from understanding what the hell it was he was supposed to do—since Charlie-Two didn't seem to know.

Before he knew it, he was hanging on to a handhold lift, descending into the sub-Triton depths.

★

As he stepped off the lift, he was some hundred meters beneath the surface, far deeper than he had been in Charlie's cavern. With vapor lamps arrayed everywhere, it was considerably brighter here than Charlie's cavern had been; but he couldn't help shivering at a certain feeling of déjà vu. As he peered down the horizontal mine shaft, he saw that the walls here contained less ice and more rock than Charlie's cavern. The ceiling had been laser-fused for structural strength, but it still made him nervous. /Does this remind you of anything?/ he asked Charlie, wondering if the quarx had memories of their first meeting.

/// Yes . . . ///

the quarx said weakly.

/What's the matter?/ Bandicut was puzzled by Charlie's abruptly subdued demeanor. /You do remember meeting me—with your translator—don't you?/

The quarx seemed to have trouble answering. He clearly found this place disturbing, for some reason.

/Say, you aren't claustrophobic or anything, are you?/

/// No, I— ///

Bandicut frowned, beginning to wonder if something really was wrong with the quarx. /You lived in a cavern smaller than this, for millions of years. Don't you remember?/

/// Yes . . . I remember . . .
But this . . . reminds me of . . .
something else . . . ///

The quarx's voice trailed off.

Bandicut realized that the other men from the van had gone off somewhere and disappeared. They probably had assumed that he knew where he was going. /Reminds you of what?/ he asked absently, wondering where in the hell he was supposed to go now.

/// . . . of . . . ///

The alien couldn't seem to finish its thought. Someone who looked as though he might be the mining foreman was walking in Bandicut's direction along the corridor shaft. Down at the far end of the tunnel, Bandicut glimpsed a flickering of light and shadow, men working. */What's* it remind you of?/ he muttered.

/// Of the war, ///

Charlie whispered.

Bandicut felt a sudden chill. /What?/ he asked softly. Something had been touched deep in the quarx's memory, something very sharp and painful, something that fitted with this underground image of tunnels in the rock and ice. Before he could ask, he felt a sudden sense of memories falling into place like the tumblers of a lock, and the quarx murmured,

/// It reminds me of . . .
our burrowing deep, very deep
to avoid the destruction
at the end. ///

Bandicut fought off a wave of dizziness. The quarx's voice carried great waves of sorrow and fear. Images flickered in Bandicut's mind, too quickly to follow; but he recognized glimpses of what the first Charlie had shown him—memories of Triton millions of years ago, in another star system, at war. The end of the Rohengen civilization. This time the memory seemed to carry a keener sorrow—as if the sight of this mining tunnel touched a nerve that ran darker and deeper than any he'd touched before. /Charlie? Are you okay?/

/// What do you mean? ///

the quarx whispered hoarsely.

/You don't sound so good. Are you having some kind of flashback or something?/ He felt the quarx flinch, and an image flickered in his mind of someone running, desperately running, fleeing from approaching explosions. The image vanished, squelched at its source, and he sensed that it was not gone, but hidden from him. /Charlie?/ There was no answer. He had a fleeting impression of the quarx burrowing, curling into a ball, pulling away from him. Great, he thought.

He heard a voice on the comm. "That you, Jimmy?" It was the suited man, approaching. "Who is that?"

"Bandicut!" he called back. "Herb sent me down."

"What the hell for?"

"How the hell would I know? He said you were shorthanded. I'm supposed to help out."

"Aw, you mean I'm supposed to train a new guy, on top of everything else? Man, I need this like I need hemorrhoids—"

"Listen!" Bandicut flared. "I didn't ask to be sent down here! Who is that—Jones?"

"Yeah, it's Jones." The foreman waved for Bandicut to join him. "Hey, nothin' personal, Bandicut. I'm sure as a miner you're a helluva good pilot. It's just that we're a little busy here. We're on a bum streak and the man up in the office is tellin' us to move our butts and get the output up, and what does *he* know about mining? Know what I mean?"

"Yeah. I know." Bandicut could now read the man's name stenciled on his suit: JQ Jones. At that moment, he felt a shiver run up his spine. It had nothing to do with Jones. It had everything to do with where he was, and why, and the fact that he was separated by a pane of cryosafe plastic from everyone around him. No connection . . . linkage . . . neurowarmth . . . neurostim . . .

Oh no. /Charlie!/

He couldn't feel the quarx; Charlie had withdrawn into his own memories; but he felt something else, something disturbingly familiar. There seemed to be a distance growing, not quite physical or tangible, but a distance nonetheless, between himself and the foreman, himself and the cavern, himself and anything else that might touch him. The silence-fugue was just in its beginning phase, but he already felt a certain comfort in the familiarity of the sensation.

"Here y'go, Bandicut. Want to help us out here?" Jones stopped beside a bank of equipment which, as far as Bandicut could tell, might have been used for drilling or for dishwashing. Was he going to be expected to operate this stuff? Then he saw that Jones was pointing not at the equipment, but just beyond it to what looked like a pile of rock rubble. A small, hunchbacked robot was picking its way across the pile. "Quasimodo here is sorting through these tailings for traces of metal that might have gotten through the big processor. You want to help it?"

Bandicut's head was buzzing. He wasn't sure he had heard correctly. "Say again? You're joking, right?"

"Naw, our big sorters sometimes miss bits that are worth as much as half a crawler load."

"And you just dump it here and let a robot claw through it?" Bandicut felt great bubbles of disbelief billowing open in his head. He'd thought he understood how things worked around here, but was it possible they were even more idiotic than he'd supposed?

Jones shrugged without apparent humor. "Quasimodo here does a pretty good job—bit of a perfectionist, really. He'll show you what to do."

Bandicut's vision flickered with little tongues of flame. He was to be a servant and apprentice to a *robot?* "Now, wait a second—"

"I tol' you, I don't have anyone here to train you." Jones grinned. "If you get real good at this, maybe we'll promote you tomorrow. Now, I gotta go. Lunch break is at eleven-thirty Zulu."

Bandicut stared at the foreman's dwindling back and thought, time is fleeing, and *this* is what I'm doing? *Charlie?* He turned to stare at the little robot. It was dusty and nondescript, with a couple of flickering lights and three eye lenses. As it rose from a crouch, it looked like a tiny, ancient man, plucking at the rocks. It examined the chunks one by one, then flicked them aside into the shadows. Bandicut brushed off the top of a small boulder and sat down, blinking.

He was casually aware that the robot was looking almost alive to him, and for that matter, the corridors were starting to remind him of a hive maze, and his safety-net Charlie was nowhere to be found; and he was dimly aware that he was teetering on the brink of a potentially major silence-fugue, perhaps as bad as the one that had sent him careening toward Charlie's cavern in the first place. He had no power to take any action, but he watched what was happening in his mind with keen interest and an avid curiosity. Spectator mode: the kind of silence-fugue that he liked best, really . . .

He felt a little shiver from Charlie, but nothing more.

He was suddenly aware that the robot was utterly still. It was watching him. It extended one telescoping arm and poked at a chunk of rock. "Yeah?" Bandicut said dreamily. "What do you want?"

The robot raised its arm and pointed at him. He chuckled, "Get outa here."

The robot hooted softly.

Bandicut squinted at the metal creature, and imagined an army of them crawling around, scrabbling at loose rock in search of stray grains of metal which they would deposit in a small pile. He imagined a storm gathering up the meager collection in a whirlwind and blowing them away as fast as the robots could collect them, all of their efforts coming to nothing as they dug and probed and toiled, for nothing at all.

Beware your state of mind. The warning thought—from Charlie?—flickered past and vanished as he rose and joined the robot, giggling silently.

A remaining sane corner of his mind recoiled in horror, then spun away in the wind. He reached out past the robot and picked up a rock. "I got one, too," he murmured. "Pretty, isn't it?"

The robot seemed to shake its head in disgust. It took the rock from him and turned it over in its mechanical hand. "Scanning," it muttered. "No metal." It turned and tossed the rock onto the refuse pile. "Next?"

"Next? Next *what?*"

The robot stared at him expectantly.

"You want me to stand here and hand you rocks? So I can look like a furgin' hunchback, too? Whaddya think we invented robots for, anyway?"

Quasimodo peered at him a moment longer, then gave a little jerk which might have been a shrug and turned back to its work, paying him no further notice.

Bandicut heard laughter. He saw Jones a little way up the corridor, walking back toward him. "Okay, Bandicut—I wasn't really gonna leave you there all day. Come on, I got something better for you to do." Jones waved him onward.

Following Jones, with a dark glance back at Quasimodo, Bandicut swiveled his head back and forth, glaring at the faces peering down at him from the walls, the ghosts maybe of all the aliens who once lived here, billions of years ago. He imagined them falling in behind him. No, no, he wanted to tell them. This is taking me *farther* from the answers! Go back! But he decided to say nothing. They would be gone soon, he knew. And so would the fugue. Soon.

13

SILENCE-FUGUE

"DOWN HERE," JONES said, pointing to a shaft. Bandicut stepped carefully forward and peered down into the shaft. It was ten or twenty meters deep. A cable descended from a hoist overhead, down through the center of the shaft. He could see movement below, the shadows of men working nearby, and occasionally an elbow or backpack jutting into view. His nerves jangled; he imagined fish with large teeth swarming down there. He stepped back. "Uh-huh."

"It's a little makeshift because the main hoist is broken, so we've got this rig here for the time being."

"And you want me to . . . run it?"

"Naw—hell no!" Jones laughed. "You think we can afford to have someone here running a stupid *hoist?* We got real work for you to do, down in the laser shaft."

Bandicut swallowed, and said nothing.

"Let me just show you how this thing works, so you can get yourself in and out." Jones pointed to a grimy panel of knobs and levers.

Bandicut peered and saw the knobs turn to little faces. He thought one of the levers waved. *Hi,* he thought. He had just enough presence of mind not to wave back.

Jones was activating the hoist. After glancing down the

shaft to see that the way was clear, he pushed a lever and the cable began rising. "Here you go. Up. Down. Keep the tension even here. Simple enough?" He turned his shiny visor toward Bandicut.

"Simple," Bandicut whispered.

"Then let's go." Jones grabbed the cable and swung out over the shaft. He sank quickly. Bandicut stepped after him and clung as they descended deeper into the mine.

The shaft surrounded him like a tomb, then opened out into a cavern full of lights and suited men. There was very little headroom once clear of the hoist, which gave a closed-in feeling to the place, even though the room opened out horizontally for tens of meters. Mining holes were being bored outward in a radial fashion from the outer circumference of the cavern. Vapors from probing lasers periodically boiled out in great clouds, obscuring the view. Bandicut shivered with a sudden feeling that this was where the real heart of the Triton operation was located. It was in these deep mines that the most promising concentrations of Tritonmetal had been detected, the melted and twisted veins of living communities . . . of buildings, technologies, and people . . . of the Rohengen, before they had been consumed by their war. And no one else here—no one human, anyway—had the slightest inkling of the history that he saw in this place.

He shuddered with a sudden intensity, and realized that the quarx, deep in his mind, was reacting violently to those last thoughts. He had a sense of tightly contained memories and feelings on the verge of erupting.

"Bandicut, for Chrissake, come on!" Jones was gesturing impatiently from halfway down a work line, where a dozen men were operating panels for the remote mining equipment.

"Right—"

"Hey, Bandie—how you makin' out, man?" He heard a familiar voice, and swung around, looking for its source.

Finally he spotted Gordon Kracking waving from behind a large computer console.

"Okay, uh . . . What are you doing here, Krackey?"

"Helpin' 'em straighten out this mess of a control system!" Krackey shouted, gesturing. Behind him a plasma laser flickered in a horizontal shaft. A conveyor belt was carrying a continuous load of rock and ice past a sensor bank for scanning and sorting. Bandicut blinked, imagining his friend as a great bird, flapping his wings and flying away in frustration from this place. He imagined Jones's gaze as a great invisible laser beam, cutting Krackey down and then turning on *him,* if he didn't move—

"*Comin', JQ!*" He hurried after the foreman, ignoring the curious glances of the other miners.

Jones was standing just beyond one of the main tunneling stations. He was fiddling with a portable control stand connected by cable to a small drilling laser. The laser, mounted on a self-propelled dolly, was parked just inside a small, fresh-looking horizontal opening. The shaft in the cavern wall was about a shoulder's width across. Its interior was dark. Jones turned his helmeted head toward Bandicut and hooked a gloved thumb toward the small shaft. "We'll be setting up a boring and extraction station here in a coupla' days, but here's the pilot hole so we can get some readings on any veins along the radial. This oughta be right up your alley, Bandicut. The instruments here're just like the ones on your survey rigs."

Bandicut stepped cautiously past the mining operation situated just to the left of the new shaft. The flashes and boiling vapors of the mining laser gave him a feeling of walking through the set of a holomovie, but he knew better. This was serious business down here; deep mining was the most dangerous operation on all of Triton. The lasers were mounted on stationary pedestals, their radiant output focused and guided by mirrors. The powerful beams glowed and shimmered within the shafts like exotic weapons beams, glittering dully off the sluglike vapor-exhaust ducts.

One of the men operating the laser was Mick Eddison, the miner who'd given him such a hard time in the dorm the other day. Bandicut shuddered, thinking, they let people like *him* control these life-threatening machines? He hoped Eddison hadn't noticed him.

Jones was flipping switches. Bandicut stepped close and peered at the instruments. Actually, they bore little resemblance to the readouts he was used to, but he assumed he could figure out how they worked. "Okay," he said.

"What you're gonna do is, walk this baby straight into the pilot shaft, and just drill straight out on a narrow beam. It's autoguided. You record the findings here." Jones pointed to the instruments, then looked at him. "Think you can handle that?"

Whether it was John Bandicut responding or some inner creature released by the silence-fugue, he answered casually, "No problem." Before Jones could say another word, he flicked on the laser.

Jones backed hastily out of the way. "Be careful with that thing," he yelled, then vanished back into a swirling cloud of vapor.

✳

Be careful? Bandicut thought, driving the laser forward into the shaft, guided by images on a small monitor. What could be simpler? He thought he heard a faint, mewling protest somewhere deep in the mines of his own thoughts; but perhaps that was the quarx, working out its own problems. But he couldn't count on the quarx; the Charlie he knew was gone, and he was on his own.

The tunnel was not yet very deep, reaching only a few meters. The guide beams glinted red, sparkling through the thin haze that filled the tenuous air, marking the track of the invisible infrared and ultraviolet beams that bored and probed and sent back reflections to the sensors. The rock and ice layers scintillated, sparkling of emerald and ruby and sapphire; it was a pretty show for Bandicut, but also information for the recorder. If there were veins of metal, even trace residues, the spectra would be detected in the return beams.

For a time, he was boring through rock, his laser slowly deepening and widening the hole before advancing. Then he struck ice and a vapor cloud billowed out of the shaft, obscuring his view. As the exhaust vent drew the cloud away, he glimpsed a dancing display of fluorescence and refraction in the monitor, deep in the hole. He was dazzled by the sight; it reminded him of the image Charlie had shown him in their first meeting—what a quarx might look like, if it existed in material form.

Was he imagining it, or did he feel Charlie-Two trembling? He blinked as the laser licked at ice and rock, melting and vaporizing, hollowing out the tunnel. He glanced up from the monitor to peer directly into the borehole. He saw faces peering back from the inner walls of the shaft. There was Charlie-One as he might have appeared as a human: a trifle pudgy and world weary, with thinning flyaway hair, but a gleam in the eye and a quip on his tongue. And there was Charlie-Two, narrow and stern, with dark, strictly kempt hair, and eyes that bored into Bandicut's, trying to understand—

Both faces flickered and melted in the laser heat, and turned to a hazy, gauzy light, with jets of fire spurting out to the sides.

"Bandicut! What the hell are you doing?"

He started and realized that his hands were working the controls of their own accord. Jones strode out of a cloud of steam like a creature from an old movie. What *was* he doing? "Are you falling asleep at that goddamn thing?" he heard, and he blinked and saw that he had taken the laser off autoguide and let it wander, hollowing out the walls, creating a pool of melted ice that was now hardening to a slick surface. He snapped the laser off and backed it out. He peered into the tunnel in dismay. It was now almost big enough for a man to walk into, if he got up there and crouched low. Too big.

Jones stared into the tunnel, shaking his head. "Jesus, Bandicut, I thought I could trust you to do this simple little—"

"Did I ever say I was a miner?" Bandicut protested weakly.

"Even a goddamn *pilot* ought to be able to see—!" Jones gave up with an audible sigh. "All right, never mind. Now that you've got it so big, we need to get a robot in there to check it out." His voice sharpened. "Commlink Echo, Robot Delta Mike Four, report to my location. *Copernicus*—you got that?"

Bandicut heard a drumtap in reply, and a few moments later, a small, upright robot with four cone-shaped wheels lumbered out of a cloud of vapor at the next work station and stopped in front of Jones. "With you, boss," it twanged.

Jones pointed. "I want you to go into this borehole and do a short-profile type-B spectrascan. Got that?"

Copernicus drumtapped acknowledgment. Using its upper appendages, it lifted itself into the shaft, then reconfigured itself into a horizontal attitude, one pair of cone wheels stretching forward. A cluster of lights on its nose blinked on, and it rolled forward into the borehole.

Bandicut watched, befuddled, as the robot's scanning lights glinted and reflected back out of the tunnel. Another memory was being touched here; he felt Charlie twisting in pain.

/You okay there?/ he whispered nervously.

An image flickered in his mind: the quarx, in its Rohengen host, sprinting down a passageway, lights flashing and ground trembling. They were under attack, underground, running for cover; but this was the wrong direction. There was a synthetic creature ahead of them; they were trying to save it. For some reason it was special . . . it was a co-worker, a *friend.* They ran, hoping to catch it, to bring it back to safety. There was a blinding light, and the ground shook—

And everything changed forever for the quarx. It was all gone in that flash: not just the robot-friend and the corridor it had been running through, but all hope for the Rohengen, for the future of quarx and host alike. The image blurred, as though obscured by tears, quarx and host fleeing back the other way. But the host was injured and dying. It barely made it through quaking underground corridors to the deep shaft where the quarx's translator was hidden. Then the host died, releasing the quarx to the translator, and quarx and translator were falling, falling . . . plunging toward the center of the moon, away from the battle and the terror . . . but it was all gone, everything that it had lived and hoped for, its only friends . . .

A squawk on the comm made Bandicut blink. It was the robot, chirping. Through the haze of confusion, he heard it calling . . . *loss of traction, adhesion to ice* . . . caught . . . trapped . . .

Trapped, and it needed help. Before Jones could respond with any sort of instruction, Bandicut pushed the laser-probe aside, clawed for purchase on the lip of the borehole as he climbed up, crouching as he made his way into the tunnel to help the robot . . .

"—what the flying fuzzookie are you doing?" Jones yelled.

No need to answer, got to get to the robot before it was injured, damaged, destroyed . . . lights flashing here, rock trembling . . . there it was, glinting just beyond the narrow constriction where the tunnel was carved out of rock, before the ice pocket. Bandicut crouched and stretched forward, and yes, it was *awfully* icy here, he'd really burnished it to a slick surface, but he could almost reach the robot . . . give it a good yank before the big flash came to end everything. He had his hand on it and felt a sudden flush, and a tingle going down his arm . . . the quarx was stirring, with some kind of reflex, trying to reach out to communicate with the thing.

"BANDICUT!" Jones bellowed.

And he finally, dimly realized what he was doing. It was sheer idiocy; he could get stuck here himself. He was caught in the quarx's memory of a desperate need to save a robot . . . but Copernicus was in no real danger. And even if it was, so what? /Charlie,/ he whispered, /did you want me to do this—?/

The answer rattled up faintly, from somewhere deep in his mind:

/// No, but . . . what are you . . . ? ///

The scanning lasers on the robot suddenly rotated and flashed back off the ice, dazzling him. The quarx writhed . . . *the destruction of everything* . . .

Bandicut shuddered and squirmed back. He twisted, glimpsing where Jones was standing at the entrance to the borehole, yelling at him.

"Are you delirious? Get out of there!"

Bandicut shuffled, crouching, toward the foreman. He heard himself croaking, "No, no, not delirious—" he gasped. "It's this damn *alien* in my—"

/// NO! ///

shrieked the quarx, and did something inside Bandicut's head.

His vision flickered off and on once, then went black as he fainted. It was only for an instant, but long enough for him to lose his balance, for his feet to shoot out from under him on the ice. He skidded feet first toward the end of the tunnel and Jones's head—and the mining laser just beyond Jones. He clawed futilely—so light in this gravity—

He flew out of the shaft, airborne, and Jones hit him with a body blow to deflect him, and he careened into the cavern wall and bounced back toward the blazing light. He screamed and stuck out a foot—and caught it on the laser's pedestal, then slammed into the pedestal before dropping in a crumpled heap to the floor. Pain blazed up his leg, and he cried out, once—

—before the quarx, panicked, shut off the pain impulses; and then his consciousness, too.

14

STRANGE FEVERS

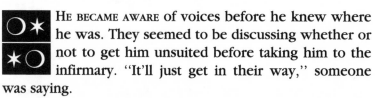 HE BECAME AWARE of voices before he knew where he was. They seemed to be discussing whether or not to get him unsuited before taking him to the infirmary. "It'll just get in their way," someone was saying.

"This monitor says he's got a broken ankle," someone else answered. "Whaddyou think we'll do to that if *we* try to take this suit off? They got nano-shit that can do that, in the infirmary."

A heavy voice cut in, "I don't want this suit ruined down there. *They* ain't gonna give a flyin' horse-moke about the equipment."

"Have a little heart, Herb! The guy's hurt!" That sounded like Krackey.

"Yeah, well, he may be hurt, but that don't make him any less of a *dumb* fucker," the heavy-sounding voice retorted. "Imagine goin' on shift with a fever of a hundred 'n' four and not tellin' anyone! Serves him right he almost got hisself killed."

Massengale. That last idiot was Massengale.

"Hey, come on, will you? He was probably too feverish to know he was sick."

Bandicut's eyes blinked open. His visor had been pushed

up, and he was staring up at the ready-room ceiling. How'd he get here? he wondered vaguely. He groaned aloud and fended off the hands that were trying to remove his helmet. With a Herculean effort, he shoved it off himself. He felt a region of numbness around his left ankle. He tried to recall what had happened, and found his memory a feverish muddle. He remembered the silence-fugue. And he remembered the quarx shutting him down like an overloaded circuit.

/// You were in severe pain.
It seemed the best course of action.
Are you okay now? ///

"Awww, too bad! He woke up," Massengale remarked.

Bandicut tried to raise his head to glare, but the supervisor was already on his way out of the room. "Stupid stoker," he grunted. He shifted his gaze to see who else was here with him. Krackey was the only one he knew. "Ah, man!" he sighed.

"Take it easy, there, Bandie," Krackey said worriedly. "You got a fever *an'* a broken ankle. It must hurt like a bastard, but we don't want to do nothin' until the meds get a look at you."

Great, he thought. The meds. The same meds who'd tried to fix his neuros. He wondered if the quarx could do anything to help.

/// I can keep the pain turned off,
as I'm doing now.
That's about all, I think. ///

He sighed and forced a grin in Krackey's direction. "It's . . . not too bad," he said, realizing suddenly that it was true. He felt disoriented, but there was very little physical pain, except for a hollow sort of emptiness below his left knee. He wondered if that was what a phantom limb felt like to someone who'd lost a leg.

"Ho, man, Bandie! If you're not in some serious pain, it must be because of that fever." Krackey looked at the first-aid monitor and shook his head. "You got yourself one whale of a fracture there. What happened? And what the hell *were* you doing, working, if you were sick like that?"

Sick? he thought. Fever? Had he actually been delirious with fever, instead of silence-fugue? That, somehow, would be easier to take.

/// Uh, no—sorry.
I gave you the fever
as an excuse for your behavior.
What were you thinking of,
trying to pull a robot out by its hind legs? ///

/Thinking? Didn't you notice, I was out of my mind with fugue?/ He remembered the quarx's flashback-induced silence. /Anyway, where were you? You're supposed to help me out when these things happen./

/// I am?
I don't have much recollection of that.
I suppose . . . I was a trifle indisposed
for a while there. ///

Bandicut felt movement, and realized suddenly that he was on a gurney, being rolled toward the door. Krackey was walking alongside him. The door opened and two med-techs came in and took the gurney. "You guys can't go walking out of here like that," one of them said. "Your boss said to tell you to go back to work," said the other. That was when Bandicut noticed that the miners were all still suited, except for their helmets.

"I'll check in on you as soon as I can," Krackey promised, with a wave. "Don't worry—these guys will have you riveted back together in no time. Just take it easy and get over that flu!"

Bandicut blanched as the techs sped him through the door and down the corridor.

✶

"No way!" he yelled, shaking. "No nanomeds!"

"Oh, come on, Bandicut. We can have you back at work in two days if you just let us—"

Bandicut flailed an arm, clenching a fist in warning. He started to sit up, but a pair of strong arms grabbed him and held him down on the table. *"No—nanomeds—!"* he wheezed, against the pressure on his chest.

Dr. Switzer's face came into view over him. He was a stocky man with thinning silver hair, probably in his late fifties. What the hell a man his age was doing out here on Triton, Bandicut hated to think. Probably barred from practice on all the other inhabited worlds. Switzer peered at him through his black-rimmed glasses, frowning. "Still can't forgive and forget, eh, John?"

Bandicut grunted. "Yeh," he managed, holding back a dozen harsher answers. "I guess that's it."

"Tsk, tsk." Switzer moved away, shaking his head. "Well . . . we wouldn't want to give you something that would cause you any *psychological* side effects, I suppose."

Bandicut raised his head suspiciously. He didn't like the sound of that. As senior medical officer on Triton, Switzer approved or disapproved everyone's fitness-for-duty status. Medically *and* psychologically. "What's that mean?"

"It doesn't mean anything, John." Switzer turned back with an alarming-looking clamping device in his hand. "I'm just trying to save you pain, that's all. Now we'll have to set that bone the old-fashioned way, and it'll take you a good four or five days to heal well enough to work. I suppose you can use the time to catch up on your reading. Jean, give him the injection, please," Switzer said brusquely.

Bandicut swiveled his head, but the nurse had already jammed the syringe into his leg. He felt a rush of giddiness. What the hell was *that?* he managed to think, before the sensation swept him away like a flickering holochannel, removing him from any awareness of his surroundings.

★

/// May I ask a question? ///
/What question? What's going on here? Why can't I see anything? Did you do that to me?/

/// *It was the injection.*
I merely organized the effect slightly,
so that we could use this time to talk.
You can't do anything else now, anyway. ///

/Thanks a bundle. Look, I need to know what they're doing to me. I don't trust them. They aren't shooting nano-meds into me, are they?/

/// *I don't think so . . .* ///

A small, framed image flicked on, like a monitor in one corner of a darkened control room. He could see the doctor and nurse and medtechs moving around him, stretching his leg out in some sort of tension device enclosed within a sensor array. It was fascinating to watch . . . until he remembered that it was his broken ankle they were stretching and twisting. Suddenly he preferred talking with the quarx.

/You said you had a question?/

/// *Yes.*
What are these nanomeds?
Why are you so afraid of them? ///

Even in the darkness and peace of the anesthesia-gloom, he would have winced if he could have.

/// *Your reaction to them is pronounced.* ///

/Yeah,/ he muttered. /Yours would be, too, if nanomeds had done to you what they did to me./

/// *I can't . . . locate the memory.*
What are they? ///

/Submicroscopic repair units—self-replicating robots the size of large molecules, programmed with medical instructions and injected into the body to make repairs. There's practically nothing they can't fix—/

/// *Then what—?* ///

/—in theory,/ he finished acidly.

/// *Oh. Then they don't always work?* ///

/No, they don't./ He tasted the bitterness and anger all over again. /They're only as good as the programming patched into them, see. And these quacks used them to try to fix some damage to my neurojack implants./ Even his mind-voice trembled as he remembered, for Charlie's benefit, what had happened . . . as he remembered the terrible shearing away of his ability to connect, to link in to that infinite world of . . .

/// And the attempt failed? ///
the quarx interrupted.

/You saw it,/ he said savagely. /You saw the silence-fugue! They screwed up the nanosoft programming, and butchered the job so badly that I can *never* use a neuro again! Do you know what it's like to have that . . . *taken from you* . . . once you've . . ./ His words failed him, as he remembered the pain and the humiliation of losing the neurolink that had made him a highly valued survey pilot, equally skilled in the cockpit and the datanet.

/// I believe I can imagine your pain, ///
the quarx answered softly.

Bandicut was startled by the answer; then he glimpsed an impression of what it was like for a quarx to lose a host, to lose his only direct connection to life, to the rest of the physical universe except through the mechanical translator, to lose the one being who provided intimacy and immediacy of thought.

/// And my predecessor . . .
helped you to bridge that gap.
Is that correct? ///

/Yes,/ Bandicut whispered, envisioning the link that Charlie-One had created to the datanet. /Yes, that was very . . . satisfying./ He swallowed, almost afraid to ask the next question. /Do you think you could—?/

He felt the quarx's thoughts shifting and adjusting—and he realized that Charlie-Two had been growing, unfolding, remembering, and learning ever since his awakening. Perhaps this Charlie had potential, after all.

/// I don't know. ///

/Oh./ He sighed softly. /I guess I shouldn't have expected—/

/// *But I'd be willing to try.* ///

Bandicut felt his heart skip. It took him a moment to remember that it was as much a part of the quarx's plan as his. But that was okay. Why shouldn't the quarx benefit, too?

/// *But now,*
I think you need to pay attention to the docs.
It looks like they're trying to wake you up. ///

/Mm?/ He looked back at the little monitor that the quarx had given him, and saw the faces of the nurse and medtechs peering down at him. He felt a stirring of sensation, and . . . a lance of pain. /Owww!/

/// *Sorry.*
Wrong connection. ///

The pain faded, and in place of it he felt the stirrings of muscular ability. His eyelids were fluttering. The small monitor image grew to fill his vision.

"You okay there?" someone was saying.

"Ahh—" he grunted. It wasn't the pain that made him grunt, it was the difficulty of regaining control over his body.

"Take it easy," said Switzer's gravelly voice. "It's going to hurt some, until you heal."

Bandicut nodded, his head heavy on the table. "What *was* that stuff?" he breathed.

"Hah. Escalomethorphin. Worked like a charm, didn't it?" Switzer stepped up, beaming. He seemed proud of the way they had knocked him out in a matter of seconds. "We got your leg set, and you're wearing a fastract unit. If you don't mind a little pain, we can let you walk out of here." He shook a finger at Bandicut. "Just don't plan on working or doing anything hard for at least four days, maybe five."

"I wasn't—*ow!* What the hell was that?" He looked

down at his leg, ignoring Switzer's cackle, and saw that the nurse had just stuck him with another syringe, a big one.

Switzer clapped him on the shoulder. "Just some hormone and mineral supplements, to help the fastract do its job. Here, try standing up." He grabbed Bandicut's right arm and motioned to one of the medtechs, who grabbed the left. "Swing your legs off the table—atta' boy."

Bandicut nearly fainted as they spun him around and sat him up. Charlie's command over the pain pathways was uncertain, and for a second he felt a searing pain roar up his leg until it tingled in his ear. "Uh—"

"That's it. Can you stand?"

/// Slowly! ///

He slid from the table with a grunt, wincing as his feet touched the floor. Charlie managed to kill the pain just as his weight came down on both legs, so it was mainly the anticipation of pain, rather than pain itself, that made him shudder. Still, he was grateful for the low Triton gravity.

"Okay?" asked Switzer.

"Yeah," he whispered.

"Good. Here's an instruction sheet on the fastract." Switzer waved a paper at him. "You've got to keep it at the right tension level, or you'll be back here in even worse shape. And no centrifuge until I say so."

"Right." *What do you think I am, a moron?*

"Just follow those instructions, and take these—" Switzer handed him a huge bottle of pills "—and come back in two days so I can see how you're doing." He hesitated. "Sooner—only if you have to."

Bandicut nodded, glancing around at the otherwise empty infirmary offices. He wasn't exactly monopolizing the doctor's time. He recalled that Switzer was rumored to spend extensive periods of leisure time in the VR facilities. Some sort of golf game, apparently. "Right," he answered. "Only if I have to. Wouldn't want to impose upon your services—"

Switzer's gaze darkened almost imperceptibly.

/// Are you baiting him now?
This is a very interesting dynamic. ///

Bandicut sighed. /Oh, shut up, will you?/ To the doctor, he said, "Just joking, you know."

"Yes," said Switzer, who clearly understood exactly what he'd meant, and didn't much like it. He squinted at Bandicut and said, "I wonder if we should have you come back in for some neurological retesting. I wouldn't want to think that you hadn't completely recovered from your prior . . . unfortunate . . . accident. Perhaps we should make sure that there's nothing funny going on." He tapped the side of his head meaningfully.

/// What's he mean by that? ///
Charlie asked in a panic.

"What do you mean by that?" Bandicut asked simultaneously.

"Well, you were picked up with a temperature of a hundred and four. By the time you were rolled in here, you were down to one-zero-two. Now you're back to ninety-eight point seven." Switzer shook his head, turning away with his clipboard. "That's just not natural."

/// Oh. ///

Bandicut shifted his attention. /You did that, too? You shut it off that fast?/

/// I, well . . .
I was trying to give you a cover for the accident.
I didn't think you needed it anymore,
once we were on our way here. ///

Bandicut nodded—and stopped the movement of his head when he remembered he was nodding to the quarx, not the doctor. /I suppose there's no way you could have known./

/// I still have much to learn, ///
the quarx admitted.

Switzer turned back, glaring. "You still here? Go on, get

out of here. Go take in . . . whatever it is you like to do." He coughed and hurried into his office, leaving Bandicut standing, wobbling slightly, with the nurse.

With a faint smile at the nurse's bemused expression, he turned and hobbled with a low-gravity bounce out of the infirmary.

✶

/I think I want a beer,/ he said, working his way toward the rec lounge.

The quarx was silent for a moment, before saying,

/// I find I have some pharmacological data
in my memory.
I'm not sure that it would be a good idea,
with that medication you're on. ///

Bandicut frowned. /Can't you just take care of any side effects?/

/// I'm not a miracle worker.
I'm just an alien. ///

/Ha ha./ Bandicut chuckled, then realized that the quarx had not meant the statement as a joke. /Well, okay—if not a beer—what, then?/

/// Well . . . at some point,
I'd like to see that game again.
EineySteiney pool. ///

/All right./

/// But first,
how about taking me to the place
where my predecessor . . . ///

/Yes?/

/// . . . linked you in. ///

Bandicut smiled and hobbled a little more quickly down the corridor.

15

DATAFRY

 Settling into a booth just off the lounge, Bandicut put on the headset and waited for the quarx to begin. /Well?/
Charlie hesitated.

/// *Actually,*
I don't seem to remember how he did it.
Do you? ///

/Me? Hell, no. I didn't understand it when he was doing it./

/// *Well, did he say* anything about
how he did it? ///

Bandicut thought back. /He said he was . . . altering the neural matrix of my brain. He said it was something like the way he talked to me . . . directly in my brain./

/// *Ah.* ///

/Does that help?/

/// *I'm not sure.* ///

He felt the quarx scrabbling in his mind, trying to fit together fragments of memory.

/// *Wait . . . here's something.*
Not a direct memory, but a hint.
Altering the matrix—?
Wait, I think I've got it. ///

Bandicut stared at the console, imagining the quarx's face peering back at him.

/// May I try? ///

/Go ahead. You have the con./

/// Stand by . . . ///

He nodded and closed his eyes. Nothing happened, and he was about to question the quarx, when he was startled by an eruption of sparks in his closed eyes.

```
>
    >>>>>>>>>>>>>>>>>>>>>>>>>>>>
      >>
        >>>>
    >>>>>>>>>>>>>>—<alpha-connect>—>>>>>>
    >>>>>>>>>>>>>>—<alpha-connect>—>>>>>>
    >>>>>>>>>>>>>>—<alpha-connect>—>>>>>>
        >>
        >>>>>>
      >>>
>
    ——<mode shift>>>>>>——
>
```

He shuddered at the jarring entry.

A burst of fireworks expanded in his vision, then crystallized into a network, which hung against the darkness for a heartstopping instant. Then it melted and drained like rivulets of glowing water toward him, into his vision, his eyes, his brain, his consciousness . . .

★

For several minutes, streams of silvery data branched and flowed and shifted, like mercury flowing over an uneven surface. The quarx dived into the datastream, carrying Bandicut faster than he could follow with his thoughts. He was grateful for the surge and tug of the neurolink, but Charlie was taking the data far too fast for him to follow. The quarx darted from stream to stream, dipping and sampling, siphoning information that left Bandicut dizzily bewildered.

Finally he asked, /Do you know what you're looking for?/

The quarx hummed distractedly.

/// Not specifically.
I have an intuition that he might have
left something for me. ///

/Left something? Like what?/

/// I wish I knew.
If he knew he was dying,
he might have anticipated this situation. ///

/You think he left you some kind of instructions?/

/// I would have, in his place. ///

Bandicut watched the datastream blur. What could Charlie-One have left in the datanet that wouldn't be incriminating? The quarx was now rummaging through Earth history files. A minute later he shifted to a summation of the mathematical proofs of the last two centuries. He riffled through them with blinding speed.

/// Nothing.
I find nothing.
You're going to have to help me. ///

/Okay. How?/

/// Well . . . there's a lot about him
that you know better than I.
What did he like?
What were his concerns?
What interested him? ///

/Well . . . the mission, of course./ Bandicut shrugged mentally. /Have you put the pieces of that together yet?/

/// We have to stop something from hitting Earth.
It's quite urgent. ///

/Right. Was that from your memory or mine?/

/// A little of both.
And you have some essential data in your head
which we have to relay to the translator. ///

/Right./ That little detail had almost slipped his mind. /Can you—do you see the data okay? Is it still there?/

/// I haven't actually found it yet,
But that doesn't mean it isn't there.
What else—about Charlie, I mean?
Maybe not related to the mission. ///

Bandicut thought. /Well—he was a big TV nut. He loved the old-time stuff. Was always quoting stupid lines at me. Is that what you mean?/

/// Maybe . . . ///

/In fact, now that I think about it, he used an old TV show as camouflage when he fired that first bunch of data to the translator./

/// Ah.
That's precisely the sort of thing
I was looking for. ///

The quarx shifted in a silent whirlwind to a whole new branch of the datastream, one bearing endless thousands of hours of TV and holo programming.

/If it helps, he said the program he used for cover was—/ Bandicut stopped, realizing he didn't remember. The name had meant nothing to him.

/// "Father Knows Best."
It's right there in your memory.
I'll check,
but I doubt he'd use the same cover
for instructions. ///

The scanning was a mottled brown blur, the mud of a trillion frames of imagery swirled together in a river of video history.

/// I didn't think so. ///

/He liked westerns,/ Bandicut noted.

/// Westerns?
Okay, let's check. ///

The river jumped and billowed, and for an instant, Bandicut thought he saw spinning images of cowboys riding and shooting and dying and rescuing, and then it closed together again—

/Well, I guess that didn't—/

—and *opened* again to reveal a cowboy on horseback, gazing at a sunset from some unnamed mountain ridge. The cowboy turned, grinned toothily, and the viewpoint shifted to closeup, and in the dark pupils of the cowboy's eyes Bandicut saw the exploding fire of a quarx in its native reality. And his heart skipped, because he *felt* the first Charlie's presence in those fiery eyes. /Hi, pardner,/ murmured the cowboy, in obvious recognition. /I *thought* you might find your way to me. Let's see if we can help each other out a little, shall we?/

/Uh—yeah—/

/I'm guessing that you have a new quarx-manifestation, and you need information. Well, that's what I'm here for— to help you fill in the blanks. Let's go for a little ride, shall we? Come along./

Bandicut felt himself riding beside the cowboy/quarx— along the ridge, and then suddenly pitching over the edge of a precipice into a bottomless canyon, its walls glittering with points of information. He was falling into darkness, and coruscating fire . . .

And voices began murmuring somewhere close to the center of his mind . . . babbling with information and greetings from one quarx to another. . . .

✳

/// You okay? ///

/Huh?/ He blinked in the cool twilight of the normal datastream, viewed from a height. He wasn't quite sure what had happened, or how he had gotten here from where he'd just been.

/// We got it. ///

He blinked again. /Got what?/

/// I guess you really blacked out there.
He left me the key to the database,
and told me how he'd managed the uplink. ///
/Are you serious?/
/// Why wouldn't I be?
Do you have any objections if I prepare
to make the uplink? ///
/I guess not./ Charlie-One hadn't even bothered to ask. Bandicut squinted at the fuzzy topography of the datanet. He was still trying to get things back into focus; he couldn't quite figure out where he was.
/// Let me just check a few things here. ///
The view went black; then he saw orbital projections, and images of spacecraft—moving in orbit, moored at the space station, and waiting on the surface of the dim, icy moon.
/// This is Triton, isn't it? ///
/Yah, sure. There's Neptune in the background in that one. Most of these look like monitor images from the Triton orbital station, where the interplanetary shuttles come in./
/// Orbital station?
What all do they have there?
Just big interplanetary shuttles? ///
/Well, they have a number of scout craft, as well. Big ones and little ones./
/// Hm. I see. ///
Bandicut felt drawn to the images. Space—that was where he was supposed to be. He wondered if the quarx could make it possible for him to return someday. Now there were some images of the mining encampment, viewed from orbit with a telescopic lens. There were scars visible on the surface from the mining operations; but on the whole, from space, the human presence looked pretty puny and insignificant. /Does this stuff mean anything in particular to you?/

/// For the future—perhaps.
Right now, I'm just filling gaps in my knowledge. ///

He didn't answer; while the quarx was scanning datastructures, he was enjoying the chance to see Triton from space. Cooped up in these pressurized cans on the surface, it was easy to forget the big picture. One of the images coming in now was from a monitor in polar orbit around Triton. The ice caps gleamed pinkish white in the augmented light of the distant sun.

/// There's something I'd like to try, ///
Charlie said, cutting off the images.

/What'd you do that for?/

/// We can go back to it later. ///

A loud buzzing static filled the dataspace. The quarx seemed to be monitoring some sort of communication channel. Or maybe not just monitoring. He seemed to be switching, encoding, and diverting entire streams of data.

/Charlie,/ Bandicut asked nervously, /are you sure you know what you're doing?/

/// Well, not altogether.
But this seems to be working.
I think . . . there we go! ///

Something flickered deep in his mind, and before he could blink or gasp or do anything to stop it, he felt a sudden eruption of data, bubbling up out of his mind like a great geyser of sparkling vapor, streaming into the ether. He reeled, and caught a breathless glimpse of where it was going. It was shooting in a shimmering stream up to Triton Orbital, riding encoded on one of the regular comm beams. It wasn't stopping there, but turning and flashing back down to Triton on another beam—deflected, ever so slightly, toward a silent alien receiver hidden in a deep subsurface cavern.

It was working, he realized dizzily. All that information from the ephemeris was streaming to the translator. But it was doing more than that. He heard, dimly, the jangling of alarms somewhere in the local datanet. /*Charlie,*/ he muttered over the hiss of data, /are you setting off those alarms?/

                    /// *Alarms . . . ?* ///

/Yes, *alarms.* If you can't shut them off, you'd better stop what you're doing, *fast*—and get us out of here, before they trace it to our connection. They are *not* going to be happy if they find us—/

The alarms cut off abruptly. But instead of relief from the quarx, he sensed great worry. Along with the alarms, the streams of data had cut off. Not just the data from Bandicut's mind, but *all* the data.

                    /// *Uh . . .* ///

/Oh, shit. Charlie, you didn't . . . just bring the system down, did you?/

                    /// *Um—*
              let's get out of here—okay, John?
              I'm not sure what *I did . . .* ///

Much of the local datanet seemed to have gone dark. Bandicut felt tempted to investigate, to see what the quarx had done, to see if there was any way to undo the damage. But he dared not. Instead, he squeezed his eyes shut and willed the connection between him and datanet to part.

>
—<**mode shift**>—
>
   >>>
     >>>>>>
        >>>>>>>>>>>>
                            ✷

The sparks in his vision darkened, and he slid the headset from his temples, rubbing his eyes. /Charlie—/ He remembered, suddenly, that Charlie-One hadn't intended to send the data that way; he'd meant to wait until they could go in person.

/// I've—caused problems,
haven't I? ///

/Yeah./ Bandicut got up, wincing from pain in his bad leg. He opened the door to the booth and peered out.

Somebody was yelling across the rec lounge: "Datanet's down, people! Anybody who's got an automatic linkage, get to your terminals for damage control—right now!" A loud murmur rose, and half the people in the lounge ran out of the room. Bandicut watched them go, clicking his teeth nervously. /Charlie—/

/// I couldn't have . . .
caused permanent damage, could I? ///

/Let's hope not. Let's just mokin' hope not./ Bandicut hobbled over toward the refreshment bar. /And I don't care what damn pills I'm on, I'm having a mokin' beer right now!/

16

JULIE

 As he sipped his glass of the watery stuff that passed for beer here on Triton, he shifted unconsciously into observer mode, guiltily watching those who remained in the rec lounge. There weren't many, to his relief. He felt a profound desire not to interact with anyone. He was angry with Charlie, and angry with himself, for what they had done to the datanet. And he was terrified that he would somehow be connected with it.

The first half of the first beer went quickly, before he slowed down, remembering the painkillers he was on. His gaze wandered to the far corner of the EineySteiney area, where two women were playing. He blinked, realizing with a start that the two women were Georgia Patwell and her friend, Julie Stone. How had he not noticed them before?

/// You've been . . . distracted, ///
croaked the quarx, who seemed more than a little distracted himself.

/I guess so./ In truth, this wasn't exactly a time when he *wanted* to see anyone he knew—though as he watched them play, he found his isolationist resolve softening ever so slightly. Still, there was a weightiness surrounding his thoughts. Oddly, he found himself more interested in the women's EineySteiney shots than in the women them-

selves. The table-holo was programmed with some fairly so-
phisticated gravity-well combinations, and the two women
were making slingshot banks through the maze of curves
and valleys. The tabletop was a vibrant grass-green color,
and the balls winked with faces that Bandicut couldn't
quite make out; probably it was the cartoon-character
program.

It was strange enough, his choosing to ogle trajectories
instead of women—but odder still was the fact that he
found himself not only following the motions of the balls,
but visualizing practically impossible trajectories for them,
with an extraordinarily sharp inner eye. Suddenly he realized what was going on, and it didn't make him happy.

He turned away and drained his glass and walked
around the bar for a refill. /Charlie, quit mokin' with my
brain! If I want to look at women, I'm going to look at
women! You have any idea how long it's been since I was
with a woman?/ He returned to his barstool and continued
watching.

Georgia made a nearly impossible three-body shot, and
he found suddenly that he didn't care so much about the
shot.

/// Sorry.
I guess I got carried away.
What they're doing is very . . .
interesting. ///

Bandicut grunted. The weight lifted from him a little,
and he found a new appreciation of Georgia's graceful
movements around the table. She was married, of course,
so it was just harmless appreciation; but Julie wasn't married, and Julie moved with a quickness and intensity that he
found even more appealing. He watched as she lined up a
shot—and missed spectacularly, sending the ball on a loop
off the far end of the table, where it vanished in midair with
a great burst of stars. Julie laughed good-naturedly. It should
have been an easy shot. He liked her laugh.

He cleared his throat, suddenly self-conscious. /You don't have to go to the other extreme,/ he muttered. /I can generate my own interest without your doing anything. Okay?/

/// I wasn't doing anything. ///

/Oh./ He took a sip from his glass and studiously looked elsewhere around the lounge, so as not to be caught staring.

When next he looked back at the EineySteiney table, he saw Georgia pointing her cue-wand in his direction as she said something to Julie. Julie grinned and looked the other way when she saw that Bandicut was watching. Georgia moved toward the bar, waving her cue-wand at him. What was she going to do? he wondered dimly. Whack him with it?

He felt a brief flurry of lust, and then embarrassment. Down, boy. Julie was following Georgia now, and he felt different-colored sparkles of lust. *Now?* he thought, remembering what had brought him here to drink in the first place.

"Hey, Bandie—I have to leave," Georgia said, offering him the wand. "Want to step in for me? Julie's a good player."

Bandicut swallowed, eyes darting from Georgia to Julie and back again. Say something, idiot.

/// Aren't you going to say anything? ///

He cleared his throat. "Uh—yeah! I saw! Looked good out there!"

Julie rolled her eyes as she stopped her low-gravity lope to stand at the bar. "Thanks for the reminder. That last shot wasn't my best."

Bandicut blushed. He hadn't been thinking about that last flub, at all. He'd been thinking of how she *looked.* He felt like an imbecile who couldn't talk to women without tangling up his words. He forced himself to try to relax, and was aware at once of the dopey smile he probably had on his face. "Oh, I didn't mean—I mean, yeah, that last one was—"

"I know." Julie grinned. "But I seem to remember you popping off a couple like that the other night."

"Yeah," he admitted.

Georgia laughed and handed him the wand. "So are you going to play with my friend here or not? I told her you were good company, Bandie."

"Right, right!" Bandicut slid off the barstool, accepting the wand. "Okay, you're off the hook, Georgia. You can get lost now. That is, if you want to, Julie," he added hastily.

"Let's go," Julie said, as she loped back to the table.

/// This I want to watch, ///

Charlie muttered.

/You can get lost, too,/ he said cheerfully as he stumped after Julie.

✳

"You break."

Julie nodded and split the starting formation with a *crack,* sinking a dwarf and a mermaid. Bandicut watched admiringly as she sank three more faces in a row. She missed and it was his shot. Sighting down the cue wand at the Cheshire Cat, he found himself focusing beyond the grinning teeth on the ball to Julie's intense gaze, watching from the far side of the table. She smiled and moved out of his sight line.

The cue was wobbling in his grip. He drew a breath. /Help me out a little, okay?/

/// I thought you wanted— ///

/I just mean, help me steady the shot, all right?/

/// No problem. ///

He suddenly found his aim, and felt a clear understanding of the gravity path that he was about to try. The wand flashed at the cue ball, and it spun away, looped around a well, and clacked into the Cheshire Cat. The silver cue ball drifted slowly away from the impact, and the Cat's grin skidded and vanished into the side well. /Great!/ he thought.

/// *It's good practice,* ///

the quarx acknowledged.

"Nice shot!" Julie cheered. "Can you do it again? How about putting Dinky Duck down the table into the end well?"

He squinted along the path between the cue ball and the diminutive yellow duck. There were two gravity wells in the way of the shot she'd suggested. He'd have to slingshot the cue around both of them, just like a spacecraft picking up a gravity-assist from a planet.

/// *We can do it,* ///

Charlie assured him.

/I'm trusting you./ He cleared his throat and grinned at Julie. "If I make it, will you stay and have a drink with me afterward?"

She allowed a smile on one corner of her mouth. "Only if you make it *and* promise to stay a nice guy . . ."

✳

Apparently he managed to retain his vestiges of niceness, because her smile remained as the game continued. He began to lose track of the time, what with one part of his mind lost to a great, flowing tide of hormones, a fresh surge coming every time her lips cracked a smile; and the other part of him entranced by the joy of firing cartoon-faced balls into long, wholly improbable trajectories. He heard himself suggesting, at the end of their third game, that perhaps they ought to let someone else use the table for a while, and retire to a more comfortable spot for that drink. She agreed, with an almost bashful smile.

"What do you guys *really* do, down there in exoarch?" he asked, once they were settled in a booth with a semi-privacy-curtain drawn—enough to feel cozy, but not so secluded as to feel threatening.

Julie leaned back against the headrest and half-closed

her eyes. Her short hair drifted back from her face. She had, he realized, a very small nose, and a pretty neck. Her blue eyes were intense, even half closed. "Oh, you know—mostly we wait for you guys to bring us something exciting," she said.

"Us guys?"

She opened her eyes. "Well, I don't know if it's the surveyors or the miners who are more likely to find something bigger than a melted lump of metal—but if any of you ever do, that's when we can really get to work. In the meantime, it's mainly geology for us. And frankly, I'm getting pretty sick of geology." She grinned brightly. "So how about finding us something intact, okay? How about the head of an alien—or at least some nice alien artifacts?"

Bandicut swallowed, his heart almost stopping. A moment ago, he was reeling with attraction; now he was petrified of speaking. Charlie was ominously silent in his brain. "Well—" he croaked. "I guess—we'd all like to find something . . . exciting . . . wouldn't we?"

/// Careful— ///

Julie gazed at him as though she heard more in his words than he'd intended to convey. "I guess we would," she agreed. She sipped her drink, and a look of curiosity came over her. "So . . . ," she murmured, "what exactly do you pilot types do for excitement, when you're not on survey missions?"

Was that a suggestive huskiness in her voice? He realized that he was sweating a little, and he had probably drunk too much beer. He took another sip. "Well, I, uh—" and his voice caught a little, because now, he thought, he was going to have to explain how it was that he wasn't actually flying survey missions anymore, or even driving them, for that matter. And then he thought, no, no, she already knows about that, doesn't she? "Well, I, uh—tried my hand at mining," he joked. "And it got me this—" He pointed to the cast on his left ankle.

"Ah so," said Julie. "How'd that happen, anyway?"

He tried not to wince as he groped for a suitable explanation, preferably one that wouldn't make him look like a moron. "Well—I slipped on some ice, and this ankle was the only thing between me and a big laser beam. So the ankle lost."

"Did you really try to pull a robot out of a mining tunnel?" Julie blurted, and then immediately looked sorry for broaching the subject.

He groaned inwardly. Did *everyone* know about it already? "Well, yeah," he admitted sheepishly. "It *was* pretty dumb. I don't . . . know what came over me." He stirred at the little white lie.

/// Good, good . . . ///

Julie kept a straight face, but it obviously took some effort. "I guess . . . it must have been pretty embarrassing."

He nodded and shifted his eyes away, feeling self-conscious all over again. When he looked back, he saw that she was studying him with quizzical interest. "Well—?" he murmured, turning his palms up.

Julie's face cracked in a grin. "You know something? You're not like the rest of those pilot types! You're . . . different."

"Is that good?" he asked uncertainly.

She nodded, and an odd look came over her face. She took a long pull on her drink and seemed to be trying to decide something. The grin started to return, as she shifted her eyes one way and then another, as though looking to see if anyone was watching. Then she leaned forward, biting her lip. "Georgia tells me she bets you're a good kisser," she blurted.

He blinked, startled.

Her face immediately darkened with embarrassment. "Oh, God, I can't believe I said that!" She averted her gaze with a groan, then hesitantly sidled a glance back at him. She giggled and peered down into her half-empty glass. "I must not be holding my alcohol very well," she said rue-fully. "Please excuse me."

His mind was awash with libidinous possibilities. When he answered, his voice wasn't working too well, and it came out more or less as a croak. "And how would Georgia know? Who's she been talking to, anyway?" *And are you anywhere near as horny as I am? Do you know how long it's been?* He grinned, helplessly aware of what a perfect goak he probably looked like.

"Who should she be talking to?" Julie asked shyly, blink-ing at him over her cocktail glass.

Nobody on Triton, that's for sure. He swallowed with difficulty, and couldn't find any words. *Kiss her, you idiot. What do you think she's asking for?* He cleared his throat and carefully moved his mug of beer out of the way.

/// You aren't thinking of . . .
you aren't planning to— ///

/Shut up. This would be an excellent time for you to shut up./

/// But I—you— ///

/SHUT UP!/ His smile was turning weird-looking. He could feel it, but he couldn't stop it.

Julie cocked her head, those intense eyes gazing at him with thoughts that he could only wonder at. "John, what is it? Is your leg hurting—?"

Yes yes yes, that's it . . . "Um, a little, I guess." He forced what he hoped was a warmer expression onto his face. What he was actually conveying, he couldn't imagine. She smiled, and his heart thumped. "I guess, um, if that's her . . . theory . . . maybe we ought to test—I mean, there's nothing like firsthand—"

She leaned across the little table and stopped his words with a kiss, hesitant at first, then more confident.

Time shuddered to a halt. His heart nearly stopped from the pressure of her lips. She pulled back, smiled—and he leaned farther to kiss her again. She returned willingly, lips firm for a moment, then softening. He rose up in his seat, as if weightless. His breath struggled to find release in the back of his throat, and he felt her sighing with nervous pleasure . . .

/// John—
John, please— ///

A year of pent-up loneliness welled up in him, making him want to cry out. He raised a trembling hand to touch her hair, ever so gently.

/// Please don't do this, John! ///

She seemed to like that; she kissed harder, and he felt her tongue dart out and touch his lips . . .

*/// **STOP IT!** ///*

A sheet of white static flashed across his brain . . .

17

XENOPHOBE

He PULLED AWAY from Julie with a jerk. /What the mokin' hell—?/

/// Please—I can't stand this! ///

He blinked helplessly at Julie, trying not to turn red with humiliation. /Can't stand *WHAT?*/

/// This— ///

"What's wr—? *John?* Is something wrong?" Julie was staring at him, flustered and wide-eyed. She sat back abruptly, wrapping her fingers around her cocktail glass. "Was I—I mean—hey, I hope I wasn't too forward!"

"No, no!" He struggled to think of an explanation, an apology.

"Oh, well—did I kick your leg or something? I'm sorry, I didn't even think—"

Desperate for something to say, he gulped, "No, no, but I—I just—wrenched it a little." Feeling his face burn, he struggled to recover his dignity with the lie. "I'm—uh—sorry," he croaked. "It wasn't *you.*" Inwardly, he raged. /What do you think you're doing, you meddling little—?/

/// I'm sorry! ///

Charlie screeched.

/// I apologize!
But I couldn't let you— ///

/WHAT? ENJOY MYSELF?/ Bandicut roared. He shook, grimacing—and immediately realized that he had just made an audible, rattling sound of anguish. He struggled to put a normal expression back on his face.

"John, are you in pain?" Julie asked worriedly.

/// No, I—I—I— ///

the quarx choked, radiating waves of consternation.

/You you you *what?* Why don't you just *shut up?*/ He made a prolonged clearing-of-the-throat sound, focusing his eyes on Julie with an effort. "I—*ah*—no, no, I'm *fine*—"

She peered at him for a moment, then lifted her glass and took a long drink, rattling the ice cubes. Her blue eyes appeared dark and beautiful, and utterly unreadable. She seemed to be assessing his answer. "Well," she sighed, "if your leg is giving you trouble, the last thing you need is to have me coming on to you."

"No, really, you weren't—" he wheezed. "It was fine!" He swallowed. "It was . . . uh, pretty nice, actually."

A smile cracked through her unreadable expression. "Yeah, it *was* pretty nice, wasn't it?" She laughed nervously.

He nodded, momentarily incapable of speech.

/// It's just that I
couldn't risk your telling her . . .
or getting too distracted, ///

the quarx whispered desperately.

"Yes—" he croaked to Julie.

/// There's just too much at stake. ///

He flushed with anger. /The only thing at stake right now is whether I'm going to get more than a wink and a handshake for the first time in two years, dickhead./

/// Huh?
Well, I know,
but I just couldn't—
I mean, I— ///

/Shut up./ He drew a ragged breath and finally managed

to return Julie's smile. "I guess I . . . didn't quite live up to Georgia's . . . prediction, did I? You think I should go back for more training?"

Julie chuckled self-consciously. "Well, Georgia never actually said she was making a personal report. Anyway, for a warmup, it wasn't too bad. But yeah, I'd say the jury needs to hear more evidence." She blushed. "So look, do you need some help getting back to your dorm room, or what? Or is this where I exit graciously, and, you know, let you make your moves elsewhere?"

"Elsewhere?" he said, with feigned bewilderment. He peered around as though to scan the entire lounge, then sat back again, trying to keep his grin. *Oh, real smart! Why not just say she's the only game in sight, or else you'd hustle right up to someone else?*

/// I do not *understand this interplay, John— ///*

Julie laughed, but whether it was because of, or in spite of, his idiocy he couldn't tell. "Ri-i-ight," she said. "Well, look, methinks I'd better get some sleep anyway. Dawn comes mighty early in this town." She started to slide out of the booth.

He rose up from his seat in quiet desperation. "Wait! Let me at least walk you—er, *limp* you—home."

"Well—"

He held out a hand in invitation.

/// But there's so much we have to do! ///

/Speak for yourself./ He gazed at her imploringly. "Please?"

Julie's eyes sparkled again the way they had earlier. "Compromise. You may walk me to the end of my corridor. And you may have one discreet good-night kiss." She raised a warning finger. "One only. So as not to injure your leg further."

He lifted a fist in mock triumph. "Score!"

She swatted his arm. "Score, nothing! I am not a fast

mover, I warn you." She slid out of the booth and extended a hand to help him stand.

★

True to her word, she permitted him one brief kiss at a bulkhead door near her room, then turned away with a whispered, "Good night." Before the door could close between them, she leaned back, causing the door to spasm in the middle of its cycle. "Will you be there tomorrow evening?"

He nodded, without even thinking about whether it would be true; he decided then and there that it *would* be. A moment later, Julie had fled down the corridor to the women's dorm, and he was standing facing a closed bulkhead door.

/// *I thought we were operating*
with an understanding, ///

Charlie sputtered—accusingly, he thought.

He snorted as he turned toward his own dorm section. /What understanding?/

/// *That the mission was paramount,*
that you wouldn't let yourself get sidetracked— ///

Bandicut chuckled bitterly. /Give me a call when you're ready to start the mission, all right? In the meantime, butt out of my love life./

Charlie's sputtering faded to silence.

He returned to the dorm room and found Gordon Kracking getting ready for bed. "Bandie—are you okay?" Krackey cried when Bandicut walked in.

Before Bandicut could answer, a crack opened in one of the bunk curtains, and Mick Eddison stuck his head out, peering at the two. He didn't say anything; he just guffawed, then ducked back into his bunk and snapped the curtain shut again.

Bandicut glared silently, before turning to his friend. "Yeah, Krackey, I'm okay. You guys make out all right without me?"

Krackey ran his fingers through his wildly unkempt

hair. "Yeah, yeah, sure. What a day, though, huh? First that happens to you—how's the ankle, by the way—do you still have a fever—?"

Bandicut shook his head.

"—and then I no sooner get back in than the whole fr'deekin' datanet crashes and I have to go help them try to put it back together! Man, I don't know *what* went wrong with that—hey, you haven't been drinking on painkillers, have you—?"

Bandicut realized he was swaying a little. He shook his head.

"—but I've been *telling* them all along that it's a fr'deekin' house of cards, and sooner or later *something* was gonna happen."

"Uh-huh."

Krackey was shaking his head, putting some clothes away in a drawer. "Yeah, all the safeguards failed at once, and a lot of stuff that wasn't too well protected got trashed when the thing came down."

Bandicut focused on emptiness and tried to draw a breath.

Krackey looked up at him, furrowing his brow. "Say, you weren't havin' one of your damn—" he caught himself and whispered, *"episodes* today, were you?"

Bandicut shook his head absently. He pulled himself up to the upper bunk, swinging his injured ankle in carefully.

Krackey shrugged. "So the question, I guess, is whether it was failure or sabotage."

"Sab—otage?" Bandicut croaked, leaning back out.

"The datanet crash. That's what they're sayin', anyway—maybe some disgruntled employee. Probably just a crazy rumor. It's hard to figure why anyone would want to sabotage the datanet—unless maybe the environmental nuts from exoarch, tryin' to slow things down. But naw, even they need the net. How else they gonna get their info in and out?"

Who would want to sabotage the datanet? Bandicut thought . . . unless maybe some alien who wanted to control what was happening on this moon. Some alien who had won the trust of a human accomplice.

/// *That's not it,*
not at all! ///

"If it *was* sabotage, they'll nail the sucker's hide to the wall," Krackey went on. "You can't get away with something like that for long, not in a place like this. Especially not after knocking out traffic control and causing a near-collision up at the space station." He shook his head. "But hey, you're sick. Never mind all that stuff, just get some sleep, okay?"

"Okay." Bandicut pulled his curtain shut and fell back with a wordless groan, eyes closed. He breathed deeply and rapidly for a moment. /I hope you're ready to talk./

/// *You don't really think—* ///

/I don't know what I think. I just know that you blew down the whole damn datanet, *and* you nearly caused a crash, which you hadn't bothered to mention to me—/

/// *I didn't know!* ///

/You didn't, huh? I don't really think someone as smart as you does something like that by accident./

/// *I—no!*
You've got to let me explain! ///

/I'm listening. I haven't heard much that's convincing, so far./ He scowled angrily in the dark. And to think he had actually begun to *trust* this . . . this alien.

/// *John!*
I *didn't* mean *to do any of that!*
Honestly! ///

/No? I figure, if you're smart enough to tie into the net like that, you ought to be smart enough to keep from screwing everything up in the process./

/// *No—I mean,*
it's not that I'm so smart.

Really.
There's a lot I don't understand.
Yes, I had the ability to make the connection,
but it doesn't mean I can predict
everything that's going to happen in your datanet.
Please believe me! ///

Bandicut lay silent, thinking. Believe the quarx? Why should he? Hadn't the quarx just prevented him from having a very pleasant, and totally harmless, interlude with Julie?

/// Look, John—about Julie. ///
/What about her?/
/// Well, I'm sorry I messed things up for you. ///
/Oh./
/// It's just that . . .
certain things are very difficult for me. ///

He thought he sensed acute embarrassment in the quarx's thoughts, but he couldn't quite make out the reason for it. /If you want me to believe you,/ he said, /I think you'd better explain what you mean by that. The whole truth./

The quarx hesitated.
/// It's hard to talk about. ///
/Talk anyway. Or I walk./

Charlie's reluctance was almost palpable.
/// Can't you just trust me? ///
/Trust?/ he snarled. /You want *trust?* You better start trusting *me* enough to tell me the truth, damn you./

Several seconds passed before Charlie spoke again. Bandicut felt a wave of shadow pass across his visual field. He steeled himself for confrontation.
/// It's not what you think, ///

Charlie said at last, in a voice tinged with an emotion that Bandicut did not at once recognize. And then he did. It was shame.

The emotion rolled over him like an ocean swell. He

was suddenly aware of fragmented bits of memory of other living beings, races that the quarx had touched at some point in its various lives . . . nothing visual, nothing that would help him recognize the beings in a dark alley . . . but visceral impressions of carnality, of organic ferment, the rich scents of sexuality, of decay, of *unclean material life.* He struggled to follow.

///// *This must shock you.* /////

/What?/ he whispered.

///// *Just that—* /////

The quarx hesitated, as though trying to let go of something bottled up inside. Suddenly he erupted with a yell:

///// *HOW CAN YOU STAND IT?* /////

Bandicut reeled.

///// *The chemistry!*
The oils, the smells, the dirt, the sweat!
The eggs and sperm!
The pheromones and the damp breath!
The skin! /////

Bandicut was stunned silent. The quarx was shivering in his mind. /But that's part of life,/ he whispered at last.

///// *It's not part of MY life!*
How can you live in the midst of it, John?
How can you? /////

The quarx was weeping in his mind.

/I couldn't live *without* it,/ he whispered.

///// *Yes, yes—I know.*
But it's so . . . so . . . /////

If the quarx couldn't find the words, Bandicut could. /You're fucking *xenophobic!* Is that it?/ He blinked in disbelief.

///// *I—* /////

/That *is* it, isn't it?/ Bandicut whispered. /You can't stand the thought of any kind of life that isn't like yours!/

Charlie moaned,

///// *No, I—I really can't.* /////

/But you *live* inside other people! You're living inside *me!* Does that mean you can't stand me, either?/

/// *No, no, you're different.* ///

/Like hell I am./

/// *No, really!*
A host is always . . . different. ///

/I'm so touched./

/// *But*—coupling— ///

The quarx practically shuddered in his brain.

/// *It's too . . . organic.* ///

Bandicut held his breath. /You mean coupling, as in . . . sex?/

/// *I really can't . . .*
it makes me . . .
John, I can't STAND the thought! ///

Bandicut let his breath out in a slow sigh. /Well, isn't that just wonderful,/ he said bitterly. /And that's why you interrupted me?/

/// *I'm afraid so.*
Yes.
I'm sorry, John. ///

/I'm sorry!/ Bandicut mimicked savagely. He drew a deep breath, and then another. /What the hell gives you the right to dictate what I do or don't do?/ he exploded, shaking with rage.

/// *Well, I—just couldn't help it.* ///

/I didn't invite you to take up residence here, you know! I can't believe this! Not only have I got a fr'deekin' alien, but he's a fr'deekin' *xenophobe* who can't stand to see humans . . . have a little . . ./ He ran out of words, with a gasp.

/// *It's not something I'm proud of,* ///

the quarx muttered.

/I should hope not. I should damn well hope not./

/// *I'm going to . . . try to improve.*
That's all I can do.

It's the way we're made, that's all.
I hope . . . you're not angry, are you? ///

He began laughing bitterly, and laughed until his eyes were full of tears. Then he abruptly fell silent, flat on his back in his bunk. /Get out of my brain,/ he whispered. /Just get out of my brain, you miserable, disgusting little creature . . ./

✳

The quarx seemed to retreat into a tight ball in his mind. Bandicut tossed and turned, trying to forget the whole thing and go to sleep. It was impossible. Though he'd never been married, he wondered if this was what it was like to try to sleep with a partner with whom you were furious. The gloom of his bunk seemed to surround him with an angry glare.

He sighed bitterly, wondering whether to say something to the quarx. Not that he wasn't still angry; but they were, after all, stuck with each other. He supposed he was going to have to make the best of it.

But what was there to say?

After a time, he found his thoughts blurring. He thought, at one point, that he sensed a tiny tendril of presence reach out and touch something in his mind. Somehow it was a calming touch, and a few moments later, his thoughts quieted like a fading storm, and he drifted to sleep.

✳

He dreamed of balls, EineySteiney balls. He dreamed of balls colliding and rebounding, tracing strange and impossible trajectories around a vast pool table, spinning past gravity wells and sliding, floating, never quite coming to rest. He felt that there was some strange and wonderful order in the way that they moved, some chaotic pattern that was not order as he knew it, but another kind of order . . .

He dreamed of planets and planetary bodies spinning in strange and impossible trajectories, in a chaotic dance of the spheres that only the most perceptive could fathom . . .

He dreamed of fire, consuming fire, the fire of a thousand suns . . .

18
JUST THE FACTS

HE WOKE GRADUALLY, with fantastic imagery passing before his eyes: moving fractals and spinning chaotic attractors. He knew what the images were, though he didn't understand them. Some of them looked like exotic alien landscapes, and some like exploding crystals; he knew that they were neither, but rather mathematical representations. After a while, the images changed to color impressions that held no meaning for him whatever. He sensed that these were something from the quarx's personal experience.

/// Are you awake? ///
the quarx asked tentatively.

He blinked his eyes open. For a moment, the images hung like transparent holograms in front of him; then they faded, and he was left with his own vision. /Yah—I'm awake./

/// Are you still . . . mad? ///
He sighed, remembering last night. /Yeah. I dunno. Are you making a peace offering?/

/// I guess . . . you could say that. ///
He thought of Julie.

/// I really am sorry, you know. ///

/Sorry enough to stay out of my way the next time I meet up with Julie?/

/// I'll try. Very hard.
I'm not sure . . . I can promise to succeed. ///

/Mmm./ Bandicut decided that that was probably the best he could hope for. He sat up, banging his head on the bunk overhead. "OW! Damn it!"

/// Would you like me to stop you
when I see you getting ready to do that? ///

/I would appreciate that very much./ Bandicut sighed, thinking that as long as he and the quarx were together, then he was going to have to make the best of it.

Charlie cleared his throat.

/// About the mission . . . ///

/Yes? Are we going to get moving on that?/

/// Well, we still need to get
back to the translator,
to find out exactly what we have to do.
And the sooner the better. ///

Bandicut grunted. /I can't control that./

/// I know. I don't think any of us
anticipated the difficulty we would have in returning.
But until we do,
we can't pinpoint the danger
that we have to stop. ///

Bandicut rubbed his eyebrows wearily. /So maybe it's time we *told* somebody about the danger. Then *they* could look for it, and take care of it, and we could quit worrying./

/// I'm afraid that's not a viable option.
The social turbulence factors are too great,
the time is too short.
And I know Charlie-One
didn't trust your superiors. ///

/Yeah, well . . ./ Bandicut couldn't argue with that. /Did he tell you all this in that little meeting we had?/

/// A lot of it.
And he helped me put together some pieces
that I already had.
But the important question is,
do you believe that we can't go public—
at least not yet? ///

Bandicut pulled the privacy-curtain open and slid out of his bunk. His ankle ached fiercely. /All right—yes—you win./

/// You're still mad, aren't you? ///
the quarx asked softly.

/Yeah./ He stumped toward the lav. The dorm was deserted. He realized that he had slept past the start of the workday, and then he realized that it didn't matter, because he was on the injured list. /I'll get over it. So what do you suggest, if we can't tell anyone?/

/// If you have nothing else to do . . . ///
/You already know I don't./

/// Then may we do some library research? ///
/In the datanet?/ Bandicut blanched, thinking of the havoc the quarx had wreaked last night.

/// If it's up, yes.
But I promise—no more meddling. ///
/All right. After we eat./ Bandicut dressed quickly. /But if you're lying about meddling . . ./

/// Hm? ///
/I'm gonna cut your balls off./

/// Uh . . . okay . . . ///

✳

As it turned out, a portion of the datanet was back up, though not the connection to the inner solar system. Bandicut saw nothing to suggest that any connection had been made between the net crash and his own presence, which was a considerable relief. And Charlie was presently only interested in the general history files, which were easily available in the local library.

The quarx spun through chapter after chapter of human history, while Bandicut, feeling a bit like a kid tagging along after a more knowledgeable older kid, glanced at some of the more interesting bits as Charlie scanned. From time to time, Charlie asked him for further illumination on historical questions, and almost invariably, he had to plead ignorance. History had never been a great interest of his.

/// But you know that your history
is full of violence among your own kind,
don't you? ///

/Of course. So what?/ Bandicut answered in irritation. They had covered all four of Earth's world wars, then jumped back to the Roman and Greek wars, then ahead to the crucifixion of Christ, then forward again to the Inquisitions and the Crusades. /What are you looking for exactly?/

/// Information . . . understanding.
For the social-attractor analysis.
And, to be honest, my own curiosity.
Look at this—
Nation after nation destroyed, subjugated,
entire peoples living under coercion . . .
murder, mayhem, rape, thievery.
It goes on and on,
all through the history of your species. ///

/Are you reciting all this just to make me depressed?/

/// No, no, I want to know your thoughts.
Do you know why this is true?
None of these experts seem to agree. ///

/Yes, well, what do you expect from experts? No, I have no idea. Just human nature, I guess. Isn't it like that everywhere?/ He was surprised by the quarx's puzzlement.

/// Actually, no.
I mean, it happens—yes.
But many sentient races reserve their violence
for outsiders. ///

Bandicut thought about that. /Really? You mean, we're more violent than most?/

/// Among yourselves, yes.
The odd thing is that you seem to accept it—
even relatively nonviolent individuals like you. ///

/I—well—now, just a mokin' minute. I don't *accept* nothin'—but that doesn't mean I can do anything about it. How would *you* change a whole race's behavior pattern, if you're so damn smart?/

/// I have no idea.
Fortunately, that is not my problem.
Not this time, anyway. ///

/Well, aren't you just the lucky one!/

/// I didn't mean to be critical, John.
Anyway,
there's much about your race that's admirable.
Your art and literature.
Okay, some of it stinks.
Rock and roll music, for instance.
TV.
But there's your science, such as it is— ///

/What's that supposed to mean?/

/// —your philosophies and religions,
and individual acts of sacrifice and genius.
But I'm puzzled by a certain . . .
suicidal instinct. ///

Bandicut scowled ineffectually. /Are you done making your point? What do you want to look at now?/

The quarx hesitated.

/// Well, I hope this doesn't upset you, but . . .
I need to know about your planetary defenses. ///

Bandicut nearly jerked them out of the neurolink. /Hey!/

/// Moke, I knew it would upset you.
John, I'm not planning an invasion.
I mean your defenses against natural *disasters. ///*

/Oh./ Bandicut glared suspiciously for a moment, then reflected that anything on the public boards was probably not very critical in terms of security, anyway. He unclenched, and they dived together into a new area of the library files.

/// This is unbelievable, ///

Charlie said after studying the civil and planetary defense systems around Earth.

/What's unbelievable?/

/// Your complacency!
You settle on floodplains,
on earthquake faults,
on mud cliffs;
you leave your skies undefended . . . ///

/That's not true! Not that last part, anyway./

The quarx dismissed his objections.

/// You defend yourselves against each other, yes.
But against natural calamity?
What would you do if your sun *became unstable? ///*

/How the hell would I know? Run around waving our hands, I suppose. What *could* we do?/

/// You'd be surprised at the solutions
some races have come up with.
But your people seem to think, on the one hand,
that they're helpless—
and on the other, that they're immortal. ///

/What's your point, Charlie?/ Bandicut demanded angrily.

/// My point is,
your vulnerability to a comet or asteroid strike.
You have no defense! ///

/Well—/ Bandicut swallowed, trying to think of a way to argue, but there was none. /There were some defense systems for a while—but I guess they were too expensive to maintain./

/// Expensive?
How much is your civilization worth? ///
/I don't know. What the hell kind of a question is that?/
Charlie brushed aside the protest.
/// Do you know what killed off the dinosaurs? ///
Of course he knew. A large asteroid strike. /But that was
millions of years ago,/ he said feebly.
/// You see?
That's exactly what I mean.
You never think it'll happen to you.
The K'loing were like that, too.
You want to know what happened to them? ///
/No./
/// They're dead now. ///
/I said I didn't want to know. Look—don't blame me for
my race's failings./
/// I'm not.
But your own scientists have pointed out
that the same thing could happen to humanity.
And yet nothing is done. ///
Bandicut squirmed. /Well, I suppose most people think
the danger is too remote. I'm not defending that—exact-
ly—but anyway, most of the hazardous asteroids are
tracked routinely./
Charlie was silent a moment, troubled.
/// But it is *going to happen—*
unless you and I stop it. ///
Bandicut swallowed. /So . . . you say./
/// Charlie-One said it.
And you trusted him—more than you trust me. ///
/I—/
The quarx chuckled with surprising ease.
/// That's all right.
We both know it. ///
Charlie was silent for a moment, then said softly,
/// I fear that time is growing short. ///

Bandicut suddenly shivered with fear. /Then shouldn't we—I mean—what about the translator?/

 /// *The translator is aware of the time,* /// Charlie said reassuringly.

 /// *It would find some way to let us know,*
   rather than let the Earth be hit
     . . . I think. ///

/You THINK?/

 /// *Well, I know it plans for us*
    to take action.
 But it has to let us know what *action.*
   And unfortunately,
 it strongly prefers to remain unseen. ///

Bandicut nearly erupted with frustration. /Why doesn't it just tell us in the open, for God's sake?/

The quarx was silent another moment.

  /// *Its creators desired*
 that its existence remain concealed
  from most of those it serves.
 I do not know the reason. ///

Bandicut could only stare helplessly into the silent, winking dataspace. /Oh, well, that's great . . . just great . . ./

✱

When Bandicut went to the lounge that evening, looking for Julie, he was thoroughly depressed. He glanced around, and saw no sign of her, which was perhaps just as well, considering his mood. Georgia Patwell was playing Einey-Steiney with her husband and several other friends. He opted to remain by the bar, sipping a beer and resting his aching ankle. It occurred to him that he hadn't checked in with Cole Jackson today, either in person or on the system board, but by then he was into his second beer, and after thinking about it, he just shook his head and said screw it. So what if it cost him a demerit or two? What was the good of being on the disabled list if you had to check with the boss every time you turned around?

During a break in her game, Georgia came over to the bar to say hi. "I hear you and Julie hit it off pretty well last night," she said, with a gleam in her eye.

"Uh—yeah, until I turned into a cripple here with my ankle," he said, indicating his fastract cast to try to hide his blush.

"You'll be out of that soon, won't you? We miss you in ops." Georgia chuckled. "Especially Lonnie."

"Oh yeah, I'll bet. Lonnie must be dying for me to come back."

"Well, he hasn't had anyone to abuse lately." Georgia glanced back at the pool table where her husband was waiting. "Anyway, I hear you're getting your rover back, as soon as you're off the hit list."

"Really? No one's told me about it."

"Well, I'd check with Cole, if I were you." Georgia picked up her refilled glass. "By the way, Julie asked me to tell you she can't be here tonight—in case you were waiting for her. She said she left you a message, but wasn't sure if you'd get it before you came."

"Oh, uh—thanks." He blushed again.

"Don't mention it. She was going to come, but it turned out she had to work overtime to reconstruct some files that went *ffft-t-t* when the net crashed. She'll probably be here tomorrow, though."

Bandicut bobbed his head.

Georgia looked at him slyly. "I think she likes you. Anyway, catch you later. Come join us, if you want." With a wave, Georgia wandered back to the pool table.

Bandicut continued to bob his head for a moment, then took a swallow of beer and turned back to the bar, moving his left foot carefully.

/// I had nothing to do with Julie not coming.
I hope you realize that. ///

He rolled his eyes and didn't bother to reply.

/// Why don't you check and see if it's true. ///

/What, whether Julie's working overtime?/

/// No—about you getting your rover back. ///

/Oh./ He shrugged. /Yeah, I suppose that's a good idea./ He took another swallow.

*/// Instead of sitting here making yourself miserable,
I mean. ///*

/Stop making sense, will you?/ Hoisting his glass, he drained his beer. /All right—you appear to have a one-day reprieve. I hope you're getting ready for it./

/// Beg pardon? ///

/One day. And then I will have my crude, tawdry animal fling. Comprende?/

/// Oh. Uh— ///

/What?/

*/// Do you really intend to . . . have sex?
Just like that?
I thought it took more,
I don't know, buildup . . . ///*

/Aw, shut up about the facts and just let me keep my fantasies, will you?/ Bandicut got up and walked from the room, leaving the quarx puzzling silently in a back corner of his mind.

✱

Checking the system board from a comm booth, he found two messages from Cole Jackson, asking him to check in; one message from Julie, saying exactly what Georgia had just told him; and the job assignments for survey section for the next few days. Sure enough, he was back on the roster—for northeast recon, starting the day after tomorrow. That wasn't exactly going to give him much time to heal. But he was out of the mines. And, though it didn't say so, he had presumably been exonerated by the inquiry.

Studying the assignment more closely, he noted that it covered a fair amount of territory that he had already mapped. You don't suppose, he thought, that all that recon data was kept unanalyzed, and unbacked-up, and evaporated when . . .

He didn't bother to complete the thought. He just shook his head, and felt the quarx flinch. /Guilty, guilty, guilty,/ he whispered.

✶

He went to bed early and slept like a rock.

First thing in the morning, he went to Jackson's office. Cole wasn't in yet, so on an impulse, he sat down at a terminal and tried to pull up his job performance report. The system honked and refused to admit him. He sat for a moment, thinking.

"Bandicut! Where the hell have you been?" Cole Jackson strode into the office, carrying a large steaming cup of coffee. It reminded him that he hadn't eaten yet.

"I got . . . your message," he stammered, then added, "Since Switzer put me on the disabled list, I've been taking it easy, trying to rest."

"Yeah, okay," Jackson said, walking around to his desk. "There was no need to come in person. You aren't going to get that ankle healed by doing a lot of unnecessary walking, you know."

Bandicut nodded. "I see you've put me back on the job. What was the outcome of the inquiry—if you don't mind my asking?"

"I don't mind. Why should I?" Jackson rocked back in his chair, sipping his coffee. "They gave you credit for the field repair, just like I said they should."

Oh, Bandicut thought.

Jackson added, "My people know how to do their jobs. I've always said that. So what you did was something neither more nor less than expected."

Bandicut allowed a half-smile to cross his lips. Cole, if you knew . . . if you only knew . . .

"So," Jackson said, eyeing Bandicut expectantly. "Are you going to be in shape tomorrow?"

Bandicut suppressed a chuckle. "I doubt that Switzer will okay it so soon after the accident. He said five days. You know how these company quacks are—sticklers for medical detail—they like people to be at least *half* recovered before they put them back on the job."

Jackson frowned and sat forward. "Well, you take care of the recovery, and let me handle Switzer, okay? Are you well enough to come in and do some desk work?"

Bandicut shrugged. "I guess so, as long as I don't overdo it." He hesitated. "I notice we're redoing some of the original survey."

That brought a scowl from Jackson. "Why the hell you think we're in such a hurry? Maybe now they'll start listening to me when I tell them the damn datanet is vulnerable to sabotage. I've been saying that all along."

Bandicut kept a poker face. "Sabotage? You think someone . . . sabotaged . . . the system?"

Jackson's face darkened further. "Why? Do you know something about it?"

Bandicut shook his head, not trusting his voice. He felt his face going blank.

/// *What are you* doing?
Are you trying *to draw suspicion
to yourself?* ///

"No," he managed finally. "How would I know anything about it? I've been on the sick list." /Of course not. I just—/

Jackson glared. "Bandicut, why are you looking like that?"

He flushed. "Nothing. Just—the painkillers, I guess. I suppose I should go lie down or something."

"That's what I just told you. Anyway, go see Switzer and let me know what he says. We need you out there. Now, get some rest, will you?"

Bandicut rose and limped carefully from the room.

19

EXOARCH

DR. SWITZER SHOOK his head, chuckling. "Your boss called and said he wants you back at work tomorrow. I told him that was ridiculous. What does he think this is, anyway? I couldn't possibly approve sending you out in less than three days after a broken ankle. Now, if you'd taken the nanomed treatment like I told you—"

Bandicut started to answer, but the doctor had already turned away to consult his computer screen.

"Actually," Switzer said, returning, "you might have done the right thing, refusing that particular course of treatment. We discovered another batch with faulty programming just yesterday. Instead of bringing a fever down, it gave some poor guy chickenpox." He barked a short, harsh laugh. "I don't know why they can't quality-control the stuff better than that. Here, now, let's have a look."

Bandicut watched, none too confidently, as the doctor hoisted his ankle and jacked a monitor into the fastract cast. "You been taking those pills I gave you?" Switzer asked.

"I think I forgot once." Actually, he'd forgotten more often than he'd remembered.

Switzer grunted, snapping a few switches. "Well, then, don't blame me." He glanced at Bandicut with a chuckle.

"Here we go." His eyebrows contracted as he studied the machine. "You're not doing too badly here. According to this, your cast can probably come off in two more days."

Bandicut nodded. "I guess Cole is going to have to be disappointed."

Switzer scratched the back of his head. "Well, now—he did make it sound pretty urgent, didn't he?"

"Not that urgent, I'm sure."

Switzer seemed not to hear him. "I guess maybe we could work something out. As long as you're just going to be driving. I mean, you won't be getting out and stumbling around out on the plain, will you?"

Bandicut stared at him, thinking, *that's probably exactly what I'll be doing.*

Switzer chuckled, as though they had just shared a joke. "Look, I'll tell you what—check in with me first thing in the morning, and I'll see what we can do for you."

"You don't have to do anything special for *me.*"

Switzer chuckled and clapped Bandicut on the shoulder. "I like to keep my workers on the job. That fever of yours hasn't come back, has it?" When Bandicut shook his head, the doctor shrugged. "Okay, I guess we'll let sleeping dogs lie on that one. Come back tomorrow, and don't forget to take the rest of those pills."

You don't like embarrassing mysteries in your office, do you? Bandicut thought, sliding off the table. He knew he should be glad that Switzer wasn't pursuing the question of the fever, but he couldn't help wondering what the old quack would say if he knew Bandicut was possessed by—or rather, was harboring—an alien.

*/// Thank you for that correction.
It's going to remain an academic question,
isn't it? ///*

/Does this guy look like someone I would trust to tell about you?/ Bandicut loped off down the corridor, his cast thumping lightly and rhythmically on the deck.

/// Good point.
Where to now? ///

/To find Julie./

/// Oh . . . ///

/Prepare to hold your gorge, Mr. Xenophobe./

There was no answering remark from the quarx, which suited him just fine.

✴

The lounge was deserted. He thought a moment, then decided to try the exoarch group offices. If this was going to be his last day off, he wanted to make the best of it. Charlie seemed nervous as he made his way down to the lower level. Bandicut had the feeling that the quarx was afraid that he would blow their cover with the exoarch people, but was determined to demonstrate his trust by resolutely holding his quarxian tongue. The thought flickered across his mind that it would be interesting to see how far the quarx's trust could be pushed. He did his best to dismiss the thought.

The exoarch department was marked with a hand-inked sign taped to an olive-drab door. He rapped twice, and entered when he heard a muffled voice from within.

"Well, hi there!" said the voice, which turned out to be Julie's. He had to peer around a filing cabinet to locate her, sitting behind a narrow desk, with a computer console to one side.

"Hi, yourself. All alone here, hard at work?"

She waggled a hand noncommittally. "Alone, yes. Hard at work, maybe. I've already gotten everything restored that mattered. It was no big deal—I had good backups. But—" She hesitated, and suddenly looked embarrassed.

"What?"

Julie shrugged, chuckling. "Oh, I've just been toying with a crazy notion of mine, about the datanet crash." She glanced at her console monitor.

"Oh yeah? What is it?" he asked, his heart quickening as

he walked around the cabinet to her side of the room. "Can I peek?"

She thought a moment. "Well—there's nothing to look at, really. But sure, okay." Julie flipped some pages of text and diagrams back and forth on the screen. "You'll think I'm nuts, but what the hell, so will everyone else. I might as well try it out on you."

"Okay," he said, squinting across her desk at the screen. He couldn't quite read it from where he stood. "Come on now, it couldn't be any crazier than some things I've come up with."

Her eyes sparkled. "I don't know about that. You tell me." She tapped the screen, then swiveled her chair to face him. He sat down in a chair directly across her desk from her. "Okay—now this is just an idea, and it's not even in my area of expertise. I haven't got one shred of real evidence to back it up, okay?"

"Okay." Suddenly he felt very nervous.

   /// Are you thinking what I'm thinking? ///
/Mm./

Julie nodded. "Okay—well, then—everyone keeps talking about how it could have been sabotage that made the datanet crash. But no one's found proof, and no one's been able to explain who would *want* to sabotage the net. It could be a competitor to MINEXFO, except that MINEXFO doesn't have any competitors."

"Well," he pointed out, "there are some who would *like* to be competitors, back in-system. There's the South America group, and the Mars group. MINEXFO's monopoly doesn't last forever."

Julie waved off the objection. "Sure, but I mean, there's no one else here *right now* trying to mine the turf. Okay, it's *possible* that someone here is a plant from one of those groups, I suppose—"

"I've heard people say it could be the environment

lobby, trying to screw up the system." He tried to say it in a jocular tone, but it came out sounding forced.

Julie rolled her eyes. "If I, as an admitted wacko environmentalist, wanted to screw up the system, I sure wouldn't do it by bringing down my only avenue for getting news and propaganda out, and support in. That makes no sense. And anyway, the disruption was so temporary, what would it have accomplished?"

"What if you were an *incompetent,* wacko environmentalist?"

Her eyes twinkled. "I think we left all of them at home."

"Ah." He cleared his throat. "So that leaves plain old system malfunction through shoddy design and poor workmanship. Right?"

She shrugged. "Maybe." Despite his unease, he couldn't keep from meeting her eyes. He suddenly, intensely, wanted to kiss her. "Or," she said softly, her voice a throaty murmur, "it could have been interference from an outside agency. An agency that no one has even considered, despite the fact that we're all here for the purpose of excavating the remains of an alien technology. Have you ever thought about that?"

He cleared his throat again, more energetically. Steady, boy. Think before you answer.

/// John—don't! ///

/I'm not—/

"No answer?" she said, with a quizzical smile. "Is that because you'd never thought about what you think I'm thinking, or because you're deciding that you've just dropped in on a fruitcake?"

He laughed nervously. "I admit, I hadn't thought about it . . . in quite that way. I mean, I suppose it is . . . possible." He swallowed. "But you said yourself, there's no evidence, right?"

She rocked forward, resting her elbows on her desk, and gazed thoughtfully at a point just over his shoulder. He stared at her, at those intense eyes lost in thought, and wondered frantically what he was doing here. She turned back to her screen. "Not *real* evidence, no. But there is one thing I found in the report . . ." She glanced at him. His heart was racing. "It has to do with a deflection in the comm beam from Triton Orbital to the surface."

"Uh—?" he croaked.

She brushed her hair back from her eyes. "The transmission beam was deflected slightly, just before the datanet came down. It was reaimed about seven kilometers to the northeast of us, out beyond navpoint Wendy on the charts. We have no explanation for that."

"Uh—part of the datanet failure?"

Julie shrugged. "Could be. But it seems kind of odd to me. Nobody's been able to explain how that particular thing could have happened. It appears to have been done by a software command, but no one's been able to trace the source of the command."

/// Thank God for that. ///

Bandicut nodded impassively, trying to look curious.

"But that doesn't mean it couldn't yet be traced," Julie continued. "Of course, it's just a wild idea. But it seems to me that if you're investigating alien remains, and weird things start happening, it at least makes sense to *consider* the possibility—" She interrupted herself in midsentence to cock her head at him. "Wait a minute. I've been wishing I had some way to trace the datanet records myself. But someone like you could do it. Someone who can link right in."

He swallowed hard. "I can't . . . do that, anymore. I mean, I've . . . lost my neuro capability."

She looked puzzled. "But I saw the records of people connected to the net at the time it went down, and you were on the list."

His heart skipped. He felt Charlie squirming in fear. "I, well, yes—I can connect to a very limited extent. But I mean *limited,* compared to what I used to be able to do. Say—" his voice caught, and he tried to make it a laugh "—you don't suspect me, do you?"

She smiled disarmingly. "Of course not. I suspect *aliens,* I told you. I'm just looking for someone who can . . . look for evidence, where I can't."

He suddenly wished he hadn't walked into this room; he wished he could take Julie home with him; he wished he could—

On a sudden impulse, he glanced quickly around the room, making sure there was no one else here. He hitched his chair close to her desk and leaned forward, biting his lip. "Listen, do you—do you want to—?" His voice caught, and her eyes blinked, and the corners of her mouth turned up as she leaned toward him. His heart hammered. "Do you want to go get some din—do you mind if I kiss you?"

/// John!
You aren't really going to— ///

/Clear out, ether-brain!/ He felt Charlie twitch away, and his heart stopped as he waited for Julie to react.

Her eyes widened, but when she moved, it was to lean farther across the desk toward him. She closed her eyes, and he rose to meet her halfway, and their lips touched, brushing lightly. He smiled against her lips; she smiled back against his. As her breath sighed out, he pressed just a little harder, and her lips met his more urgently. His heart was beating full tilt now, and he felt Charlie squirming and contracting into a ball as his blood grew hot with arousal.

·   "How's your ankle?" she whispered, brushing her lips over his cheek and then his temple.

"My . . . umm . . . fine," he whispered back, suppressing a little shiver. "It's the rest of me that—"

"Shhh," she said, drawing away a little and putting a finger to his lips. "Not here." She peered into his eyes. "Do you want—?"

"Dinner?" he croaked.

She grinned and looked at the clock. "At noon? How about lunch?"

"Oh—"

"We could take it back to . . . my place. I have a private—"

"Let's go," he murmured huskily.

★

They slipped down the corridor like a pair of thieves, strolling casually whenever anyone else was in sight, and hurrying with suppressed excitement when the way was clear. They darted into the cafeteria and loaded a takeout tray with sandwiches and drinks, and hurried away.

He felt suddenly awkward as they crept into her dorm compartment and slid the privacy-curtain closed. Julie seemed to feel it as well, but when she put the tray down on the tiny desktop, and turned, and he put his arms around her in a prolonged hug, the awkwardness didn't seem to matter anymore. She pressed her hands against his chest and whispered, "I know this is crazy. But you made my toes curl, the other night. Will you do that to me again? Please?"

/// John— ///

There was a note of desperation in the quarx's voice.

He ignored the voice. He struggled to find words. Julie answered the silence by stretching up and kissing him . . .

★

"Julie?"

It was the longest, deepest, throatiest kiss yet, tongues and lips dancing, breath whispering, hands moving over half-unfastened shirts, bodies lurching in the one-thirteenth gravity.

"Julie, are you in there?" The voice was female, and sounded concerned.

"Damn—!" Julie whispered. She broke from the kiss and slumped against him, arms holding him limply. For a moment, they were silent and still together. Then Julie raised her head and called out, *"Yes!* What is it?"

"Can I come in? It's Georgia."

Bandicut groaned softly and straightened up. He began to refasten his shirt front, but Julie stayed him with one hand. "What is it? I'm—" Julie gulped "—not feeling . . . too well. I'm, uh, trying to take a nap." She looked at Bandicut and grimaced, then hiccuped with suppressed laughter.

"I need to talk. It's about John. It won't take long."

About John? he thought.

Georgia rattled the curtain fastener, and it popped open. She started to step in. "Ohh—" she croaked in sudden mortification. "I, uh—"

"I thought I *locked* that thing!" Julie snarled, hurriedly readjusting her clothing. She looked apologetically at Bandicut, and he shrugged silently. He glanced at Georgia, and caught her hiding a grin. He blushed and averted his eyes.

"Sorry—!" Georgia murmured, backing out of the doorway.

"Oh, hell, you might as well tell me what you wanted," Julie sighed. She cocked her head. "You said it was about John?" She glanced at Bandicut.

"My John. Not you, Bandie," Georgia said wryly.

"Ah," said Julie.

"I, uh—it can wait. I'll talk to you . . . later." Coughing politely, Georgia added, "I'm sorry . . . you're not feeling well." She closed the curtain again, but Bandicut thought he heard her chuckle.

Julie sighed deeply. She wrapped her arms around Bandicut's chest, and finally turned her eyes up to his. "Well— how's that for a mood-breaker?"

He grunted, and managed a grin. "What do you suppose are the, uh . . . chances of . . . getting the mood back?"

Julie pressed her lips together fretfully. "You could ask me to . . . dinner," she suggested.

Bandicut turned his head to peer at the tray of food. "Want to have dinner at a gourmet restaurant?" he squeaked. "Or—" his voice deepened again "—do you want to kiss me again?"

She smiled. "It's not dinner time yet. But I like the second idea, I think." She leaned back toward him.

★

The comm buzzed once, and they ignored it. It buzzed again, insistently. This time when they broke from their embrace, they were both cursing. Julie snarled and pressed the talk button. *"Yes?"*

"It's Kim. Can you come down to the office right away? We've got something from the latest scans that you've got to see."

Julie furrowed her eyebrows. "What is it?" To Bandicut, she muttered, "Kim's with exoarch."

He nodded.

The voice from the comm said, "We may have a find. It's an object of some kind, buried about thirty meters deep, just within buggy range to the northeast. I don't know how we missed it before, but it showed up when they repeated some of the orbital scans yesterday. It just came in. We're trying to analyze the data now. We could use your help."

Julie froze, electrified. Finally she murmured, "Out near—navpoint Wendy, by any chance?"

"Yeah. How'd you know?"

She looked at Bandicut with a mixture of excitement, apology, and pleading for forgiveness. He shrugged helplessly. "I'll be right there," she said into the comm, and snapped it off. "I'm *sorry!* I'm really sorry! But this could be—" Her voice caught.

"Just what you've been waiting for, right?" he croaked.

She nodded, swallowing. She looked breathtakingly beautiful as she buttoned her shirt and ran her fingers back through her hair. "I'll let you know what we find," she promised, leaning to touch his lips with a parting kiss. "You're so sweet I almost can't stand it." She gave him another parting kiss.

He stood up, readjusting his clothing. "I'll call you," he promised. "Or you call me. Or something. Okay?"

"Okay," she whispered. "Bye."

"Bye," he murmured, and slipped out the door.

20

A TIME TO HEAL

/// John, if that's my translator they found,
we could be in trouble. ///

Bandicut shrugged irritably as they made their way
back toward his own dorm. He was concerned, in
the sense that he felt as though things were moving farther
and farther out of his control; but deep down, he was having trouble sharing the quarx's worries about the translator.

/// I hope you noticed
that I didn't interrupt you this time.
I tried really hard not to be a
"miserable, disgusting little creature." ///

Bandicut grunted. He was remembering Julie's third-to-
last kiss, the one interrupted by the call. It made him shiver
to remember it. It also made him depressed. Why did something *always* go wrong anytime he started to like a woman?
/Who said you were a miserable . . . whatever you just said?/
he muttered.

/// You did.
The other night. ///

/I did? I must have been mad./ He entered the dorm and
climbed into his bunk with a groan, snapping the privacy
curtain closed. /I wonder how Julie managed to get a pri-

vate room, anyway. Who'd she get cozy with, I wonder?/
He was madder than he'd thought.

/// *No one. That's one area*
where the exoarch people made out.
They came late,
and management wanted to keep them separate.
Thought they were a bunch of meddlers.
Some extra cubicles were converted into dorms,
and they were too small to be multiples. ///

Bandicut blinked. /How the hell do you know all that?/

/// *Just something I picked up*
scanning the net. ///

/Before you wrecked it, you mean?/
Charlie answered softly.

/// *Yes.*
And I have a feeling that
the new orbital scan that took Julie away from you
was prompted by my blunder.
So we both lost out today. ///

Bandicut closed his eyes, alternately trying to forget,
and then to recapture, the memory of Julie. /Yeah,/ he said.
/Look, I'm sorry I called you a perverse, stinking little pip-
squeak—/

/// *That's not what you called me.*
You called me a— ///

/Never mind. I'm just sorry, okay?/
The quarx was silent for a moment.

/// *Okay. Hey, John—*
it's really important that we get out
to the translator before anyone else does.
Really important. ///

Bandicut scowled. /Why? It can protect itself, can't it?/

/// *Sure.*
But possibly at the cost of our *being able to reach it.*
It might decide to sink out of reach, to avoid contact.
We can't let that happen. ///

/I thought you said it would do what it had to, to stay in touch with us./

/// I said I thought .
But I can't be absolutely sure. ///

/Well—I don't see what I can do about it, anyway,/ Bandicut muttered. /Say, you know, it might be a good idea for us to browse the system board and see what people are saying about sabotage. To see if anyone's onto us./

/// Getting back out there is more urgent. ///

/Well, I *can't* get out there until my ankle's healed. Even if Switzer signs me off, I won't be ready for hopping around subterranean caverns./

*/// That's why I was thinking,
maybe there's a way to make you heal faster. ///*

Bandicut snorted. /How? By magic? That reminds me, I haven't taken those stupid pills./ He sat up and groped in his bunk storage cubby for the bottle of pills that Switzer had given him. He shook three of them out and took them with a swallow of water from a half-empty drinking bulb.

*/// Not magic.
But it's occurred to me that maybe,
with my help . . . ///*

Bandicut wished he could see the quarx face to face. /Physical intervention? Can you *do* that?/

He almost felt the quarx frown.

*/// At first, I didn't think so.
But I've been thinking about the fever I induced
by touching your nerve impulses.
And I've been remembering some meditational
techniques
that I believe could help you
focus upon your ankle's healing
and speed it up from within. ///*

Bandicut blinked. Mind-techniques? Even if it were true . . . /Would you know how to heal a human body?/

/// Not precisely.
But your body knows what to do.
I would just help it concentrate
and do it faster.
I've done it before, in past lifetimes. ///
/But never with a human./
/// Obviously not. But
I'd never done it with a Peloinang, either.
Or a Fffff tink.
But it worked with them.
And on tougher hurts than broken bones.
I remember parts of it vividly. ///

Bandicut suddenly felt like another player in a long line of players, in a game he didn't understand. /Are you in the habit of getting your hosts badly injured?/

The quarx sighed and didn't answer. Instead he began to hum a low, rhythmic chant.

/What are you doing?/

But it was obvious what he was doing, and Bandicut's protest died of its own accord. The sound was oddly compelling, not just soothing and restful, but evocative as well. Despite his own resistance, Bandicut found his thoughts filling with restful images of water and dappled sunlight and green leaves on trees, and he felt a female presence nearby, not arousing but comforting, a pair of feminine hands stroking and kneading tension out of his muscles. The sensation was so real that he began to feel cries of relief from his knotted muscles, and he thought, go up just a little, now to the right . . . *ahhhhh.*

The imagined hands found just the right spot. Charlie's humming chant changed in timbre and pitch, and Bandicut could have sworn that his muscles were responding with their own minds to the sound—relaxing, and allowing oxygen to flow where tension had blocked it before. He experimentally tightened his left shoulder; it responded, but as he released it, it relaxed again into the swell of the hum.

*/// The more you surrender control,
the better. ///*

For an instant, he thought of asking for a nice, relaxing image of Julie to surrender to; but he could hear the tsk, tsk of the quarx leading him in more restful directions, and in the end he gave up to it and imagined that he was floating in a hot, swirling mineral bath . . .

He began to see new images, gazing inward into his own mind/body/being. He glimpsed a welter of tensions and frustrations and longings—shuttered windows onto deep pains and sorrows of the past, like the loss of his parents and brother and sister-in-law, and the one comfort that was his young niece Dakota. He flickered upon a memory of sitting with her parents, watching her play in a VR booth, her seven-year-old face frowning in tight concentration as she worked at piloting a ship through an imaginary space-warp, trying to reach . . . what was it? . . . the universe of rainbow snow. He wondered wistfully if he would ever see Dakota again. He was suddenly aware of the years of loneliness that had built up inside him, and his occasional feelings of emotional exile, which the neurolink had done so much to assuage, until it had been torn from him . . .

He began to tighten up, pulling back from the images; but the quarx's mutterings moved him through them with a whispered,

*/// Not now.
Those things take time to heal.
We have simpler business now. ///*

A new image took over, a vision of a stream of golden light pouring into a room, bathing away the hurt of the memories, not changing what had happened, but soothing those hurts and others that rose to find balm. The golden light flowed toward the physical injuries in his body.

Skeletal muscles relaxed and tightened again, gently; the muscles holding the bones of his left ankle began to draw themselves into a natural conformation that put just the right tension on the half-healed fracture that ran through one of those bones . . .

What are we doing? he thought dreamily.

/// Trust your body to know. ///

Moments later he glimpsed the actual break, and the edges that needed joining, and he saw the places where the alignment was imperfect. He felt his muscles contract slightly, until the edges shifted into the best fit. Nerve endings fired at the movement, but the signals were stroked into something that said, this is right . . . and the flow of histamines stopped, and calcium and phosphate ions and oxygen and glucose flowed more freely and accurately . . . and he could almost see the cells bathed in the nutrient sea, churning out new bone. And in the break, the bone was knitting itself together without a trace of a scar, following blueprints held within each one of those glowing cells . . .

✴

When he woke, it was to the sound of the quarx saying,

/// . . . got to get something to eat.

You need fuel . . . ///

He blinked his eyes open, startled to realize that he'd gone to sleep. For a moment, he could not identify what he was feeling. Then he realized he was ravenous. He hadn't eaten a thing last night; he had slept straight through from late afternoon to morning. Pushing himself up, he felt a wave of lightheadedness. He felt drained and hung over. /What have you been doing to me?/ he whispered.

/// Healing you.

We demanded a lot of your body, while you slept.

After you eat,

we've got to see the good doctor. ///

It took an effort to get down from his bunk, but once he'd been upright for a few moments, he felt better. /I would hesitate to give Switzer the benefit of that title,/ he grunted, testing his ankle. He felt nothing—but then, with the cast on, he hadn't felt too much anyway.

/// Well, whatever we call him,
he's going to be mighty amazed . . . ///

※

Switzer stared at the readouts, scratching his head. "Bandicut, I don't think you even need that cast anymore. Ol' King Cole is going to love you."

Bandicut blinked. "Say again?"

"Jackson. I'm telling him that you're cleared for driving duty today. But," Switzer added, frowning as he tapped Bandicut's ankle through the fastract cast, "I'm leaving this thing on for one more day, just to play it safe. There've been too many damned weird things about you lately." He gave the cast a good rap with his knuckles. "Feel anything?"

Bandicut shrugged. "I feel you hitting me."

"Do you feel any *pain?*"

He shook his head.

"No fever? Never mind, I can read it right here." Switzer pulled the readout plugs out of the cast. "You can go to work. Hell, you can play *soccer,* for all I care. Come back tomorrow to get the cast off." He shook his gray-haired head and turned away with a dismissive gesture. It was clear he regarded Bandicut as an annoying enigma, and the sooner the man was out of his sight the better.

Bandicut was happy to oblige him.

As he walked to the exo-ops center, Bandicut conceded, /That's pretty amazing, what you did. The ankle feels great. It seems silly to still have this cast on./

/// I'm glad you're pleased.
But now, my friend, comes the time for us
to earn our keep. ///

Bandicut started to give a jaunty reply, but swallowed it when he realized exactly what the quarx meant. He'd met the translator once before, and he hadn't liked the experience, not at all.

21

TRANSLATOR DREAMS

THE DEEP BLUE Neptune was a comforting companion in the midnight sky, as he drove toward navpoint Wendy. In the week since he'd last been out
in a buggy, Triton had completed slightly more
than one tidal-locked orbit of Neptune, and the mother
planet was once again in crescent phase, a slender scythe in
the sky. Whatever misgivings he had about the surreptitious
mission he was about to undertake for Charlie, he could not
resist the pleasure of the solitude, and the view. He knew
there were not too many other people who would have
considered this a scenic drive, but he loved the rugged des-
olation under Neptune's regal presence. He sometimes
wondered if there was something wrong with him, that he
didn't become as jaded by it as everyone else.

*/// Do you ever get this sort of feeling
for your homeworld? ///*

Charlie asked, as they bobbed and bumped over the landscape.

Bandicut squinted, picking out a course through the
hilly nitrogen ices. /I dunno. Sometimes, I guess. Why?/

*/// You don't seem to think of Earth that often.
Or of people you left behind. ///*

Bandicut shrugged. /Didn't really leave a whole lot of

people behind. My family's gone—you already know that. Except my niece, of course. And a few friends. But not really any close friends, I guess./

/// Is that hard for you to accept? ///

/What are you, a damn shrink? I'm alone. So what? Lots of people are alone./

For a few moments, the quarx didn't reply. Bandicut tried to concentrate on his driving. He glanced off to his left and watched Napoleon galloping over the dunes, paralleling his route. It was about time for the robot to check in with them.

/// What about Dakota? ///

Charlie asked suddenly.

Bandicut growled in annoyance. /What about her?/ He waggled the control stick, making the buggy veer left, then right. He was annoyed because he was feeling distracted and guilty; he'd gotten a message from Julie, saying that exoarch seemed to be onto something exciting, but they couldn't send out a team until more orbital scans had been done. He felt as if he were lying to her.

/// I'm trying to understand, that's all.
Dakota's your niece, right?
So you don't have a relationship with her
the way you would, say, with Julie. ///

/Obviously./

/// Therefore,
this thing that you're doing,
putting your earnings in trust for her,
is something that you're doing
for no other reason than that you care for her? ///

/Yeah, so? What's your point?/ Bandicut braked suddenly, realizing that he was veering from his plotted course. He sighed, noting that Napoleon was heading his way, probably to check on him. He flashed a signal to Napoleon that everything was all right. They were getting close now.

/// We're just under a kilometer from the cavern.
I'm skirting the point, I know.
But here it is:
Would you miss Earth, John,
if you were never able to return? ///

Bandicut felt a sudden chill. He instinctively pulled back on the power. /What the hell is that supposed to mean, Charlie? Yeah, I'd miss it. I'd miss it a lot. Why?/

Charlie stirred with an unusual restlessness.

/// Nothing . . . exactly.
Let's hope the question never comes up. ///

/Then why'd you bring it up?/

/// Just . . . trying to understand your emotions. ///

Bandicut grunted suspiciously and gunned the motor. The buggy crested a rise with a dim puff of snow, and on his console, two arrows converged. Time to get started. He keyed the comm. "EXO-OP CONTROL, UNIT ECHO. AP-PROACHING NAVPOINT WENDY. BEGINNING SURVEY RECORDINGS." He touched several switches on the console, turning on the mapping-sensor recorders.

/I hope you've got this figured out. If I cross the STOP HERE line again—even Stelnik and Jackson will be smart enough to figure out that something is going on./

/// Time to ask Napoleon to help us, ///

the quarx said, as they began their sweep over the assigned territory.

/// When you reach your turn up ahead,
could you ask it to come alongside? ///

/You're the boss. Let's just do it right./

✳

Bandicut stood with his hand tingling on the robot's outer case. He wanted to ask Charlie exactly what he was doing to Napoleon's programming, but he sensed that the quarx was too deep in his work to answer. He only knew that fairly complex instructions were passing through his skin and glove into the robot's central processor. The tingling fluctuated for a moment, then faded.

/// Okay. You can take your hand away. ///

Napoleon made a creaking sound over the comm and stared with its black holocam eyes. "Of course, John Bandicut, I will assist as requested."

"Yes, good," Bandicut said, clearing his throat. Charlie had apparently just instructed the robot to carry on with the survey in his stead while they set out on foot to the cavern. /What now?/

/// Starting in nineteen minutes,
we will have a forty-nine-minute period
in which there will be no spacecraft or satellites
overhead. ///

Bandicut took a slow, deep breath. /All right. Hey, Charlie—if we do pull this off? You'll tell me everything the translator says, right? No secrets?/

/// No secrets, John.
We're in this together. ///

Bandicut set the rover into motion. Napoleon bounded alongside on its gangly grasshopper legs. When they reached the easternmost corner of the assigned sector, fifteen minutes later, he brought the buggy to a halt. They had four minutes to kill before the last of the overhead satellite eyes dropped below the horizon. Bandicut opened his visor and ate a chocolate bar. He tried to ignore the butterflies in his stomach. He knew it had to be done, but he was starting to feel like a criminal.

/// Time. Let's go. ///

Bandicut opened the bubble canopy and climbed out. Napoleon had already clambered up onto the side of the rover and plugged in its probe. As soon as Bandicut stepped clear, the robot drove off, hanging from the rover like a monkey. /That thing better be back here on time,/ Bandicut said uneasily.

/// It will. Let's go.
Bearing zero-five-four. ///

Bandicut sprang ahead in the one-thirteenth gravity and loped across the uneven icy surface, across the invisible STOP HERE line, into the unauthorized sector where he and Charlie had first met.

※

/// Right here. ///

Panting, he came to a stop. He had been jogging for ten minutes at the most, but it felt more like an hour. It wasn't easy, stumping across that distance with a cast inside his left suit leg; it would have been impossible in Earth gravity. He peered around over the frozen nitrogen and methane surface. /Is this it?/ It looked vaguely familiar; but a lot of places out here looked like a lot of other places. And the last time he was here, the translator had been busy rearranging the landscape.

The quarx didn't answer. But an instant later, he felt his feet sinking slowly into the ice. Then he was falling, and he was suddenly aware of sparkles of light whirling around him, and his vision and the rest of his consciousness went cottony and vague . . .

※

He blinked in darkness, and found just enough light to see that he was standing directly in front of the translator—the same machine, with its pulsing, squirming, not-quite-solid black and iridescent spheres, which had started him on this crazy path. He felt that he was dreaming, but knew he wasn't. The translator looked even more alive than before—this *thing* that belonged, not to the alien Rohengen who had occupied Triton millions of years before humanity, but to some other race lost even deeper in time and space. Bandicut felt that he was underground in the ice cavern, but saw nothing to confirm it; his vision was completely dominated by the spinning globes moving around each other and through each other.

He felt a palpable and urgent sense of *purpose* in the translator. He also saw something now that he had not before, a curious point of darkness floating inside one of the iridescent spheres, like a tiny shadow in the light. It caught his attention, because it did not seem to be just a fleck of physical matter, but more like a pure geometric point. The word *singularity* flickered in his mind, and he had no idea if that was what it was; but even as he was wondering, it caught his gaze with a wrench. He felt his vision telescoping down into that point of blackness. His breath escaped with an explosive rush.

He was falling into a microscopic universe of darkness, and deep within that universe, he saw dancing fire—and found it disturbing to look at. These were not chemical flames, but something far more fundamental, something burning and fusing deep in the uttermost building blocks of space-time . . . and whatever it was, it was bright, painfully so. And yet it was not the brightness so much as the *strangeness* that tore at his eyes. He wanted to call out to Charlie, but could not. It felt as though he were peering into the heart of a quantum black hole; nothing here quite fit anything that he knew or understood. It was almost as if he were being pulled into some tightly compacted dimension of reality, a corner of the universe that the human eye was never intended to see.

—It wasn't—

whispered a voice, which might have been the quarx's, or his own imagination. It was suddenly lost in a rising babble of voices, chaotic voices, speaking no language he knew, but reverberating in his mind, coming from within, coming from the fire, coming from God knew what source within this quarxian madness.

He was suddenly feverish with a rush of knowledge flowing into his mind, carried on the tide of voices. He was faint with it, he was dizzy and bewildered; he didn't know if he could hold or comprehend it all, and he could only hope that the quarx could. Charlie . . . was Charlie still here?

Images were building within him, images formed by knowledge gathering like atoms around a nucleating body, and soon they would crystalize abruptly into a vast clarity of—

—(what?)—

—*You will see*—

—*the chaotic movement, the danger*—

—a ticking molecular pendulum, marking time—

—a glimpse of tumbling rock and ice, perturbed from its orbit, far from the sun—

—falling inward, across endless space; hurtling close to the sun and then away—

—(is this?)—

—*yes*—

—a glimpse of a blue-and-white planet, floating serene in the darkness, a living world—

—the comet rising like a tremendous curving fastball, streaking toward the planet; and striking like a cosmic hammer, and erupting with—

—fire—

—*fire!*—

The fire seemed to spin around him, or he was spinning, and he felt himself caught in a transformation of time and space, and for a terrifying moment he thought this was nothing but silence-fugue, not alien wisdom or knowledge at all . . . except that now the previous images vanished and he saw a figure of coruscating fire, alive and aware, in the heart of the darkness, and he could not tell if it was the quarx or the translator, or both. Before he could ask, three blazing points of light erupted from the figure of fire and spun toward him, circling into tight orbits around his head, and then dropping into his pockets.

—*these you will need*—

He tried to focus on the points of light, but could not.

Something new was building around him like a pressure wave, and with it was a growing sensation of unreality, and he felt himself wanting to scream, but he could not. He opened his mouth and darkness billowed out, and it was filled with a lance of fire—

—and he glimpsed cavern walls flashing and shimmering—

—and he heard a quarx crying out—

—and the darkness shrank down to a penetrating point—

—and spun away—

—and everything blurred—

He thought he heard a deep gong ringing in the darkness, but this darkness was of a different sort. It was the darkness of space, and there was a blue planet arching over his head. He blinked dizzily, trying to stand. He saw ice under his feet, and realized that he was standing on the surface right where he had begun this madness . . .

/// Don't faint! ///

the quarx barked.

He caught himself stumbling. Whatever he had just been through, he felt as drained as he had this morning, after his healing.

/// Start walking—to your left!
Breathe, John—breathe! ///

He gulped air and shuddered, chilled to the bone. He had the presence of mind to call out to his suit for a system-check, and was reassured to hear that his life support was fine.

/// You've got to keep moving.
We meet Napoleon in nine minutes. ///

Napoleon . . . yes. He rasped in a lungful of air, trying to remember.

/// Do you understand what just happened? ///

/Not . . . no./ He started to stumble and caught himself before pitching over onto the cryogenic surface.

> /// *Keep walking.*
> *It'll help you recover.*
> *You did well.* ///

/I did?/ he whispered, moving his feet like lead weights, one after the other. Slowly, mindlessly, he pushed himself to a cautious jogging speed. He thought he remembered visions of . . . it was so hard to remember, like a dream, dancing tantalizingly at the edge of his memory. He knew it would come back, if only he could . . . focus. But he couldn't focus while running.

> /// *You've just experienced a connection*
> *not meant for corporeals.*
> *I was afraid we'd lose you.*
> *But you held together.*
> *We got what we needed.* ///

He followed the gentle directional nudges from the quarx, sensing that Charlie didn't want him to try to comprehend it all now, but just to recover first, and get back to the rover. But he thought he would go mad if he didn't recapture what had just happened. He was up to a full, loping run now, panting steadily, letting the quarx direct his feet as he ran toward their rendezvous with the robot, all the time trying desperately to focus on the memory that was rising now toward the surface . . .

It was a planet, blue and white, Earth, homeworld, floating serene and vulnerable through the vast eternal night of space; it was oblivious to the motions of certain bodies from the edge of the solar system, one of which was now tumbling inward at hellbent velocity.

He stumbled on a ripple of ice and pitched forward, gasping. He pushed himself back up to his hands and knees, the image quaking with crystalline clarity in his mind:

The Earth burning.

> /// *John, don't stop.*
> *You've got to keep moving.* ///

He struggled to get up, but his legs and arms felt like

putty. He looked up at blue Neptune over his head and saw another blue planet, its atmosphere clouding over with smoke and ash.

/// *John, please—* ///

/Charlie—/ he gasped /—is that really going to happen?/

/// *Yes, if we don't stop it.*
It's closer than I imagined. ///

/When?/ he croaked.

/// *Impact in forty-seven days.*
Now get up and run, damn it!
RUN! ///

22

VIRTUAL TRUTHS

THE ROVER CAME over the hill to the north, kicking up a cloud of ice particles as it sped down the slope. At any other time, Bandicut would have been terrified by the sight of the robot driving his buggy that way, hanging off the side like a remora fish, the buggy slewing to come straight toward him before braking to a stop. Now, he was simply too numb to care.

"John Bandicut, survey strips three-A through five-B are completed. What further needs do you have?" Napoleon squawked, raising itself up on the cowling of the rover as Bandicut climbed back in. It looked as though it were trying to peer into the driver's compartment to see what he was planning to do next.

/Charlie?/ he asked, buckling himself in.

/// Place your hand on the robot, please. ///

Bandicut reached out and touched Napoleon. He found the gesture oddly calming, like petting a dog. /Are we releasing it now?/

/// Yes.
Recon Thirty-nine,
terminate and delete special programming Beta.
Confirm. ///

"Termination confirmed," squawked the robot. "John Bandicut, do you have further needs?"

"Ah . . . negative, Nappy. Go ahead and take up your regular station, I guess."

As the robot unjacked and let itself back down onto the moon's surface, Bandicut suddenly realized that, according to his work orders, he was to stay out here for three more hours before returning to base. He didn't think he could stand to wait that long. /Charlie, if that's really true, about the comet—/

/// It is. ///

/—then we've got to get back! Do you have all the orbital data? Is that what all that gibberish was, from the translator?/

/// Some of it.
And yes, I can give you the figures,
but they're a complex interaction.
I'll be able to show you better in the VR room. ///

/Never mind showing me. Can you show the people who can do something about it?/

/// John—remember?
There's only one person
who can do something about it.
And that's you. ///

Bandicut swallowed, his blood rushing. /Charlie, what can I do? We've got to *notify* somebody!/

/// We've been through this before.
Your planet has no defense.
Not against this. ///

Bandicut had trouble catching his breath. /No, but—what about—fusion warheads—?/ He was clenching and unclenching his fists. Napoleon was looking back at him from the top of the knoll.

/// Perhaps you should start driving.
I'm afraid, John, that warheads are not the answer.

It is likely they would only split the comet,
and make its effects all the more devastating. ///

/But we should at least warn people,/ Bandicut whispered.

/// Please start driving.
Your people would not believe a warning from us.
The comet is behind the sun, hidden
from the only stations that might confirm its orbit.
Please *start driving. ///*

Bandicut snapped the joystick forward, and the buggy lurched ahead, wheels churning on nitrogen ice. "Exo-op control, Unit Echo," he croaked, pressing the long-range comm. "I'm coming in early. This ankle cast is killing me. Copy?"

"COPY, ECHO. HI, BANDIE. SHALL I ALERT, AH, ANY-ONE IN PARTICULAR?" answered the cheerful voice of Georgia Patwell.

Bandicut sighed. "Negative, control. See you soon." At least he was grateful for Dr. Switzer's casual treatment. If he hadn't had an excuse to come in early, he would have gone crazy for the next three hours.

He thought, actually, that he might go crazy anyway.

✳

/// Don't forget the daughter-stones. ///

/Eh?/ An image flickered, and he remembered the three points of light from the translator flying to him and dropping into his suit pocket. /What *was* that, anyway?/ he asked, driving into the hangar area.

/// Daughter components of the translator.
They're essential for what we have to do.
Keep them with you at all times. ///

/Uh, okay./ Rolling to a stop, he secured the buggy and hurried inside. After dressing, he reached into the suit outer pocket to find three small, translucent stones. They looked like glass marbles, one obsidian, one ruby red, one glittering white. He thought he saw a faint sparkle of light glowing within the white one, but it died immediately, and there was no other sign that they were anything other than glass stones. /What should I do with them?/ he asked, rolling them in the palm of his hand. He immediately envisioned dropping them and watching them disappear under various immovable objects.

/// They'll stay in your pocket
if you direct your thoughts to them,
asking them to.
I'll tell you more about them later.
Let's go. ///

Bandicut shrugged and dropped the stones into his pocket. Then he grabbed a terminal to submit his field report, and called Switzer's office to say that he wanted the cast taken off. He was told to come by in two hours. Perfect. He headed straight for the lounge.

Locking himself into a VR room, he switched on a solar-system realtime program and perched on a stool, surrounded by a panoply of stars, with a glowing sun floating in space some distance away. At Charlie's request, he put on a neurojack headset and adjusted the controls until all nine of the planets were enlarged enough for their features to be recognizable in the dark interplanetary gulf—the outer planets with their cloud bands and rings, Mars a rusty pebble, Earth a blue-and-white gem. He dimmed the stars, so that they hung in the background like an infinite tapestry, while allowing him to see clearly the movements of the planets.

/// Splendid.
The translator can make do with raw numbers.
But this makes it much easier to visualize,
doesn't it? ///

/I guess so. What exactly are we visualizing?/

/// In a manner of speaking . . . EineySteiney pool.
I'm downloading the orbital data now.
Waiting for the VR program to process it . . . ///

EineySteiney pool? Bandicut thought.

/// There we go.
First I want you to see the orbits of
the planets and all significant tracked objects
as they were several years ago.
This is based upon the information
we took from your library. ///

The image dimmed; the planets shifted positions in their orbits as the program made the time-based adjustments, and there was a momentary blurring of the myriad of tiny points of light that represented known asteroids, comets, and satellites. When everything became clear again, the overall picture looked much the same.

/// Now—I want you to see the gaps
in your routine observations,
based upon the locations of your
telescope and radar stations
which would be tracking the movements
of small bodies. ///

The holoimage was suddenly crisscrossed with swaths of soft illumination, emanating from various points on the Moon, Mars, Ceres, and several other stations. Some of the swaths were moving. A significant portion of the solar system remained in shadow, however—more than half the sky.

/// A century or two ago,
Earth-based amateurs might have spotted the danger.
That was before air and light pollution
made it impossible.
Now let's subtract the coverage
from two solar-orbiting sats
that are no longer being monitored. ///

/Wait,/ Bandicut protested, as two swaths of light blinked off at locations a third of the way around the sun from Earth. /Are those sats really out of service?/

/// As far as I know, they're still functioning.
But their transmissions have been turned off.

Because of budget cuts,
no one was analyzing the data. ///
/Well, damn it—/
/// I'm just laying out the facts.
Now, look here— ///

Bandicut watched, as the quarx rearranged the solar system. Everything blurred, then stabilized. A small pointer winked on and tracked a tiny point of light as it drifted through the dark emptiness far outside the orbit of Pluto. /What's that?/

/// That's your planet's nemesis,
a dark comet as it was some years ago,
orbiting in the Kuiper Belt.
I'm going to give you brief snapshots
of its movements since then. ///

The image changed, in shifting freeze-frames, as the planets spun around the sun, the nearer planets moving quickly and the outer planets swinging with ponderous slowness.

/// As you can see,
it has passed through observation swaths
several times.
It has never been named,
but its presence is recorded in your astronomers'
compressed databases, as one among thousands
of extremely faint transitory objects
whose orbits have never been calculated.
If its orbit had been derived,
it would have been listed as safe.
Indeed, here it floats
at the edge of interstellar space,
bothering no one. ///

/So where's the problem?/ Bandicut stirred restlessly.

The image changed, and zoomed across the solar system to bring that one comet's movements into closer relief. Bandicut felt his heart skip a beat as the comet's course seemed

to bend inward suddenly, then a little later, bend inward
again. He watched nervously as it fell toward the sun,
across the solar system. /What's happening? What diverted
it?/

/// Its companions out here . . . ///

A pointer blinked momentarily at several other points of
light, jumping from one to the next.

/// The chaotic movement
of half a billion bodies, John.
I've compressed the effect here,
because it would take hours to show you
all the tiny changes to its orbit
over the millennia.
Our data become more uncertain
the farther back we go,
but our projections right now are quite clear.
Even if your people had been watching,
they could not have predicted
these course changes.
You have not yet mastered the necessary nuances
of dynamical chaos. ///

Bandicut bristled. /But your translator has?/

/// Yes. ///

Bandicut grunted. /But are you saying that all of this is
just a projection? You don't have actual observations?/

/// We have verified the first part of the prediction,
from your most recent databases.
Earth has not noticed the course change,
but it has occurred,
and the data are there in your libraries. ///

/So they could find it from that, after all,/ Bandicut said
hopefully.

/// No.
At the time of these observations,
the orbit was still innocuous.
It had not yet passed close to Uranus. ///

He watched as the point of light zoomed inward, toward the gaseous green planet, represented here as a grape-sized ball of light. The object's course bent sharply as it passed through Uranus's gravity well and spun out again, toward the sun.

/// *There's the slingshot.* ///

/I'm sure they would have seen that!/

/// *Afraid not.*
That passage occurred while Uranus was
out of observation.
See?
It's in the shadows.
And the only active Uranus probes
were looking the other way.
We checked. ///

Bandicut swallowed nervously. It all made sense, if the image here were accurate. /But how did *you* see it, then?/

/// *We didn't.*
This is a projection,
based upon the earlier data.
But it's a good projection.
John, I've never known the translator to miss
—not even once—
on its orbital projections.
You could say it's a sort of specialty. ///

Bandicut cleared his throat. He wanted to believe the quarx, but all of this was making him very uneasy. /So . . . when do we see it again?/

/// *Earth-based observations*
won't catch it until a few weeks before contact.
Now look at this— ///

The comet sped inward through the patchwork of observation swaths, neatly missing all but the very edge of one field of view. Bandicut had to admit that the chances of its being noticed at that point were slim, at best.

> /// *It* wasn't *noticed.*
> *We're still in past tense, here.*
> *But there was one datapoint*
> *dismissed as noise*
> *that was consistent with our projections.* ///
> /Still—if we told them where to look for it—/
> /// *It's too late for that, John.*
> *And even if it weren't,*
> *you know,*
> *we'd still have this little problem*
> *of credibility.* ///

/What problem?/

He heard a sigh, and felt something strange, and was aware that the quarx was doing something through the VR neurolink. /Charlie, you still there?/

"Right here," said a voice in front of him. A hologram blinked on: a bizarre-looking creature wielding a teacher's pointer. It looked vaguely like a dinosaur, with a knobby head and bent-looking fins running down its back.

"What the fr'deekin' hell is *that* supposed to be?"

"An alien presence," rumbled the monster. "I searched the records for an indication of how your fellow humans might view me, if they believed in my existence at all. According to your VR library, this is typical of what humans conjure up in their minds when they think of aliens." The quarx-dinosaur turned awkwardly. "This representation is called 'Godzilla.' Now tell me—do you think your people would listen to a warning about impending disaster from—"

Bandicut shook his head angrily. "Stop, Charlie! Is this a serious discussion?"

"Very," said the lizard.

"Then conjure up another image. Look human, for Chrissake. We would *not* transmit a message from some goddamn antique monster holo."

"Okay, but do you understand what I'm saying?" The

reptile blurred and vanished. A man's image appeared, a salt-and-pepper-haired, vaguely jovial, grandfatherly figure. It was probably an image of some actor, or American president—but thankfully, Bandicut didn't recognize the face. The human gestured with the same pointer. "Can we . . . talk like this?" he rumbled throatily.

"Yes," Bandicut said tensely.

"Good." Charlie turned and pointed to the image of the comet, now plunging slowly, it seemed, toward the sun. "Okay, then. Let's assume your astronomical union caught a glimpse of this before it disappeared behind the sun. Even then, they couldn't have established its orbit with certainty, and if they had, they wouldn't have thought it a danger."

"Why not?"

"Because there's a final change that will be occurring, very soon, with the comet behind the sun." The Charlie-image rapped its pointer in the palm of its hand. "The translator has predicted a solar flare which is occurring now on the far side of the sun. That's been confirmed by sat readings. That flare is affecting the solar wind and radiation through which the comet is passing. That will be causing propulsive outgassing of vapors as the comet passes close to the sun. This projection was made by analyzing course-change behaviors already observed, in conjunction with certain mathematical chaos-functions which are not in your scientific lexicon."

"Charlie—?"

"I understand your feelings. But I'm not bullshitting you, as your people might say. The translator *has* predicted it, using functions which your astronomers would not understand and would not believe."

Bandicut glared. "If these functions are so useful, how about explaining them to *me!*"

The quarx-human turned up his hands. "John, I can't explain the math. But I can show you a few of the metaphase-space projections." He gestured, and a graphics window opened in one corner of the solar system. Within it, complex three-dimensional attractor patterns twisted and circled.

"That's helpful. Let's see . . . I'd say it looks like a serpent on heavy drugs, sewing a button on a cape," Bandicut responded sardonically.

"Well, it's a temporal-probability path of the comet, mapping tumbling characteristics and derived analysis of the thing's physical structure, based upon known data and a complex stacked array of behavior patterns, cross-correlated with the projections of solar activity."

"Charlie—"

"The thing is, all of these apparently random factors are not really random; they're just chaotic—extremely sensitive to tiny changes. This form of chaos analysis uses a lot of minute detail—but it also uses patterns and metapatterns, and derives still deeper patterns from those. The truth is, John, your language doesn't have all the words necessary to explain it. It comes perilously close to—well, I have often wondered if it is not so much predicting the future as *viewing* it. The translator denies this, but—" The quarx-human shook his head.

Bandicut stared at the alien, and felt very much like a dumb animal. He hated the feeling.

Clearing his throat, Charlie turned to look soberly back at him. "Anyway, this is the kind of thing on which the translator just doesn't miss. It really doesn't. It's been doing this sort of thing for about a billion years."

Bandicut gestured noncommittally. "Okay. The translator doesn't miss. But they still might spot it coming around the other side."

"They might, indeed." Charlie nodded vigorously. He turned and sped up the image. "I'm sure they will, in fact. But too late. There are only forty-seven days left, John. *Forty-seven days.* The thing is in a fast, highly elongated orbit. Here, look." He pointed to Earth. "I've programmed in everything Earth has that could conceivably reach the comet and change its course. The comet will start blinking when it's too close for the best course change to be good enough. Watch."

"I'm watching," Bandicut said in irritation.

The comet emerged close to the sun, arcing toward Earth's orbit. An armada of ships began to climb out of Earth's gravity well, curving toward the sun. The fleet was barely a fourth of the way from Earth to the comet when the comet began blinking.

"This is an optimistic assessment," Charlie said, as the blinking point of light continued closing with Earth. "The ships just aren't fast enough—and they don't have the clout we need. The best they could do is change the point on Earth where the impact will occur." The comet and Earth converged, and there was a flash. "Boom." Charlie threw up his hands.

Bandicut didn't say anything for a moment. He had no idea what to say.

"How bad would it be, you're wondering?" the quarx-human said. "History is littered with end-of-the-world scares, after all—right?" Bandicut didn't answer. The quarx was reading his thoughts accurately. "So how do we know this isn't just another false alarm?" Charlie gazed at him. "Think of the dinosaurs. Think of nuclear winter. That comet is about seven kilometers across—almost as large as the one that turned the dinosaurs into fossils. If it hits the Earth at that speed, it will explode with a thousand times more energy than all of the nuclear weapons ever amassed on Earth going off together."

"But—"

"Think of so much dust and soot in the atmosphere that photosynthesis ceases—and all food-bearing crops die out. Then think of war."

"You can't know this," Bandicut insisted.

The quarx-human shrugged sadly. "Forty-seven days. I

know it's difficult for you to hear. And your reservations are correct, in the sense that all of humanity will not necessarily become extinct. There will no doubt be pockets of survivors, including those off-planet. But Earth's population will be drastically reduced. Probably by ninety percent or more.''

Bandicut was swaying dangerously on the stool. He stood, stumping slowly around the solar system, trying to get a handle on the situation. "So . . . I seem to recall that you . . . had a plan?'' He cocked his head. A feeling of extreme surrealism was coming over him, almost but not quite like silence-fugue. "Isn't that what you said?'' he asked. There was no reason to be angry at the quarx, he thought. But it made no difference; he was angry.

Charlie nodded stiffly. "That's what this is all about, John. That's why we're going to have to—'' he hesitated "—steal a ship.''

Bandicut stared at him for a breathless instant, then barked a laugh. "I'm glad you have a sense of humor, Charlie, I'm glad you have a sense of humor. Because that's about the most inane thing I've ever heard in my life.'' He shuddered to silence, because he knew that this Charlie *didn't* have a sense of humor like that. "What do you . . . *really* . . . have in mind?''

The quarx-human stepped toward him. "We have to steal a ship, John,'' he said softly. "We have to steal it, and go out there and stop that comet from hitting Earth.''

Bandicut swayed dizzily and wondered if he was getting enough oxygen. Was he still underground in the cavern, dreaming all this? He took a long, deep breath. "That's ridiculous,'' he said finally. "You just showed me how ships from *Earth* couldn't possibly get there in time. And we're about a hundred times farther away than any of them.''

"True,'' Charlie agreed.

Bandicut erupted angrily. "So you claim you have these wonderful orbit projections, but you don't even know that someone out here at fucking *Neptune,* even if he could somehow steal a ship that could *make* it that far, couldn't possibly reach the inner solar system in time. That's just—"

"The others don't have the translator," Charlie interrupted calmly.

Bandicut clamped his teeth shut. "What?"

"They don't have the translator."

"That's your fr'deekin' answer?"

"That's my answer," said the wide-eyed hologram. "The translator can do what your ships can't."

Bandicut sat speechless, staring at the unblinking alien.

♭

IMPOSSIBLE THINGS

 "WHAT DON'T YOU understand?" asked the quarx, studying his face.

Bandicut laughed harshly. "Are you crazy? I don't know which is more ridiculous—the idea of stealing a ship—or the idea of what we would do with it if we *did!*"

The holoimage nodded, scratching its cheek in thought. "Look in your pocket, John."

Bandicut scowled at the quarx and drew out the three stones he'd gotten from the translator. He squinted at them. They had changed; they were much smaller than before—more like gems for finger rings than marbles. He shook them in the palm of his hand—a ruby, a diamond, and a black-something. They didn't look very alien, or very powerful. On the other hand . . . they were from the translator. Who the hell knew *what* the thing could do? "Okay," he murmured.

"Those daughter-stones will, among other things, enable you to channel the energy of your spaceship in ways that I guarantee you have never imagined."

"You make them sound like magic."

The quarx shrugged. "To you, they might well seem that way."

"Don't patronize me, Charlie!"

"Sorry—I didn't mean to. They represent an extremely advanced technology. Please keep them safe. Ask them to stay in your pocket."

Bandicut returned them to his pocket. Stay, he thought.

The quarx-human frowned, nodding. "John, about this . . . *idea,* as you put it . . . of stealing a spacecraft. I want you to know—I do not suggest this lightly. Nor do I ordinarily condone stealing—"

Bandicut laughed. "Oh, no?"

"—but these are extraordinary circumstances."

Shaking his head, Bandicut walked through the display of the solar system. He reached out to touch the fragile little ball of the Earth. His hand passed through the hologram. "Do you know what would happen if I got caught trying to steal a spaceship?"

"I expect it could be unpleasant," the quarx admitted.

"Unpleasant? Yes." Bandicut stared at the images of the other planets. "I would spend the rest of my life in prison. If I didn't get killed in the attempt."

The quarx cleared his throat. "It is true that I'm asking you to take a very great risk."

"I'm glad you admit that much. What is it you're intending for us to do, exactly? If you don't mind my asking."

"I don't mind. What we're going to do is make a high-speed flight, using a process known as 'spatial threading,' culminating in a massive . . . energy conversion."

Bandicut blinked. "What's that mean?"

"It means we're going to intercept the comet at about a quarter of the speed of light, and hit it head-on—"

"*WHAT?*"

"—and the threading field will convert roughly a fifth of the mass of the comet to energy—"

Bandicut swallowed.

"—at a safe distance from Earth." The quarx-human paused, gazing at the holographic Earth, and turned back to

Bandicut. "And that will terminate the danger to your homeworld. If all goes as planned."

Bandicut stared at him in disbelief. "And what about us?"

"Well—" Charlie considered his words. "There is a significant possibility that we will die. But I estimate we have, perhaps, a fifty-percent chance of surviving the collision. Which is rather high odds, considering the energy we plan to release."

Bandicut could only shake his head. "Right. And if we do survive, with this fifty-percent chance of yours?" He stopped and thought about it. He didn't know *how* to think about it; it seemed beyond reasoning. "Have you figured out what we do then? Have you figured out how we're going to *get back here?* How we're going to—forgive me— take up our lives again? Have you figured that out? Charlie?"

The quarx-human gazed at him in dismay. There was some emotion disturbing his face—and stirring in Bandicut's mind as well—that he could not identify. Finally, Charlie turned away, saying softly, "No, I'm afraid I haven't worked that out yet. I guess I believed that saving Earth was more important than our getting back here."

Bandicut swallowed, suddenly feeling selfish and ashamed. And angry at Charlie for making him feel that way.

"But John," said the quarx, turning. "We won't be without resources. I can't tell you exactly where the explosion will put us, or in what condition . . ." He hesitated, and seemed to realize that he wasn't satisfying Bandicut. He shrugged helplessly. "But I can say this. If we survive, we will have . . . resources . . . provided by the translator."

Bandicut furrowed his brow and said, darkly, "Well, that just reassures me all to hell. We'll have resources. You mean to call for help, so someone can come and pick up our pieces?"

"No, it won't be like that—"

"Tell me something," Bandicut snarled, losing patience. "Why couldn't you have found someone *qualified* for this harebrained scheme?"

"What do you mean?"

"Someone who *wanted* to be a hero."

"John—" The quarx cocked his head and actually chuckled. "Far fewer beings than you imagine actually want to be heroes. Why you? Because you're in a position to do it, and no one else is. And—" the hologram cleared its throat "—I might add, time is fleeing, as we sit here and debate the inevitable."

Bandicut turned away in anger, then wheeled back toward the quarx. "Tell me this—are we at least going to send a warning to Earth, to let them know what we're doing? It would have to be better than nothing."

The human figure shrugged. "Define 'better.' You might prompt a worldwide panic. If we succeed, they need no warning. But if we fail, you would only give some people a short reprieve. There will still be tidal waves and earthquakes, dust and smoke clouding the atmosphere, global cooling, and a die-off of plant life. And in the end, if we fail, billions will die."

Bandicut walked aimlessly under the stars, batting at the planets as they floated by. And I'll probably die, doing what you want, he thought. When he spoke, his words were tinged with surliness and guilt. "Everyone dies, right?"

"Yes," said the quarx, "but I note that *you* seem to want to live."

Bandicut jabbed at the air and sighed. "Well, why all this cowboy stuff? Why not get an authorized ship, one equipped for the flight—and then go do it?"

"John—" The image made a stiff, pleading gesture with its hands. "We have to leave within forty-eight hours. Do you seriously think we could persuade your authorities—in two days—to give us a ship?"

"We could try," he said stubbornly.

The image shook its head. "They'd say you were crazy and lock you up. And we would have lost the element of surprise we need for taking a ship."

"Do you have a plan for that, too?"

"Only a partial plan, I'm afraid." The quarx-human studied him. "I can see that you're still not convinced. John—could I ask you a hypothetical question?"

Bandicut shrugged.

"If you knew your niece Dakota would be among those to die—"

"Now, don't you start in with—"

"Would you do it then? It's a distinct possibility, you know. She might not die at once. She might die later, along with all of the others dying of starvation or disease. I'm not trying to manipulate your feelings, but—"

"Jesus, Charlie!" Bandicut slammed his balled fist into the cushioned wall at the edge of the solar system. "Not trying to manipulate my feelings?"

"Well, it is true that I'm appealing to things that matter to you—"

"Look, just leave my niece out of it, all right?"

Charlie was silent for a moment. "Does Dakota not live on Earth? In Iowa City?"

"What did I just say?" Bandicut yelled. "Leave her out of it!"

"I am merely stating facts—"

"*Damn it!* This discussion is not about *facts,* asshole! It's about . . . whether I *believe* you enough, *in here*—" and he thumped his chest "—to make a completely *irrational* decision to do something that will either ruin my life or end it!"

"You're saying that it's an emotional question, as well as a factual one?" The human-image made stiff hand gestures. "I believe I understand that, John. But—" He paused, stopped by Bandicut's glare. "It's just that I am poorly equipped to—"

"Yeah, yeah . . ." Bandicut was pacing now, bounding about in the low gravity like a caged wildcat, ankle cast and all—a wildcat loose among the planets and stars. A rogue comet. He was about to explode from nervous tension.

/// Is there any way I can
help you work this through? ///

the quarx asked nervously, inside his head.

He turned at Saturn and loped back across the solar system toward Earth. He spun around as a sudden, compelling idea came to him. "Yeah," he drawled. "You can." He felt a bitter edge creep into his voice, and it made him shiver with pleasure.

"Please tell me." The quarx-human, near Neptune, peered across space toward him.

"Step into the middle of the room and make yourself solid. No transparency, full physical feedback. Can you do that?" Bandicut spoke in a low tone, which he attempted to keep nonthreatening. He crossed the room to the lockers, and took out the tactile-feedback gloves and jacket.

"Are you—planning to—?"

Bandicut balled his fists inside the gloves. "I'm planning," he said, letting his anger out in a long growl, "to address the *emotional* component of this discussion." He strode to where the quarx-human was standing, and planted his feet as solidly as he could in the Triton gravity. "I'm planning to make a point about you and your mokin' pompous arrogance—"

"My what?"

"—and your assumption that you can just decide for people what they're going to do with their lives." Bandicut squinted at him. "Tell your programming to follow real physical norms for this room. Gravity, solidity, everything. Now put up your fists."

"John, you aren't—I mean, I—"

"Yes, I am! And you can't say you didn't ask for it, you fokin' goak!" Bandicut swung as hard as he could. His fist crashed into Charlie's chin, and even as he spun around from the recoil of his own swing, he glimpsed the quarx-human toppling past Uranus and crashing back into the wall. Catching his own balance with some difficulty, Bandicut stumped back on his cast and glared down at the fallen quarx-human, as it clumsily picked itself up from the floor. "You and your damned secrecy—and your damned crazy schemes to save the world! You might be right—*I'm sure you probably are right!* But you've been using me, and I don't like it!"

Charlie looked up with chagrin. Starlight glinted in his eyes. "John, I—didn't think you would do that."

Bandicut balanced on the balls of his feet. "No, I don't suppose you did. You want to stand up so I can do it again?"

"Is this—really—necessary?" Charlie asked, rising slowly.

"YES, DAMN IT!" Bandicut shouted. He swung again, and Charlie went crashing through the outer solar system to the floor. This time, Bandicut went down too, rolling in a twisting somersault, because he hadn't braced himself at all properly. "Yes, it's goddamn necessary!" Gasping, he rose, and as the quarx got up too, he lunged across the room to catch the quarx in a flying tackle. "I'm gonna NAIL you, you mokin' fokin'—!"

The illusion failed at that point, and he sailed through the quarx-image and crashed with a bone-jarring thud into the padded wall. "Uh—" he grunted, stunned, and drew a couple of gasping breaths from where he lay on his back. "Ah hell," he groaned. After a moment, he rolled to look at the holographic human form crumpled nearby.

Charlie slowly sat up and gazed at him, with what emotion he couldn't even guess. "That hurt me, John," Charlie said softly. "You wanted to cause me *physical* pain, didn't you?"

"*YES!*" Bandicut roared, swinging one last time and

knocking the quarx over like a bowling pin. "Yes, I wanted to hurt you!" he wheezed in satisfaction.

He sat back suddenly and sighed. "You can turn that damn thing off now. We have an appointment with Switzer. We mustn't keep the good doctor waiting."

Charlie sat back up. "John, if this is important to you . . . I notice that there are programmed boxing scenarios in the VR system. We could have a—"

"No. It's over," Bandicut said wearily, getting up and pulling off his gloves, jacket, and headset. "Shut that thing off, and let's get going."

/// You don't want to fight anymore? ///

Bandicut turned off the whole VR display, including the human. /I don't want to fight anymore. Now let's get the hell out of here./

★

They spent about ten minutes total in Switzer's office—just long enough for Bandicut to tell Switzer that he had come in from his survey run because the cast was driving him crazy. Switzer peered at him suspiciously, but instructed one of the techs to remove the cast. He probably figured that Bandicut was sandbagging on the job. Bandicut couldn't have cared less; he just wanted to leave the cast behind.

As for Charlie's "proposal"—Bandicut refused to discuss it further right now. There was, he said, much to consider; and he needed to sleep on it and let his subconscious work on it. He also badly wanted to see Julie. And to the quarx's protest, he replied that if Charlie didn't want to take this on his terms, then he, Charlie, was free to leave anytime he wished.

Charlie was quiet after that.

Returning to the dorm to shower, Bandicut found a message waiting for him on his bunk terminal. It was from Julie, on audio. He couldn't tell if she was being apologetic or enticing. "Sorry that these discoveries keep wrecking our dates, but if you want to come by later, I may be able to show you something. And . . . if you're not too fed up, maybe I can get you to have dinner with me again. I promise not to take any calls tonight. Well . . . unless . . . oh, you know what I mean. Bye." She made a sound of blowing a kiss.

He stared at the comm, imagining the possibilities. He knew, but did not wish to admit to himself, that he had to devote serious *conscious* thought to Charlie's proposal. He was frozen with conflicting urges, and he sensed Charlie quivering with tension, a coiled spring waiting for action. Charlie was asking him to take a terrifying leap of faith. But what if the quarx was right, which he almost certainly was? Probably, it was crazy even to be thinking about Julie tonight. But wasn't he entitled to *some* life before he threw it all away?

/// Do you . . . ///

/What?/ he snapped.

/// . . . intend, well . : . ///

/None of your damned business. Okay?/

The quarx sighed, and didn't ask further. Bandicut showered and changed in a blur, and got out of the dorm area just before the work shifts ended and everyone started coming back in. He went straight down to the exoarch office. He opened the door and met a short, stocky man who looked at him curiously. When he asked for Julie, the man hooked a thumb toward the back of the room.

Julie was poring over a computer display, which he recognized as radarsat scans of the Triton surface from low orbit. She looked up and beamed at him. "See this?" She tapped the screen where a dark series of contour lines converged in a small area. "This is it. It's a total anomaly in the scan. It represents a reflection pattern completely different from anything we've ever seen,—anywhere. All we know for sure is that it's very compact and very high density."

"Huh." Bandicut felt his temples start to throb with

guilt as he swallowed a dozen possible replies. "That's . . . interesting."

"Interesting?" Her eyes were alight like a child's on Christmas morning. "You bet it's interesting. It's especially interesting that it has *just* appeared, at a time when *our* activity is increasing in a nearby area. You want interesting? I think we really might have us a genuine—" She hesitated, suddenly looking abashed.

"What?" he asked, huskily.

"Well—we don't know yet, of course." Her eyes glinted as she sat back in her chair, finger to her cheek. "But we're going to find out, real soon."

"You are?" he croaked.

"See this?" She pointed to the area immediately surrounding the anomaly. "This is an underground cavern which apparently contains the object, or mass. It's not that deep, and we think there's a chance we could cut through and climb down in to have a look."

"Sounds—exciting," Bandicut stammered. "Of course, you never know about that sort of thing until you actually go look." He wondered why he was so dismayed. If someone had to find the translator, better it should be exoarch than the miners. At least they'd look at it before they tried to melt it down.

> /// *John—we dare not let*
> anyone *get to that translator—*
> *not until we're on our way.* ///

Bandicut hmph'd, though his heart was thumping anxiously. He hadn't said anything to the quarx about having made a decision to go.

"Well, we'll find out tomorrow. We have permission to go out and take surface readings." Julie suddenly made a face, corralling her enthusiasm. "But don't tell anyone," she said hastily. "I'm not even supposed to tell you. But I had an idea." She looked at him conspiratorially. "Do you suppose you could arrange to be the one to go out and do the survey? Georgia says you're more familiar with that area than anyone else.''

He bit his lip, at a loss for words.

/// It's an idea.
You might be able to sabotage the effort
for a day. ///

/I thought you said you wanted to get going. /

/// Well . . . that's true, too. ///

Bandicut cleared his throat, realizing that Julie was waiting for an answer. If he was still on Triton tomorrow, he would be going out on survey, anyway. "I could try," he said finally.

"Good! I see you have your cast off. Are you okay now?"

"Ah—yes!" he croaked. "Yes—I'm doing great."

She peered at him intently, with those penetrating blue eyes. "John? Are you *sure* you're all right? You seem—I don't know—upset. Or distracted."

He shook his head, but could not wipe the insipid busy-talking-to-an-alien grin from his face. "I just know," he managed, "that you invited me to dinner. And that it's about time we stopped talking about . . . alien artifacts . . . and started talking about . . . well, whatever." He blushed, but felt better when he saw an answering glimmer in her eye.

"Okay," she said. "Just let me put in a good word for you for tomorrow. If you'd really like to."

"Sure," he whispered. "I'd like that. A lot." He tried not to wince at the insincerity in his own voice.

★

Dinner in the cafeteria seemed as unromantic as ever, so they opted for sandwiches and beers in the lounge. Julie suggested a round of EineySteiney, but Bandicut's head already hurt with images of balls hurtling through Einsteinian fields. "Could we just talk, instead?" he asked nervously.

"Sure," she said, eyes laughing. "Imagine that! A man, wanting to just talk!"

"Aw, come on. We're not that bad, are we?"

"Well, you might yet qualify as a credit to your species. I'll let you know later." Julie took a bite of her club sandwich and said with a mischievous grin, "Want to see my holos, back in my place, after we eat?"

He smiled and didn't answer.

/// *Not now—please!*

Not when we have so much to— ///

/Go to hell,/ he thought cordially. /Tomorrow might be yours—but tonight is my own./ He grinned at Julie, and she returned it with her eyes.

✳

"Nice," he said, as her tiny compartment opened into a mountain vista, stark barren peaks at the summits, with caps of snow, and forested bases lying under blankets of white. The sky seemed infinitely deep overhead. "I like that. It's almost better than the VR room."

"You can't walk around in it, but this image is one of my favorite retreats," Julie said, settling into a cross-legged sitting position beside him on the bunk. She lifted his arm and placed it around her shoulders.

"Mm," he said, leaning back against the wall. He had her pillow tucked behind his back, but it was so small as to be useless against the hard wall. He decided to ignore the discomfort.

"Tell me what your favorite memories are of Earth," Julie murmured, gazing at the holo.

"Mm?" He swallowed uneasily. He imagined the question being asked after the Earth was destroyed, when the planet of his birth was only a memory.

"I mean, what do you think about when you think of Earth? What do you miss most? Where do you come from?" She hugged closer, still gazing at the snowy landscape.

"Ah. Well, I'm North American—"

"I know *that*!"

"Oh—well, let's see." He thought a moment, his tongue

feeling thick and awkward. "I grew up in Ohio, small factory town, couldn't wait to get out. I—fell in love with the Rocky Mountains the first time I saw them—just like this."

"Really? Me, too," Julie said, nodding against his shoulder.

"But . . . I never got to live near them, except for a few months in piloting school. I lived on the East Coast after school, until I shipped up to L5 City and got training in space piloting." The words brought back a surge of memories; he didn't think of his past very often, and when he did, it was like letting in a dizzying rush of air.

"What did your family think about your heading out into deep space?" she asked, turning to peer up into his eyes.

"Well—uh—" His eyes watered.

"Uh-oh, did I ask the wrong question?"

"No, no, I just—well, my family all died before—I mean, in the Chunnel collapse . . . the English Channel . . . ?"

"Oh," she sighed softly. "I'm sorry, John."

"It's okay, I'm over it now." He laughed falsely. "I still have a niece, back in Iowa."

She looked up again, and her blue eyes seemed dark and liquid and full of mystery and life. "Yes," she said, touching his nose with her finger. "I can see that you're over it." She smiled and settled back against his shoulder. "My parents *hated* the idea of my going to space. They said it would age me prematurely. They said it was too dangerous. They said there wouldn't be any decent men there." She chuckled softly. "What do you think? Were they right?"

"About the men? Definitely," Bandicut said, clearing his throat.

"Maybe most men," she admitted. "But there are a few—"

"Nah. Stay away from 'em. There's only one thing they want."

"Oh? And that is?" She looked up, wide-eyed.

"Er . . . to kiss your knuckles," he stammered. "Every

one of 'em. That's it. Anything else, they couldn't care less. Oh sure, they'll *tell* you they want your whole body, and even your mind, but knuckles is it. Take my word for it."

Eyebrows arched, she raised her hand and offered him her knuckles. He took her hand gently, and nibbled on the first joint of her middle finger. She giggled. "You said *kiss,* not nibble."

"Oh—sorry!" He took a breath, dizzy with desire. "I meant, nibble." He carefully kissed and nibbled all of the knuckles on her right hand. She hummed, laughing softly. When he was finished, she raised her left hand. "Knuckles?" he said. "Did I say knuckles? I meant . . . er, ears."

"Ohh." She carefully pulled back her hair and offered him an ear. He kissed it lightly.

"Ears?" he murmured. "I meant . . ."

"Mmm?" Her eyes widened, pupils dark and beautiful.

"Lips," he whispered, and moved to kiss her.

"That's what I thought," she said, touching his mouth with her fingertip, before kissing him suddenly. "Men," she said, after the first kiss.

"It's all we want," he whispered, and then they didn't say anything more.

Until the comm chimed.

They paused, looking at each other. His hand was poised over the front of her shirt. Julie started to giggle, then stopped. Bandicut shook his head, thinking, *it's never going to happen, is it?* Julie turned slightly to touch the buttons on the comm. She killed the sound, and activated the message receiver. "There," she murmured, turning back to him. Her eyes, her smile, her tousled hair dazzled him. "Now . . . tell me again what men want?" she sighed, touching his hair.

"I think you should tell me what women want," he murmured, touching her lips.

She pulled him down, a slow slide in the low gravity. "An honest man who knows how to treat knuckles," she murmured, kissing his hand and then his ear and then his mouth. "And ears. And . . . lips." His hand moved and settled on her right breast. "And . . . I think you've . . . mmmm . . ."

He was aware, as Julie pressed close to him and he smelled the warm musky scent of her arousal, of the quarx stirring unhappily in its corner of his mind. But if it said anything, he didn't listen, and he certainly didn't answer.

24

AFTERFUGUE

As THEY LAY together in silence afterward, he gazed over the contours of Julie's body, admiring the silhouette of her shoulder and arm and stomach against the flames of a holocampfire flickering beneath a tree canopy. He stroked her skin gently, touching the perspiration on her breasts, thinking that there was something magical about this moment that he would never feel again. Julie was still, her dark eyes gazing into the fire, only occasionally shifting to look at him. She touched his nose, smiled faintly, then turned to the fire again.

He felt the quarx coming out of hiding, like a frightened animal.

/// Is it safe? ///

Bandicut chuckled to himself. /Safe to look, but don't touch. What did you think of all those pheromones?/

/// Ugh . . . ///

Bandicut squinted into the fire. /If that's all you can say, you may return to your hiding place./

/// Well, you asked. ///

/Well, maybe I didn't really want to know. If you'd like to take the rest of the night off and get some sleep, I'll call you in the morning./

"Anything wrong?" Julie asked, her gaze shifting to study his eyes.

He shook his head as the quarx vanished back into seclusion. "Just a little internal dialogue I have every time I make love to a beautiful woman. Very boring stuff."

"I'll bet," she said, rolling toward him with a laugh. "You don't look bored to me." She reached down and stroked him, and he felt himself rising with unexpected excitement.

Not again! he heard a distant, muffled voice cry. Then the voice was gone, and he heard only his own heartbeat and Julie's murmurs as they pulled each other close once more.

✶

There was a frantic desperation to their lovemaking this time; and when it ended they fell, entwined together, into silence. Within minutes, Julie had fallen asleep, and he found himself alone with his thoughts, musing over the woman at his side.

Would he ever see her again? he wondered. He was astonished by how powerfully he felt drawn to her. The thing was, he genuinely liked her, and not just because of pheromones or hormones or raw animal passion. He liked the way she talked and walked, the excitement with which she seized upon thoughts, the way her eyes blazed, the way she looked when she made love. When was the last time he had felt that way about a woman? Maybe never. It was a wonderfully satisfying feeling—and it was about to be ripped from him, probably forever, if he did what Charlie asked. What would Julie think, if she learned that the man she had just made love to had, hours later, gone out and stolen a multimillion-dollar spacecraft, in some insane messianic pursuit? Would he return a hero or a criminal? Would he return at all? He wondered if Charlie even cared about the price that he would be paying for this crazy mission . . .

This mission to save the Earth.

He felt a disjointed sense of urgency, as he was brought back to the decision he had to make. It was almost as if the quarx had reminded him with a stern warning; but it wasn't the quarx's voice, it was his own. He knew that if he didn't make his decision tonight, it might be too late to make it at all. How far did he trust the quarx? What he had seen of the translator's powers suggested that it all could be true, and probably was.

But what if . . . Charlie were lying, for some unfathomable reason? What possible motive could he have for tricking Bandicut into stealing a ship? To get to Earth? There were easier ways to do that. Besides, Charlie wasn't even talking about flying *to* Earth, merely to its defense, on the far side of the sun.

No, the lying scenario just didn't make sense. Even as he contemplated it, he waited for the quarx to leap forward with an indignant defense. When he heard only silence, he grunted to himself and turned his head to study Julie's sleeping form again, silhouetted against the flickering flames. What a thing to think about, so soon after making love! But there was no stopping the train of thought; Charlie had set it in motion, and there would be no stopping it until he had made his decision. But it seemed unlike the quarx not to be right there trying to convince him.

Still there was no response—and in fact, no stirring of the being at all. Charlie seemed to have completely isolated himself, leaving Bandicut to work things out for himself. Which was okay, except that with Julie asleep, it seemed a little lonely just now. Lonely . . .

Just himself and the flames, flickering . . .

And EineySteiney balls careening through space, and colliding, and flames consuming them . . .

He felt the silence-fugue creeping over him like a whispering fog, obscuring his vision of the world that lay before him, and superimposing another view, a sense of invisible shapes and presences and forces. He felt a great awareness of *gravity,* of the shaping of space by the presence of mass and gravimetric fields; he felt as though he were *becoming* space, his mind and spirit stretching out into emptiness, but that emptiness was being warped and twisted by the presence of objects hurtling through it. Then, moments later, he felt himself transformed into one of the objects, a comet, and ahead of him now was the fantastic blue and green and white form of the Earth, and he was plummeting toward it . . . there was no stopping him, the Earth was growing, swelling before him . . . he saw death rising up to greet him like a leering specter, not just his own death, but the death of a planet's civilization . . .

The feeling of horror within him swelled like the Earth, until he could no longer breathe—

And then the fugue-nightmare snapped away, and he was floating in darkness, gasping for breath. A broad array of information slowly came into focus surrounding him. Elements of it gleamed faintly in the darkness like toy soldiers creeping silently out of hiding in the night to surround and capture him. His heart beat rapidly, anxiously, until he realized what it was. It was a summation, awaiting his inspection.

He had warned the quarx not to trouble him about it anymore tonight, and Charlie had obligingly vanished inward. But he had left behind the answers to many of the questions that Bandicut might ask, if he were of a mind to.

He wanted to flee, to avoid the questions. But he was penned in by an army of information: gleaming datapoints that revealed the evolution of the quarx's plan. He saw, without real comprehension, the threading of space that would speed him across the solar system; and he saw the breathtaking simplicity of the translator's power to intercept the comet and destroy it. He even saw the numbers, the probability that the maneuver would cost him his life, the one-in-two chance that he would buy Earth's life with his own. And he saw what was perhaps the greatest uncertainty in the plan: the actual theft of the ship, because that involved human unknowns that even the quarx and his translator's science could not clearly fathom.

Not for the first time, he found himself wondering, what's in this for Charlie? Why does he care so much? Why's he willing to take this risk for Earth?

And the questions floated away over a windswept plain, and he caught glimpses of Charlie's past lives like luminous ghosts in the night, trying to help hosts with whom Charlie had found himself partnered. And he glimpsed Charlie himself at times wondering, how did this come to pass? There again was that murky sense of loss in Charlie's past, the sense that he was somehow in search of . . . what? Answers? Redemption?

Bandicut felt a heady, rushing dizziness as the fugue-images vanished back into the darkness; and he struggled for breath again, and found a moment of quiet and peace, a feeling that he was floating on calm, lapping waters in the gentle darkness. He gathered his thoughts there, thinking of Earth, thinking of obligations and responsibility, thinking of young Dakota hunched over edu-sims beyond her age level because she so desperately wanted to go to space, thinking of a rain of death that only he had the power to stop. And he thought of Julie, with a bitter ache, almost wishing that he were angry with her instead of feeling what he felt, because if he were angry, it would be so much easier to leave . . .

＊

His eyes opened, as the last waters of the fugue ebbed away. His gaze drifted from the ceiling, to the fire, to Julie's partially naked form. And he knew, not logically, but in his heart, that the quarx was telling the truth and that he had, really, no choice.

For a few moments, he just gazed at Julie and let his troubled feelings revolve through his mind. Finally he sat up and climbed carefully over her to stand beside the bunk. He checked his pants pocket and made sure that Charlie's stones were still there; then he went to Julie's comm terminal and began quietly typing.

✳

"*. . . I am telling you all this because I desperately want someone to know the truth of what I have done. And because I trust you more than I trust anyone on this godforsaken moon—or maybe anywhere else, for that matter. And because . . . I'm so sorry that I have to leave this way. Julie . . . If only I had time to know you better, I think I might just . . .*" What? Fall in love?

He hesitated, trying to decide how to finish. He didn't want to sound like an idiot, after all. Was it just infatuation, or need, or was what he felt the beginnings of the real thing? Anyway, he was leaving, perhaps forever, so what difference did it make if he made a fool of himself? A stray thought occurred to him and he wondered, if Charlie could still communicate with the translator, whether it might be possible to arrange somehow for Julie to be the one whom the translator allowed to find it. It would be nice if he could leave her that much as a parting gift, at least.

Finally he typed: "*. . . well, I think a lot of things, and there's no time now to tell you about it all. Too little time, too little. Please trust me, even if you're shocked—even if you're angry. You can tell anyone you want, after I'm gone. Please be well, Julie. And do go and find that alien device! It's out there! Love, John.*"

He felt that it was a pretty ineffectual close, but he couldn't think how to say it better. He saved the letter to Julie's private files and tagged it to be sent to her on the day after tomorrow. He was tempted to let her see it sooner—it tortured him to think of keeping the secret from her even that long—but he didn't dare. Julie might wonder, for a day, just what sort of monster she had slept with, but she would find out soon enough. He hoped his explanation would salvage her opinion of him.

He gazed down at her and ached to climb back into the bunk, to wake her, to make love to her again. Reluctantly, instead, he answered the powerful urge that was building somewhere deep inside him, an urge that he had no doubt was a signal from the quarx. With a sigh, he picked up his clothes and began to dress. Julie stirred in her sleep and mumbled something inaudible to him. He bent and whispered, "I have to go now. I have urgent things to do." He kissed her on the forehead, and her eyelids fluttered for a moment. "I think you're wonderful," he whispered, so softly he could scarcely hear his own voice. And before his resolve could vanish altogether, he straightened and hurried from her room.

On his way to the comm booth off the lounge, he spoke to the quarx with mounting anxiety. /All right. Now please tell me—how do you propose to steal this ship?/

Charlie had given no indication of his conscious presence for some time now, and several seconds passed before he responded to Bandicut's question. When he did speak, it was in a distant whisper, as though he had buried himself so completely that he had to call up out of a great depth.

/// I am pleased by your decision.
We must use the datanet,
and hope that it is restored enough
to do what we must do. ///

Bandicut nodded. That much he had assumed already.

/// First we must
change your job assignment
to Triton Orbital Station.
Then we must look carefully into the
scheduling of ships . . . ///

/What, are we going to get ourselves a reserved seat?/ Bandicut asked doubtfully, adjusting the headset on his temples.

/// Something like that, ///
Charlie murmured, and as he spun out the connection to the gleaming points of energy in the neurolink, he seemed to Bandicut to be humming with anticipation.

25

FINAL PREPARATIONS

THE MORNING CAME too soon, and not soon enough. Bandicut woke up restless and nervous, at once wishing he had spent the night with Julie, and wanting to get on with Charlie's scheme before he lost his nerve altogether.

/// You still have the stones? ///
Charlie asked, as Bandicut dressed.

He felt in his pants pockets and drew out the three tiny stones: a glinting ruby, a tiny coruscating diamond, a fleck of coal. /Okay?/

/// Okay. ///

Bandicut replaced the stones in his pocket, and suddenly felt lightheaded as he realized: I am leaving Triton today. I am going to attempt to steal a spaceship. /I suppose I should pack a bag./

/// Okay.
But travel light. ///

He scratched behind his ear. /What time's the shuttle leave?/

/// Oh-eight-hundred.
That doesn't give us much time. ///

Bandicut grabbed his travel duffel and stuffed it with clothes. He hesitated, thinking of Julie, and felt a large lump forming in his throat. He felt an urgent nudge from Charlie—quickly tossed in some books, holos, and other personals, without sorting. He paused in midmotion, remembering last night. He wished that there were some way . . . but no. /Charlie,/ he murmured almost plaintively, /is there *any* chance we'll . . . make it back here?/ He already knew the answer.

The quarx seemed to draw a deep breath, and seemed very far away as it answered,

> /// *The chances are . . . slight, John.*
> *I wish I could say otherwise.*
> *I will miss the translator, too, you know.*
> *But it is the sacrifice we must—* ///

/Okay, okay,/ Bandicut muttered in annoyance. /You don't have to go on and on about it, for Chrissake./ He zipped his bag and blinked a few times, trying to clear his eyes. He turned away from his bunk.

"Hey, Bandie, what is this?" Krackey demanded, walking into the room, waving his hands in dismay. He pointed to the duffel bag. "You aren't leaving, are you?"

"I, ah . . . actually, yes," Bandicut stammered. He thought frantically. He'd hoped he wouldn't meet anyone else he knew on his way out. "I'm glad I . . . didn't miss you, Krackey. I just got new orders. They're shipping me right off for some orbital work—Lord knows why." He tried to grin, and felt the effort failing.

"C'mon, Bandie. I saw the orders on the system board this morning, too," Krackey said. "Obviously it's a screwup. Did you talk to anyone in person?"

"No, but—"

"Well, check it out before you go all the way up, man!"

"Well, I can't just—" Bandicut's breath caught. "I mean, it's—" He felt his face reddening. /HELP!/

> /// *I don't know . . .* ///

Krackey scrutinized his face, as though wondering at Bandicut's mental competency. "Let *me* check into it, Bandie. Hell, here you are just getting back into the groove. I'll bet I can straighten this out in no time. I mean, what would Cole Jackson do without you?''

Groaning silently, Bandicut turned away.

''Bandie, come on! Let me fix it for you! The datanet's still screwed up, that's all. If you take the shuttle upstairs, you're just going to have to come right back down.''

''Krackey,'' he said, mustering the only excuse he could think of, ''I'm sure you're right. I'll probably be back here tomorrow, and we'll all be laughing about it.'' He gestured casually. ''So, I'm going to have a holiday in orbit, for a day! One mokin' day! Don't you ever want a change of scenery?''

Krackey's face changed from a look of bewilderment to one of suspicion. Suddenly he grinned wolfishly. ''Why, Bandie, you old son of a gun—you didn't *rig* this to give yourself a day off in orbit, did you?''

''For God's sake! No, I didn't *rig* the thing!'' Bandicut protested. ''I wouldn't know how, even if I wanted to.''

Krackey grunted and eyed him doubtfully. ''Well, I believe you. But if you *were* to try something like that, lemme just tell you, you'd get yourself in some pretty deep shit.''

Bandicut shrugged, wanting desperately to leave the room before he erupted with any more lies.

''Oh well, enjoy yourself.'' Krackey clapped him on the shoulder and chortled.

''Yeah. Say, look—Krackey.'' Bandicut swallowed, realizing that he was about to say good-bye to Krackey for the last time. He started to stretch out his hand, but quelled the impulse. ''Listen, if anything—well, what I mean is—you take care, okay?''

Krackey peered at him oddly. ''Yeah, I'll take care. You just get back down here soon.''

Nodding, Bandicut picked up his duffel and hurried from the room. /Charlie, I hope I don't run into anyone else. I don't think I can stand it./

/// Let's just hope you don't run into Julie, ///
the quarx said, naming the one person Bandicut desperately hoped he *would* run into.
/// I sense your feelings.
I don't think it would be good for you to see her. ///
/Why not?/ he demanded.
/// I'm not sure you could handle it.
We might never make it off Triton. ///
/Give me some credit, will you?/ Bandicut retorted, knowing full well that the quarx was right. And yet, as he strode down the corridor, he realized that he intended to see Julie one more time anyway, risk or no risk.
/// John, no—it wouldn't be wise! ///
/Tough,/ Bandicut said, glancing both ways in the empty corridor before heading toward the lower-level dorm section. He paused at the bulkhead door where Julie had said good-night to him with a discreet kiss, just the day before yesterday (or had it been years ago, which was what it felt like?). He pushed through the door, stopped at Julie's room, hesitated, and rapped three times. He heard the sound of someone stumbling on the other side of the privacy-curtain.

"Who is it?" said a sleepy-sounding voice.

"It's Band—John," he stammered.

"Bad John?" The voice sounded slightly more awake.

"It's *John.* Can I see you?" He was trembling, afraid that someone might come walking along and see him in the corridor, afraid that he had made a terrible mistake coming back here, afraid that he wouldn't have the courage to leave.

The curtain opened, and Julie stood before him in a thin bathrobe, her hair tousled, her eyes red with sleep. "You left," she said, squinting. "I hate it when men do that."

He swallowed and nodded. "May I . . . come in?"

He couldn't read her expression as she stepped aside and closed the door behind him. Then he realized that she was staring at the duffel bag in his hand. "Are you going somewhere?" she asked, puzzled. He nodded silently, unable to trust his voice. "Ah," she said and peered at him with those blazing eyes. He felt pinned, like a butterfly to a mount. "You *were here last night,* weren't you?" she asked suspiciously. He nodded again. "I wasn't imagining that, in some crazy dream?" He shook his head, trying to laugh to break the tension, but he couldn't; he was afraid of what might come out instead. His face felt frozen like a block of ice, unable to convey any expression.

She nodded. "And it was . . . *good.* Right?" Her eyes and the corner of her mouth were twitching, as though trying to decide what it was she was feeling.

He glanced longingly at her bunk, wishing he could climb back into it with her. *"Yeah,"* he said hoarsely. "It was . . . good. *Real* good. But I've . . . just been ordered up to Triton Orbital. Today. I might be gone a while. I . . . oh moke, I wish I . . . ."

"Didn't have to go?" she asked.

He nodded numbly. She was still trying to decide whether to laugh or to be sad or angry, he thought. He didn't know how to help her.

Julie nodded to herself. "That's the usual line, isn't it? Usually, though, I don't drive men to pack their bags and leave the fucking *planet.* What about the survey run today? Who'd they give it to?"

"I don't know. And it's not a planet, anyway, it's a moon," he said, cracking a smile.

"Oh, excuse *me*—"

"And Julie—it's not a line, and I don't usually . . . do this, either. I'm sorry about the survey run. But I'm more sorry about—well—you know." He felt his face burning.

"No, I don't know." She peered at his blushing face and said in a hurt voice, "What aren't you saying?"

"I'm sorry about *us,*" he croaked.

"Us," she echoed. She nodded, as though completing a

mental readjustment. "Well, it's not as if we've *known* each other all that long, when you get right down to it. So we shouldn't have any expectations—right?"

"No, but I—I really—" As he hesitated, she tugged her robe more snugly around her, which only made him want her all the more. "I really thought we might—I mean, I'd hoped we—"

"Yeah," she murmured, shrugging. "Me too."

/// John! ///

His voice caught. He sighed and changed the subject. "Well, look, I—I really hope you—find something out there. On the plain, I mean. I hope it makes you famous. But I have to get . . . going, and . . ." He swallowed hard, then dropped his bag and opened his arms, and after a heart-beat's hesitation, she moved reluctantly into his embrace. She suddenly surrendered to whatever she was holding back and hugged herself to his chest. They were both trembling, and he squeezed her, as if that would somehow stop it.

"Who are you leaving me for, really?" she whispered finally, looking up into his eyes.

The lump in his throat grew larger. "An alien," he whispered back.

She nodded, and hugged him again. "Figures. Why do men always do this to me?" He felt himself growing hard against her, and knew that she felt it, too.

"What, leave you for aliens?" he croaked.

"Yeah."

Clearing his throat, he muttered, "I, uh—don't know how long I'll be there, I was just told to pack a bag. I don't even know—" he hesitated "—just exactly what I'm going to be doing there." Which wasn't *exactly* a lie.

"How like a man," she said, with a hoarse laugh. "Couldn't you have appealed the assignment? Told them you had this hot new love affair?"

"I *wish*," he said honestly. "But look—I'll—"

"Write?"

He chuckled, trying to break the spell of gloom. "Yeah, I'll write. Guaranteed. I'll send you word when I know—" he swallowed "—when I'll be back."

"Okay, sure." She squinted, studying him. "You really had no idea, before this? You weren't just . . . holding off telling me? So you could have a little fling?"

His face burned again as he shook his head. "I . . . knew there was a *chance* I'd be reassigned. But I didn't know when, and it . . . wasn't posted until today."

She drew back from him, perhaps sensing the lie. "Does this have anything to do with our find?" she asked suspiciously.

He shook his head vigorously. "No," he whispered. Not with *your* finding it, anyway.

/// John, damn it—we have to go!
The shuttle! ///

He didn't answer the quarx. He didn't know what to say to Julie. He only knew that he had blown it totally now, and he wanted somehow to make amends to her before he left. "Julie, it's really true—"

"I believe you," she sighed. "I guess maybe you should get going, huh?"

"I—"

"You're just making it harder, you know. I mean, it's not as if you're going away forever, right?"

"R-right. Good . . . bye, Julie." He bent to pick up his bag, then dropped it and seized her in another hug before she could back away again. She was shaking as he held her. He felt her body, awkward against him, and her hair in his face. "I . . . really meant it . . . when I said I wished I didn't have to go," he said thickly. "I *will* send word."

"Okay," she said, reaching up to touch his cheek. She pulled her hand away and smiled. "Bye," she murmured.

"Bye." He picked up his bag and fled from her room.

★

"Bandie, where are you off to?"

He nearly cried. He was twenty feet from the airlock leading to the shuttle boarding tube. Turning, he saw Georgia Patwell. "New assignment," he called. "Up at Orbital."

She looked puzzled. "Does Julie know this? And how about Cole Jackson? I thought he was expecting you—"

"Georgia, I gotta run! I'll see you later!" Cringing, he turned and ran for the shuttle.

"Bandie?" Her voice trailed off, and he sensed her bewilderment, and could imagine her shrugging and walking away as he entered the lock. He rested his forehead against the bulkhead and prayed that no one else would see him.

/// You're almost there. ///

/I'm not even close./

/// I didn't think you were going to make it . . .
from Julie's, I mean. ///

/I'd rather not talk about Julie right now, if you don't mind./

/// I'm sorry. I really am.
Let's get on that shuttle. ///

He nodded and hurried through the passenger tube to the waiting spacecraft.

★

Liftoff was abrupt, and momentarily jarring, until the shuttle settled into smooth acceleration into orbit around the moon. He got only the briefest glimpse of the ground complex, and tried but failed to identify the general location of the alien cavern, before the landscape turned out of sight past the edge of the window. He felt himself breathing a little hard under the .7 gee of acceleration, and realized how delinquent he had been in keeping up his exercise program.

He was the only passenger on the shuttle, and was outnumbered by the crew. He recognized the male copilot by sight from his first arrival at Neptune orbit, but the pilot was a hard-eyed woman, unfamiliar to him. He avoided meeting their eyes; the last thing he wanted was a conversation. He stared out the window, as though he might never see the surface of Triton again, with its cratered plains of nitrogen and methane and its tiny plumes of carbon. He tried to imagine what this moon must have looked like twenty or thirty million years ago, or whenever it was that Charlie had ridden it into orbit around Neptune. He sensed that the thought stirred old, and painful, memories for the quarx.

/// We have to plan our next move. ///
Charlie said abruptly.

/Okay./

/// I've never stolen a ship before.
I'm counting on our being able to alter flight orders
to give us the diversion we need. ///

Bandicut moved his head, trying unsuccessfully to catch more than a glimpse of Neptune, as the shuttle rolled in a course-change maneuver. /If you're looking to me for advice, you've come to the wrong place. I thought you knew what you were doing in the datanet last night./

/// Well, I've isolated two ships
that appear to have the energy capacity
and life support that we need. ///

/That's a good start./

/// And I hope I've figured out
how to rig the departure control . . . ///

Bandicut sat back in his seat and closed his eyes. /You don't sound all that confident, partner. I thought you had this planned./

/// I do.
Just remember, when you steal the spacesuit—
transfer the red stone to your outer pocket. ///

Bandicut swallowed. /Now I'm stealing a spacesuit, too?/ He pressed his hand against his pocket, feeling the small stones. /Why don't I just pick a ship that's hooked up to a boarding tunnel?/

*/// You have to go outside, anyway,
to throw that stone into the engine exhaust port. ///*
Bandicut took a breath. /Say that again?/
*/// I'll explain when we get there.
Now, as soon as we dock,
make a beeline for the closest neurojack input.
Meanwhile, maybe you should rest up
while you can. ///*
Eyes closed, Bandicut shook his head in bewilderment.
It didn't matter how unreal this felt to him; he was sure it
would become even stranger before it was all over.

26

TRITON ORBITAL

HE GOT ONLY a momentary glimpse of the station, before a wall came up alongside, blocking the view. Docking took just a few minutes: some thumping and jostling, and a metallic clang, followed by a hiss of air. He unbuckled his seat belt and floated toward the baggage compartment, trying to get his zero-gee legs under him. /I should have brought some spacesickness pills,/ he thought, suddenly intensely aware of his stomach.

/// If it's vestibular disorientation,
I may be able to help
with neural feedback signals. ///

For an instant, he felt twice as dizzy and nearly threw up. As quickly as it came, the feeling cleared. /Okay, that's good,/ he gasped. /Don't do anything more./ He opened the compartment and gave his duffel bag a tug, then shoved its weightless mass ahead of him toward the exit hatch.

He drifted down the mating tube into the station, grateful for the lack of passenger amenities, which meant there weren't a lot of people around asking embarrassing questions. Still, he had to ask directions to the nearest comm-center with neurojack inputs. If the loading officer who pointed the way thought his question odd, she didn't say anything; she merely looked puzzled by the frantic urgency that he was undoubtedly radiating. He sailed awkwardly into a booth, wrestling his bag in behind him. Closing the door, he paused to take a few deep breaths, realizing that he had let his adrenaline get away from him. Better to go slow than to create attention.

It took only a few seconds to connect with the station datanet and locate the traffic schedules. Charlie showed him specs on two ships presently docked which he had identified as possibilities. One was named *Orion,* a large interplanetary transport. According to the listing, it was scheduled to depart in-system for Mars, twenty-three days from now. The other was a planetary surveyor, *Neptune Explorer,* which was scheduled to leave in four days on a much shorter run, a series of research orbits around Neptune proper, before returning several weeks later to Triton Orbital.

/// Which one do you recommend we take? ///

Bandicut blinked. /Is that a rhetorical question? I don't see how we can get either of them. But if you must dream, then I'd go for the big one. At least it's made for interplanetary flight./

/// Hm.
It may be less practical. ///

/Charlie, the whole damn *idea* is impractical!/

/// You know what I mean.
The problem with Orion *is that*
it's not fueled and provisioned yet.
Also, it'd probably be
harder to get away with. ///

/May I point out that the other one isn't even designed for a long voyage? It probably doesn't have the necessary stores, and it certainly doesn't have the fuel range or power!/

/// All that, I think, we can finesse.
It's designed for a crew of six,
and life support supplies are already on board.

If they allowed a decent reserve,
that should give us enough. ///

Bandicut felt his eyebrow twitch. /What about propulsion?/

/// The least of our problems.
The red daughter-stone will convert
the energy of your reaction-rocket
into translational threading potential. ///

His eyebrows twitched harder.

/// Never mind—you'll see.
But that's why we have to introduce the stone
into the exhaust outlet.
All we need is for your powerplant to provide
a reliable source of high-temperature heat. ///

/It can do that, all right,/ Bandicut answered numbly. /Listen, if you've already thought of everything, why bother to ask my opinion?/

/// I'm sure I haven't *thought*
of everything. ///

/Oh. Well, have you planned how we're going to pull off the actual heist?/

/// I think so, yes.
Watch. ///

A schematic appeared, displaying the movements of all spacecraft in the vicinity. The survey craft was highlighted, along with two tugs that had just finished guiding it from the fueling depot to a tether-stop near the station's departure dock, where a boarding tube would soon be attached. Several other vessels were in motion nearby—two shuttles undocking and a third, a supply ship, approaching from higher orbit. As Bandicut studied the array, wondering what Charlie had in mind, he noticed the stream of messages going out from Docking & Traffic Control. He felt a sudden rush of fear. Was Charlie proposing to . . . he wasn't thinking of interfering with the safe movement of local spacecraft traffic, was he?

Bandicut began to protest, but he felt the quarx's reassurance. Okay, he thought. This must just be a demo simulation. Let it play out and we'll see what he's planning.

The two local shuttles were moving in accordance with the instructions from DTC. One maneuvered outward, into a higher orbit, while the other dropped down away from the station toward Triton. On the far side of the station, the supply ship was approaching, coming from higher orbit toward dock, closing with the forward part of the station as it matched velocity. The supply ship and the outbound shuttle pilots could not possibly have seen each other through the station; it was the role of DTC to keep them separated. But Charlie was proposing to alter the control instructions. Bandicut felt his stomach turning, and it wasn't the weightlessness.

/Charlie, you can't do that!/ he yelled, as the two vessels emerged from opposite sides of the station. He must have yelled just as the pilots of the two ships got their first clear view of each other. And at that moment he realized with a shock that this was no simulation.

/// We need the distraction.
I've calculated it to keep it gentle. ///

/Gentle!/ Bandicut watched in horror as the two vessels maneuvered in an effort to avoid a collision. Emergency calls were already flashing out on the voice channels. But it was too late—the ships came together like pieces of driftwood in a glancing blow, clung for a few moments, then parted again—the smaller of the two spinning slowly. In the image, the collision was silent and schematic. But Bandicut could imagine the impact, the grinding of hull upon hull, the whistle of escaping air. /What have you done? CHARLIE, WHAT HAVE YOU DONE!/

The neurolink showed him: emergency telemetry, damage reports, voice commands overriding the flawed DTC datastream, tugs changing course and diverting to the aid of the stricken vessels. What about injuries?

/// *We're all set,* ///

Charlie barked.

/// *Get going and*
grab a spacesuit from the EVA dock. ///

Bandicut exploded. /What do you mean, we're all set? Do you know what you've just done? You son of a bitch, you can't DO that to people! Charlie, you son of a bitch—/

/// *I wanted to run a sim on it first,*
but there was no time.
We HAD to do it for real. ///

/You bastard, you can't—/

/// *John, we NEED THAT SHIP!*
There's no time to discuss this— ///

/No time—?/ he choked, running out of words. He felt sick. It was not just Charlie who had caused the collision; it was John Bandicut who was linked to the datanet. If they tracked the cause, which the system was probably doing right now, it would be John Bandicut who would be named, Bandicut who would be nailed. /Christ, Charlie!/ he whispered.

/// *John—DISCONNECT!* ///

Everything shifted, and he saw another schematic, the datanet searching backward for the source of the altered DTC commands. The lines of the search were leading toward this comm booth, despite Charlie's efforts to misdirect it. /Damn you!/ He broke the connection and yanked the headset off and stared, disbelieving, at the comm board, as though he expected it to erupt with lights and sirens.

Charlie flashed an image in his head: directions from the comm booth to the Extravehicular Activity suit-up area.

/// *GO!* ///

He went, clutching his duffel bag to his chest as he pushed off from one wall after another, sailing down the intersecting corridors to the suit-up area. /I can't believe it, Charlie. I can't believe you did that!/ He was in despair as he found the EVA room.

/// It was the only way.
Now, listen—you need to grab a suit.
Pretend you're part of the damage control team.
And be ready to do what I say,
without hesitation. ///
/Why the hell should I—?/
/// You're got to trust me.
Please, John! ///

He had no answer. He had trusted the quarx this far, and it was a little late in the game for second thoughts.

The suit-up area was in chaos. At least a dozen men and women were frantically trying to get outside to render emergency assistance. People were shouting back and forth, and no one paid any attention to Bandicut as he crammed his bag into a locker and made his way through the confusion to the stores. He grabbed at the racks for a spacesuit close to his size and floated back to the locker with it. He dressed facing the locker, hoping that his presence would continue to go unnoticed—not just by the workers, but by the safety-and-security cameras on the walls.

"Hey—come 'ere a second, will you?"

He turned his head cautiously. The man just to his right was floating perpendicular to him, helmet in his hands. He was talking to Bandicut. Hooking a thumb over his shoulder, he pointed at his life-support pack and said, "Check my stats, will you? My readouts aren't working, and I don't have time to screw around with it. Just tell me if I have two hours' worth."

Grunting nervously, Bandicut floated up over the man's left shoulder, opened the direct readout panel, and squinted at the tiny green numbers displayed there. "Yeah," he said finally. "You look okay for . . . well, if you aren't a big oxygen pusher, maybe two and three-quarters hours." He floated back to his locker.

"Thanks." The man started to turn away—but another

man, lanky and sharp featured even in his partially donned spacesuit, appeared over the first man's shoulder. The name "Jensen" was stenciled on his suit; he looked like a foreman or supervisor.

"Hold it," Jensen said, staring at Bandicut with penetratingly dark eyes. "Lemme double-check that." He held Bandicut in his gaze, as if to say to the other man, *Do you know this guy?* Then he performed the same check that Bandicut had. "Yeah, you're okay."

The first man shrugged, clamped his helmet on, and pushed off for the airlock. The one named Jensen glared at Bandicut for a moment longer. "You're new here." Bandicut nodded without answering; he didn't trust his voice. "Well, if you don't know what you're doing out there, stay the hell out of the way of the people who do." Without waiting for an answer, Jensen turned away to finish his own suiting up.

Bandicut followed him uneasily with his eyes. Jensen's suspicions were totally justified; he and Charlie were responsible for all of this. If anyone died out there . . .

/// Quit thinking and
get your fr'deekin' suit on, John!
We're doing this to save lives,
remember that! ///

/Tell it to the crews who are out there twisting in vacuum,/ he thought darkly, pulling his suit on with deliberate speed.

/// Hopefully, no one's seriously hurt. ///

/Hopefully,/ Bandicut said acidly.

/// Don't forget to put the red stone
in your outer pocket.
In fact, put all three in. ///

Bandicut frowned and reached inside his suit's zippered opening to fish the tiny daughter-stones out of his pants pocket. He stared at them for a moment, wondering how he could carry them in a large utility pocket without losing them, especially when he would be fumbling for them with gloved hands.

> /// *Just stick them in and*
> *ask them to stay put.* ///

Bandicut popped them into his spacesuit pocket. /Stay./ He raised his eyes and saw Jensen watching him. Turning back to his locker, he tried to ignore the stare.

By the time he was suited, most of the ready room had cleared out, except for Jensen. Bandicut tried to avoid meeting the man's eyes, but as he finished his checklist and crouched to push off for the airlock, Jensen called out, "Hey, you—stop for a buddy check!"

> /// *What now?* ///

Bandicut hesitated. "Right," he said, and swung himself toward Jensen. He turned to present his back to the man, thinking, *Don't interfere with me, damn you.*

"Okay," he heard. "Remember what I said."

"Right," he repeated, and launched himself toward the lock. When he reached the airlock door, he punched the cycling button and flipped himself into the chamber even as the door was sliding open. He did not intend to look back, but as he caught a handhold and swung around to punch the inside airlock control, he found himself gazing back through the window into the ready room. Jensen was watching him with a scowl. Past Jensen's head was the gleaming eye of the safety-cam.

The airlock cycle seemed endless. The outer door opened onto vacuum, and at that instant he remembered his duffel bag in the locker. /Charlie! My bag!/

> /// *Leave it.*
> *You can't go back.* ///

/But it has everything I own!/

Charlie's voice grew more urgent.

> /// *You can't go back!*
> *NO TIME!* ///

He knew Charlie was right—but that didn't make him

feel any less miserable as he launched himself out into space.

/// Straight out.
Then left about forty degrees
and up thirty.
You have thruster control on this thing? ///
/Yeah./ He was rotating slowly as he emerged from the airlock. "Suit control—give me attitude stability and thruster control at the right wrist." He felt the thrusters popping, stopping his rotation, and he bent his wrist slightly to the left as he drifted out past the end of the station wall. The thrusters flared and he yawed, and he pointed with his index finger and the thrusters jetted him forward.

Ahead was an array of vessels, some clamped to docking ports on the side of the station, others tethered at in-between points. Most of them had once gleamed white and gold and silver, but were now smudged and weathered with age. As he scanned around to his right, he spotted—at a distance of perhaps a kilometer—the diversion that Charlie had created. The two damaged ships were surrounded by a cluster of tugs. Suited workers were crossing over to the site like flying insects. It was impossible to judge from here the seriousness of the collision. He was tempted to listen in on the comm, but felt a strong opposing urgency from Charlie. Too distracting, too much to do.

/// That medium-sized ship, John—
just beyond the container ship. ///
Bandicut nodded without answering, coasting through the weightless silence of space. He veered past the cargo carrier, then on toward the survey ship. He could see a part of the name *Neptune Explorer* stenciled on its aft section. It had a configuration like a squashed hatbox, with modest-sized engines on the end nearest to Bandicut. It was tethered, not hard docked. /What do I do when we get there?/

/// Get behind it. Float
right up to the nozzles of its main engines. ///

Bandicut grunted. Charlie's instructions ran contrary to all of his instincts for safe operation around a live spacecraft. What if those engines came to life without warning? He didn't even have his comm on. Nevertheless, he aimed for the point that Charlie requested. He was a little rusty at zero-gee maneuvering, and in his haste he overshot, braking frantically, then had to coax himself back with slow, careful bursts on the thrusters. In the meantime he sensed Charlie's urgency growing. /What's the matter?/ He came to a stop directly in front of one exhaust bell of the fusion drive. /You're making me nervous./

/// Sorry.
That guy in the ready room
made me nervous. ///

/Why, do you think he's following us?/ Bandicut started to rotate to look, but felt Charlie's desire that he desist. No time for distractions. He peered instead into the dark muzzle of the fusion rocket.

/// Forget him—even if he is following.
Now, take the red stone out of your pocket. ///

He reached blindly into his waist pouch with a gloved hand. /How am I supposed to find the red one? You better hope they don't float away./

/// Ask for it.
Now take your hand out of your pocket. ///

Bandicut withdrew his gloved hand. Stuck to the tip of his middle finger was a point of ruby light. It was larger now, and pulsing visibly with some kind of internal energy. He wiggled his finger, but the stone seemed glued to it. /I'll be dipped in—/

/// Throw the stone into the rocket engine. ///

/Wait. It's stuck to—/

/// Just do it. ///

He drew his arm back, and made a flinging gesture, trying to flick the stone loose with his thumb. It remained stuck to his finger. He held it up to his visor. /It isn't coming loose./

/// Don't try to flick it.
Just pitch it like a ball. ///

He pitched it. The stone twinkled and flashed, and sailed from his finger, straight into the empty chamber of the rocket engine. For an instant, it seemed to hang in the center of the chamber, a tiny light straining to cast illumination in the dark space. Then it flashed out a series of sharp red beams, thin spikes of light spinning out to probe, in microsecond bursts, every shape and surface within the rocket chamber.

Bandicut's heart skipped. Before he could ask what was happening, a gout of fire erupted from the stone. He stifled an outcry, raising an arm involuntarily to shield himself. But the light was already subsiding, and he lowered his arm to see the tiny stone now the size of a basketball. It glowed with a self-contained fire that reminded him of the nerve-wrenching energies he'd glimpsed in the translator.

He looked away, blinking. But out of the corner of his eye, he had an impression of the fire unfolding, like the petals of a flower. As he looked back, the sphere turned to liquid light and began streaming out along the inner surface of the chamber. It flowed in a great wave. He had a sense that the engine and even the spaceship itself had become translucent for an instant, the wave of light flashing from stern to bow, then vanishing. When it was over, the ruby-stone was gone, but *something* remained, a twinkling and pulsing presence high in the throat of the rocket. He stared at it dumbly.

/// That's it, John.
Let's go. ///

/Go where?/ he asked faintly.

/// To the nearest airlock.
That would be . . . uh,

*at two o'clock,
right around the stern. ///*

Bandicut moved slowly, too stunned to concentrate on the quarx's directions. A wink of light in the upper right corner of his vision prompted him. He pointed with wrist and finger and jetted around the stern of the ship, then forward along the side facing away from the station. As he turned, he glimpsed—just before the hull of the ship intervened—a spacesuited figure coming in his direction from the station. /Charlie—?/

*/// I saw it.
Don't stop, but you'd better switch on your comm
and find out what's happening. ///*

"Suit—comm on, receive only! Sort all frequencies."

His helmet filled instantly with barking voices, some synthesized, some human . . .

"TUG TANGO, COME TO ZERO FOUR EIGHT MARK—"

"Sort!" he snapped.

"WORK CREW BRAVO, WE'VE GOT A MAN TRAPPED IN THE MIDSECTION OF THE SUPPLIER. WE NEED CUTTERS AND TORCHES—FAST."

"Sort. *Mokin' foke, Charlie.*"

"—JENSEN. THAT GUY I SAW HANGING AROUND *EXPLORER* IS MOVING UP TOWARD THE AFT AIRLOCK. SOMETHING *VERY WEIRD* JUST HAPPENED OUT THERE—A FLASH OF LIGHT. I'M GOING TO HAVE A LOOK."

Bandicut tensed as he listened for a reply. He was accelerating now toward the airlock. He cut off the thrusters, realizing that he was going too fast. He was also getting warm in his suit, and short of breath.

"ALL RIGHT, LET US KNOW IF YOU NEED HELP. WE'RE A LITTLE SHORTHANDED RIGHT NOW."

"THIS GUY MAKES ME NERVOUS, CONTROL. IF I HOLLER, GET SOME PEOPLE OUT HERE FAST."

/Terrific. What do we do now?/ Bandicut was braking, closing feet-first with the airlock.

/// Move like hell
and hope we can beat him out of here.
According to the datanet,
there's no one aboard the ship. ///

/Good./ He landed and swung around to the airlock controls. He breathed a prayer of gratitude that the chamber was already evacuated. The door began to move, sliding open with painful slowness.

"YOU THERE—DON'T ENTER THAT VESSEL!" echoed the voice he had heard a moment ago. It was Jensen, and he was angry.

Bandicut swung into the airlock and hit the control. The door slid closed. /I'd say we have about four minutes before he gets here./

/// Can you lock this entryway? ///

Bandicut fretted as the airlock pressurized, and the inner door finally opened. /Maybe./ He searched the controls, and when the inner door was wide open, snapped the DISABLE toggle to freeze the controls. /If he has the right code, he can probably override this from the outside. But it should slow him up./

/// Then let's get to the flight deck, fast.
How soon can you light the rocket? ///

/That depends on how secured everything is. Anywhere from three minutes to three hours. If you want me to do any flying, I'd better get out of this suit. At least the helmet and gloves./

/// No time!
Wait till you get there! ///

The urgency in the quarx's voice was mounting.

Bandicut vaulted down the passageway. He didn't know the inside of the ship, but it seemed to be laid out in a reasonably sensible manner. There were a few cabins, and a kitchen—he saw them flashing by as he careened, diving far faster than was safe, down the narrow passage. It was not that large a ship, and most of the rest looked like lab and engineering cubicles. The flight deck, he figured, should be at the far end.

He slid open a bulkhead door and dived through, loosening his visor. He floated into an observation deck—a dead end. /It must be below this!/

/// Hurry! ///

He backed out, found a crossover passageway, dropped through it with sickening turning movements, and found a door marked COCKPIT. He wanted to yank off his helmet to gulp some fresh air, but he needed both hands to push himself through the bulkhead door. He floated straight into the flight deck—and there were the controls and the maneuvering windows right in front of him. /Here we are. I see some green lights on. I may be able to able to fire up the maneuvering thrusters pretty quickly, at least./ He seized the back of the left seat, intending to swing his legs around into it.

He sensed a movement to his right and turned dizzily. A woman in a jumpsuit was facing him, brandishing a screwdriver in one hand and a wrench in the other. Startled, he froze. When he could breathe again, he flipped up his visor to talk to her. "What the furgin' fuck do you think you're doing in my ship, mister?" the woman yelled, before he could say a word. She elbowed a comm switch and shouted, "Station, *Explorer!* He's here in my cockpit! Get me some help, fast!"

Bandicut opened his mouth to reply, but could not speak against the wave of fear that rose up in his throat.

27

DEPARTURE TIME

/// Don't give in to it! ///
The quarx's yell brought Bandicut up short as he fought back the fear-bile in his throat. The woman was advancing on him. He hadn't bargained on hand-to-hand combat, especially not with a woman. /I thought you said there was no one aboard!/ he croaked.

/// The ship was listed as empty!
Can you defeat her—
or talk to her? ///

He tried to make his voice work. "I—*wait!*" he cried through his open visor. *"Don't wave that thing at me!"* Sweat from his forehead was getting into his eyes, and he was having trouble seeing properly. But he could see the glinting point of the screwdriver well enough.

"Listen!" she snapped. "You assume the fucking *position* against the fucking *wall,* mister—or I'm gonna stick you in the belly with this thing. Who are you and what are you doing on my ship? Did you have anything to do with that collision?"

"Uh—" he grunted. "No . . . *no!*" His protest sounded weak, even to him.

"No? Well, I just heard on the comm that *they* think you did. *Someone* messed with those traffic codes. Let me tell you, I don't put up with that kind of shit, mister. I've got friends out there in those ships. So you better tell me—"

"I—" He reached out an imploring hand.

"GET UP AGAINST THAT WALL AND SPREAD 'EM!" The woman loomed, waving the screwdriver.

He floated back from her. /What the hell do I do?/ he hissed to Charlie. He had no desire to fight—but he was afraid he would have to try to knock her out.

/// *The white stone!*
Get it out! ///

Bandicut blinked, groping in his pocket.

"HANDS IN SIGHT! And no sudden movements!" The woman's voice was growing a little shrill, with just an edge of panic. She undoubtedly thought he was reaching for a weapon.

/// *Do as she says.* ///

Bandicut swallowed and drew his hand out slowly. There were two stones on the tip of his finger, one black as night, the other a dazzling point of white light. The white stone flared dazzlingly, directly into his eyes. He felt as if a sheet of light were writhing against him, molding and transforming his face.

"What the fr'deekin' hell—?" The woman's eyes bulged, and she grabbed a panel edge to stop her movement toward him. "Who the fuck *are* you?" she whispered. "*What* are you?"

"I don't want to hurt anyone," Bandicut pleaded, but what came out was a harsh, guttural rasp: "HARKK-AHHH DERRK-K-EN GRAK-K-K-NEESH'N." Stunned, he fell silent. /What was *that*?/

/// *The white stone—*
it's translating you into Krenz.
I think it's giving her pause. ///

Bandicut's mind was reeling. Without thinking, he raised his hand to look at the stone. The woman screamed. The black gem had expanded into a huge, squirming ball of living darkness, engulfing the white one, yet glimmering with inner energies. Before he could ask Charlie what *that* was, the thing erupted with knife blades of light, flashing out, crackling, striking the wall on all sides of the woman.

She started to cry out again, but caught herself and backed toward the comm panel, hand over her mouth. "DON'T!" he warned, not knowing what he would do if she disobeyed. His voice reverberated inhumanly in the cockpit.

She stopped her movement. "Please," she whispered. "Wh-what . . . do you . . . want?"

He felt the quarx encouraging him to speak. "I want you to leave the ship," he said, and his words came out resonant, but fully human. "Call them and tell them to keep everyone clear, including the blast area. I want all tethers freed, and I'll give you five minutes to get away from the ship to safety." His temples were pounding, his eyes watering. He could not believe what he was saying. "Is there anyone else aboard?"

He was interrupted by a burst of static from the comm, and a voice saying, "WE'VE IDENTIFIED HIM AS JOHN BANDICUT, A SURVEY DRIVER. WE DON'T KNOW WHAT HE WANTS, BUT WE'RE TRYING TO CONTACT PEOPLE WHO KNOW HIM. HE MAY BE HAVING A PSYCHOTIC BREAKDOWN. BE EXTREMELY CAREFUL IN DEALING WITH HIM!" His breath caught, hearing that; he felt a protest, a denial rising in his throat.

The woman froze with indecision, and Bandicut finally erupted angrily, "You're wasting time! If there's anyone else on this ship, *get them off*—or you're signing their death warrants! Do you hear me?"

Her eyes widened, and she shook her head. "There's no one else aboard."

"Good. Call the station!"

"You're—you're—"

Crazy? he almost said, but instead snapped, "DO IT!"

His hand traced the air, and the undulating black ball fired a new volley of crackling beams of light.

As she moved toward the comm, her voice was fearful and strained. "You can't just . . . where can you *go?*"

He opened his mouth, and for a moment pondered how insane this must look. They were in orbit around Triton and Neptune. Where could *anyone* go from here? He didn't know how to answer her. "Watch it on the holos," he whispered at last, and his voice came out as a threatening hiss. "Now MAKE THAT CALL!"

She fumbled for the comm switch. "Triton Orbital, this is . . . Captain Schroeder. He has—he has—some sort of weapon—bomb—I don't know what."

"EVERYONE AWAY FROM THE SHIP!" Bandicut boomed.

"Everyone away from the ship," she whispered.

"FREE ALL MOORING TETHERS AND CLEAR THE AREA."

"Free all . . . did you copy that?" she croaked.

An incredulous voice answered in the affirmative.

"HAVE SOMEONE READY TO HELP THIS WOMAN TO SAFETY, WHEN SHE LEAVES THE SHIP!"

She looked startled. "Is that all?"

"Yes," he said, more softly. "Now get the hell out of here, Captain." When she still hesitated, he raised his voice one last time. *"GO!"*

She fled from the flight deck.

/// Good work!
Let's get this thing powered up! ///

Bandicut swallowed hard and stared at his finger. The ball of darkness had contracted to a black jewel again. Hesitantly, he removed his gloves and started to put them in his pocket, fearful of dropping the two stones. To his astonishment, both jewels sprang away from the tip of the glove's finger and flew to his wrists, just under the suit cuffs—the white one to his right wrist and the black one to his left. His skin burned as the stones, like sparks, embedded themselves in his flesh just below the hand joint. /Oww!/ The pain subsided slowly. /Jesus, Charlie, what—?/

/// Never mind the stones now.
John—power up! ///

Stunned, but responding to Charlie's urgency, he pulled himself into the pilot's seat and peered at the control board. There were some differences from the panels he knew, but he didn't think he'd have any trouble maneuvering the ship away from the station. He began snapping switches, initiating the computer-controlled launch sequence. /What about that woman? I wonder if we can trust her to leave. Is there a camera in the airlock?/

/// Can we jack in and take a look? ///

The board was designed for both manual and neurolink control. He looked frantically for a headset. Finally he checked the overhead compartments, and two headsets floated out. He snatched one from the air and plugged himself in.

The transformation was abrupt. He felt himself in a hollow, echoing ball surrounded by inputs. He could still see the instruments on the panel, but his attention was focused inward. /There's the launch sequence . . . we have to shortcut some of it, or we'll be here for hours./

/// All I need is a fusion fire in one chamber.
Can you get that much going? ///

/I think so. You find anything on the airlock monitors?/

/// One moment.
Yes, here it is. ///

The quarx showed him an interior shot from near the midships airlock. An angry-looking Captain Schroeder, suited except for her helmet, was studying a panel in the corridor wall. It took him a moment to realize that it was probably an environmental control panel. What was she thinking of?

/Give me an intercom channel—fast./ He felt the con-

nection open, tied to his throat mike. "CAPTAIN, YOUR
TIME IS RUNNING OUT. TOUCH THOSE CONTROLS AND
YOU'LL BE TAKING A VERY LONG, ONE-WAY RIDE!" He
could feel his voice booming through the ship's passage-
ways. He saw Schroeder stiffen, looking around. She fled
into the airlock, fastening her helmet as she went.

/// How's that launch sequence going? ///

/It's coming./ He scanned the checklist, cueing the computer to compress or eliminate everything possible. The
ship was fully loaded with isotopic fuels for the engines,
and life-support stores registered three-quarters full . . . except the galley, which was only half stocked. /Is that going
to be enough?/ he thought worriedly.

/// It'll have to do.

We can't send out for pizza now. ///

He nodded unhappily.

/// We can manage.

As long as we have some *food,*

we can make more.

John, when can you light this thing off? ///

/In about nine minutes. Chambers are heating now./ He
glanced nervously at the external monitors, half expecting
to see a platoon of space marines boarding. He saw no one,
but the cameras didn't give full coverage, either. /What
about a course? Are you doing the navigation in your head?/

/// For now, yes.

We just need to get clear of the station,

for starters.

We can't start the spatial threading

until we're clear. ///

/Uh . . . huh. Are we undocking normally?/

/// I'll augment the thrusters a little.

You can steer normally,

but expect a slight translation forward. ///

/Uh?/

/// You'll see.
Oh, and we have two passengers to pick up.
Be ready with the midships airlock. ///

Puzzled, Bandicut readied the airlock, noting that the captain was clear now, crossing back toward the station airlock. Several other figures were joining her, escorting her in. He didn't have time to ask Charlie about it, because the fusion chambers were approaching critical heat and temperature, and the magnetic pincers were fluctuating just enough to worry him. He didn't like rushing it. But if he lingered, they would never get away.

And, he realized suddenly, they were still tethered.

"Station! Get those tethers freed!" he snapped.

"BANDICUT, STOP NOW BEFORE IT'S TOO LATE!" squawked the comm. "WHATEVER'S WRONG, TALK TO US! YOU'RE GOING TO KILL YOURSELF DOING THIS!" There were some rustling sounds, then the voice added, "IF YOU TELL US WHAT YOU WANT, MAYBE WE CAN HELP YOU."

"You can help me by not interfering."

"PLEASE—"

"Cut those tethers!"

"WAIT—BANDICUT—WE'VE GOT SOMEONE HERE WHO WANTS TO TALK TO YOU. WE'RE PATCHING HIM IN NOW."

"Forget it—" he said, but a familiar voice was already booming out of the comm. It was Krackey, from Triton.

"BANDIE, WHAT ARE YOU DOING? I *THOUGHT* SOMETHING WAS WRONG, THIS MORNING! THIS IS CRAZY, MAN. THERE'S *NO PLACE FOR YOU TO GO!*"

"I'm going to save Earth," Bandicut muttered.

"WHAT? SAY AGAIN? BANDIE, IS THIS ANOTHER GODDAMN SILENCE-FUGUE? DAMN IT TO HELL, I *KNEW* WE SHOULD HAVE TOLD SOMEONE ABOUT THOSE! BANDIE, CALL THIS OFF BEFORE IT'S TOO LATE!" Krackey sounded frantic, as if he were about to burst into tears.

Bandicut drew a deep breath. "Krackey, I'm not in fugue, and I'm not crazy. At least I don't think so. I want you to watch my trajectory—all the way"—his voice caught—"across the solar system."

"BANDIE!" Krackey wailed. "THAT'S JUST CRAZY! PLEASE, IT'S NOT TOO LATE TO SHUT DOWN!"

Bandicut grunted. He wanted to turn off the comm, but couldn't bring himself to do it. "Krackey," he said, "talk to Julie Stone, tomorrow! I've explained everything in a letter to her! About the alien artifact and everything else. She'll get it tomorrow. Tell her I said it was all right to show it to you." His voice was starting to tremble; he clamped his mouth shut.

"JULIE STONE? ALIEN ARTIFACT? WHAT THE HELL—? WAIT, BANDIE—JUST WAIT A MINUTE—LET ME GET HER PATCHED IN FOR YOU!"

Bandicut shuddered, closing his eyes. He opened them again. "It's too late. I have no time to argue, Krackey. I hope I'll see you again, but if I don't—just trust me." His voice became harsh. "Station, damn it—CUT THOSE LINES! I am about to fire thrusters."

He saw a series of flashes along the station's mooring points, and the cut tether lines began drifting toward the ship. He suddenly realized that *Neptune Explorer* probably had releases of its own. He searched for the software control, found it, and fired the tethers loose on his end, as well. The lines writhed like snakes in the open space between the ship and station.

"AW, MAN—!" he heard Krackey mutter, then a click as that connection was broken off.

The chambers were ready to fuse hydrogen. He had only to feed it, as soon as they were a safe distance from the station. "Everyone clear. I'm about to fire thrusters."

"BANDICUT, WAIT!" cried a panicked voice. "WE'VE STILL GOT A MAN OUT THERE."

He cursed and held off thruster ignition. "You've got

one minute," he warned, checking the monitors. If their man was already aboard, he might be stupidly giving them the time they needed to stop him. He looked up from the controls, mind still mostly in the neurolink—and nearly jumped out of his seat. A man in a spacesuit was hovering directly in front of him, staring in through the maneuvering window. It was Jensen, and he was waving angrily.

"JENSEN, GET THE HELL OUT OF THERE!" called the voice from the station.

"NEGATIVE. HE'S GOING TO HAVE TO GO RIGHT THROUGH ME. I DON'T THINK HE'LL DO IT."

"CHRIST, JENSEN—THE MAN'S INSANE!"

"Thirty seconds," Bandicut murmured aloud. He gestured with an angry hook of his thumb, wondering what he would do if Jensen refused to move. He snapped his visor shut, thinking, I don't want to hurt him—but I also don't want him crashing through that window . . .

"BANDICUT, WE'RE TRYING TO GET JULIE STONE PATCHED IN!"

Don't, he whispered silently. Please.

/// Pop the thrusters backward. ///

/Huh?/ Then he realized what the quarx meant. He gave the forward-pointing thrusters a half-second burst. The ship began moving backward, away from the suited figure—and toward the station, stern-first. "TEN SECONDS!" he yelled.

Still, Jensen didn't move clear. He jetted toward the window again.

*/// Give me a few joules of power
in fusion chamber four.
ONLY number four! ///*

/But Charlie—the station!/ He was going to have to thrust forward in a few seconds to avoid colliding with the station, Jensen or no Jensen.

*/// Let me try it.
I won't harm the station. ///*

He fed chamber four a tiny squirt of fuel. In the rear

monitors, he saw a great bloom of light. The ship began to glide forward, toward Jensen. The entire station behind the ship appeared to be on fire.

"JESUSGODALMIGHTY—!"

The comm circuit was filled with panicked outcries and static.

/What have we just done, Charlie?/

/// *Very little. Trust me.* ///

In front of the ship, Jensen was turning frantically. He lit his thrusters and fled sideways, away from the ship. *Neptune Explorer* continued moving, but the blaze of light died away, and Bandicut took control with the maneuvering thrusters. They were moving not quite parallel to a wing of the station, at close quarters—and closing. He had to fire a burst or they'd collide. *Pop. Pop. Pop.* The ship stopped closing with the station. In one of the monitors, he saw Jensen tumbling away, caught by a thruster blast. He cursed, but there was nothing he could do except get farther from the station.

/// Wait!
Open the airlock.
Maintain this distance
until we pass that hangar up ahead. ///

Bandicut obeyed, terrified that armed men would leap across into the airlock—even though he knew that they were moving fast enough relative to the station to make that unlikely. He pointed one of the external cameras toward the hangar at the end of the station—and was unnerved to see two small figures spring away from the hangar, into space. They didn't appear human.

/// There they are.
As soon as they're aboard— ///

/Who are they?/ he demanded. /Quit screwing around with me, Charlie!/ The tiny figures were drawing close enough now to see with magnification, and he felt a flutter of astonishment as he recognized them. He'd half expected them to be aliens.

/// Napoleon and Copernicus.
I programmed them to respond to a
priority call from us. ///
/But we didn't send any call—/
/// Yes, we did—
in the datanet, last night.
I didn't want to make a big deal of it.
But they came up on the shuttle with us. ///
/Why?/ Bandicut whispered.
/// Allies.
You never know what we'll need help with.
They're good workers. ///

Bandicut couldn't think what to say. If Charlie had told him about this earlier, he probably would have protested that he didn't need to steal any more property.

/// Okay, they're in.
Let's close the airlock and move away,
before anyone else
decides to come after you. ///

Swallowing, Bandicut gave a long maneuvering burst on the thrusters. The ship passed the hangar, and then the entire station was behind them, slowly receding. /Charlie,/ he asked, painfully aware of the tightness in his chest. /What happened back there, a minute ago—when I lit the fusion chambers?/

/// You mean the light show? ///

/Light show? It looked like we were incinerating the station! What kind of radiation were we throwing back at them?/

/// Visible light only, John.
The stone converted your fusion output,
mostly for dramatic effect—
plus enough spatial translation to slip us forward
through the continuum.

They might have felt some ripple-tremors behind us,
but mostly I expect they just wondered
what the hell happened. ///

Oh, Bandicut thought. /What about Jensen? We hit him with a thruster./

The quarx was silent for a moment.

/// I don't know, John. ///

Bandicut nodded unhappily. He realized that the comm circuit had been turned down to a murmur. Had he unconsciously done that, to avoid distraction?

/// I believe there are some tugs chasing us.
I think it's time we powered up
for the long haul. ///

Bandicut hesitated, reluctant to take the final steps. Before he could respond, he heard a muted yell to him on the comm, and he raised the volume again.

"BANDICUT, ARE YOU LISTENING? WE'VE GOT JULIE STONE PATCHED IN. WILL YOU TALK TO HER?"

His heart seemed to fill his throat. Julie? Now? Please, God, don't make me go through this . . .

"JOHN, THIS IS JULIE!" He could tell at once that she was trying hard not to cry. He closed his eyes, imagining how she must have felt when told what he was doing. "JOHN, PLEASE TALK TO ME!"

Julie, please—what can I say? he whispered soundlessly.

"I'VE READ YOUR LETTER—"

His eyes blinked open. "Julie? You've—read—"

Her voice quickened at his response. "YOUR FRIEND— GORDON KRACKING—BROKE IT OUT OF STORAGE FOR ME TO READ. JOHN, I—I DON'T KNOW WHAT TO SAY, THIS IS CRAZ—IT'S—"

I know . . .

"IT'S . . . INCREDIBLE, IT'S . . . I DON'T KNOW . . ."

"What to say?" he whispered, supplying words to her faltering voice. He tried to make his own voice strong. "Julie, I know what you're thinking," he croaked. He tried again, and this time his voice held. "Julie, every word of that letter is true! The artifact . . . the alien . . . the comet . . . the danger to Earth . . ."

"JOHN, I . . . BELIEVE YOU." Her voice was full of doubt. "BUT YOU CAN'T JUST . . . HIJACK A SHIP!"

His eyes were starting to well with tears. "I can't *not* do it, Julie! Do you think I want to? I know you can't believe me—not really—not until you find the artifact yourselves."

/// Or until they see what this ship can do— ///

He blinked the tears from his eyes. "Or—the alien tells me—" he said huskily, over the sound of Julie struggling to find words, "until you see what this ship—can do—"

/// —when we start threading space. ///

"—when we start threading space."

For a few moments, there was no answer, but several rasps of static—probably the result of someone cutting Julie in and out of the connection while they argued over who should talk to him.

*/// We've got to accelerate.
Those tugs are gaining on us. ///*

/Yeah./ He gave the thrusters a blast to increase their velocity away from the station. "Julie—?"

"JOHN," Julie called, her voice barely holding together. "IF IT'S REALLY TRUE . . . AND I WANT TO BELIEVE YOU, THAT IT IS . . . CAN'T YOU WAIT JUST A FEW MINUTES LONGER, SO WE CAN TALK? SO YOU CAN EXPLAIN?"

He closed his eyes again, squeezing them shut. No, Julie, I can't. And I'm so sorry, more than I can tell you. He cleared his throat, several times. "Julie, I—I wish I could. But I have to go—*now*. Please trust me. This must be . . . done. I hope you'll see why." He swallowed with difficulty. "Good . . . bye, Julie."

He shifted his thoughts inward. /*Do* something, damn it!/

/// Give me a squirt of fuel. ///

He touched a control and watched in the monitor. The

station, and the pursuing tugs, receded at an impossible rate. He felt no sense of physical acceleration. His heart had not stopped pounding yet. He wasn't sure it ever would.

/// Okay, that's enough simple translation.

Let's pour it on, John.

We have a long way to go. ///

"JOHN? WHAT'S HAPPENING?" whispered Julie.

Unable to breathe or speak, he opened the flow to chamber four, trusting the quarx to know what he was doing. In the rear monitor, he saw a sunburst of concentric colors expanding outward: white in the center, radiating to blue, to green, yellow, orange, and deep red on the outside. For a few seconds, he couldn't see the station at all. Then the quarx pointed it out—a tiny point of light, vanishing behind the horizon of a shrinking, orange-grey disk of Triton. /Charlie? How are we—?/

/// We're threading space, man.

Say good-bye to Neptune. ///

His heart almost stopped as he realized that the great blue ball of Neptune was also shrinking visibly, and with frightening speed. He could not tear his eyes from it. He wondered what the people on the station had seen, what they thought now. What Julie thought. He imagined a choir of voices . . . he felt his thoughts spinning toward silence-fugue. He felt the quarx putting the brakes on the process.

/// Stop it, John!

Just say good-bye.

Think of what's ahead.

Think positively. ///

He could not breathe, could not swallow. /Good-bye, Neptune. Good-bye, Triton,/ he whispered. /Good-bye, Julie./ And after a moment: /Good-bye, life./

28

SUNWARD BOUND

A HALF HOUR later, Charlie announced that the course was set, he'd confirmed their trajectory via one last linkup with the translator back on Triton, and Bandicut could relax. Relax? Bandicut watched the white diamond in his right wrist flicker one last time. The black one on the left had throbbed with heat during the linkup. Other than that, he had felt nothing. But he stared at the stones suspiciously, rubbing his wrists.

/// *They're intelligence and communications*
accessories.

We're passing out of range of the translator,
but we'll be using the stones again, I'm sure. ///

Bandicut nodded slowly. He didn't really care about the stones. All he cared about was what he had left behind. The solar system was a vast, cold, dark, and lonely place and he had just set course for himself across its enormous emptiness. How the hell was he supposed to relax? He was feeling severely depressed. He struggled to get out of his cumbersome spacesuit.

/// *John, it's going to be a long flight.*
I hope you can find a way to unwind. ///

/You can hope./ Bandicut shook his head angrily and hurled the empty suit away. He settled back into the pilot's seat and stared at the monitor images of the planet he had left behind. He kept increasing the magnification as the planet dwindled. Out the front window, he saw only darkness and a few of the brighter stars. He knew if he dimmed the cockpit lights or turned up the light augmentation, he would see more stars; but just now he didn't care to. He knew he should get busy. There was plenty to do, including checking the ship over from stem to stern. He had only Charlie's earlier datanet access to assure him that the ship was ready for space. He wanted to make sure that some hardware problem or missing supply wasn't going to doom them from the start. For that matter, he wanted to make sure no one else was aboard. The datanet had been wrong about that once already.

/// I suggest you enlist
Napoleon and Copernicus in your inspection.
They seem well equipped for the job. ///

Napoleon and Copernicus—he couldn't believe that the quarx had thought to bring him a pair of mechanized companions, but no one human. He knew why, of course; it was bad enough to be risking one human life on a suicide mission.

/// I would like to claim that as my only reason.
But actually, John,
who would have come with you? ///

He sighed, not answering, and checked the instruments again. He couldn't quite make himself leave the pilot's seat. He couldn't help wondering just what the translator-stone was doing, back there in the rocket's belly.

/// I've tried to explain that to you. ///

/Yeah./ Charlie had told him that "threading space" meant that they were weaving in and out of the "normal" space-time continuum many hundreds of times per second. With each fraction of an instant that they were in "secondary" space, they slipped forward so that they reappeared in the normal continuum at a point considerably displaced from their previous position. The effect created the illusion, to human eyes and instruments, of astonishing forward velocity.

> /// *It's not totally an illusion.*
> *We're picking up energy*
> *with each passage through the spatial boundary.*
> *Plus, as we fall toward your sun,*
> *we'll gain some hefty gravitational acceleration,*
> *which we need, too.* ///

/Need?/

> /// *For the actual destruction of the comet.* ///

/Ah./ Somehow, that did not make him any less depressed. He could well imagine the outcome of all that energy being released. See Julie again? Not likely.

He wanted desperately to send a transmission back to Triton, but Charlie had told him that it was impossible while they were threading space—and indeed, his brief efforts had met with a tempest of static. Charlie's final link with the translator had been via a spatial-thread connection that human communications equipment could not pick up, and even that link was no longer possible, at the present distance.

Nevertheless, Bandicut ached to explain again, to justify himself to Julie, to beg her forgiveness and her blessing. He wanted to tell her to wait for him. He didn't want her to think of other men. He wanted her to dream of him the way he dreamed of her. He wanted her to—

> /// *Stop it!*
> *You're making yourself miserable!* ///

/Then find a way for me to get another message to her,/ he said miserably. The letter hadn't been nearly enough; he wanted a chance to say it right.

> /// *John, I'm afraid your letter will have to do.*
> *There's simply no way we can transmit right now.* ///

/Well, when can we transmit? You never told me it would be like this. There are some things I'd like to make clear to the rest of them, too. I don't want people to think I'm a criminal, damn it!/

/// *I understand.*
Maybe they'll find the translator.
We'll just have to see.
It depends on when we break out of threading,
and I don't know when that will be yet. ///

He grunted, and swiveled in his seat to start another checklist of the instruments. After a minute, he stopped and sighed heavily. /Where are those damn robots, anyway? I might as well get some work out of them./

/// *Good.*
That's really the best way to approach it. ///

/Go jump in a lake./

∗

The two robots were parked just inside the airlock, using magnetic anchors. He floated down the corridor and touched them for a moment without speaking. He realized that he actually felt some comfort in their presence. They weren't exactly what he had in mind for companionship— and they weren't even very smart robots, just clever at what they were designed to do—and yet he had already been through some difficult times with them, and in that sense they felt like old friends. "Hi, Nappy," he said finally. "Copernicus. Long time no see."

"I am at your service, John Bandicut," Napoleon answered, raising itself slightly on its ungainly legs. Two lights winked on its holocams.

Copernicus answered with a series of drumtaps. "With you for the mission, Cap'n Bandicut." The robot rolled forward and back a few centimeters on its conical wheels.

"Thanks," Bandicut said softly. "Look, you two. I have to tell you right now that you've signed on for a . . . difficult mission. But I'm glad you're here. I want you to help me inspect the ship. I didn't have time to give it much of a preflight."

"Preflight inspection is mandatory before all operations," rasped Napoleon. "We should suspend—"

"Stow it, Nappy. We're in flight already. And I need your help."

"You are in command, John Bandicut," Napoleon answered. "Would you like a class-one detailed inspection of all systems, a class-two inspection of only vital systems, a class-three—"

"Just *check the fr'deekin' ship,* will you?" Bandicut roared. "Look first for any other human aboard, then check vital life-support supplies, then power systems, then anything else you have time for in the next forty days, before we all cash it in. I'm going to stick close to the bridge. Just check in with me from time to time, okay?"

"Understood," said Napoleon.

"Wilco," said Copernicus with another quick drumtap.

> /// *Could you touch them again*
> *for a moment, please? ///*

Bandicut pulled himself close and laid a hand on each robot. His hands tingled. /Reprogramming?/

> /// *Just fine-tuning.*
> *Okay. ///*

Bandicut removed his hands. "Get going," he said. He watched, frowning, as they clicked into motion and started down the corridor—Napoleon swinging like an angular monkey on its magnetic feet, and Copernicus rolling smoothly down the side wall of the corridor. Bandicut sighed and returned to the cockpit. It made him nervous to be away, even though there was no piloting for him to do. If he was to be captain of his stolen ship, he just thought he damn well ought to be on the bridge.

> /// *You'll get used to it, John.*
> *You might as well spend some of the trip*
> *coming to terms with what you've done,*
> *don't you think? ///*

/I thought I told you to go jump in a lake,/ he said, not meaning it at all kindly.

✳

It took some time, watching the two robots at work on the monitors, before he was willing to believe that they were capable of inspecting the ship far more easily—and more thoroughly—than he could himself. What finally moved him to quit worrying about it, more than anything else, was hunger. He hadn't eaten in many hours, and he was anxious to take a look at the food supply aboard ship.

He left the cockpit with Napoleon and Copernicus hard at work on the propulsion deck. Locating the galley again was easy. Finding something he wanted to eat was more difficult. The fresh food had not been loaded; what he had to choose from was freeze-dried, irradiated, and other nonperishables. He finally made some instant macaroni and cheese and a large flask of coffee. He was rusty at handling food in zero-gee, too, and he created a fair amount of mess floating in the air.

*/// Would you like me to adjust the local gravity
to something more comfortable? ///*

Bandicut stared at the leaking bulb of coffee and the globs of black liquid writhing in the air. /You can do that? Why didn't you say so sooner?/

*/// I didn't think of it.
But it's a fairly simple adjustment to the
threading field surrounding the ship. ///*

There was really no reason to be amazed, he thought, but he was, nevertheless. /Sure. How about one-twelfth gee for starters, and maybe we can work our way up so I can get back in shape./

*/// Excellent idea.
I suggest you find the proper vertical. ///*

Bandicut turned his feet to the ship's acceleration axis. He felt a twinge in his left wrist and slowly drifted down to the deck. The coffee globs hit at the same time, splattering quietly. He sighed and mopped up, then took his dinner to the cockpit. He sat, chewing slowly, watching the robots on the monitors, watching a brightness-enhanced view of the stars before him, watching the silent and effectively disabled comm, thinking about what he would like to say if only Charlie could give him a chance. And wondering if anyone would listen.

※

The time passed with numbing slowness. He learned to use the shipboard laundry, and found some clothing in stores that fit him, more or less. He'd finished his speech to Triton and to Earth at least a dozen times, before Neptune vanished into the darkness behind him. How many times he'd finished his speech to Julie was beyond counting, as were the times he'd come to, with a start, realizing that he'd been dreaming that she was here with him. By now, she might have had time to go looking for the translator. Would it allow her to find it? Would she believe him then—really believe him? Would she forgive him?

He ached to know, to hear her voice.

*/// I didn't expect
that you would form such intense attachments
so quickly. ///*

/I guess there's a lot you don't know about me,/ Bandicut thought gruffly. /I'd like to know if that guy lived, too. Jensen. And the people on those two ships./

/// Yes, ///

was all Charlie said in reply.

※

They were eight days inbound from Neptune when Bandicut felt a sudden trembling in the air, a coiling in his gut, a shiver.

/What the hell was that?/

*/// We've got a fluctuation in the
threading field.
We've got to shut down. ///*

Bandicut felt a leaden weight of anxiety, then weightlessness as he floated up out of his seat. /What's wrong?/

*/// I think we've damaged your
number four fusion chamber. ///*

Bandicut studied the monitors, and saw nothing. He switched to the neurolink for a closer look. /Seems fine to me. Normal wear and tear./

*/// If we were using it as a fusion rocket,
it would be fine.
But the wear is causing a separation in the
threading field. ///*

He didn't like the sound of that. /Which means what?/

*/// We've got to remove the translator-stone
and move it to another fusion chamber. ///*

Bandicut said nothing. The last thing he felt like doing right now was going EVA on a solo flight across the solar system. If anything went wrong . . .

*/// We can send Napoleon out to do it.
No need to risk yourself. ///*

Bandicut nodded, frowning. Of course. Napoleon could do the job just fine. But it gave him another idea. /Listen, Charlie—as long as we're stopped—/

/// Okay, ///

said the quarx, without waiting for him to finish.

/// I guess I owe you that much. ///

They first had to program Napoleon and get him on the job. Then they powered up the long-range comm, to see if they could raise Triton. Bandicut nervously waited as the computer initiated the call and monitored for an answer. At this distance from Neptune, the signal lag was going to be almost half an hour each way. Time had never crawled quite so slowly. After a few minutes of that, Bandicut decided to transmit blind; they didn't have time for back-and-forth chitchat, anyway. He sent a focused beam to Triton, and a weaker omnidirectional signal as backup. "Triton Orbital, or any other station, this is *Neptune Explorer,* John Bandicut speaking. I do not know if you are picking up this signal, so I will just say what I have to say, and hope that it gets through."

He hesitated, clicking his teeth. All his carefully rehearsed speeches had evaporated from his mind. He struggled for words. "I—apologize for the theft of *Neptune Explorer.* If there had been any other way, I would never— but really, there wasn't. I guess by now, you all know what I said in my letter to Julie Stone. It was all true. I'm—sorry, Julie, I didn't mean for it—" His voice caught. This wasn't coming out right.

He drew a breath.

"To repeat: The reason I took *Neptune Explorer* is to prevent a . . . catastrophe . . . to Earth. I know that sounds crazy. But you must . . . well, ask exoarch, they know where the alien artifact is. Perhaps you've found it by now."

He squinted, thinking—if that damn translator hides itself, they'll never believe me. He took another raspy breath. "I just want to be clear. It is through that alien . . . presence . . . part of which is still with me here . . . that I learned of the comet which is on a collision course with Earth. I am on my way to intercept it."

/// Perhaps if you tell them where you are . . . ///

/Huh? Why?/

/// Could you have gotten here yourself? ///

/Oh./ Bandicut cleared his throat. "My present position—" He leaned to check the nav and read off the numbers. He was almost halfway across the distance between Neptune's orbit and Uranus's. "You understand that I could not possibly have traveled this distance using only the fusion drive. If you doubt that I am using a nonhuman technology—" He hesitated. "Oh, Christ, just *believe* me!" He rocked back in his seat, growling helplessly to himself.

/// It's not an easy thing to convey. ///

/I had this all worked out in my head! I should have re-corded it!/

He sighed and continued: "Please convey the following to Julie Stone, exoarch department, Triton Surface: 'Julie, I'm sorry I couldn't have told you sooner. If you find the artifact, you will know that everything I told you is true. If you don't find it, keep looking. It is capable of . . . hiding. And *please* believe me. I don't know what else I can say. You probably all saw me vanish into space like some kind of goddamn holo effect. Maybe you all thought I was dead. Well, I'm not—yet, anyway. I will return—if I can—after Earth is . . . safe. I . . . I lo—, I miss you.' " He hesitated, trying to swallow back the lump in his throat. "Unquote," he muttered. After a moment he added, "Just for the rec-ord, Julie Stone had nothing whatever to do with this. She didn't know."

He paused again. "Oh, and Julie, could you please pass on everything I've told you to my niece, Dakota Bandicut, in Iowa City? Tell her . . . that I am not a criminal, and that I miss her, too. Thanks." He pondered saying more, and fi-nally croaked, "End transmission."

Something was tingling in the back of his mind, the quarx's reaction to something he had said. Even without hearing it, he felt his stomach knotting tighter. /What?/ he muttered.

/// Well . . .

I just want to be honest with you. ///

He waited, words frozen in his throat, in his mind.

The quarx stirred, and he thought he sensed guilt.

/// I don't really think . . .

that there's any chance you'll ever return.

I wish . . . I could say differently.

But I can't. ///

Bandicut closed his eyes, hard. He couldn't speak. This

was hardly news to him. Except, there had always been a tiny grain of hope remaining.

> /// *It's not as if I told you otherwise.*
> *Did I? ///*

/No,/ he whispered. /I don't know. I don't remember./ He shook his head and squeezed his eyes shut harder, but he couldn't keep the tears from leaking out.

Finally he gave up, wiped his eyes, and got back to work.

★

Napoleon had no difficulty changing the placement of the stone. Bandicut watched in the monitor as the robot emerged from one exhaust bell, glowing ball in its grip, and disappeared into another. It came back out empty-handed, and a moment later, Bandicut felt a momentary dizziness, which he assumed was the stone expanding its field to encompass the ship again. As soon as Napoleon was back aboard ship, Charlie suggested that they resume threading flight at once.

/I want to wait and see if we get a reply from Triton,/ Bandicut insisted. He was feeling morose, but also stubborn. The quarx reluctantly agreed to wait another hour.

Fifty-one minutes later, the comm picked up a signal. Bandicut strained to hear. It was a voice signal, but faint with static, as though improperly aimed. ". . . *EXPLORER* . . . CANNOT CONFIRM YOUR POSITION. PLEASE SAY AGAIN. IF YOU CANNOT RETURN . . . STABILIZE YOUR ORBIT . . . ATTEMPT TO ASSIST. WE DO NOT UNDERSTAND, BUT . . . GAME . . . OVER . . ."

Bandicut stared at the comm panel in disbelief. The message continued, repeating itself over and over. Was it possible they didn't believe him—even after the way he'd departed? He swallowed, knowing that it was all too possible. Even if Julie and exoarch believed him . . . he could just imagine the rulers of MINEXFO trying to wrap their small minds around something like this.

/// I'm sorry.
But I'm honestly not surprised.
Shall we continue? ///

He shook his head, his vision blurred. /Just a minute./
He cleared his throat to transmit, and squeezed the switch.
"Triton Orbital, *Neptune Explorer.* This might be the last
transmission I can make. I'm about to accelerate again—
threading space, they call it. So listen to me, and listen
good. Are you listening?" He took a breath, then shouted,
"YOU DUMB MOKIN' *GOAKS!* PUT A MOKIN' *TELESCOPE*
ON THE MOKIN' COORDINATES I JUST GAVE YOU! IF
YOU DON'T BELIEVE ME, BELIEVE YOUR MOKIN' EYES!
BANDICUT OUT!" He gasped with anger as he punched
the comm off.

/// Well said, John . . . I think. ///

/Charlie, punch it. Let's get moving,/ he said wearily.
/And give 'em a good light show, okay?/

As the fusion chamber ignited, he felt a gentle push of
returning gravity. And in the rear monitor, he saw an eruption of concentric rings of light and color behind them, as
Neptune Explorer threaded space inward toward the sun.

29

LONELY CROSSING

 BANDICUT'S ANGER DID not diminish, and it was only a matter of time before he turned it inward, upon the quarx. /You weren't exactly honest with me, were you, you bastard?/ he said, after stewing in silence for a while.

/// *What . . . do you mean?* ///

The quarx's voice sounded weak. Defensive?

/You said there was a fifty-fifty chance we'd come out of this alive. Now, you tell me we're goners. You care to explain that?/ It had taken a little while for it to sink in, that the quarx was changing its tune, now that they were under way and it was too late to turn back.

/// *No, I said . . . well, I mean . . .* ///

/You just said—/

/// *—that we won't return to Triton.*

But I . . . ///

Charlie's voice was quivering. He seemed to be straining for words.

/// *I never said we would return, John.* ///

/Fifty-percent chance! That's what you said./

/// *I didn't mean, to return!*

I meant . . . to survive, in some form. ///

Bandicut squinted out the window, imagining a great orrery of planets encircling the sun. /In some form?/ His mood was not improving. /You implied that we might be rescued. Now you're saying, what? We'll survive, but we won't be rescued?/

/// Not by . . . your people . . . no. ///

His heart skipped a beat. /What the hell are we talking about, then—the goddamn afterlife? Is this some kind of goddamn theological prediction?/

/// No, no!

I meant survival.

But I have to admit, the chances might be less than I predicted before. ///

The quarx's voice was definitely trembling.

/// I think I was . . . optimistic, before. ///

Bandicut caught a glimpse of his reflection in the window. His face was contorted with fear. /*Charlie?* Where the hell will we be—if we're not dead?/

Charlie's voice dropped to near-inaudibility.

/// I can't . . . say for sure.

But it will be a journey.

Possibly a most magnificent journey . . . ///

Bandicut's breath caught, and he sat staring at his own terrified reflection in the maneuvering window, thinking about Charlie's journey of millions of years that had brought him here to the solar system. And he suddenly knew that the quarx was not talking about a journey to the other side of the sun. The quarx came from beyond the stars, and that was where he intended to return.

Charlie was quiet for a few moments.

/// Not home, *if that's what you're thinking.*

That I cannot do.

But . . . beyond the stars . . . yes. ///

Bandicut swallowed. /Then where—?/

/// Well, that's the thing.

I really can't say.

But, John—?

Looking at our present situation,
the chances are probably more like ninety percent
that we'll die,
and that will be the end of it. ///

Bandicut stared blankly for a moment. /WHY THE MOKIN' HELL DIDN'T YOU TELL ME THAT BEFORE?/ he thundered.

/// I was . . . afraid you wouldn't agree. ///

/You were afraid—/ Bandicut felt his breath go out. /You mean, you . . . *lied* to me? You flat-out lied?/

/// Well, I . . . weighted some uncertain odds.
I guess, in that, I misled you.
I'm sorry. ///

/Thanks, asshole./

/// I said, I'm sorry.
It really would be better, John,
if you just went into the final phase of our mission
expecting to die. ///

Bandicut bit back a sarcastic reply. /Well, you haven't answered my question. If we don't die, where do we go? Alpha Centauri? Sirius? Where? Don't I have a right to know that much?/

/// John, I really don't know. ///

/How can you NOT KNOW?/ Bandicut yelled, his emotions sliding completely out of control.

There was no answer.

/CHARLIE?/

After a moment, the trembling quarx whispered,

/// John, didn't you understand from the beginning
that you were giving your life to this?
That nothing would ever be the same again? ///

/Are you crazy?/ Bandicut pounded the console savagely. Maybe the quarx had made it clear enough *then*, but that didn't help him accept it now.

From the quarx, there was silence. Charlie had shut himself off, and retreated into some private purgatory of his own.

⋆

In the absence of the quarx's voice, Bandicut found himself starkly alone and at a loss for purpose, drifting toward, but not quite into, silence-fugue. He watched the instruments and the stars, and did little more for the rest of the ship-day than tap the armrests on his seat and listen to the vague choir of fugue-voices tuning up for action, just beyond the edges of his consciousness.

Eventually, drawn by hunger, he drifted out of his borderline state and went to prepare a grim, lonely dinner. He mouthed some tasteless soyloaf, thinking about all he had left behind, even his duffel bag with all of his photos, books, memories . . .

/// You still have your memories.
Those other things were only possessions. ///

He grunted. /You're back, huh?/ The quarx might have been right, but he very badly wished he had those possessions. He thought he might find them comforting, at the end. To say nothing of the people he would have liked to see.

And that thought was enough to send him skidding over into real fugue . . .

⋆

Dakota's voice made him turn. "Uncle John?" Her green eyes were welling with tears as she prepared to board the train with her grandparents, after the heartbreaking funeral. "When you're back on Earth, will you still come see me?" She glanced at her grandmother, beckoning from the train portal. His heart ached as he chucked her under the jaw. He felt like a hopelessly awkward uncle, and wished he could somehow find a way to show his niece how much he cared. " 'Course I will, kiddo," he murmured. "And I expect you to come visit me in space, when you're a little older. Deal?" Deal, she whispered.

He saw her just twice after that, before shipping out to Triton. But he set up the trust fund before he left, in a sudden impulse that in retrospect seemed almost prescient.

"I know what you're going through," Julie murmured, leaning to kiss his cheek. "I'll find Dakota and explain everything to her, don't worry. And I'll wait for you right here, for as long as it takes you to come back. I love you, John—"

/// Your act must be its own reward, ///
Charlie said, breaking through the soft borders of the fugue-dream.

Bandicut started. /Platitudes, Charlie. Tell me—will anyone believe that I really did this? Will they even see the comet go kaboom? Will there be *any* evidence?/

*/// Depends on their willingness
to believe what they see.
Maybe they'll see the flash. ///*

Bandicut grunted. He suspected that the quarx had not even the slightest expectation that his act would be recognized even if it were seen. /I always thought,/ he muttered, /that when people died heroes, they at least got a little credit for it./

The quarx didn't answer. In the silence, Bandicut drifted back into his own dreamy fugue.

★

The sun grew steadily as the days passed. They were plummeting inward in a steep, S-shaped trajectory, aiming to loop around the sun in the direction opposite to the movement of the planets. On day twenty, they swept through Saturn's orbit and inward toward Jupiter's and Mars's. Not that they would be stopping off, or even able to *see* those planets, other than as remote telescopic images, since the orbits were merely abstract tracings on the nav-screens and the planets themselves were elsewhere in their great elliptical tracks around the sun. Nevertheless, Bandicut imagined conversations with the outposts on and around those worlds, imagined stopping off to have a beer on Ganymede or Phobos, before continuing his mission . . . imagined Julie at his side . . .

Their velocity extrinsic to the threading environment was quite impressive now, close to a tenth of lightspeed. It would, Charlie acknowledged, make for a pretty good bang when they hit the comet. It gave him greater hope—if not of survival, at least that their collision would be seen.

Life aboard ship grew increasingly quiet. Charlie increased the shipboard gravity by small increments, and Bandicut exercised twice a day in an effort to get back into shape, and wondered why he was bothering. Charlie made periodic, unsuccessful efforts to cheer him up. The quarx seemed unusually distracted. Bandicut wondered if something was bothering him, but didn't wonder very hard. Bandicut's own thoughts were growing more and more disjointed as they streaked inward toward a close approach to the sun, and a rendezvous with the comet soon after. He was aware that he was slipping in and out of a semipermanent silence-fugue, and he wondered vaguely, from time to time, why Charlie didn't do something about it. He wondered if Charlie was just getting tired, or if something else was wrong. But by the time he thought to ask, he had forgotten why he cared.

✳

Perhaps, if he had been clearer headed—or if Charlie had been more alert—the accident on day twenty-four would not have happened. But at the time, working on the engineering level checking some power systems with Napoleon and Copernicus, he was already having trouble distinguishing what the robots were telling him from what the fugue-voices were saying.

"Award for best leap yet across the solar system!" cried an ethereal spectator in the asteroid belt, clapping at Bandicut's amazing feat of celestial navigation. Bandicut bowed, jumping across the propulsion deck from one instrument panel to another, puffing lightly with the exertion. The shipboard gravity was now at about one-fourth gee, but in his present dreamy state it felt like much less.

"John Bandicut," Napoleon interrupted with a metallic rasp. "If you wish us to inspect the secondary fuel-pump assemblies, it will be necessary to move these cylinders. They are blocking our access." The robot swiveled its head from a rack of compressed gas tanks that had been clamped up in an apparently temporary storage location during the servicing of the ship.

Bandicut peered up at the robot, hanging high on the wall, and the tank rack that it was poking at. One of the tanks was labeled "Barium"; it probably contained gases intended for injection experiments in the atmosphere of Neptune. "We won't be needing those, I guess," he muttered, waving his approval. "Sure, take care of it." His decisiveness brought another wave of applause from his asteroid-belt spectators, and he leaped across the deck again, with a graceful twist.

/// John, are you sure you should be . . . ///

/What's the matter?/ he muttered to the quarx. /Don't you trust the robots to do their job? I thought you were the one who—/

/// No, I mean your jumping around.
Your fugue seems to be getting out of hand. ///

Bandicut snorted. /If you can't help me control it, what am I supposed to do?/

/// I'm having trouble, John.
I'm very tired, for some reason. ///

/Then don't mind me . . . *huh?*/ There was a screech of metal, and he squinted up at the robots' efforts. Napoleon was releasing the tanks from the rack, and Copernicus had its manipulator-arms extended upward to bring the tanks down; but neither one of them seemed to have very good control.

"Pinball!" yelled someone from the audience, waving from the shadows. "All riiiight!"

"John Bandicut—!" squawked Napoleon. It was interrupted by a bang and a metallic shriek—and an avalanche of cylinders, cascading directly toward Bandicut.

He had only a momentary awareness of alarm and danger—and an abrupt shift in the gravity field, but too late to stop the fall—before the first tank glanced from his temple, and the second hit him squarely in the ribs, and everything went black.

∗

The sensation of pain was pervasive. He flickered in and out of consciousness, in a haze of red. His eyes refused to focus, but he was aware of two shadowy shapes moving nearby, and metallic drumtaps and voices. Then he blinked, and both of the shapes were gone.

He tried to turn his head, and felt a flash of new pain.

/// Don't move! ///

gasped the voice in his head.

/What—?/

/// I'm healing.
It's very difficult . . . ///

and then the voice faded away.

He had a dim memory of heavy objects falling toward him, but he couldn't quite place what had happened. He began to sigh, but it hurt too much. He breathed in slow, shallow waves . . .

When awareness came back to him, he found that he could focus on a ceiling overhead. He couldn't quite identify it. He didn't think it was his bunk, or Julie's . . .

He felt her hand on his forehead, cooling and soothing with her touch; he was burning with fever. She was speaking softly, not in words, but with comforting sounds. His chest hurt, but he was able to breathe a little more easily. Now Julie was leaning to kiss his forehead, and now his lips . . .

When he blinked and focused, he realized that he was on the deck of the engineering compartment, staring at the ceiling. He recalled at least two or three heavy metal cylinders hammering into his body. Where were they now? Weren't there supposed to be robots around to help? What about the mission? He felt nearly weightless; the gravity must have been cut back; maybe he could just turn . . .

/// Very carefully, ///

whispered a fatigued-sounding voice. Who was that? Charlie? He'd never heard Charlie sound so tired . . . except once . . .

/// Never mind that.
Can you move your eyes? ///

He tried, carefully. It made him a little dizzy, but he managed to refocus on another part of the ceiling.

/// Can you move your head slightly? ///

He tried. His head and neck blazed, but he was able to turn his head slightly to the left. Blinking his eyes back into focus, he saw a black-eyed robot peering down at him.

"John Bandicut—are you well?" squawked the robot.

The sound of its voice made his ears ring. He didn't try to answer.

/// I think we've repaired
the most critical damage . . . ///

/I—what—happened?/

The quarx's answer seemed to require an almost overwhelming effort.

/// Do you remember . . .
the tanks striking you? ///

/I—think so./

/// The robots . . . didn't compensate properly . . .
for the change in gravity.
They couldn't support . . . the tanks. ///

He felt faint for a moment. /That's stupid,/ he whispered. /I should have . . ./

/// They are unsophisticated machines. ///

/But I should have . . ./

> /// *You were in fugue.*
> *I'm sorry.* ///

/Sorry?/

> /// *I wasn't . . . feeling well . . . couldn't help.* ///

/Oh. You sound tired now./ He shifted his gaze from the waiting robot to the ceiling again.

> /// *Yes . . . very.*
> *The healing . . . getting you out of critical danger . . .*
> *demanded . . . much of me.*
> *It's not done, but I . . .* ///

Bandicut felt a flicker of alarm. /You aren't hurting yourself, are you?/ His head throbbed with the effects of the sudden surge of adrenaline. /Charlie—?/

> /// *Yes, well I . . . I don't know how much . . .* ///

Bandicut closed his eyes and counted to four. /Charlie,/ he whispered slowly and carefully. /Don't put *yourself* at risk—not even to heal me. I can't do this thing alone./

The quarx sounded wearily unconcerned.

> /// *Your survival . . . is paramount.*
> *Your skills will be needed—* ///

/No, listen. I—/

> /// *—at the end.*
> *Absolutely essential.*
> *I am . . . expendable.* ///

/Charlie—/ His head was buzzing with a confusing welter of physical and emotional pain. /Don't. You hear? You've . . . saved my life. That's all you need to—/

> /// *There are still . . . repairs . . .*
> *I must facilitate . . .* ///

Bandicut drew a breath and prepared to try to sit up. /If you mean this pain, I can live with it./ He gasped, pushing himself up from the deck.

"John Bandicut—are you injured?" squawked the robot.

"Nappy—help me—sit up!" he croaked.

The robot clicked and hummed, and a pair of metal arms awkwardly levered him into a sitting position. He was dizzy, and his chest hurt like hell; he must have had some cracked ribs that weren't healed yet. God, what sort of damage had those tanks done to his body? He sat, panting, gathering his strength, before telling the robot, "I want—to go—to my cabin. Help me—stand up."

"John Bandicut—we should summon medical assistance," advised the robot. "I have been calling on all frequencies, but with no response."

"There *is* no one, Nappy. Just us. Come on, now." Bandicut started to get up, swaying dizzily.

/// John, I'm not sure . . . ///

/I'm going to . . . lie in my bunk, damn it./

There was no further protest from the quarx. The robot awkwardly stretched to its full height, supporting him under his left arm. Hobbling painfully, Bandicut made his way to his cabin. Through a blaze of fire in his chest, he managed to get himself onto his bunk, and he gasped instructions to Napoleon to go to the galley and get him some juice and crackers.

Then he fell into a troubled sleep.

✴

When he awoke, the pain in his chest was considerably lessened, and his head was relatively clear. /You didn't listen to me, did you?/ he asked Charlie. /Well, never mind. Thanks./ He turned his head and saw Napoleon waiting patiently, juice-pack in one mechanical hand and a half-crushed box of matzohs in the other. Slowly, Bandicut sat up, managing without assistance. "Thanks, Nappy," he croaked, taking the juice and flatbread. He tore into them like a starving man, scattering crumbs everywhere and dribbling orange juice in his lap. He didn't care; he drank greedily and stuffed his mouth with what felt like dry flour and tasted like ambrosia. He could feel his body screaming for sustenance.

/Charlie, am I in shape enough to go to the bridge?/ he asked, when he paused for breath.

The quarx's answer was nearly inaudible.

/// Don't know. Try. ///

Bandicut slid down from his bunk. The robot backed out of his way. He glanced in the mirror, and was shocked by his gaunt appearance. His body must have ravaged its own reserves in its quarx-guided healing. /You burned yourself out doing this, didn't you?/ he asked the quarx accusingly.

/// I . . . just tired, really.
Yes. ///

Bandicut shook his head and made his way carefully to the cockpit. He ached, and felt some dizziness, but he suspected that the quarx felt worse than he did. /Well, rest, damn it. And that's an order./ He squeezed into the pilot's seat.

/// Yes . . . ///

Charlie said, and a moment later, added,

/// John, it's time to switch. ///

Bandicut blinked. /What?/

/// To, uh . . .
fusion chamber two. ///

Bandicut shook his head dreamily. Fusion chamber two—the second to last. What day was this? He squinted at the inertial nav. Day twenty-nine. He drew a breath. /Shall I send Nappy out?/

There was a pause.

/// Yes . . . that would be good. ///

Bandicut reached to shut down the fusion reaction. /Are you turning off the threading field?/

/// What?
Yes, yes—the stone knows what to do.
Don't worry. ///

Scowling, Bandicut called Napoleon and gave him instructions to go out and switch the location of the stone. He closed his eyes and held his breath as the threading field cut off, along with the gravity. But he vowed to stay alert, even if the repair was completely out of his hands. He was determined to keep an eye on Charlie.

Not that he had the slightest idea what he would do if the quarx needed *his* help.

✶

While they were out of threading, he tried to transmit to Mars, focusing on one of the relay sats. He also tried Earth, via a different relay sat; then he tried beaming to Earth direct. He received no response, though he did pick up a hashy commercial broadcast. Charlie noted that it was likely that their antenna had gotten degraded from the high-speed threading. Chances were, no one could receive their signal anymore. Still, that wasn't going to stop him from trying. For an hour, he transmitted a recorded message over and over, stating his position and progress, in the faint hope that he might be heard.

Eventually he gave up and strained to listen to the commercial broadcast. After a few minutes, he realized that he was picking up the BBC Interplanetary News Service. He listened eagerly for word about himself—or the comet.

He made out something about renewed political instability in the Middle East, and a threatened breakaway of New Brazil from the Union of American States, and continued secessionist agitation in L5 City. Holo star Jason Landru was dead at ninety-five . . . and a new, unusually eruptive comet had been spotted coming around the sun in a highly eccentric orbit, one that would fling it out in a *very* close approach to the Earth. ". . . Speculation that it might have had . . . unreflective surface before its solar . . . not seen until . . . ices volatilized . . . no hazard, but if this one brightens . . . comet of the century. Get out your cam-goggles . . ."

/// Is Napoleon back in yet? ///

/SHUT UP, Charlie—I want to hear this!/
/// Sorry . . . ///
At that point, the news cut to a long interview with a politician from New Brazil. Bandicut listened impatiently, and finally gave in to the urgent twitchings of the quarx and turned his attention to the robot's progress. Napoleon was back in the airlock, and there seemed no excuse not to press on. Still, Bandicut lingered over the staticky broadcast.

/// John . . . it's time. ///
Sighing, he reached out to turn off the comm. As his hand touched the panel, he heard the interview end, and one last, scratchy news item: ". . . word from Neptune's moon Triton . . . discovery of an intact alien artifact, still active with an unknown energy source. Exoarchaeologists disagreed on the significance . . . whether this could have any connection with the *Neptune Explorer,* stolen from Triton . . . rumors that . . . predicted the appearance of the comet have been denied by officials of MINEXFO . . . also denied reports of a later . . . predicting a flash of light in Uranian-Neptunian space. Other sources differed . . . flash identical to the effect when *Neptune Explorer* vanished . . . believe . . ."

There was a loud hiss of static, and when the broadcast became audible again, it was in the middle of a soft-drink commercial.

"They're trying to keep people from believing me," Bandicut muttered under his breath. "I can't believe it! They'd rather sit on the truth than admit it. I'll bet they're afraid they'll lose control over the translator. But they found it! Do you think it was Julie?"

/// I . . . put in a good word for her.
That's all I can . . .
John, I'm . . . ///
/What?/ Bandicut whispered.

/// I think . . . John . . . I'm dying.
I'm sorry.
Can we go now? ///

Bandicut blinked, stared, and hit the fusion igniter. He waited for gravity to return, pressing his aching body back into the seat, before he tried to speak again. He wanted to ask Charlie if that was just a figure of speech he had used, about dying—if he had just meant that he was very, very tired. But somehow Bandicut knew the answer even before he asked. He had feared that it was coming, but prayed that it was not. Charlie, don't! he thought. You shouldn't have sacrificed yourself to put me back together! But you did, didn't you?

Dear God, he didn't want to die alone.

30
COMET

 /YOU STILL THERE?/ he asked, as he watched the numbers flicker endlessly on the nav.

/// Still here. ///

/You okay?/

/// No. ///

/Want to tell me about it?/

/// I think . . . no. ///

Bandicut felt a pain in his left side. /Don't try to fix that,/ he snapped. He felt a sudden burst of unreasoning anger. /You're just going to leave me, then? Get me into this, then check out before the closing act?/

/// It is my intention . . . ///

the quarx gasped,

/// . . . if possible . . .
to stay till the very end. ///

Bandicut grunted, vaguely reassured. He didn't know how he would manage the final plunge if Charlie were gone. For that matter, suppose they actually survived this crazy dive across space—what then? Wherever he would be, he sure as hell didn't want to be without Charlie. /If you don't make it, Charlie, will you be . . . reborn again?/

/// Maybe.
How the hell should I know?
I don't suppose even quarx . . . go on forever. ///

Bandicut opened his mouth, stunned by the quarx's anger. Maybe Charlie really was fearful that he'd miss the end of this drama that he had set into motion.

/// Don't worry . . .
the translator-stone . . . knows what to do.
You can do fine without me.
Just hit . . . the blasted comet. ///

The thought sent shudders down his spine. /I don't want to do it without you,/ he whispered. /You might be a pain in the ass, Charlie—but you're all I've got now./

Charlie didn't answer—then, or for many hours afterward.

✶

By the time they were inside Mars's orbit, they were moving so fast that Earth's orbit seemed to be mere minutes away. Bandicut scarcely had time to readjust his thinking. Before, time had crawled; now it was running away from him. The inner planets were much closer together than the outer planets. Earth would be next, then Venus, then they'd whip across the orbit of Mercury to skim the sun, and from there it would be a smooth arc out . . . smack into the comet. Boom. They would nail it somewhere outside the orbit of Mercury, on the far side of the sun.

He hoped he wouldn't spoil the show for all those people on Earth who were dusting off their cam-goggles. With luck, he might produce an even better show, if a briefer one.

The sun grew large and bright and hot in the viewer. He kept Napoleon and Copernicus busy running checks on the ship's systems, particularly as they drew inward toward the sun. It was unlikely that *Neptune Explorer* had been designed to survive the kinds of conditions he was about to put her through—such as the intense heat of a close solar approach. The translator's threading field was capable of excluding excessive radiation, but if they dropped out of threading during their approach to the sun, he'd be fried long before they reached the comet.

An hour after they crossed Earth's orbit, Bandicut roused Charlie and asked him to darken the threading field; it was starting to get uncomfortably warm inside the spacecraft, and nastily hot on the outer hull. Charlie, muttering to himself, passed on the request, and told Bandicut that next time he could just address the translator directly.

/// *Talk to the white stone.*
It's the communications element. ///

/Oh./ Bandicut noted, on the instruments, a drop-off in ambient radiation. He fingered the silent stone in his right wrist and muttered, "Can you darken it a little more, please?" There was no answer that he could hear or feel, but he saw a sparkle of red fire in the black stone in his left wrist, and the field darkened a little more.

Venus's orbit flashed behind them, and he began to think seriously about preparing for the end. He found himself worrying about how he was dressed. He imagined the planets gathered around, watching and applauding as he smashed straight into the comet, and he wanted to look right for the event. He hurried amidships to put on clean clothes for the final plunge. He was amazed at his own calm in the face of near-certain death.

The glowering image of an enormous sun swam in the window, filtered by the threading field, as they streaked in past the orbit of Mercury. Bandicut imagined himself a performer on stage in some great cosmic theater, spotlights beaming and dancing upon him as he spun and sang. The planets loved his song and clamored for more. He was into his third song when he heard the quarx shouting hoarsely,

/// *John . . . can you hear me?* ///

He reeled back in his seat, trying to sort fugue from reality, as the quarx wheezed at him,

/// You have to get ready! ///

/Eh, what?/ he gabbled. /I'm ready! I'm ready! But for what?/

/// To do the flying . . . ///

The quarx's voice faded a little.

*/// . . . get ready to link with
the translator! ///*

/What?/ he asked, thoughts spinning back down into reality. He felt a burning sensation in his wrists, and he looked down and saw both stones pulsing with light. /I thought you guys were flying./

*/// I can't anymore.
John . . . you have to take over now. ///*

He felt a knife blade of fear, as the quarx gasped an explanation. He didn't want to hear it—*really* didn't want to hear it—especially once he understood what the quarx was saying. All the nav data had been going to the translator-stones through Charlie; but it was getting too hard—Charlie was weakening fast and didn't trust himself to get it right anymore. /Are you telling me that the translator can find its way through spatial threading, but it can't track a comet around the sun?/

*/// It can follow it . . .
but not if it can't see it.
And we have some . . .
equipment problems. ///*

/Equipment problems—?/

*/// We, uh . . . burned out the main . . . nav sensors.
I guess I shouldn't have pointed them . . .
at the sun . . . ///*

/You wha—?/ He gulped back his own question and looked at the nav display. Charlie was right. The sensors had failed, and the navlock was lost. /Why did you do that?/ he gasped.

> /// *We didn't know.*
> *Sorry . . .*
> *it was . . . a mistake.* ///

He felt his hopes sliding. /How do you expect me to fly without any nav?/

The quarx struggled to answer.

> /// *The basic trajectory's . . . fine.*
> *It's the final approach . . . we need you . . .*
> *to steer us, at the end.* ///

Bandicut blinked, trying to absorb Charlie's words.

> /// *Think of it as . . . docking . . .*
> *high-speed docking.* ///

He couldn't answer. Was Charlie telling him that he was supposed to *eyeball* the ship in to impact—that it was all going to depend on his being personally linked to the stones?

He thought of his linkup with the translator in the cavern and shuddered. Don't worry, came a whisper from Charlie. It would be just like a game of EineySteiney, only here the stakes were a little higher.

A little, he thought. Indeed. But if there was no other way . . . /What do you want me to do?/ he whispered.

The quarx's answer came in broken words.

> /// *As soon as we're . . . outbound . . .*
> *past the sun*
> *. . . use the telescope to find the comet.*
> *I'll link you . . .*
> *you make corrections through the translator . . .*
> *biggest game of . . . EineySteiney . . .*
> *you ever played.* ///

Bandicut swallowed hard and turned to the computer charts to determine where to point his telescope to find the comet. They would be at perihelion—closest approach to the sun—within the hour.

∗

The threading field was so dark now that the windows were effectively shuttered. But Bandicut could see the sun in his mind's eye as vividly as if he were staring at it through the clear quartz-plex window. The sun roiled and fumed, like some terrible volcanic cloud churning over his head in the blazing glow of sunset. It was like some astonishing drug-induced hallucination, and in fact it *was* a hallucination—he was in full-blown silence-fugue now. But he was also locked in a bewildering feedback embrace with the translator-stone; he sensed its vast power glimmering and flickering, just out of his reach; and it seemed that the clearer the solar image grew in his mind, the more powerfully hallucinatory it became, reverberating back and forth between his mind and the stone's. The quarx did not interrupt the fugue; maybe he was content to let it run, or maybe he was no longer capable of intervening.

In Bandicut's mind, a great solar prominence crested, erupting downward out of the sun to lash into the dark emptiness of space. Somewhere beyond that prominence was the comet that it had become his destiny to destroy, or destroy himself in the attempt. Earth wasn't visible from here, but he knew that she was watching, with all the other planets, as he flew to her defense. He rode the wave of the translator's energy, and the marching flames of the sun saluted his passage.

They were arrowing straight past the sun's rotating horizon.

He noted almost casually that they were now at perihelion, and he thought he heard the applause of the planets.

Then they were past perihelion, arcing back out of the sun's gravity well. It would be just a fleeting breath of time before they shot out past the other side of Mercury's orbit. Time flowed like a fine wine, intoxicating him as he bobbed his head, watching the movements of the planets like the fabulous, dancing movement of balls on an enormous EineySteiney table.

As the sun shifted out of his view to the stern, he grinned savagely and unshuttered the forward windows and unlimbered the telescope. He pointed the thing where the computer, using the last known orbital data, said the comet would be; and in his mind, the coruscating near-consciousness of the translator-stones whirled and followed his focus like a swarm of fiery bees.

✴

It was a blazing ball of ice and stone, viewed from the sunward side—with a great luminous tail that stretched outward from the surrounding gaseous coma, the tail blown not by the comet's movement but by the streaming particles of the solar wind. The comet was a breathtaking sight, glowing through the filters and lenses of the telescope. It looked like an angel, or a cosmic sign, anything but a planet killer.

Overtaken by sudden self-doubt, Bandicut ran a new computer analysis of the comet's orbit, urgently trying to see if it really was going to hit the Earth. His measurements were uncertain, and he could see the comet emitting jets of solar-heated gas, which were bound to affect its trajectory, even if very slightly. But he suddenly had to know: Was he doing this for nothing? Did he really *have* to throw away his life? Or . . . was it possible he could veer away from collision, and ride herd on the comet all the way to Earth? Instead of dying, perhaps he could return home . . .

/// John— ///

croaked the quarx.

He calculated furiously, the fugue pushing back the bee-swarm of the translator-stones in his head, and he found that his results fell short of proving what he needed to know. The comet was going to make a terrifyingly close encounter with Earth . . . but would it be a collision? Was the translator right? Would the jets change the comet's course enough to slam it into his home planet? Was it conclusive enough to die for?

He wondered if authorities on Earth had realized the risk yet, wondered if they had called for evacuations or preparations, wondered if they had gotten his messages, wondered if they believed him even if they had. He couldn't listen to any broadcasts while they were threading space; anyway, he doubted that they even had an antenna left on the ship. He wondered if he would know, afterward, if he had succeeded in destroying the comet. He lobbed his wondering thoughts, like glowing coals, at Charlie, but the quarx answered with stony silence; he was hunkered down, saving his strength.

The calculations had left Bandicut breathless with indecision. Probably the translator was right . . . but what if it wasn't? Couldn't he wait just a little longer and see?

The quarx stirred feebly.

/// John . . . ///

If he plunged into the comet, he would never know for sure. He longed for a chance to run a deep simulation in neurolink . . .

/// John . . .
I'm going to do something . . .
to stretch out your . . . apparent time flow . . .
to give you more time to . . . react . . .
at the end. ///

They were beyond the orbit of Mercury, outward velocity in excess of two-tenths of lightspeed. He switched to the low-power telescope and began nudging the translator into small corrections as he tried to peer through the vapor shroud surrounding the comet's core. They needed to penetrate that vapor shroud; it was the nucleus in the center they would have to hit, in order to destroy the comet.

The time-shift hit him, with a sudden feeling that his fingers were moving like molasses. A bitterly icy calm swept over him, even in the heat of the fugue. He'd played this game of EineySteiney dozens of times in his mind already—the sudden veers and accelerations that might be needed to zero in on the target. It always played out just right in the fever of his imagination. In real life it would be harder— orbital docking maneuvers were tricky, even at slow speeds. But he still had Charlie with him, and Charlie was the best EineySteiney player in the universe, and even if he screwed up, the quarx could do it.

If he decided to do it. He peered at the comet and imagined *Neptune Explorer* moving in a nice, slow pirouette around it, escorting it to safety. He listened as the planets murmured with uncertainty at his thoughts, and broke into scattered applause.

Now he was gazing straight out the window at the comet. It had grown, in direct view, from a pinpoint to a luminous, vapor-shrouded tennis ball.

/// Are you . . . ready . . . John? ///

He nodded absently. He felt a growing tingle in his mind, and a burning in his wrists, and the fugue-state was in the full flower of heat and . . . this was it . . . he felt the time-shift kick in even more powerfully . . . he watched his own eyes blink like shades rolling up and down . . . and it was dizzying, but he knew that they were falling toward the comet at a fabulous speed . . . falling . . . but not too late to veer off . . .

The quarx suddenly convulsed, and he felt a sickening shudder.

/// John . . . oh, mokin' foke . . . ///

/Punch it in, Charlie,/ he whispered. /You take it. It's your shot./

The comet grew astonishingly fast now, slowed time sense or no. Wisps of vapor were obscuring the stars beyond . . . in a moment they would be in whiteout, inside the vapor envelope.

/// Ohhhhhhhhhh . . . . . . ///

He felt more than heard the wail, reverberating off the walls of his consciousness, and then he heard the quarx's voice echoing off into a great distance. /Charlie? CHARLIE?/

/// The con . . . . . . is yours . . . . . .
do it . . . . . . for both of us . . . . . . ///

He felt a gasp of breath go out; it was his own, and yet not. Something went silent inside him, and he felt a bottomless emptiness where the quarx had been, like a well into forever. /CHARRLIIIE!/ he screamed. /CHARLIE, GOD DAMN YOU!/

The fugue snapped away, leaving him breathless but clearheaded. Was he going to destroy the comet or not? The hard ball in his stomach told him: of course, he had no choice. He could not wait and see; he and the comet were flying headlong toward each other and he had only this chance and no other.

He stared at the growing coma, holding his terror at arm's length. The stars were gone, there was nothing except white cloud before him, and an enormous, planet-busting nucleus of ice and rock somewhere inside it, and he was still threading space, accelerating. He wanted to curse, and weep, but his wrists were on fire, telling him that the translator was waiting, he was at the controls . . . and the retarded time-sense could give him only a precious few moments to think.

In the whiteout he searched for the killing form of the nucleus. His fear and despair churned through him, then fled. He glimpsed his parents and brother and sister-in-law for the last time; and Dakota, hunched over her sims; and Julie, eyes wide and blue and intense; and he felt a final piercing grief . . .

And then the dark nucleus of the comet tumbled out of the fog into view, *and it was off course to the right, and they were about to miss it.* The translator-stones flashed, and he gave the ship a hard kick; but the time-shift was deceptive, and he overcorrected and had to kick sharply back the other way. That was it; he had it right. He felt an upwelling of light around him as the translator-stones unfolded to transform the kinetic energy of the collision . . .

The nucleus lunged toward him, and he knew then that he was going to die. It mushroomed into an enormous mountain blocking his way. For a timeless instant, he seemed to hang directly in front of it, as though he might hang there for a cosmic *forever;* then, without any sense of the movement of time, he slammed into the mountain like a hydrogen bomb. He felt the hellish light and energy of a small sun, blazing into space; he was *aware* of it, but coldly, dimly, aware of time frozen, aware of his body and soul bathed in the fire of a trillion-megaton explosion.

Then the daughter-stones blossomed into cool, iridescent halos, and all consciousness was taken from him.

31

TRANSLATION

 It was the quiet of a dream, the quiet of death. He was lost in darkness, he was plunging into the core of a sun. Darkness and light, all soundless. An explosion, frozen in eternity. This was the afterlife, said a quiet part of his soul, and no one spoke up to disagree. He was surrounded by bursts of fire, concentric rings, in colors he had never known. He was falling through them, or perhaps floating motionless, and these ethereal crowns of light were falling past him.

It was impossible to tell.

Impossible to understand.

He was submerged in a deep ocean of surprise. Never a firm believer in an afterlife, he had always assumed that if there *were* an afterlife, then some loved one would be there to greet him. Mom? he thought absently. But there was no Mom. There was only the fierce, strobelike movement of the rings of fire, in colors he did not know.

He remembered a comet . . . and a creature not human . . . but his thoughts were like chunks of ice in a packed floe, vibrating with energy, but too jammed together to move.

A little later he wondered, could this be silence-fugue instead of death? He remembered silence-fugue. But there was no feeling of madness, exactly. Time and space didn't quite seem to exist around him, or perhaps they too were frozen. And yet he was aware of a sense of *passage,* and suddenly it seemed to him that time was crinkling around him, like a crystal shattering in slow motion. What did that mean?

Annihilation.

The thought appeared in his mind, unbidden, unspoken.

He was aware of two points of light blazing close by, pulsing, one white as diamond and one coal-red out of blackness. He felt a burning pain.

Transformation.

Bewildered, he stared at flickering zigzag images, like fractals forming and disrupting, dancing at the periphery of his awareness. What? he whispered into the silence and emptiness of silence-fugue, or death.

Translation.

Suddenly the rings of fire exploded into darkness, and his breath erupted in a gasp so violent that it sent a stab of pain through his chest. He lurched up against seat restraints, then fell back, panting, against a headrest. He blinked in confusion. He sensed the dark shape of a cockpit around him, and heard the hiss of life support. He was alive, and not in silence-fugue. He glimpsed instruments, and a window. Out the window, he could see blackness, space, and a sprinkling of stars. He blinked again, trying to focus. It looked different somehow.

He remembered suddenly, sharply, what had happened. EineySteiney. The comet. Attacking it like a suicidal cue ball. And Charlie dying before he could see the ending . . .

The ice floe came unstuck. Memories came tumbling loose in dizzying numbers, cascading backward through space and time, the dive toward the sun, the stolen ship, Triton, Julie.

Julie!

He glimpsed her face, her eyes, her kiss . . . and then she was gone, leaving him with only the memory, the emptiness, the knowledge that he had left her forever.

Through the cascade of pain and emptiness, he remembered an aching truth: In leaving her, he might have preserved a living Earth for her to return to.

If he had succeeded.

Annihilation . . .

The word sprang again into his mind. Meaning what? That Earth was annihilated, or the comet? Or was this all still part of some cruel death-hallucination?

Charlie? he thought—and remembered again, Charlie had died.

He did not think this was a hallucination, though he wished it were. He thought of the passage he had just been through; and he felt a sudden icy wind blowing through his thoughts, and a certainty that he had left his past irrevocably behind, not just in space perhaps, but in time, as well. The thought made him tremble at the edge of tears. Was he eons from Earth now, centuries from Julie? He found himself weeping at the thought, gasping, unable to stop the bitter tears that were suddenly rushing down his cheeks.

He felt a stab in his wrists, and glanced down. Something was flashing—the translator-stones. The white diamond was pulsing, with unmistakable urgency. /What do you want?/ he thought, with no real hope that it would answer him. /Charlie?/ he whispered, with no greater hope. The quarx was gone, his life spent saving his human host, in order that Bandicut could do . . . whatever he had just done.

The stone pulsed insistently.

/Stone,/ he thought, resting his head back, staring out the window through his tears. /Can you tell me, did we succeed? Did we destroy the comet? Or was all this . . . for nothing?/

He cursed quietly, bitterly—not so much for the loss of

his past life, as for the terrible loneliness that had come to take its place.

Wait.

A window blinked open in the vision of his inner mind. For an instant, he thought it was Charlie, back again, preparing to show him something with one of his visual displays. But there was no hint of Charlie; there was only a flash of something like a graphical display, very complicated, but dimly familiar. When it vanished, he was left blinking. Elements of it burned in his memory like an after-image; and finally, he realized that it looked like an energy curve. An energy curve with a tremendous spike in it. A spike so sharp that he found himself wondering if it didn't represent the annihilation of a large chunk of matter. A comet, perhaps.

Annihilation and transformation.

The words hung soundless in his thoughts.

Transformation and translation.

The white daughter-stone? It was still pulsing on his wrist. Was it speaking? He shut his eyes and glimpsed coruscating particles of fire. /Are you telling me the comet was destroyed?/ he whispered.

Twenty-four-point-seven percent of mass was transformed into energy, breaching with a five-point-six percent reserve the quantum threshold for metaspatial translation.

He hesitated. /Does that mean yes?/

Yes.

He grunted. He had saved the Earth, then; he must have. /What . . . did it look like?/ he asked. There was no answer. He stirred, peering out the window, looking for some familiar patterns in the arrangement of the stars. He found none. /Can you tell me where I am?/ he whispered, suddenly more frightened than he had ever been in his life.

There was no answer.

Before he could ask again, he felt a sudden angular rotation. He glanced at the instruments. The fusion tube was still firing, at low power. But the ship was being turned, as though the attitude control system had been activated. The black stone in his left wrist was flickering red; it appeared to be in command.

He studied the star patterns as they revolved past, straining for something, anything, familiar in the sky. How many light-years would one have to travel before the constellations became unrecognizable? He hadn't the faintest idea. He grabbed the telescope and swung it into place for a wide-field scan. He grunted in surprise. Some of those stars didn't look like stars at all; they looked blurry, like galaxies. In fact, most of them did. But that was crazy, unless . . .

Unless . . . he was . . . outside . . .

No. He refused to consider that possibility. Just the thought of it caused a burning sensation deep in his chest.

The ship had turned about ninety degrees when the curved edge of a great platter of light came into view in the window. Only it wasn't . . . a platter of light, exactly. It was more like a vast, swirling ocean of stars. He blinked, not quite focusing on it; he couldn't, didn't want to focus on it. Didn't want to let the pieces come together in his mind. There was something else, too, like a shadow across his gaze. He blinked, trying to refocus his eyes.

There was something out there, dark, floating in space. At first he mistook it for a part of the great swath of stars, but it seemed to be intruding somehow from the darkness of space itself, and at last he realized it was *in front of* the starry sea. It was hard to make out, a shadowy silhouette against starlight; but it was a structure, perhaps a very *large* structure. He squinted, his heart pounding; as the ship continued to turn, he brought the telescope to bear with trembling hands. It was too dark to focus on clearly, but he glimpsed enough to guess that whatever it was, it was artificial.

He looked up from the telescope, and gasped at the vast

swath of stars behind the structure. The ship's rotation had brought a much brighter feature into view: a blazing galactic center, partially wreathed in dark dust lanes. The sea of stars was, unquestionably . . . a galaxy.

Bandicut couldn't breathe. His diaphragm spasmed, trying to draw breath into his lungs. He heard himself making little involuntary crying sounds.

This is frightening me, whispered a thought somewhere in the back of his mind.

He blinked, searching inward for the source of that thought. But it was only his imagination, his subconscious.

Something inside him released—and he gasped in one frantic breath, then another. He began to hyperventilate as he wrenched his gaze closer to the enormous structure shadowed against the light . . . and then back out to the majestic ocean of stars, tilted toward him. As he gazed at it, and its great glowing center, he knew with a sudden, terrifying certainty that this was the Milky Way galaxy. His galaxy.

And he was viewing it from the outside.

He blinked, and swallowed, and clamped his eyes shut against an uncontrollable rush of tears.

✶

It took a long time before he could bring himself to gaze again at the sight of the Milky Way; and then he did so with a kind of anguished fascination, imagining that he might locate the sun, lost in that sea of light—or even identify the portion of the spiral in which the sun lay. It was impossible, of course. He knew that Earth's sun lay in the Orion spiral arm of the galaxy, but even that was impossible to identify from this perspective.

When he drew his gaze back in to focus on the nearer structure—now a hard-edged shadow cutting across most of the breadth of the galaxy—he realized with a start that it seemed closer than it had been just minutes ago. Was *Neptune Explorer* moving toward it? The silhouette angle seemed different. He turned to check the sensor array, then remembered that Charlie had burned the sensors out pointing them at the sun.

Wait.

He felt the daughter-stones sparkling in his wrists.

Look outside.

Frowning, he peered out the window, shifting his gaze along the length of the mysterious object. He felt a flicker in the back of his mind, and realized that the stones were making calculations, steering by his eyesight. /Are we still threading space?/ he whispered.

Translating.

Translating, he thought—and *almost,* for an instant, caught an understanding of this non-Newtonian movement across space.

Bandicut blinked at the shadowy . . . ship, or space station, whatever it was, against the fiery galaxy. Half the Milky Way was blocked by it now, and he seemed to be flying directly into its galactic-light shadow. Any chance he might have had to perceive its shape or dimensions was gone; he was too close now. Its form vanished into darkness to his left and his right. He thought of L5 City, humanity's largest self-contained structure in space, and knew somehow that it was a toy compared to this. On impulse, he flicked on a forward-pointing spotlight. Its effect was invisible; the thing was still too distant. And yet it felt as though he ought to be able to reach out and touch it.

His heart pounded, as he began to pick out some surface detail: just a fine spiderwebbing of lines, and vague shapes, all of them black, but some blacker than others. For an instant he thought he glimpsed a winking light from the shadows. The spiderwebbing slowly resolved into a very broad, shadowy, sectional layout of surface structure. Some faint illumination was coming from somewhere behind him, perhaps the light of other galaxies. Idiot! he thought suddenly, and switched on the window's light-augmentation. The view brightened, and more detail emerged from the shadows: architectural sections within sections within sections. There was an almost fractallike quality to the dark, sculpted complexity. As patterns grew, they revealed finer patterns of equal complexity.

/What *is* it?/ he whispered, rubbing his wrists. /Is this the translator's home? Or Charlie's?/ Apparently the stones were too busy flying, because they gave no answer, except:

Maintain visual link.

He obeyed, and wished that he could somehow tell Charlie what was happening. Or Julie. He blinked back more tears.

The surface loomed closer, closer . . . he felt as if he were falling into a vast maze of canyons. His wrists burned; he felt the ship's gravity fluctuate momentarily; he was growing dizzy as he fell . . .

The structure rushed up to meet him, and he could just make out the yellow blur of his spotlight on its surface. For a terrified instant he knew he was going to crash . . . and then something directly below him began changing shape, a shadowy cat's eye dilating open, and inside the eye he glimpsed a flash of volcanic-red light, and then darkness. A heartbeat later he had fallen through the pupil, and was swallowed in the darkness.

Prepare for docking.

He moved his hands helplessly over the controls. He had no idea what to do. His spotlight had gone out. He could see nothing. /Please—tell me what—/

The ship's gravity lurched, and pitched its angle up sharply, and increased abruptly. He fell back against his headrest, grabbing his armrests with a gasp.

A blazing crimson light strobed in through the window, blinding him. The hull shuddered. He felt, or perhaps imagined, a *clang* as the ship hard-docked.

Arrival.
/Arrival?/ he whispered. /Arrival where?/
There was only silence for an answer.

—to be continued in Book 2 of
THE CHAOS CHRONICLES—

ABOUT THE AUTHOR

Jeffrey A. Carver is the author of a number of thought-pro-
voking, popular science fiction novels, including *The Infin-
ity Link* and *The Rapture Effect.* His books combine hard-SF
concepts, deeply humanistic concerns, and a sense of
humor, making them both compellingly suspenseful and
emotionally satisfying. Carver has written several successful
novels in his "star-rigger" universe: *Star Rigger's Way,*
Panglor (both of which will be released soon in Tor Books
editions), *Dragons in the Stars,* and most recently, *Dragon
Rigger.* With *Neptune Crossing,* Carver inaugurates THE
CHAOS CHRONICLES, a sweeping new series inspired by
the emerging science of chaos. He lives in the Boston area
with his wife and two daughters.